TEACHING THE TEACHER'S PET

MOST LIKELY TO ★ BOOK ONE

SARAH SUTTON

TEACHING THE TEACHER'S PET

Copyright © 2022 Golden Crown Publishing, LLC

All rights reserved. No part of this publication may be reproduced, stored or transmitted in any form or by any means, electronic, mechanical, photocopying, recording, scanning, or otherwise without written permission from the publisher. It is illegal to copy this book, post it to a website, or distribute it by any other means without permission.

This novel is entirely a work of fiction. The names, characters, organizations, businesses, places, events, and incidents portrayed in it are either the work of the author's imagination or used fictitiously. Any resemblance to actual persons, living or dead, events or localities is entirely coincidental.

For information, contact:

http://www.sarah-sutton.com

Cover Design © Designed with Grace

Images © DepositPhotos – envivo, coprid, ihor_seamless & Krakenimages.com

*To new beginnings
and new stories waiting to be told.*

CHAPTER 1

*P*atience. It was definitely not my strong suit. And if Principal Oliphant made me wait any longer, I was going to stick a pencil in someone's eye. Maybe even mine.

My English teacher was nice enough to let me schedule this meeting in the last ten minutes of class, and that rare display of leniency wouldn't happen again. Besides, in a high school with over two thousand students, Principal Oliphant's schedule was near impossible to get on. I'd won the lottery when I got the email this morning from the secretary. *She has a ten-minute opening during fourth period at 11:50 AM.*

I glanced at the clock hanging crooked on the wall for the seventh time. In five minutes and thirty seconds, my time slot would be up. My time to make my case to her would be taken over by whatever was next on her hectic schedule. Brushed aside or swept under the rug, or another analogy that meant what I had to say didn't matter outside my ten-minute window.

Patience, Maisie, patience.

Nudging my glasses further up my nose, I studied the front of the four-page stapled stack in my hand, but really, I knew the words by heart.

Principal Oliphant, I'm short on time and I value yours, so I'll make this quick. The reason I requested a meeting with you is because I want to discuss the decision of cutting the student ranking system, therefore cutting valedictorian. As you might know, I have been maintaining my high academics since the beginning of high school in preparation for the top spot, so this is a topic I feel passionately about. Colleges consider valedictorians and salutatorians first for scholarships, and to cut it entirely may make our school less competitive in terms of academics.

Words I believed with my whole heart and soul. Heck, I might even agree to give my firstborn baby for this. And, sure, it might've been overkill to write a whole essay on it, but I didn't trust myself not to fly off the handle. Even though I inherited practically nothing else from her, my temper definitely came from my mom.

The clock ticked on. Four minutes.

"Maisie?" came Principal Oliphant's bright voice, and all at once, my bouncing leg stopped. I looked up, spotting the blonde woman standing at the mouth of her now-open door. "I'm ready for you."

And I'm ready for you, I thought in determination, shoving to my feet.

Principal Oliphant's office was sparsely decorated, with a few bookshelves lining the far wall, more of a décor piece than anything else. The dust on the ledges hinted she didn't touch it often. She liked a lot of blacks and whites, it seemed, with only the occasional splashes of color in the paintings on her wall. Neat, clean, professional. The ideal office for a principal.

But to me, she wasn't *just* a principal. The history that stretched between us was extensive, and even though our contact in the last four years had been minimal—aka, only if I was forced to interact with her—I was banking on that.

"Have a seat," she offered, gesturing to one of the basic gray chairs opposite her desk. She tucked a blonde piece of hair that had escaped her bun behind her ear. "What's this about?"

Cue intro.

Without glancing down, I started on my first lines. "Principal Oliphant, I'm short on time and I value yours, so I'll make this quick. The reason I requested this meeting—"

"Maisie." She lifted her palm to silence me, throwing me off before I could really begin. "Is this about the school board's decision to discontinue the student ranking system?"

Ookay. I glanced down at my paper, but I knew it wasn't see-through. "How'd you know?"

"Mrs. Diego spoke with me on Friday. Apparently, you two talked about it last week."

Mrs. Diego had been my favorite math teacher for three years, ever since I was able to start taking senior classes my sophomore year. Even being in the advanced classes wasn't quite enough. Mrs. Diego tasked herself with finding tough equations that would stump me. *"We have to keep that mind stimulated,"* she'd said once.

She also made for a great listening ear for me to rant to over losing valedictorian.

"I had hoped *you* would've been the one to tell me personally," I said to Principal Oliphant now, going off-script and tapping into that "passion" I probably should've kept under wraps. At least until we got further than thirty seconds into our time together. "Given the fact that we both know *I* would've been valedictorian."

I'd been nursing my GPA from its infancy, a religious routine that had ruled my life for the last four years. No, I couldn't skip school on Student Skip Day—I had homework to turn in. No, I couldn't take the elective that sounded fun—it wouldn't weigh enough toward my GPA. And now, with one bogus email sent from a Do Not Reply server, four years of progress...*poof.* All gone.

Principal Oliphant reached up and rubbed a spot above her eyebrow, an action that was familiar. "Unfortunately, Maisie, this isn't only my decision. It's the school board's decision."

"Shouldn't it be a student-voted decision?" I demanded, fighting to keep my voice level. "Since it's directly affecting the students?"

"This is the year we're testing it out, eliminating the valedictorian award. There are many reasons we've made this decision. GPA isn't the most accurate way to judge a student's performance, along with the fact that the student ranking system promotes unhealthy competition amongst peers."

Oh, *please*. She'd be hard pressed to name one person who actually took academics seriously enough to get "competitive." No one came to Brentwood for academics. Me, sure, but no one else was ready to use their protractors like pitchforks. "What would you call football, then? Or any other sport that Brentwood High idolizes?"

"Maisie." The line to her mouth took on a sympathetic tilt, eyes softening. It was almost like I hadn't spoken, or maybe she interpreted my silly questions as rhetorical, because she didn't answer. "I've watched you grow up. You've always been a dedicated, smart girl. You know that with our history, I want nothing more than to offer you opportunities to grow. This, though...I just can't swing."

Our history. Hearing it come from her mouth, the phrase "our history" sounded so much more significant than it was. Then again, I practically grew up in her house from first grade until the beginning of freshman year, so maybe it was me who downplayed the significance. At this moment, though, she was as familiar to me as a stranger on the street.

"Jefferson High has student ranking," I told her, gripping my collection of papers tightly enough to crush them. "I could always transfer."

Principal Oliphant's demeanor didn't change. It started to come off too much like pity. "If you were to transfer, you would go from being Brentwood High's top student to Jefferson's tenth best. Or lower."

My stomach dropped at her words, the sudden sensation feeling like I was on a rollercoaster. "You don't know that," I said, trying hard not to feel offended. "My grades—"

"Their classes are much more competitive. Their focus is math and science, whereas Brentwood focuses more on the arts."

Yeah, right. Brentwood didn't focus on the arts. Above all else, it focused—no, *worshipped*—sports. That was evident when the mathletes team was cut from the school's list of clubs last year. Evident even further when they gave jocks a free period during the school day for weight training. What did art students get? A dingy little studio.

And kids who liked mathematics? We got calculators that were nearly two decades old and an unlimited supply of graph paper.

There was a sharp knock on the office door before it swung open, revealing a girl that easily could've been Principal Oliphant twenty years in the past. The same blonde hair streaked with deeper layers of gold, the same thin nose and arching eyebrows, except the girl in the doorway wore a blue and gold cheer uniform. "Mom, can I *please*—" She cut herself off when she saw me, blinking. "Oh. Uh. Hey, Maisie."

Since Brentwood was a big school, my path didn't frequently cross with Madison Oliphant, but each time it did, it was enough to make me want to snap something in two. One specific day during freshman year—the day we went from planning to be in each other's weddings to ex-best friends. I stared at her now, unable to conjure an ounce of politeness to return her greeting.

"Maisie," Principal Oliphant said when it became obvious Madison wouldn't say anything more with me in the same room, "if anything changes, I'll be sure to let you know, okay?"

That was a pathetic cop-out if I'd ever heard one, but I also registered the hidden meaning behind her words: *dismissed.* My five minutes to win her over were up, and I'd lost.

I hadn't even had a chance to read my speech.

Madison stepped out of my way as I walked to the door, her eyes on her shoes. Yeah, I didn't want to look at her either.

With only a few minutes left until the class change, I went to the cafeteria, depositing my satchel onto the tabletop and all but slouching onto the chair.

What good was it being the top student at Brentwood High if I had nothing to show for it? Doing away with the ranking system completely meant that the top spot I'd been clinging to for years meant nothing. I was no better than a kid who slept through class every day and turned in their homework late. The grades and hard work and dedication I'd prided myself in were now useless.

It left me panicked, untethered in darkness and unable to find steady ground. Without the valedictorian label, would colleges even notice me in a sea of seniors? Without a ranking system, how would colleges know which students to focus on? Which students to give scholarships to?

Given the state of my college fund—depleted due to

sibling inequality and parental unfairness—I was desperate to stand out. Desperate for those scholarships.

With a lump in my throat, I brought my math book out of my satchel, spreading it wide on the table. Quickly, I fell into the mix of numbers and sentences, letting it fill all the sad spaces in my brain. Integral functions and derivatives—things that made my little math-loving heart happy. And the worksheet on the lunch table in front of me was absolutely full of them.

Name the integral function of $f(x) = sin\ 2x$. I read the problem in my head, and the answer blinked like a neon light in my mind, a yellow and bright *pick me, pick me!*

My pencil worked in overtime scribbling the formula down. $(-1/2)\ cos\ 2x + C$. Duh. What else would it be?

Finding the right answer felt like searching for treasure—I couldn't stop until I found it. How most people got an endorphin rush after exercising, I got one from working through equations. And the numbers now, after the crushing disappointment of Principal Oliphant's rejection, made the world a smidge lighter.

"Earth to Maisie?"

The sudden voice, so close to my ear, caused me to jump badly enough that I drew a line of graphite across my paper. It effectively cut through the answer I'd written down, nearly hard enough to go through and mark the table. I looked up at the chairs that had been filled since I'd fallen under my hypotenuse hypnosis.

My boyfriend, Alex Newman, sat beside me, and my two other friends, Rachel Manning and Ava Jenson, sat on the other side of the table. Rachel had her lunch tray in front of her, the bright blue plastic with a gold pawprint on it that represented the Brentwood Bobcats. Ava packed her lunch like she did every day, and her pink fabric lunch bag had been deconstructed in front of her. PB&J, a bag of ranch-flavored potato chips, and a red pop can, like clockwork.

Alex looked at me calmly in the way he always did.

"I didn't realize you'd sat down," I muttered, glancing around. Cafeteria B had filled up since I'd lost myself in the worksheet. It wasn't nearly as full as Cafeteria A had to be—which mostly consisted of freshmen and sophomores due to the proximity to their classes—but there was enough noise to fill the room. Now that I'd noticed the chatter, there was no hope of falling back into my blissful bubble of silence. "I was working on my math."

I scooted the worksheet closer to me, though, half-embarrassed I'd lost track of time.

"It's not homework," Ava said, but she grinned knowingly at me. She held her cell phone in one hand, and the screen was lit up. "I bet you already have next week's homework finished. It's extra credit, isn't it?"

"Don't interrupt the Brain while she works," Rachel said affectionately while dragging a plastic fork through her mountain of spaghetti. The sauce didn't stick to the greasy noodles but rather slid off to pool underneath them, the oil spill less than appetizing. Even though she sat across from me, the health hazard was too close. "It's not like we were talking about anything newsworthy, anyway."

I put my pencil down, smirking a little at the nickname. "It's too late. She's already been interrupted."

Alex reached over and patted my arm. "You know you don't need to worry about extra credit, Maisie. School started literally a week ago."

"Might as well boost the grade now."

Not that it really mattered anymore.

I turned toward him and then inwardly winced at the small round bandage above his upper lip, one that, instead of matching his skin tone, was a bright green. I hadn't gotten the chance to see him this morning before classes started, so the sight came as a cringing surprise. "Did you try shaving again?"

He seemed proud of himself. "I *did* shave, thank you very much. One little nick this time. I'm getting better."

Last week, Alex claimed to have found facial hair along his upper lip. I told him that, with a head of hair as dark as his, he'd be able to tell if he was growing a mustache. He made me touch the skin there, and despite my less than stellar findings—smooth as a piece of paper —he took it upon himself to shave. Apparently every four days.

"Judging by your lack of excitement, I'm assuming things didn't go well with the principal," Ava said as she leaned forward, giving me a sympathetic frown. Her recently-dyed pink hair was tied up into two space buns today, her go-to style. "She's not going to reinstate the valedictorian stuff, is she?"

My shoulders slumped. I'd texted our group chat all weekend about it. Ava even went as far as helping me create the beast of a script I hadn't gotten the chance to read, and Rachel stayed up late last night, listening to me practice. All for nothing. "She practically said my dreams of a valedictorian speech are a thing of the past."

"That's so lame," Rachel said with a huff. "You said she knows it's important to you, right? It's like she's trying to punish you."

It wasn't out of the realm of possibility.

"You know I'd write about it in my blog if it were more..." Ava trailed off, probably already regretting how her words sounded.

I knew what she was going to say, though. *If it were more interesting.* "Interesting" was relative. Readers of her school-centered gossip column, *Brentwood Babble*, really only cared about one subject—all the dirty secrets of their favorite popular crowd, the Top Tier. Consisting of jocks and rich kids, the Top Tier liked to live as if they were A-List celebrities, and Ava's blog helped perpetuate that. As soon as something hot fell into her lap, she typed up an article and posted it for the entire internet to see.

The last time we celebrated, she'd had over seven hundred registered visitors.

Despite my corrupted concentration, I tried to go back to my worksheet, focusing on the swirl of letters and numbers. *Name the derivative of the function* $f(x)=4cos2x+logx+x$.

"I can't wait until the game Friday," Rachel said, leaning her cheek into her palm. "I already have my posters made up."

"In support of *Connor Bray?*" Ava asked, adding a sing-song lilt to the last two words.

I couldn't help but frown at my best friend's latest crush. Out of all the guys at Brentwood High, she had to pick the top of the Top Tier boys, someone who was more obsessed about popularity and sports than anything meaningful. Then again, she wasn't alone. I'd be hard pressed to find someone who didn't worship the guy and his forearms.

"Shouldn't you be supporting your brother instead?" I asked her. "He's on the team, too."

Rachel's smile fell into something more serious, and she lowered her voice. "I've been holding off saying it. At least until it was, like, legit. Until he confirmed it with me. Reed quit the football team."

"But your brother was one of the best players!" Ava said with a little gasp. "Was it because he was passed up for quarterback?"

"I don't know *why* he quit. He won't tell me."

Alex let out a soft sigh. "It's his senior year. If I was on the football team, no way I'd quit."

I closed my eyes briefly, trying to block out the conversation. *Name the derivative of the function—*

"Is it okay if I put it on my blog?" Ava asked, her thumbs already typing.

"Yeah, go ahead. I doubt he'll be mad about it." Rachel's lips quirked up into a small, wistful smile. "But, yeah, my signs are for Connor. They're going to catch his attention for sure."

Or the attention of Connor's possessive girlfriend.

"He's pretty dreamy, right?" Rachel asked Ava. "Have you seen his butt in those football pants?"

"It *is* a nice butt," Alex agreed thoughtfully.

I loved my friends, but the fact that our conversations devolved into guys' butts made me ready to stab my pencil in my eye. Out of all the topics to talk about, they always decided on football and boys and popularity. Then again, they probably felt the same whenever I delved into explaining equations and functions. Not that I dove into that conversation often, unless I decided I wanted to bore my friends to death.

"Maisie," Ava said, calling my attention to her. "Can I send over an article for you to proof after your tutoring?"

Mrs. Diego asked me last week if I would be able to start my tutoring up again this year, since it was something I'd been doing the past two years now. More often than not, I met with freshmen who weren't willing to put the effort into learning algebra. It was only the second week of school, and I already had three students to meet with to make sure they started the year off on the right foot.

Teaching math was exciting to me, almost as fun as working through equations. Something about tutoring made my heart so full. Especially the moment where the math equations suddenly *clicked* for the student—it was a victory for both of us.

"You can if you want," I told Ava. "You know you don't need it, though. I never find anything."

She didn't always send me things to proof, but I

think the idea of someone reading them over first gave her peace of mind. I faithfully read whatever she sent me.

"Wait, wait, so you're starting up your tutoring?" Alex asked, eyebrows wrinkling together. "Who needs tutoring already? We've only been in school a week."

I picked up a potato chip and popped it into my mouth. "I told you I was Friday at lunch."

"No, you didn't."

"She did," Ava insisted, thumbs flying on her cell. "How else would I have known?"

Alex's lips tightened a bit now, and the bandage above his lip quirked with the movement. "You should live a little more. Do things *other* than homework."

For reasons I'd never understood, Alex didn't like it when I spent all my free time on homework. In the past year we'd been together, while I focused on academics to hold on to my valedictorian spot—R.I.P.—he'd always tried to coax me out of my introverted shell. "But I *like* homework," I said, wishing the words would sink in.

Just when I started to reread my calculus question again, Ava gave a sharp, deep gasp, a dramatic noise that almost sounded as if she'd been stabbed.

"What's wrong?" I asked. Her saucer-wide gaze was focused on her phone, and her jaw dropped. "Did you get a new submission?"

She slowly lifted her head. "Someone sent me the link to the Most Likely To list."

Any curiosity disappeared as annoyance took its place. Rachel let out a sudden shriek while Alex leaned forward. There was no missing the shock in his tone. "They sent it to *you*?"

"To *Babble*," Ava exhaled, blinking fast. "The submission asked if I could post it."

"Post it, post it, post it!" Rachel latched on to Ava's arm and gave it a shake. "Don't even bother writing an article—post the link!"

Ava didn't hesitate, because not even a second later, a colossal wave of sound cut through my concentration, a rapid fire, domino effect of noise that reverberated through the entire cafeteria. Some were beeps, some were chimes, some were fast-paced alarms. I lifted my head, as did seemingly everyone in the room, glancing around for a quick second before their heads ducked back down. Hands searched through their things.

It was straight from a *Gossip Girl* episode. All over the Most Likely Tos.

The Most Likely To list was an assortment of insanity that swarmed through the school at the start of every year. It was a list with fifty labels filled with digs and insults, such as Most Likely To: Never Be Kissed or Most Likely To: Get Dumped Before Homecoming. It was a sickness that plagued the mind of every student at Brentwood High, infecting everyone with stabs of vanity and ego.

The Most Likely To list was the first obsession of the school year, and each year's list was more annoying than the last.

Despite my sweltering animosity, I could share in a little bit of Ava's excitement. This was a big milestone for her blog, being trusted enough to distribute the list. Last year it was passed around solely on email chains.

Ava spoke first. "Nathan Tulane was voted Most Likely To: Cheat on Their Partner."

"I thought popular kids were usually excluded from these lists," Alex said with a frown.

Rachel scrolled through with her thumb. "And I thought he and his girlfriend broke up last week after the football game."

Ava nodded. "They did. It was ugly, too. Maybe that was why."

Let's talk about integrals, I thought, staring at my worksheet as my friends slowly lost their minds. *Dive into a little bit of constant functions talk. Talk derivatives to me.*

My thoughts once more ground to a halt when, in unison, as if they were still possessed by the same puppeteer, all three of them lifted their heads. Their eyes went straight to me.

I let out a sigh. "Who's on the list?"

The probability of being given a label was low. My senior class alone had over three hundred students, and since the Most Likely Tos were open to the entire high school, with only fifty labels, the odds of getting picked were slim.

However, not impossible. Last year, Alex was Most Likely To: Never Get a Girlfriend.

A lot of people, Alex included, treated getting on the list like a challenge, some sort of personal attack that they needed to prove wrong. Hence him asking me to the homecoming dance not even a month after he'd made the cut. I'd never been too worried about the sudden ask-out, though. If he had only dated me because of the list, we would've broken up a year ago.

"Are you on it again?" I asked him, trying to figure out what label it would be this time.

"Not me," he said slowly. "*You.*"

A contradictory impulse stirred in my stomach like bile. I didn't want to know what the label was—I definitely, definitely didn't want to know—but I *had* to know. I couldn't think of anything else. "For what? Most Likely To: Do Something with Her Life?"

Alex passed his phone over to me, which was warm from how firmly he'd been gripping it. A slew of names on a poorly designed PDF greeted me, and I had to blink a few times to understand what the awkward font was trying to say.

The label was a new one, because if it'd been created any years in the past, I definitely would've been named it. Every single time.

Most Likely To: Marry A Math Book.
Maisie Matthews

"Am I supposed to be offended?" I demanded, frowning at the screen. My heart was running at a strange beat in my chest, like a bird had been trapped in my ribcage. "Is that supposed to hurt my feelings? What kind of label is that, anyway? You can't marry an inanimate object."

Despite the firmness in my voice, I felt my cheeks burn.

It was the dumbest thing ever. The whole list was the dumbest thing ever. I mean, come on. *End up alone? Never get a girlfriend?* How was any of that funny?

Like Alex had said, populars never made the Most Likely To list, which was super convenient that *they* were never made fun of. It proved that they had to be the ones who made the whole thing up.

I lifted my gaze, finding the table the Top Tier claimed. They were the only ones who *weren't* looking at their phones, but rather sitting back and watching the insanity spread. I found Madison among the group, her pink lips turned up as she glanced around the cafeteria. She faltered when she spotted me, some of the amusement seeping from her features.

It was funny how high school changed people. I never would've guessed that the girl I grew up with, the girl I considered a sister, would turn out this way. Because out of all the possible suspects who might've come up with the stupid label, she was at the top.

I swiped up my worksheet and pencil and stuffed it into my orange satchel, where my calculus book greeted me spine-first. *Marry a math book.*

"Oh my gosh, did you see who got chosen for Never Get a Girlfriend?" Rachel asked, leaning toward Ava and tilting her phone screen, even though they were peering at the same ridiculous PDF. "That's so sad—he's sweet!"

"But he's never dated," Alex joined in, swiping

through. "Ooh, they've added a few more new ones this year. Look at this one—Most Likely To: Stay a Prude?"

"I'll see you guys later," I got out, but none of them noticed me gather my things. Which was fine by me, because I was sure the annoyance was clear on my face like a swipe of bright paint. Annoyance at them for being so interested in this shallow nonsense, annoyance with myself for even asking about the list in the first place.

Marry a math book. I cracked my knuckles as I stormed away from my table, passing head after head bowed into their cell screen. Was that seriously the best they could do?

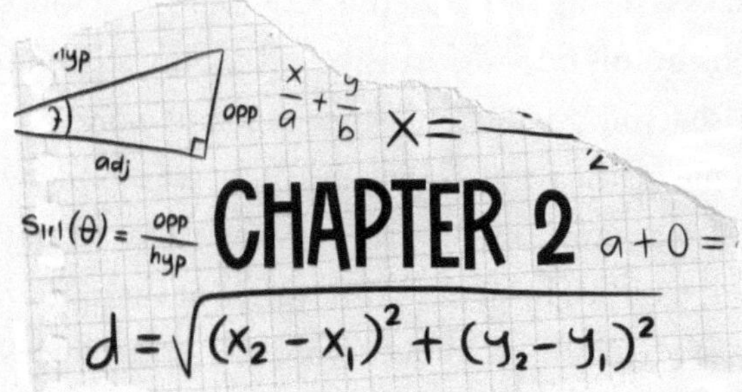

CHAPTER 2

$$d = \sqrt{(x_2 - x_1)^2 + (y_2 - y_1)^2}$$

Sometimes it felt like after freshman year, I turned into a totally new person. There was a version of me who'd lived from birth until the beginning of high school, thriving with a carefree attitude and a happy life filled with sleepovers and bike rides. Then there was a version of me who lived now—quiet, reserved, focused.

It was times like this, though, with the whispers and stares surrounding me like fog, that had me reliving freshman year all over again.

Since lunch, The Most Likely To list was all anyone talked about for the rest of the school day. Mondays were annoying on their own, but to hear every lame label parroted around during the remaining five classes nearly drove me insane.

So did the whispers.

"Did you see they made a new label for her?"

"Can you blame them? *Marry a Math Book*."

Someone laughed. "Yeah, it's so clever."

Ha, ha, ha. Yeah. *Super* clever.

I stared at the back of Mrs. Diego's head as she went over the homework for the night, trying to focus on her soothing voice and block out the peanut gallery behind me.

"I want you to do problems one through twenty-one tonight," Mrs. Diego said, scrawling the numbers on the board with her red dry-erase pen. "Odds only. Yes, yes, I know. Keep groaning. I know when I give you only even problems, you all go to the back of the book for the answers. Showing your work is required."

In the grand scheme of things, eleven problems weren't hard, especially since we were in the intro phases of calculus. If the class was groaning now, they were in for a treat for the rest of the year. I already had the homework finished. Mrs. Diego had given me the syllabus for the month last week, and I worked through it over the weekend.

"The bell's about to ring, so no in-class time today," Mrs. Diego went on, capping her marker and turning around. For a math teacher, a married one at that, she was relatively young. Early thirties. Not a single gray hair in her brown braid, and she was an expert at makeup. "You can have the last few minutes for free time."

Free time. Like the room was filled with a bunch of kindergarteners rather than seniors.

I brought my neon orange satchel onto my desk and took out my math binder. Earlier in the summer, Rachel had taught me calligraphy—more like attempted to teach me—and I had written *Calculus* onto this one. Lopsided and frumpy, but still legible. Still a win. With it in tow, I started toward Mrs. Diego's desk.

"Maisie," she greeted as I approached. "How did you find those questions I gave you over the weekend?"

"You went easy on me." I passed over the extra credit worksheet. "Speaking of, Principal Oliphant did *not* go easy on me when I met with her today."

"She said no, huh?"

"She didn't even give me a chance to ask before she shot me down."

Mrs. Diego's lips quirked to the side. "I'm sorry, Maisie. I know it must be frustrating, but don't worry about it too much, okay? I'll write you Brentwood High's best letter of recommendation."

It wasn't enough to completely lift my dark cloud of disappointment, but her words did a good job at breaking through some of the darkness. "I'll be ready for the next worksheet when you find one."

Mrs. Diego was my favorite teacher because she understood me. Even if she was the *only* person who understood me.

"Such a teacher's pet," the peanut gallery resumed once I sat back down, which caused my skin to prickle. I ducked my head, as if I could disappear into the desk. I'd never felt embarrassed about my love of math before—there'd never been a reason to. But with the list floating around, pleasantly invisible Maisie started to feel like trapped-inside-a-fishbowl Maisie.

The final bell rang, a long note that was more grating

than relieving, and the clamor of student voices rose to a crescendo now that the school day was over. Packing up my things, I escaped into the hallway, away from the whispering voices and prying eyes.

It was easier to blend in with the crowd of students filtering from their last period classes, easier to fall in step with everyone shuffling forward. Easier to feel less like a bug under a microscope.

Until I stepped to my locker, spotting something taped to the front of it. Paper. *Textbook* paper, with black words scrawled on it.

MOST LIKELY TO: MARRY A MATH BOOK.
Maisie Matthews

My brain processed the words at a snail's pace, like each letter took five seconds to work through. One of the jockstraps seriously got my name wrong? So, what—they were anti-English now, too?

Someone's hand came down on my shoulder hard, jarring me a little. "Let me know when the wedding is!"

A girl laughed directly behind me. "I can't wait to see the tux you get for the book."

I wouldn't have called myself a violent person, but in that moment, I wanted nothing more than to turn around and find out how much punching someone actually hurt. It'd hurt more than it was worth. Probably.

I ripped the paper off the locker, crumpling it into a ball while angrily turning my lock. I got the combination wrong the first two tries, fingers fumbling.

Marry a math book. Was it wrong to have something

you enjoyed doing? Were we really stuck in the 80's where the smart kids were picked on? Would I walk up to the quarterback and tell him he's most likely to marry a football? How about an art student? Most likely to marry a paintbrush? What was the big deal with math and numbers? Who *cared*?

Cracking the knuckles on my left hand, I angrily sorted through the things in my locker with my right. I didn't care what anyone thought, not anymore. I didn't.

But it didn't change the fact that I kept my head buried in my locker until the crowd behind me thinned.

"Um, hello?" The voice was so soft-spoken that I nearly missed it, and even when it did register, I ignored it. I slid my English Lit book into my satchel, right next to my calc textbook, shoving things around to make room. "It's Macy, right?"

When I turned, I was met with a wall of chest covered by a blank yellow T-shirt. Accompanying the T-shirt were the brightest eyes I'd ever seen. Not green, not blue, not brown—hazel. The intensity in the gaze lit a match in my chest, setting fire to a wave of anger.

There were two Connors at Brentwood High—Connor Wasilewski and Connor Bray. Connor W wasn't as infamous as Connor B. Wasn't on the varsity football team, didn't have the snobby head cheerleader as a girl-friend, and didn't have a fancy-schmancy house on Bleeker Avenue that he liked to throw parties in. Connor W was a great guy.

Connor B, the hazel-eyed boy standing in front of me, was not.

"Hi," he said again, a mask of superiority coating his features. Full lips, straight nose, thick eyebrows. It was like *be conventionally handsome* had been on his Christmas list or something. "Can I talk to you for a sec?"

I stared at him, fighting the urge to look over my shoulder. Surely, he wasn't talking to *me*.

But Connor persisted. "In private?"

I glanced around the hallway at the handful of students standing by lockers and chatting with their friends. It was then that I realized Connor didn't stand directly in front of me. There were about five feet of space between us, his body angled toward the lockers, as if he were having the conversation with the metal. Almost like if anyone were to glance over, they wouldn't assume he was talking to me.

It solidified my response. "No."

He blinked his ridiculously long lashes in surprise. "No?"

Gee, go figure. He'd never heard the word. "If you have something to say, you can say it right here." Not that I really cared what he'd have to say. I was surprised he even knew my name—except he couldn't have been bothered to get the pronunciation right.

"Fine," he muttered, the first sign of his perfect mask cracking. He took a baby step closer. "Someone mentioned that you offer services. I'm not sure how much you charge or whatever, but I'd be willing to pay a bit extra for...well, for discretion."

"Hate to break it to you, Mr. Star Football Player, but I'm not a prostitute."

His reaction was worth the joke, with a strangled inhale and rapid blinking. "I didn't say—" Connor stopped sharply on the word, hazel eyes flashing before he closed them. "I meant your *tutoring* services. Trust me, I wouldn't be coming to you for anything else."

The little dig fanned the flames of my anger higher, with a blistering heat spreading across my chest. Before I lashed out and said something that'd probably bite me in the butt later, I turned back toward my locker. *You are alone in the hallway*, I told myself, going back to sorting through my things. I moved on to cracking my right hand's knuckles. *Where did you put* Pride and Prejudice?

People who thought they were perfect, that every road they walked on was paved with gold, bothered me to no end. With Connor Bray, it was worse because everyone else thought he was perfect, too. He was one of the few students at Brentwood High that lived on Bleeker Avenue, the section of Brentwood nearly exclusive to lawyers and doctors. Anyone with heaps of money.

His football rap sheet began in freshman year when he blew the coaches away with his tryouts. As the best catcher and the fastest runner, he was the very first freshman ever brought up on to varsity as a relief player. Sophomore year, he got more field time than some of the seniors. By junior year, he'd turned into the best player on the team—and with all the muscle he'd put on from years of commitment, he quickly transformed into a crowd favorite, too.

And this year he and his girlfriend, Jade, were a shoo-in for homecoming king and queen. Though it was normally Brentwood tradition for the quarterback to be king, there was no doubt in my mind that Connor would get the title. He was dating the head cheerleader, of course, who was practically already crowned queen. They were Brentwood's It-Couple.

"I need help with Algebra II," Connor went on, inching forward as much as he dared. "You tutor people, right?"

I am alone in the hallway, and the annoying voice in my ear is a gnat. Or a fly. A bug to be squashed.

"Macy—"

"It's *Maisie*," I snapped, putting emphasis on the *z* sound, giving in to the burning. "And what in your concussion-riddled brain made you think 'hmm, I need a tutor, might as well go to the girl my friends voted most likely to marry a math book'?"

Instead of seeming intimidated by my reaction, by the severity in my voice, the jerk *smiled*.

Out of everything that had happened today, that irked me the most. "'Maisie Matthews, math geek extraordinaire, *must* be a tutor, and of course she'll fall at my feet for the chance to tutor *me*.'"

"Wow, you nearly nailed my unmistakable baritone."

"It's easy to nail *stupid*."

Connor tipped his head to the side, that amused smirk turning wicked. "You know from experience?"

I clenched my jaw so tightly that it was a surprise my teeth didn't shatter. "And *discretion*?" I scoffed on the word, slamming my locker shut. "Who do you want to hide it from? Your football buddies? Heaven forbid they think you have more brain cells than they do. Except you probably don't if you're needing a tutor the second week of the school year."

Connor arched a brown eyebrow, his calm demeanor cracking like a sheet of ice. "I'm flattered you know so much about me. Didn't realize I had so many fans wandering the Brentwood halls. Want me to autograph your math book?"

I slapped the crumpled piece of textbook paper against his chest, hard enough to rock him back a step. "My tutoring roster is already full," I bit out. "Find someone else."

I didn't wait to see if he caught the paper before I barreled past him. My sneakers squeaked at the hasty getaway, and I fumbled to get my satchel strap over my head.

God, who did he think he was? A frustrated scream built in the back of my throat as I stomped away, refusing to let the brief interaction jar me. Because it didn't. Boys like Connor didn't get to me. *Especially* not Connor. Come tomorrow morning, he wouldn't even remember my name. Not that he'd gotten it right the first time. *Guess Mr. Football Star isn't as perfect as he wants everyone to believe.*

That night, Alex lounged against his green sofa with his socked feet resting in my lap. I tried to breathe through my mouth since his feet were way too close to my nose, and though it was something that always irked me, I let them perch there, at least while I figured out what to say to start a conversation. *Any* conversation.

I had a copy of *Math Challenges for Future Mathematicians* open on my lap, thumb bookmarking the page. My older sister, Jozie, had gotten the workbook for me right before she left for college two weeks ago, and though it was a thoughtful present, the concepts and equations were way too easy. I hadn't had the heart to tell her that the workbook was meant for middle schoolers, but worked through it anyway.

Or tried to. My concentration now had dwindled to the barest amounts.

Alex slammed his thumbs against his videogame controller, heels digging into my thighs as he surged forward periodically. The graphics raging on the TV screen took up the air for dialogue, as did his grunts when he inevitably died and respawned. For a guy who'd been playing videogames since he was five, he absolutely sucked.

"Can I ask you a question?" I watched him as I spoke. He didn't turn toward me, but he did raise his eyebrows. I took that as a *go ahead*. "Do you think it's lame that I'm on the Most Likely To list this year?"

I hated even asking the question. It reeked—almost as bad as Alex's feet—of insecurity. But as soon as I had read the words at the lunch table, a stone-sized weight settled in my stomach, and as the day passed, it grew and grew so much that my stomach physically ached.

"It's not lame," he said, voice flat with concentration. "I was on it last year, you know. Do *you* think it's lame to be on the list?"

"Maybe lame isn't the right word." More like embarrassing. I studied him. He'd taken the bandage on his upper lip off since leaving school, but the skin was red and puckered from Shaving Incident Number Four. "Never mind."

Alex let the topic go as easily as it'd come, but then again, I wasn't totally convinced he'd really been listening. Readjusting my grip on my book, I turned to the videogame on the TV, but the gunshots and blood splatters barely registered. And then I thought of something that would get his attention. "You'll never guess who came up to me today and asked me to tutor them."

"Are you coming to the game on Friday?" Alex asked suddenly, and though he still focused on the TV, his voice became a bit more animated. "It's an away game."

"When do I ever go to football games?" I readjusted my legs so his heels weren't digging into my skin. The soles of his white socks were dirty, as if they were several days without a wash.

"You know, you're turning into a recluse, Brain. I was talking to Nate Tulane, and he told me he didn't even know I had a girlfriend."

"Nate Tulane is a terrible friend, then, because we've been dating for almost a year."

"My point." Alex emphasized each word with a

vicious swipe to his controller's joysticks. "Brentwood is a big school, but if my own friends don't even realize we're dating, that's not a good thing."

I wanted to tell him a relationship wasn't a one-way street. If his friends didn't know we were dating, Alex could've said something. He could've posted more pictures of us together. Could've invited me to hang around his friends more. *My* friends knew we were dating.

"Do you ever just..." He slumped deeper against the couch arm, shoulders losing some of their tension. "Feel like we're different?"

"Of course we're different," I said without hesitation. "We're different people."

"I meant *too* different."

I'd be lying if I said I hadn't been expecting this conversation to surface at some point. As if we'd both tied an anchor to the topic and threw it in the ocean, but sooner or later, the tide would bring it back in. His voice sounded neutral, though. Maybe a bit curious to hear my answer. It wasn't a serious enough question for him to pause his game for. "Are you breaking up with me?"

"No, no," he rushed to say, and finally, blessedly, he paused his game. The raging gunfire abruptly stopped. Setting down the controller, he worked a hand over his eyes. "I'm not. I'm just making conversation."

An odd subject to make conversation about, but I mulled the words over. No emotion surfaced from them. Almost as if my brain couldn't really compute their meaning. "I don't think we're too different," I said to his socked foot, placing my hand on his ankle, where his pantleg had risen and a sliver of skin was visible. "I think we complement each other."

Alex and I weren't total opposites, anyway. Sure, he was more obsessed with the whole "Top Tier" realm than I was. Always refreshed *Brentwood Babble* for the latest updates, whereas I couldn't care less. He liked sports, while I liked the more scientific side of things. But we both liked country music and hated pineapple on pizza. We were both introverted—albeit me a little more than him—and preferred nights in rather than going out.

When he'd asked me to homecoming last year, kicking off the start of *him and me*, it'd been fun. New. I'd been excited to have another half, to have someone else to think about. And a cute boy, at that. The honeymoon period had melted into this, though. Quiet nights, smelly feet, and few words exchanged between us. But that was normal. No relationship could stay in the honeymoon period forever.

Alex reached over and placed his hand on top of mine, and it became a weird hand-hand-foot sandwich. It took me a second to realize he was stopping me from popping my knuckles. "Maisie, I don't think it's lame you're on the list," he said, and his words held a soft, rare quality.

Relief washed over me because he *had* listened to me, and he wasn't judging me. "Really?"

"Yeah. I mean, I was voted Most Likely To: Never Get a Girlfriend last year, and here I am." He gave me an awkward half-smile, one that kind of tugged on one side of his mouth. "And it's not too late, you know? You can find a new hobby, Maisie, and it'll be okay."

His words took several moments to sink in, for my brain to understand the full meaning behind them. He patted my hand before leaning back. The rare softness in his eyes was gone as he went back to the TV screen, almost as if that'd never happened.

My thumb bookmarking the page in my math workbook twitched. *Find a new hobby*. Like it was something to fix.

I leaned my head on the back of the couch, staring up at the ceiling. There was a water spot near the corner, one that'd been there since I'd come over to his house the first time. It was shaped like a heart with a fissure down the center. "Did you know that I'm top in the class?"

"I mean, it makes sense. You live and breathe academics." Alex moved his foot to knock against my book. "You even have homework with you right now."

I slid my thumb out of *Math Challenges for Future Mathematicians*, setting it on the couch arm.

Alex swore viciously at the TV, slapping his controller. "How does this keep happening? Why isn't my team helping me?"

I wanted to say something, but his attention had already been recaptured when his character respawned. Alex slammed his feet on my lap as he sat up, cursing at the TV again as the screen took on a red tint. He hadn't even lasted a minute.

My cell phone buzzed where I'd left it on the coffee table, and I swiped it up, grateful for a distraction. It was an email attachment from Ava, subject line: **MLT PROOF.**

As soon as I opened it, I wished I hadn't.

In case you've been living under a rock, Brentwood High, the Most Likely Tos are upon us again! And let me say: this year? It's DRIP-PING with drama! Three new labels were added to the roster this year—Stay a Prude, Marry a Math Book, and Peek in High School. Ouch! Which one do you think is more embarrassing? And I spy with my litttle eye a few football hotties on the list too. Landon Settler, never to get a girlfriend? Nate Tulane, branded a cheater?

Time will tell if anyone's going to break free of these awkward titles, but let me know—who do you think will spread their wings first?!

Though I hadn't been living under a rock, at that moment, I wanted to crawl under one. I could practically hear Ava's voice in my head, an enthusiastic chatter filled with exclamation points and emphasis. *Which one do you think is more embarrassing?*

Except reading her words left me empty. Hollow. The butt of a joke that I knew she hadn't realized she'd told. She was caught up in it all, like everyone else.

MAISIE

You used the wrong peak and used three t's in little

I typed back to her numbly, the *whoosh* of the message sending echoing in my ears. I picked at the cream polish on my nails, basking in the brief satisfaction when a piece came off in a big chunk. I'd fix it later. "Mom said the lasagna would be out of the oven at seven, so I should get going."

Alex dropped his feet to the ground with a *thunk*. "Yeah, you don't want to be late. Your mom's lasagna is the best."

I had to make sure I dodged the view of the TV as I stood, stretching my stiff limbs. Judging by the ache in my butt, I'd been sitting silent for a while, working through equations while my boyfriend murdered non-player characters.

Months ago, I might've kissed him goodbye. I would've risked his annoyance and stolen a peck on his lips, and months ago, he might've kissed me back even in the middle of a game.

"Text me when you're home safe, okay?" he asked without looking over, but he did quickly lift one hand in farewell.

I watched the back of his head for a moment, mind caught up in everything. *Do you ever just...feel like we're different?*

Sure, maybe he didn't get my love of math and wanted me to try new hobbies, but wasn't that the point of being in a relationship? Helping the other grow and explore things a bit more? This was us.

I was okay with that. Hopefully he was, too.

$\mathcal{J}$nstead of my alarm waking me up the next morning, the delicate trill of a text coming through stirred me. The first one barely broke through my awareness, but the second one woke me up enough for me to slap the nightstand a few times. My fingers finally brushed against the screen, and half-asleep, I squinted at the bright display.

JOZIE

Happy Tuesday, May-May! Tell Mom and Dad I love them, but know that I love you more. xx

Don't text back tho, okay? Walking in2 class now. Love you!

Just like that, I was wide awake, letting my hand fall and my cell press against my chest. Even with my phone now locked, I could see the text behind my closed lids. Jozie had been gone two weeks now, and she never missed a wake-up text. Except since we were going on week two of the messages, they started to feel more and more ingenuine. Her messages weren't copied and pasted word for word, but the phrasing was always similar. Similar enough to let me know that my happy-go-lucky sister wasn't putting that much thought into it. But she was in college. She was busy. Too busy for her little sister.

Her absence in the house was like a grand chandelier with one of the lightbulbs missing. Dim, incomplete. I rolled over onto my side, peering at where her bed was rammed in the far corner. My vision was blurry without my glasses on, but I knew what it looked like. Stripped of her normal, cheery comforter, now covered with an old quilt. The nights were silent without her chainsaw snoring, and after seventeen years of sharing a room with her, I hadn't gotten used to the quiet.

We were close in age—only eighteen months apart—but so drastically different. She took more from Mom and Dad, falling on the free-thinking side of life, the creative spirit, artistic mindset. As a lover of analytics and numbers, I couldn't have been more different from them if I tried.

She'd told me not to text back, but I wanted to more than anything. Despite the daily texts, I couldn't remember the last time I'd heard her voice.

Instead, I threw my blankets off my legs, letting the air-conditioned air sweep over my skin, and stood. There was no going back to sleep—might as well start the day.

"Good morning," my dad greeted as I came into the kitchen after getting ready, standing near the coffeepot. He already had on a pair of tan painter's overalls and had his shirt sleeves rolled up to his elbows. "I'm about to head out for the day. Coffee?"

I shook my head. "Jozie is the one who likes coffee."

Dad topped off his to-go tumbler, nodding a little. "Ah, right. Well. Your mom already left for the gallery. She and the owner are meeting with an artist this morning."

Mom worked as an art curator at the newest art gallery in the county. Center Inspire was fighting to claim its relevancy with new showings and exhibits, which meant that most of Mom's life happened within those walls. More since Jozie left—with Mom's pride and joy gone, her mini-me, what reason was there for her to be home?

"I won't be home until late. Once I finish painting the exhibition room, they have a few sets they want me to build for next week." Dad worked in the building department for the art gallery, playing a huge role in getting everything pretty for their showcases. He took a long sip of coffee while ghosting his hand over his balding head. "You can figure out food on your own?"

I took out the chocolate milk from the fridge and poured some into a glass. "Mmm-hmm." The clock on the microwave blinked at me.

"How's it feel to be back at school for a full week?" he asked, his peppery mustache quirking up. He kept trying to deny the gray slowly taking over his once-brown facial hair, but it was getting harder and harder for him to fight the truth. "Senior year. It doesn't feel like it's been that long since we did this with Jozie."

I hadn't told them about the Most Likely To list. With how technologically challenged they were, I wasn't sure they'd even understand me if I tried to describe it. Heck, they might've even thought the list was *creative.* However, not telling them about it meant swallowing my thoughts and feelings about the stupid label.

I also hadn't told them about the losing my valedictorian spot, even though I knew I should've. We needed to plan for the loss of that top spot position, which in turn would lead to the loss of scholarships, but the thought of bringing it up made me sick.

"Time flies," I said simply, dropping my cup into the sink. "I should get to school. I'll see you tonight."

"You have to go already? I was hoping to chat with you more." He offered me a smile, one that was warm and *him,* and it made me hesitate in my beeline toward the door. "Your mother and I talked with Jozie last night. She said she's really been enjoying her classes. I told her she shouldn't have been worried—a school that's charging that much ought to have impressive classes, right?"

Dad hadn't intended for the words to stab on a pressure point, I knew. As a chronic avoider of conflict, he'd rather stay silent than deal with the wrath of the Matthews girls. *A school that's charging that much.*

The day Mom and Dad sat me down was crystal clear in my memory, as if it'd happened yesterday. "Maisie," Mom had said, her tone light and friendly, as if we were going to talk about what was for dinner. Jozie, at my left, had been stiff in her chair, but I hadn't thought twice about it at the time. "After using up Jozie's scholarship money and the money Grandmama left for her, we're a bit short for her college tuition."

It'd never been a secret that Jozie and I shared a college fund. Grandmama had started it after I was born, and since we were her only grandkids, she'd left Jozie and I each all of her savings when she passed. "Are you going to take out student loans?" I had asked, turning toward my sister.

"She doesn't need much more," Mom had explained. "So to avoid taking out loans in her first year, we were hoping we could take some out of your fund. Since you'll be valedictorian, and given your grades, you're more likely to get full-ride scholarships anyway. Would that be okay?"

Jozie had faced me then, her desperation stripped to its most obvious state. Wide eyes, puffed out bottom lip, crinkled brow. Jozie asking me for anything was a rarity, and there she'd been, probably seconds from getting on her knees to beg.

I'd said yes before I thought it through, and they'd all walked away before I had a chance to change my mind.

Now here I was, no valedictorian spot and a college fund that would've made my rattling piggy bank seem rich.

My phone dinging startled me, pulling me from my thoughts. Dad regarded me expectantly, waiting for a response to a question I couldn't remember. Instead, I peered at the text from Rachel. "I have to go," I told Dad, giving him a distracted nod. "I'll see you when you get home. Have a good day."

This time, when I headed for the door, Dad didn't stop me.

I laid my hand on the steering wheel for two seconds, the car horn filling the air with a pathetic squawk. Though it was early September, the air had a chill to it this morning, and I turned the heater on full blast. I was lucky anything puffed out, because the crappy air system had a slow-moving way of life, like it was ready to move on to its retirement home.

A classic, Dad would've said as he eyed the two-door coupe, but all I saw was rust and bad mileage.

I laid my palm on the wheel once more, but before I had a chance to press down, Rachel emerged from the cheery yellow door. She'd styled her hair into a high bun today, almost on the center of her head. As she hurried across the lawn, she worked on drawing out small little pieces of baby hairs to frame her temples.

"Sorry, sorry," Rachel rushed out, ducking her head as she fell into the passenger seat. "Thank you for picking me up. I couldn't find any of my hair ties, and then I couldn't find my Gilfman boots—"

"Real Gilfman?" I asked, peering at her black leather boots. Dew clung to them, making them shiny. They *looked* like the designer brand, but I couldn't imagine Rachel having the money to afford them.

She winked at me. "Fake, but you can't tell. All about appearances."

With that thought in the air, I grabbed the shifter and reversed out of her driveway.

"Listen, I can't thank you enough for driving me," she said, fluffing her brown hair in the crappy flip-down mirror. Even from here, I could see the dust buildup along the edges of the glass. "When we get to school, I'm chewing out my brother. He couldn't be bothered to wake me up *and* he left without me. I'm going to wring his thick neck." Her frown deepened. "*And* Ava. She didn't wake me up either."

"She slept over?"

"Yeah, but she was gone before I woke up, and that's not like her."

Weeknight sleepovers were something they did from time to time, since they lived right across the street from each other. They'd invited me a few times, but I'd always declined. As a girl who loved getting her beauty sleep before a seven-hour school day, I didn't mind skipping out on those sleepovers, knowing they were mostly gossip sessions anyway.

"We were going through the yearbook, looking for boys for her to kiss," Rachel went on, affirming my thoughts. She tilted her head to peer at me, somber. "Did you see she was on the list, too?"

I jerked my head over to her, frowning. "She was?" I *had* stormed off after hearing my name, but I was surprised Ava hadn't said anything in a group text. "What was her label?"

"Never Have Their First Kiss."

"She's not bothered by it, right?" I tried to picture

Ava reading the label, and my heart pinched. "Because she shouldn't be. It's a meaningless list." Now if only I could swallow that same pill, with the rest of Brentwood behind me. But that was just it, wasn't it? If it truly was meaningless, people wouldn't be so obsessed.

"I think she was." Rachel tugged a tube of lip gloss out of her pocket, the sparkling pink mixture making a sucking sound as she twisted the wand. "I was thinking about trying to find Ava a date. I've got a few potential candidates."

"Why not find *you* a date?"

"Because I'm swearing off partners. At least in high school."

"It's for the best," I said, flipping on my blinker to turn into the school's parking lot. "That way you don't have to always guess someone's intentions with stuff."

She peered at me from the corner of her eye. "Did Alex say anything about you being on the list?"

It was one of those moments when I could've told her the truth, or even at least a half-truth. I thought of his legs on mine yesterday, his attention fastened onto the TV as if I wasn't even there. I could've stripped naked, and he wouldn't have batted an eye. *Do you ever just...feel like we're different?* Even now, the words didn't have much of an effect on me.

Alex technically said being on the list wasn't a big deal, but he also said that I had time to find a new hobby. That I had time to change myself. I knew if I told Rachel any of that, she'd go off. "Why would he say anything? He was on it last year."

"I remember. He got Most Likely To: Never Get a Girlfriend. And then he asked you out a few weeks later."

I fought the urge to roll my eyes. "He asked me to *homecoming,* and then we officially started dating two weeks after the dance. It's not like he walked up to me and immediately asked me to be his girlfriend."

"Be honest with me." Rachel reached out and gave my knee a squeeze. The gesture lessened some of the tension compounding in my body. "The Most Likely Tos. How much is it bothering you, being on it?"

I'd only been friends with Rachel and Ava since the end of freshman year, which gave us two full years to get close, but not close enough for her to perfectly see through my lies or not. I kept my eyes on the parking lot, scouring it for a space, refusing to glance over. "Why would it? The list is stupid anyway."

"I know I'd be a little upset if I was on it."

"Well, I'm flattered, really."

Rachel checked her makeup one last time in the visor mirror. "Out of everyone at Brentwood, they noticed *you.* They even made a new label for you. That is special, I guess."

Special. If I could've blended into the background of Brentwood High, that would've been even better.

"You know what's weird?" Finally, she turned away from me. "There are a *lot* of jocks on the Most Likely Tos this year. A lot of popular people. More than usual."

With barely any interest, I asked, "Like who?"

"Well, Nate Tulane—he's the one that plays all the sports. Football, baseball, basketball. Landon Settler, which you know is the quarterback. Uh... Oh! Madison Oliphant."

My foot slipped on the brake, lurching us forward. Rachel slapped her hand against the dashboard, the jarring movement causing the glovebox to pop open. "Madison's on it? What's her label?"

"Uh." Her face scrunched up in concentration as she slammed the glovebox shut. "I can't remember. Ava would know, of course. I'd be shocked if she didn't already have the whole thing memorized. Let me check. It wasn't for anything good, though."

"There aren't any good ones on that list," I told her, turning in to a parking space. The lot was mostly filled, but we were able to snag a space between an SUV and a beat-up truck.

Rachel scrolled through her phone for a moment before passing it to me. "Madison Oliphant," she said, as if I didn't know the name.

Once again, I was greeted with the poorly designed webpage, but I barely gave it a second thought now. Instead, I scoured the names.

MOST LIKELY TO: NEVER GET A BOYFRIEND

Lacey Churchill

MOST LIKELY TO: PEAK IN HIGH SCHOOL

Madison Oliphant

MOST LIKELY TO: STAY A PRUDE

Gemma Settler

"Peak in high school," I echoed, thinking back to Ava's article last night. "That's a new label, right?"

Rachel nodded, taking her phone back. "I can't believe she was voted it, honestly. Or any of the guys. Top Tier is *never* on it. Makes you wonder who's running it."

Madison being on it didn't make any sense. She was co-captain of the cheer squad. Out of the Top Tier girls, she was easily number two, only beaten by her best friend, Jade Dyer. Madison had fought tooth and nail to be right hand to Jade's top spot, not caring about who she put down in the process.

I'd know.

It might've made her a perfect candidate for "peaking in high school," but her Top Tier status should've exempted her from it all.

As I unbuckled my seatbelt, I couldn't help but wonder how she was taking it.

Rachel and I both climbed out of the car into the chilly air, and I curled my shirt sleeves over my fingers. Rachel fluffed her cardigan. "Don't let it get to you, Maisie," she said, huddling closer to me against the rather sharp breeze. "I'm sure by next week, everyone will forget all about it. Just..." Rachel caught my arm before we got too close to the building. "Don't look at the comments on Ava's post, okay? Promise?"

I winced as if bracing for a punch, the tense feeling refusing to go away. I trailed behind her slowly, my body tense, knowing full well what I'd be doing during first period.

CHAPTER 4

I immediately knew, as soon as I loaded *Babble*, that I should've listened to Rachel.

StarBoi28: Could you imagine being labeled to marry a math book??? LOL

BrentwoodBobs: OMG, super awkward

HeartEyes422: Have you met Macy Matthews, tho? TOTALLY fits.

I wasn't the only one targeted—the Most Likely To digs extended beyond math geeks, apparently—but there were enough for me to memorize, and for them to replay on a loop throughout the entire day. Every time I locked eyes with a random student in the hall, I couldn't help but wonder if they were StarBoi28 or HeartEyes422. *Totally fits.*

I should've transferred to Jefferson when I had the chance.

To preserve my sanity, and a little bit of my self-esteem, I held on to Rachel's promise of the list dying down after a week. She had to be right. After a week, what was there left to talk about? All the punch lines and gossip threads were overused.

It was last period that left me the most unsettled. A class I'd always felt so comfortable in left me feeling too seen. I'd been comfortable in my element, and now my element made me feel embarrassed.

Especially when Mrs. Diego called on me with ten minutes left to the class.

I'd had my head down, diligently working on next week's homework, when I heard my name.

"Maisie? Can you tell me the first step to getting the answer for the equation on the board?"

My mouth ran dry as I met Mrs. Diego's stare, feeling more than a little betrayed. She never called on me. She always knew I'd know the answer. Why did she have to start drawing attention to me now?

I glanced at the equation on the board only momentarily, ready for the attention to switch back to her. "I'm not sure."

Mrs. Diego began nodding before she froze. She regarded the board, almost as if trying to spot a mistake *she* made. "You don't know?"

I ducked my head, wishing the graffitied surface of the desk could swallow me whole.

"Um, well, Jia—can you give me the first step?"

It'd come as an instinct, saying that I didn't know, a sort of self-preservation. As if getting the answer wrong would prove that I *wasn't* a math geek.

Ugh, pathetic. I was pathetic.

When the bell rang signaling the end of the school day, I'd already been expecting Mrs. Diego to ask me to stay behind.

"I'm having an off day today," I told her, unable to keep the defensiveness from leaking into my voice as I approached her desk. I readjusted the strap of my satchel against my neck, the nylon biting into my skin. "I—I wasn't paying close attention."

Mrs. Diego looked up at me from her chair. "I've heard about the Most Likely To list."

Wow, so even teachers gossiped about it. That made me feel even more embarrassed, which I didn't even think was possible. I could imagine them surrounding a table in the teachers' lounge, reacting to each label. "It's no big deal."

What I actually meant was *I don't want to talk about it*, because even though Mrs. Diego was my favorite teacher, the levels of awkwardness would be unmatched. She'd probably give me a mathematics-focused speech. *"Think of it like an equation—how can you convert this negative into a positive?"*

Which, fine, it would've been a good speech, but she wasn't old enough to come across as motherly; she also wasn't young enough for me to take her "your worth isn't decreed by a list" encouragement without feeling monumentally embarrassed.

"Oh good, I caught you."

A new voice had both Mrs. Diego and me turning to the door where Principal Oliphant stepped through. Immediately, my guard went up. The memory of her brushing me off yesterday stung, and I wasn't so certain I could muster up any ounce of politeness for her.

She glanced between us before looking around the empty desks. Once confirming that the math room was empty, she promptly shut the door. "Maisie," she greeted, venturing closer, "I wanted to thank you."

Something about her sudden presence unnerved me, especially with the only escape route closed off. "Thank me for what?"

Mrs. Diego took the principal's words as some sort of cue, because she straightened in her chair and brought out a collection of papers from her printer. Even from here, I could see the top sheet was covered in ink. "Maisie, I printed out a schedule you can follow, if you choose to, and which chapters are going to be on the test."

"*Test?*" She pulled a textbook out of a built-in cupboard by her desk. It was an Algebra II book with math equations and graph lines emblazoned on the front. A girl with black glasses grinned on the cover, and annoyingly enough, she kind of looked like me with her brown hair and freckled cheeks. Awesome. "Wait, is this for another tutoring session? Does someone else need tutoring?"

Principal Oliphant's voice came closer to my elbow. "A student needs to retake last year's final exam. We were under the impression that he spoke with you already."

Mrs. Diego nodded with slight confusion. "He told me this morning that you two had spoken yesterday after school. That I could give you the supplies."

"No one talked to—" I did a full stop, almost as if I

hadn't started speaking in the first place. Something underneath my skin began buzzing, as if a swarm of bees had crawled their way into my veins. *He spoke to you yesterday. You two had spoken yesterday after school.* I bit the word out, though I already knew the answer. "Who?"

"Connor Bray," she said, as casual as could be. "I already rearranged the three students you were set up to tutor to meet with another tutor. That way you can give him your full attention."

Principal Oliphant folded her hands behind her back. "There's also a certain amount of...discretion required."

Discretion. That was the freaking word he'd used.

All the embarrassment and humiliation morphed into something hotter, fiercer, something that could burn down a small village. Or at least one single, selfish, egotistical football player. "Listen, I'm not—"

Mrs. Diego tapped the corner of the textbook, and something intense in her demeanor had me shutting up. "It's a special situation. He learned this information last year, but he didn't end up passing the final exam."

"Why can't he just retake the class like everyone else? Why does he need a make-up exam?"

"Only one math course can be taken per year, and he's required to pass Algebra II and Statistics to graduate on time. So if he doesn't get a make-up exam—"

"Without this make-up exam," Principal Oliphant cut in, "he'll have to retake Algebra II over this next summer, meaning he *won't* graduate on time."

Here she was explaining all this when my mind still

choked on the fact that she was talking about *Connor Bray.*

"The school district's very firm," she went on. "Normally, students are given the opportunity to retake the test, or any failed class, over the summer. But there was a clerical error...Well, we didn't see that Connor scored below passing until last week when sorting out the paperwork. We're giving him another chance to retake the exam, but at the end of the month. Since he had the summer to forget the material, we're giving him a brief period to relearn."

"The end of the month?" I raised my eyebrows. "How do you expect anyone to learn a whole year of math in three weeks?" Even better question: how on earth did they expect me to teach it?

"What you'll be doing is more like a few practice sessions than true tutoring," Principal Oliphant said. "You'll be refreshing his memory."

"You said he failed the first time." My words came out slowly, and I was absolutely blown away at how calm my voice sounded. Flat. Unbothered. I should've been an actress. "Meaning he didn't understand the material to begin with."

Mrs. Diego's expression was truly apologetic, with pinched eyebrows and a scrunched mouth. "You're the best tutor in the school. Every student you've tutored has gone on to pass their classes with grades above a B. I believe you'd be able to help him."

I glared down at the book, at the stupid smiling girl on the front. "Mrs. Diego—"

"Maisie." Principal Oliphant tilted her head at me, her neutral lips turning up into a smirk that screamed of craftiness. Like we were about to share a secret. "In exchange for helping Connor pass the exam, I'd be willing to reinstate the valedictorian awards for one more year."

If I hadn't been gritting my teeth, my jaw would've dropped. It was a carrot dangled in front of a starving rabbit, close enough to smell but just out of reach. At that moment, I could see more similarities between Principal Oliphant and her daughter than their appearances. "I thought you said the decision wasn't up to you."

"It's not, but I can request that the board delay the decision for one more year. It's not too late."

Surely, she had to hear how she sounded. She wouldn't fight for *me*, but for Connor Bray she'd pull out all the stops. *Why?* I wanted to scream. *Why is he so special?*

But I didn't even have to ask the question. Connor Bray might not have been the quarterback of the football team, but he *was* Brentwood's star player. He was practically a household name to those who worshipped the Bobcats. Connor Bray, Brentwood High Bobcat running back, *senior.*

What would everyone say if Connor was held back due to a *clerical error*, something that is solely the school's fault? The Top Tier clique didn't stop with the high school students; it extended to their moms and dads as well. When one of their own was threatened, it meant war. Heck, they'd probably light torches and grab pitchforks.

Once again, like always, the popularity card held more weight than a stack of books. If it were anyone else, would they be assigned a tutor? Would they be given a month to study? I was surprised Principal Oliphant hadn't just passed Connor and swept it under the rug.

And then, just in case I had any doubts, Principal Oliphant said, "Connor's talent will take us to state championships this year. We just need to make sure he's eligible to get us there."

My nails would've dented the cover on the textbook if it were a paperback. "And Connor already told you I agreed to this?"

Mrs. Diego nodded. "Came to me this morning before classes started."

I imagined Connor Bray waltzing into Mrs. Diego's classroom this morning, confidently telling her that, of course, Maisie Matthews had said yes. That she'd practically tripped over herself to say yes.

"But we wanted to give you an incentive," Principal Oliphant cut in, "to make sure he'll pass. Of course you'll do a fantastic job as always, but we wanted to—"

"Sweeten the deal?" I finished for her, fighting for composure.

The most infuriating part of it all was that Principal Oliphant had me, and she knew she did. Valedictorian was the one thing I wanted—the one thing I needed—and after my desperate display the previous day, she knew I'd never turn an offer like this down. I couldn't only tutor

Connor, though. I had to get him to pass the exam. Those were the terms.

"The suggested learning schedule is on page two," Mrs. Diego said, and I couldn't help but feel a sting of betrayal. It wasn't only Principal Oliphant using me like a chess piece. At least Mrs. Diego had the decency to seem guilty about it. "Like Principal Oliphant said, it's more of a refresher. You don't have to teach the entire chapter, but you'll want to cover a few equations at least. It's a lot to go over, but do your best."

"We believe in you," Principal Oliphant said. "And, of course, we'll check in periodically to hear how it's going."

I didn't trust myself to speak—surely if I opened my mouth, I'd breathe fire. I gave a hasty nod, clutching the Algebra II textbook to my chest. Without another word, I turned on my heel, showing myself out into the hallway.

Did that really happen? My entire tutoring roster swiped clean, dedicated to one student. One freaking golden boy.

I'd never heard of anyone getting an extension like they were giving him. Sure, there might've been a clerical error—whatever *that* meant—but it was Connor's fault he failed the class. Knowing him, he and his buddies probably had mentally checked out after prom. He should've studied for the exam, should've passed it. Or at the very least, he should've checked his report card over the summer and noticed the error sooner.

Some students lingered in the hallways after the final bell had rung, gathering things from their lockers, but I bypassed mine. With my orange satchel bouncing angrily against my hip, I made a beeline for one place in particular. One place I'd promised myself never to go again.

The football field was a five-minute walk behind the school building, and even as I strode up to it with a vengeance, it seemed to take forever to get to. The outside air was suffocatingly hot, a sharp contrast to the cool breeze this morning. It did nothing to chill the fire in my veins.

We wanted to give you an incentive. More like wanted to have me in their back pocket.

And I could've said no. I could've told Principal Oliphant to stick it where the sun didn't shine. But valedictorian...the possible scholarships... They'd backed me right into the corner they wanted me in.

The grand gray bleachers lining the football field were riddled with a few students waiting for football practice to begin, because apparently it was super cool to watch guys practice running around in the heat.

My steps faltered at the idea of having an audience. I thought of all the comments, all the jokes. Would this spur on StarBoi28 and HeartEyes422 further? *Math geek loses it on football star?*

Football star who lied to a teacher and said I agreed to something I explicitly said *no* to. Anger renewed, I resumed my pace.

Before I had to start searching, the dented metal door to the field locker rooms swung open, revealing none other than Connor Bray. The black shirt he wore hugged his body like a second skin, outlining a set of muscles that didn't belong on a high school boy. He had his football helmet in one hand and a set of white shoulder pads in his other, and he froze when he spotted me.

I opened my mouth, and even I had no idea what was going to come out. Probably all the curse words I knew—which, admittedly, weren't many.

Before I had a chance to say anything, though, Connor dropped his equipment as if it burned. His hand closed around my upper arm as he pulled me to the side, and I stumbled to keep my balance.

"Get your hand—" I began, but his other hand sealed over my mouth before I could get another word out.

Connor dragged me into the back side of the bleachers where the shadows of the press box created a hallway of darkness. He ducked underneath a rung and hauled me after him, the underbelly of the stands and the absolute lack of sunshine creating a somewhat unnerving atmosphere.

With his hand over my mouth, I did the only thing I could think of. I bit him.

With a curse, Connor practically shoved himself away from me to cradle his hand. "Did you *bite me*?" he demanded incredulously, inspecting the wound with wide, almost horrified eyes. "You really bit me. Dear God, you broke *skin*."

"Good," I spat out, gripping the textbook to my chest, ready to use it as a weapon if he came closer. "Do *not* touch me. Ever."

"Jeez, don't worry about that. At least next time, I'll make sure you're muzzled."

"There won't be a next time!" I fired back, torn between wanting to take a step closer to smack the living crap out of him or moving away. He examined his hand, analyzing the little indents my teeth made. "You know, when you came up to me yesterday asking me to tutor you, I told you no. *N-O.* Did you fail English, too?"

Connor glanced around the dark space, and then up, as if afraid someone would be peering at us through the slats in the bleachers. "I read between the lines. Can you keep your voice down?"

"Between the lines? There was no line other than 'get lost.' I think I made it pretty clear I want nothing to do with you."

Connor's eyes met mine then, an intensity swarming in their depths. In the darkness underneath the stands, his hazel eyes seemed darker, practically a full brown. "Look," he said, staring me down with a glare that could've iced over the Pacific. "I won't pretend that I get where your attitude's coming from, but trust me when I say I wouldn't have asked if I weren't desperate."

"Why should I care?" I demanded, happy that for once, I was in the high seat. He was desperate. Good. It'd do him good to learn what it was like to want something so badly, to experience consequences for the first time in his life.

"You're a tutor, aren't you? Isn't it your job to help me?"

"You do realize how entitled you sound, right?"

Connor shut his eyes for a solid five seconds, and like me, he fought for composure. He took a step toward me, and I had to fight to keep from jolting back, forcing my feet to stand their ground. No way was I going to let him intimidate me. "I have to pass Algebra II. I don't have a choice. If I fail, I'll get kicked off the football team."

The consequences—they *were* sweet. "Then you should've studied the first time."

Connor's face twisted with an ugly emotion—a mixture of frustration and anger that pinched up his pretty-boy features—but before he had a chance to whip out a comeback, a new sound interrupted.

"Where the hell is Bray?" a voice boomed from the direction of the football field, causing both of us to jump. Connor reacted sharper, head whipping toward the field.

When he turned back to me, his eyes were glimmering with urgency. "Name your price. Anything."

In that moment, something in me lifted. The anger he'd worn a moment ago had instantly evaporated into pure desperation, and the side of me who loved tutoring, who loved helping, winced. *He needs help*, that side of my brain whispered. *You're going to let your feelings get in the way?*

I was truly, truly debating it.

Someone called Connor's name again, this time sounding much closer. Connor took a large step away from me—I hadn't realized he'd gotten so close. "Think about it, then. We'll meet tomorrow."

"Tomorrow?"

"For our first tutoring session." And just like that, he'd regained his composure enough to shrug back on the mask of confidence and condescension. As he ducked underneath the bleacher railing, he flashed a wink at me. "Don't forget that textbook of yours."

If it weren't so sacrilegious, and if I wouldn't have gotten a fine for the damage, I would've chucked *that textbook of mine* at the back of his head. I was no football player, but I had pretty good aim.

Before I had the chance, he bolted back to where he'd ditched his stuff.

Our first tutoring session. As much as I wanted to fight it, there was no use. Despite me literally biting him and yelling his ear off, he, like Principal Oliphant, had me in his back pocket.

CHAPTER 5

"Maisie." Mom's voice came as an intrusive pin to my thought bubble, drawing me away from my U.S. History worksheet. She slumped down on the other end of the couch and propped her mismatched socked feet on the glass coffee table. It was a very *Mom* look. She hadn't even been home ten minutes and she was already dressed in her comfy clothes, ready to check out for the night. "Can you do me a favor?"

"It depends," I said slowly, knowing it'd annoy her, but also knowing it wasn't a good idea to blindly agree. "What is it?"

"Can you drop a packet of paperwork off next door? It's for the student exhibition Center Inspire is hosting in a few weeks. I need Principal Oliphant's signature on a few things."

And there we go, a prime example why blindly agreeing was a bad thing. "Mom."

"It's next door," she said, smacking the TV remote on her thigh before aiming it at the console again. She blew at her bangs, but they only fell back into place. Jozie had convinced her to get those bangs, and the same style made them seem more like sisters. Whereas I inherited Dad's rounded nose and big ears and brown hair, Jozie got all of Mom's dainty features and strawberry blonde hair. "It's not like it's on the other side of town. And all you have to say is 'these are from my mom,' and come back."

"Can't you do it? I'm working on homework."

Mom pinched her ancient, tattered sweatshirt. "I'm hardly dressed to be going out of the house. And it'll do you good to have a break, Maisie. You can't do homework all the time."

Intentional or not, her words felt like an insult. I turned back to my worksheet, ready to dig my heels in.

"I'll let you off the hook for dishes tonight."

Bribery. It seemed I couldn't escape it.

A two second interaction was worth the twenty-minute dish-washing time, especially since it was lasagna night. I could do this.

Growing up, I'd never thought things with Madison would end the way they did. I never pictured our friendship ending, but if it had, I would've expected a World War III type argument, a blow-up so big and bad that it even ruined the cordialness of our families. Is it really so bad if it wasn't a big enough fight to be nuclear?

The answer: yes. It could really be that bad.

Our falling out *wasn't* nuclear. It didn't extend to our parents. In fact, after *the incident*, we simply never spoke again. Almost like we weren't best friends to begin with.

Madison's house was directly next door to mine, so close that we used to throw Barbie dolls to each other through our open windows. It felt weird approaching her porch now, the gravel of her driveway crunching beneath my feet. Almost as if I was in a dream.

The porch creaked as I stepped onto it, eyeing the *All Are Welcome Here* doormat that was well-worn. It actually read *All r Wlme re* since foot traffic had erased most of the letters.

I rang the doorbell, half debating on leaving the packet on the mat and sprinting back to the safety of my house. If it was Principal Oliphant that answered the door, I could deal with that. She wasn't my favorite person after today, but I could be civil. If it was Madison, though...

The last time I'd been in her house had been the day before cheerleading tryouts freshman year, and she and I had been practicing the group routine in her living room. Anyone who was anyone knew that being on the cheer squad offered an express pass to popularity, especially at Brentwood High, and Madison wanted us to nail our choreography. We'd shoved all the furniture to the corner of the room—angering her mother when she found that the coffee table left scratches on the hardwood—and danced from the time she got home from church until my mom was calling me home for dinner.

Back then, I hadn't cared about popularity, but my best friend had. And anything that my best friend did, I had to do too. Cut my hair the same length. Paint my nails the same color. Try out for the cheer squad.

The door swung in at the same time my stomach flipped over, because instead of Principal Oliphant, Madison stood on the other side of the threshold.

It was after six now, and though cheer practice was over, she had her blonde hair tied up into a high ponytail and still wore her royal blue Brentwood Babe cheer sweatpants. She sucked in a breath as she registered who exactly stood on her antiquated welcome mat, going from curious to shocked in an instant. "Maisie?"

"Is your mom home?" Despite feeling like I was about to hurl—which was seriously possible—my voice came out as intended: icy.

"Not yet." She transferred onto her other foot. "Why?"

"This is for her." Stiffly, I thrust the thin packet of paperwork at her as if it were germ infested. "From my mom. For some art thing." *Just take the papers.*

Madison eyed the packet for only a moment before taking it with her manicured fingers. There. Delivered in under a minute. Before I had a chance to pivot, though, she lifted her blue eyes back to mine. "How's Jozie doing? I haven't had the chance to check in since school started."

Despite our friendship falling apart, Madison and Jozie stayed friends. Chatted in the hallways, went to parties together, texted here and there. Since we were all so close in age, it'd always been the three of us. *"You're both like my sisters,"* Jozie had said right after it'd happened freshman year. *"I can't cut her out of my life just like I couldn't cut you."*

It wasn't technically a fair comparison, since

Madison and Jozie weren't blood, but I never won that argument.

"She's fine," I told Madison now, completely leaving out the part where I didn't have a clue about how Jozie was doing. Fine enough to send good morning texts, anyway. "Busy."

"You finally have a room to yourself, huh? I bet that feels nice." She gave a simple smile. Something about her words, though, made my stomach tie back up. "But then again, I bet it's lonely without her."

The conversation felt a bit like a math problem that was hard to solve—I couldn't figure out if she was making small talk or trying to actually have a conversation. "Uh, yeah, it's a bit lonely."

The awkward tug-of-war conversation stalled for a moment. I should've turned around and gone back into my house, but a thread of a thought wrapped through my mind.

The Most Likely To list. It was one thing to suspect she was behind it, but another to confirm it. But now that there was an opening to approach the topic, I found myself reeling back.

In the end, I didn't have to come up with a gawky goodbye. Principal Oliphant turned her shiny silver SUV into their driveway, offering both of us an out. "I'll give this to her," Madison said, waving the papers. "It was... nice chatting."

I turned around without a response, curling my fingers into my palms, silently cursing myself for coming over here. *Nice.* Next time, Mom could walk the papers over herself.

$$+ - \times \div$$

"Are you coming over after school today?" Alex asked the next day as we shuffled with the forward movement of traffic in the hallway.

The lunch bell had called every student between the claustrophobic walls, creating a wall-to-wall blockade that moved at a snail's pace. We'd pass Cafeteria A around the next bend, though, and most of the crowd would thin as the juniors and seniors would continue on to Cafeteria B. I walked as close to Alex as I could, my shoulder brushing against his side with each step. "I have tutoring."

"Why'd you start that again, anyway?" Alex demanded, the patience snapping out of his tone in an instant. "It sucked up all your free time last year. Why do it again?"

I studied my brown paper bag, crumpling the edges between my fingers. "I like tutoring."

"This is why you were voted for the Most Likely To list, you know," he told me, having at least a bit of decency to lower his voice so only the ten kids closest to us could overhear. "Even in your free time, you work on math homework."

"I was never confused why I was picked," I grumbled, debating for half a second telling Alex who exactly would be "sucking up all my free time." Alex, lover of popularity and social climbing dreamer, would've changed his tune real quick upon hearing that my silly passion brought me close to the most popular guy at Brentwood. "It doesn't hurt you, so I don't know why it's such a big deal."

"You don't think I'm embarrassed? Dating the girl voted Most Likely To: Marry a Math Book?"

"You don't think *I'm* embarrassed?" I glared up at him, the directness of the situation causing my heart to slam in my chest. "Dating the guy who'd been voted Most Likely To: Never Get a Girlfriend?"

He stiffened at my words, going from intense to embarrassed in the time it took to blink. It wasn't something we brought up, ever, and here I was throwing last year's label in his face. Then again, he'd thrown my label first.

We passed the doors to Cafeteria A, where many of the students were siphoned off, and without warning, someone slammed into me with enough force to send me crashing into Alex, ricocheting off his chest until I hit the floor. I dropped my packed lunch to catch my fall, the paper bag splitting on impact and scattering my lunch everywhere.

Students routed around the collision, and true to accidents on the highway, everyone slowed down to get a closer look.

"Jeez, walk much?" a snide voice demanded, one I recognized with a sigh. She would've kept walking if she hadn't seen who'd fallen. But she did a double-take at my downturned head, voice going from annoyed to a sort of saccharine gooeyness that made my insides crawl. "Wow,

Maisie, I didn't even see you there."

I wouldn't have categorized Jade Dyer as a bully. A jerk, maybe, an absolute snob, but not a bully. She had that superior-type personality, treating people as if they were beneath her, but emotional warfare wasn't really something Jade doled out.

Unless, of course, it was me.

"These hallways are always so crowded," she went on, voice smug as she glanced around. "But still, Maisie. You should watch where you're walking."

Of course, Jade wasn't alone staring down at me. Madison stood at the cheerleader's left elbow, biting down on her lower lip, but even better, Connor was there too. Of course he was. He had his hand wrapped around Jade's, but I refused to lift my gaze higher.

My boyfriend was among the people towering over me, not even attempting to help me collect my things. His hands hadn't even come out of his pockets. In fact, he was starstruck in the presence of the Top Tier, as if they were famous actors instead of mediocre high schoolers.

"Too bad algebra doesn't help with coordination." Jade folded her arms across her chest, watching as I grabbed my apple and shoved it back into the split paper bag. My turkey and ham sandwich had landed in the path of traffic, and in the midst of my fall, someone's sneaker had squished it flat. "X might not equal Y, but even after all these years, Maisie still equals clumsy."

It wasn't even a good insult, but my cheeks heated regardless. The warmth only flared hotter when Connor bent and picked up my water bottle that had rolled to a stop against his sneaker, offering it out to me. Something about the small gesture left me gritting my teeth, like he could pick up my stupid water but not keep his girlfriend from bulldozing me in the hallway. If I expected him to call off Jade based on our newfound tutoring relationship, I was sorely wrong. I snatched the plastic bottle from his grip.

"Why doesn't X equal Y?" I asked Jade as I got to my feet, using the back of my hand to nudge my glasses higher up my nose. Madison had taken a step away from the couple, almost like she was attempting to blend in with the crowd. "What are their values?"

When Jade smiled, it looked like a piece of chiffon—transparent enough for me to see the slice of steel underneath. "Huh?"

"You didn't quantify the variables, which means that it's possible that X equals Y. But you're saying that X *doesn't* equal Y, meaning you added values to the variables. I'm asking what they are."

Alex gripped my elbow then, trying—and failing—to discreetly pull me aside to whisper, "Would you stop?"

Stop what? I wanted to ask, because it could've been two things: stop talking geek speak or stop embarrassing him in front of the Top Tier. Most likely, it was both.

Jade gave an unkind chuckle as she tipped her head to the side, closer to Madison. "She makes it too easy, doesn't she?"

Once upon a time, Madison stood up for me in front of Jade. When I first switched schools, we'd attempted to make the friendship work between the three of us. It was quickly obvious that Madison's school bestie and home bestie weren't going to mesh, though—even back in the ninth grade.

"Yeah," Madison said now, blinking fast. "She really does."

In the whole conversation, that was what hurt the worst. Not Jade running her mouth just to make noise. Not even Connor and Alex, silently watching the showdown, refusing to intervene. It was the complete and utter disregard of someone who'd once been like a sister to me.

The hallway swayed a bit as I watched the three of them start toward the cafeteria, my sluggish heartbeat loud in my ears. Students still moved around us; the crowd had lessened now, but even though there were fewer prying eyes, I felt utterly exposed.

"Maisie," Alex began, loosening his grip on my elbow, but not letting go completely. He didn't go on, probably wondering, like me, what there was that he could possibly say.

"Drop it," I said sharply, juggling my broken lunch bag so the contents didn't spill out again. The pressure on my chest caved and creased, but it didn't go away.

CHAPTER 6

The next day, I stared at the door to the library with a laser-like focus, not even blinking. It was black with chipping paint and a small window inset into the metal, and every time someone walked past it, my spine prickled.

On the packet Mrs. Diego gave me, it said that we were to meet in the library after school. It'd been thirty-four minutes since school let out. Twenty-four minutes since Connor Bray was supposed to meet me. And in six minutes, I was giving up and walking out. If Star Player couldn't be bothered, neither could I.

Inhale through the nose. Exhale through the mouth.

I'd started off our tutoring session feeling okay. I'd had the entire day to convince myself that I wasn't meeting Connor Bray, the football prodigy. Instead, I pretended I was meeting some other student who needed help with their math. Someone who was kind and desperate and had a good attitude about wanting to learn. Pretending got me through the *I don't want to do this* mantra that'd been dancing around my head since I'd woken up that morning.

In the first ten minutes of waiting for Connor, I'd settled in at a table closest to the door. In the first fifteen minutes, I'd already unpacked the Algebra II book Mrs. Diego had given me as well as a few practice problems I'd organized onto a piece of lined paper. After twenty minutes, I started staring at the door.

And it was about four minutes ago that I realized he wasn't coming.

Was he really going to stand me up? After all that b.s. of lying to Mrs. Diego and forcing me to help, he was going to be a no-show? Was this some prank on me? *Ooh, get the math geek's hopes up about valedictorian?*

The door opened, but it was only a petite girl with a rainbow ponytail. Not the muscular figure I was ready to fight.

Five minutes left. Mrs. Diego could clear my tutoring roster and give Connor VIP access all she wanted, but I wasn't about to chase him down like some mom searching for her toddler in a grocery store. Where would he even be right now? The football field? Yeah, I didn't need a round two of yesterday. I barely escaped with my sanity the first time, and *he'd* barely escaped without me drawing blood.

I should've bitten him harder.

With two minutes to spare, Connor sauntered through the library door. He had his black backpack slung over one shoulder, a lazy pace to his steps. Like he *wasn't* late to our session.

The football player was so out of place amongst the bookshelves and vibrant Book Fair posters, everything around him screaming *academia* whereas everything about him screamed *jock*. Even down to the bored way he gripped his backpack strap. It was as if he'd stumbled into the wrong room.

Until he found me at the table, and his languid posture snapped into something more alert, more alarmed. Ten feet spanned between us when his footsteps stopped, his eyes wandering the entire perimeter of the library like he was noting every single student within sight.

I raised my eyebrows at his imitation of *deer in headlights*. "Uh, are you going to sit down?"

It was a blink-and-you'd-miss-it response. Suddenly, Connor strode toward me, hands hastily gathering all of my papers into a stack before shoving them inside the Algebra II textbook. Then, without a word, he picked everything up and fled in between a row of bookshelves.

I stared at the now-empty desk in front of me. Someone had etched a curse word into the top of the wood, either with a sharp pencil or a pocketknife. Coincidentally enough, it was the same word that screamed in my head.

Breathe, Maisie, breathe.

Snatching up my bag, I stalked in the direction he went, ducking to look down every aisle like we were playing a game of hide-and-seek. They were all empty except for the last one, a section of the library that had dust from the 1970s. The row was for legal texts and autobiographies of random people from obscure historical moments, tomes that must've gotten donated to the school ages ago.

And, apparently, it was also the row for Top Tier boys to sit, because Connor leaned against one of the bookshelves with my Algebra II book at his hip like he belonged there.

"Sorry," Connor said normally, as if him storming into the library—late—and whisking my things off to a dusty corner wasn't weird. He slid my book across the aisle, a spot he designated for me to sit. "I figured this area would be...easier to concentrate in."

I stared down at him with my hand gripping my satchel strap. Better that than his neck.

"You mean so no one would see you?" *Discretion* was the word both he and Principal Oliphant had used, but I still didn't really get it. "You're afraid people will find out Principal Oliphant's giving you special treatment?"

"Something like that. Are you going to sit down, or am I going to be staring up at you for the rest of the hour?"

"First of all, I *was* sitting down. At that nice table you so rudely stole my stuff from. I don't know what era you're from, caveman, but in modern day society, we usually *ask* when we want something."

Connor's lips quirked into a smile that wasn't a smile —I could see the tightness underneath. "To be fair, I—"

"And second of all." I cut him off without hesitation. "*The rest of the hour* is fifteen minutes. For a guy who's so desperate for a tutor, you should've showed up on time."

Now his features tightened, and he swiped up the textbook. "I had to tell coach I wasn't making it for practice."

"It took you forty-five minutes to tell him that?"

"What can I say? Guy's chatty."

If I was Medusa, he would've turned to stone. Seriously. "And my time is valuable."

"Did I say it wasn't?"

Actions are louder than words, I wanted to shout back, but instead I dropped my bag to the ground, my butt following soon after. The healthy three feet of space between us would keep me from doing anything murderous. "Here I thought you couldn't find the library."

"Secretaries have to be good for something, right?"

Apparently, they're not good at spotting clerical errors. Ugh.

The way he'd crammed the papers into the textbook had bent and creased the edges, and I smoothed them out with a patience I didn't feel. "So, Mrs. Diego said you failed Algebra II."

"Uh-huh."

"And that you need a refresher on everything for a make-up exam."

Connor leaned forward as if someone were about to come around the corner. His hazel eyes were always on alert. "Add that to your long list of things you know about me. Do you write it all down in your diary?"

"Here." I threw a crumpled piece of paper at him, but it didn't get farther than his ankle. "Fill this out."

Connor stared at the thing like it was a wild animal, even going so far as to tug his leg away. "What is it?"

"It's a practice exam. It'll help me get an idea of where to start. If you don't know anything, leave it blank."

He was slow to pick the paper up and even slower to grab a pencil from his backpack. A part of me had a *whatever* attitude—he could waste all the time he wanted. But the other part, the smarter part, remembered the goal. For me to snag my coveted valedictorian spot, this meathead needed to pass the exam. For him to pass, he needed to be serious. We both did.

Connor pulled out his own Algebra II textbook from his backpack and used it as a surface to write on, squaring his shoulders as he analyzed the first equation.

And then he stopped. Looked up at me. Considered me. "So, have you thought about what you want in return for tutoring?"

I stared at him.

"How much do you usually charge, anyway? Fifty bucks? I'll double it."

"I don't charge."

That seemed to intrigue him, and he made a soft *mmm* sound. He'd only turned back to his exam for a second before squinting at me again. "You're friends with the girl who runs *Brentwood Babble*, aren't you? She was sitting at your lunch table today."

"Can you please focus?" I demanded, rubbing a hand over my forehead. This guy was going to give me premature frown lines. "You need to get *something* done today."

"I'm making sure this won't end up on the site," Connor said, gesturing between us flippantly. "You can't tell her."

It was a good thing we weren't sitting at the table in the front, because with the way he ordered me around, I probably would've flipped it. "There's nothing to tell if you don't concentrate."

Connor rolled his eyes as he turned back to the paper, letting out a disparaging sigh. I leaned against the book-shelf while he worked through the quiz, every so often tilting his head as if he could shake loose an answer from his brain.

A line of concentration marred the middle of his fore-head, and the longer he worked through the sheet, the less confident his expression became. It was something I knew well—for some students, it was embarrassing to admit they didn't know things, embarrassing to ask for help.

But no way was Connor Bray embarrassed.

"All right," he said after five minutes, passing the paper back. His voice was considerably softer, less cocky. "Done."

I scanned over the questions, finding his shaky circles surrounding the incorrect answers. I blinked at them, but the circles didn't move. "I said if you didn't know some-thing to leave it blank."

Connor gave me a glare. "I thought I *did* know it."

"You got over half of them wrong."

"Gee, wonder why I failed the class in the first place."

This was more than needing a refresher on the subject. "Did you not pay attention at all last year?"

"Oh, I'm sorry that I spent an entire summer forgetting what *x* equals. And jeez, are you always so judgy?" Loathing coated his features as he pressed his fingers against his temple. "It's great that math comes easily to you, but for normal people, it's tough."

"*Normal people.* Right, because since I enjoy math, that makes me not normal." I leaned forward. "Just because I'm good at math, it means I'm the most likely to marry a math book?"

"No, what's not normal is how high and mighty you act," he fired right back, slamming the book down on the floor. "Like everyone's beneath you."

My jaw literally dropped. "Oh, I act like that? What about you, Mr. Star Football Player?"

"I've only been called that twice, and both times, it was by you."

"Excuse me!"

We both startled at the third sharp voice to enter the argument, turning to find Mrs. Juniper standing in the aisleway with both of her wrinkly hands on her hips. Through her bifocal glasses, the librarian passed each of us a glare fiercer than anything we could've conjured.

"If you don't keep it down, I'll ban you from the library," she hissed, and even in a near-whispering voice, she was threatening. "If you want to argue, find somewhere else to do so."

And with that, she disappeared back to where she came from.

I hadn't even realized our voices had grown so loud, but now that silence descended between us, the quiet was more unsettling than the fighting. Connor stared stonily down at the closed textbook on the floor beside him. He was strung as tight as a rubber band, as if any second, he could've launched back to where we left off.

I gripped the practice test tightly. If it were anyone else, I wouldn't be reacting this way. If this was some sad little sophomore, I would've been more understanding. More helpful. But everything about Connor pressed a button inside me, one that screamed *get away and stay away*. The feeling I got whenever Rachel or Ava brought up the latest jock gossip.

The feeling I got whenever *that world* bled into mine.

"You hate me," Connor said suddenly, and for a moment, I wondered if I'd said any of that aloud. "I get it. You can hate me for whatever reasons you've got, but can't you hate me and tutor me at the same time?"

Could I? Was it possible to stomach everything about him for a few tutoring sessions? Well, more than a few. He'd gotten every question wrong. And stomaching him and his over-inflated ego might've been possible as long as I had a TUMS or something ready.

"Listen," I said slowly, because attempting more than a few syllables at a time might've caused my fury to relapse. "I'm not trying to be a jerk, but it is a lot to learn before the month's over, and if—"

"You think I don't know that?" he demanded, but his voice wasn't nearly as sharp as before. A hint of defeat had trickled into his words. "I know I'm basically screwed. That I'll be kicked off the football team and held back a year. But I have to try."

"You showing up forty minutes late is *not* trying. You can't learn an entire year of math in fifteen minutes because you want to gossip with your coach."

Dragging his legs up to his chest, Connor slouched until his forehead pressed on a knee, giving up on the conversation.

There were two sides of me: the tutor side that felt bad for giving him such a hard time when he was obviously in a tough place and the side of Maisie who was dancing and skipping around because Mr. Perfect didn't have it all together, no matter how hard he tried to portray the distorted image. Ava could write *Brentwood Babble* articles about him all day long, but I'd seen the façade fracture. I'd been the one to crack it.

Tutoring Maisie won out. "Every student I've helped has gone on to pass. I'm not going to let you ruin my streak."

He didn't lift his head, but the tension in his shoulders loosened slightly. Slightly.

"But we have to meet on time. It's a lot of ground to cover in two and a half weeks. Four units with ten chapters each. It's too much to go over in two hours a week."

"I can't miss football practice. It won't matter if I pass or fail Algebra—Coach will cut me from the team."

Was he seriously more worried about football than the possibility of not graduating on time? I wracked my brain for a possible solution. "How about we meet after practice? Four days a week?"

His hazel eyes widened further. "Four days?"

"Four units, forty chapters in total. In two and a half weeks. That's not even ten chapters a week, Connor." Did he understand *that* basic math? If he didn't, I might as well dust my hands of this situation now and kiss my valedictorian status goodbye. "Some of it will be easy, but it'll take time to do a proper refresh of everything."

I focused on Connor, watched as he scrubbed his hand along the back of his neck. "Fine, fine. Four days a week after practice. Not on Fridays, though. Those are game days."

Mentally, I swiped everything off of my schedule, not that I had a lot going on anyway. Thursday night was bowling night with Alex, Rachel, and Ava, but that wasn't until six. I stuck my hand out between us. "Deal."

Connor eyed my hand as if it were covered in mud. He made no move to take it. "And you swear not to say anything?"

Him and his stupid discretion. "I swear."

"And to help me pass?"

"Jeez, yes."

My arm began cramping before Connor finally reached across the space, fitting his palm against mine. His shake was firm; Dad would've been proud.

Connor stretched his long legs out in front of him once more. His shoes nearly touched the opposite shelf. "Who was that guy with you in the hall today?"

At the mention of the scene his girlfriend caused, my skin prickled. I tried not to let my discomfort show. "His name is Alex."

"You got a crush on him?"

His words punched me in the stomach. Of course, it made sense that Connor wouldn't know about our relationship—Connor barely knew who I was and had no idea who Alex was—but it stung that he couldn't tell Alex and I were a couple. That he'd have to ask. "Well, he's my boyfriend, so I'd hope so."

"*Boyfriend.*" He turned the word over in his mouth, savoring it with a visibly suppressed grin. I wanted to knock the look off his face. "I never would've guessed."

"Oh, I'm sorry we weren't jumping each other while your girlfriend berated me," I shot back at him, ready for this stupid tutoring session to be over. "Let's get back to studying." *Before I lose my patience.*

"We only have five minutes left." He rubbed his thumb along his lower lip in a way that Rachel, in her Connor Bray infatuation phase, would've gushed over. Ava would've scrambled to get it caught on camera. "Not nearly enough time to get started with the actual tutoring. How long have you two been dating?"

Cue dramatic sigh. "We've been together almost a year."

Connor's reaction was the exact opposite of what I expected. Instead of nodding affably, like a polite person, he made an *oof* face. Scrunched eyebrows, crinkled nose, avoided eye contact.

"What?"

"You haven't even been together for a year, and he's already treating you like that?"

It felt like I was moments away from snapping at him again. "Like what?"

"Like you're his annoying little sister." Connor leaned back against the bookshelf, expression like a doctor's who'd given a patient a grim diagnosis. "That's rough, Macy."

"He does *not* treat me like I'm annoying!" I shouted, risking the wrath of Mrs. Juniper. "Or like a little sister. And it's *Maisie.*"

"Hey, the spark between you two faded, that's all. If you're that into Alex, you need to amp it up."

Okay, it was a little eerie that I'd had that same thought a few nights ago—that Alex's and my spark had dulled. Hearing it come out of Connor's mouth now, though, made me want to punch something. "Yeah, because that's the easiest thing in the world."

I wasn't sure what it was about my words, but something triggered the bright smile that spread across Connor's mouth. It displayed a set of teeth that were sparkling white, but slightly crooked. The blip of normalcy felt more out of place than his presence in the library to begin with.

After he started to rub his hand across his mouth, remaining silent, I squirmed under his stare. "Why are you smiling?"

"*Love advice.*"

"Excuse me?"

"In exchange for tutoring me, I can give you love advice."

He'd spoken clearly, but surely I heard him wrong.

Connor's amusement didn't fade, though, and neither did the feeling churning in my stomach. "Love advice?" The laugh I barked out was obnoxiously loud and filled with nervous tension. "From you? Yeah, no thanks."

"It's fitting. Tutoring the tutor. I like it."

Fitting? *No*, it wasn't. Love advice from Connor Bray? I mean, yeah, he had an on-again, off-again girlfriend, but it was *Jade*. That *Heathers* wannabe wasn't the girl next door. Not exactly the epitome of a healthy relationship there. If I wanted love advice, he'd be the last person I'd go to.

But then a new thought trickled in, an insidious whisper that took the voice of the person who should've been the most accepting of me. *Do you ever just feel like we're different?*

When it came to Alex, it felt like I was clinging tightly to a rope tugging out of my grip. The friction burned my palms, but I couldn't let go. The newness of our budding romance wore off like dew evaporating in the morning sun, fizzling out to a content time together. And it *had* been content.

Do you ever just feel like we're different?

"We shouldn't meet here tomorrow," Connor said, dragging me from my thoughts. "If Mrs. Juniper heard us, someone else could've too. We should find a place more private."

"Okay, whatever." His desire to keep this a secret irked me, but then again, did I want anyone to know I was hanging around him? Ava and Rachel would probably give me a list of questions to ask him if they found out, ranging from his favorite shampoo to what color underwear he wore. "Any ideas where?"

"Your house?"

"My hou—*no*. I live next door to Madison Oliphant."

My excuse only slowed him down for a fraction of a second. "Meet me at the corner of Main Street and College Avenue at four-thirty. Practice should be over by then."

The intersection he mentioned was one a few blocks down from the school, the very public corner near the heart of Brentwood. "Meet you there?"

"Yeah, wait for me there. And don't worry," he added, tucking his textbook under his arm and walking back-ward toward the end of the bookshelves. His eyes glinted with amusement and mischief. "I'll make my own curriculum tonight. Your lessons in love start tomorrow."

"I don't need—" I began, but cut myself off when he disappeared around the corner, slamming the door shut on that conversation.

I sat motionless amongst the omnibuses and dust bunnies, trying to process the whirlwind of the last twenty minutes. Connor's practice test was on the floor beside me, his terrible handwriting the only indicator that he *had* swept into the library late, that he *had* taken the test—and bombed it—and that he *had* offered me love advice. *Love advice.* Because he took one split-second interaction with Alex and thought, "hmm, these two need a love doctor."

The guy failed math—no way he was smart enough to have a PhD in romance.

I mean, sure, he had more experience than I had when it came to relationships. Whatever tips Connor could conjure up...what if they worked? Yes, I'd be lowering myself to the bottom of Connor's stupid football cleats if I took his advice, but what if it ended up *amping up* my relationship with Alex?

With a sigh, I grabbed my textbook and satchel and stood up. A promise of love advice or not, it was going to be a long two and a half weeks.

CHAPTER 7

om was already lounging on the couch when I came home, her tablet balanced on the arm of the cushion. It'd been a Christmas present from Jozie and me years ago, back when Jozie worked part-time at Sailor's Cinema, and she'd pitched in more than my meager chore-money piggy bank could allow. The tablet wasn't the latest model by any means, but Mom cherished the thing like it was her third child.

She tapped her stylus in her grip, analyzing the picture in front of her, her artistic eye no doubt being overly critical. So much was evident by her curved posture.

"I'm home," I told her as I appeared in the living room doorway, and she turned around.

"Maisie." Her voice was an exhale of relief at the sight of me, and she waved me closer. "Come give me your opinion on this. Are these colors working? I can't tell anymore."

"You know I'm not good at that kind of stuff." I took a step closer anyway. "Have you asked Dad?"

"He went straight into the shower after work. Covered in paint, I tell you. Like he was painting himself today instead of the wall." She beckoned me with an oscillating hand. "Come here."

She had to zoom out from the section she'd been hypnotized by, exposing the whole image of...something. Mom's passion was "semi-abstract," but I couldn't figure out what about it was "semi." The image was a bunch of dots and different sized shapes in several shades of green, yellow, and orange. "I think it looks fine."

Mom's mouth twisted further, my answer clearly not pleasing her, but she went back to dragging her stylus across the screen. "Where've you been?"

"At the library. I was tutoring."

She murmured distantly, her attention only half-present. "Are you doing something *besides* tutoring and homework? You should have more of a social life balance, Maisie."

Yeah, this was a conversation I *so* wasn't in the mood for. "Yes, Mom."

I could recite half of my calculus textbook in my sleep, but watching Mom go through the settings of her little art app made my head hurt. She'd tried to explain the different levels of shading and complexity to me once —or, really, she explained it to both Jozie and me, and Jozie was the only one who understood a single sentence. It had something to do with switching brushes and opacity. She could've been talking gibberish and I wouldn't have known. It was one of the rare times where I realized people probably felt the same way when I mentioned polynomials.

Even though it was still the two of us in the living room, Mom had tucked herself away into her little tablet, consumed by the greens and yellows and oranges. I kicked the edge of the sofa with my socked foot, lightly enough for it to not make a sound but hard enough that it stung a little. "By the way, do you know how much is left in my college fund? Some of the scholarship applications will ask about it."

Mrs. Diego had been the one to tell me that I should know how much I was going to be able to contribute to paying tuition, so I knew what kind of scholarships to apply for. Even though I loved school, I couldn't deny that the college stuff went over my head a little.

Mom's stylus never faltered. "I'd have to check the paperwork. I thought scholarships meant you got tuition for free, though."

"Not always. There are partial scholarships."

Much like how she'd beckoned me over, Mom waved her hand again. "Please. You'll be getting a full scholarship—you don't even have to worry about it with the grades you have."

"It's not all about grades." My voice started to sound like a wrung-out towel—any ounce of patience effectively twisted dry. Principal Oliphant's words came back to me. *GPA isn't the most accurate way to judge a student's performance.* "It's about participation in extracurricular activities—"

Mom cut me off. "Tutoring."

"Leadership qualities—"

"Tutoring."

I felt more like the parent than the child, and still, she pored over her tablet like I wasn't even there. I might as well have been a TV she'd forgotten to turn off. "Mom. It's more than tutoring and grades."

It kind of felt like the tables were turned in this conversation—usually it was Mom preaching the sentiment at me. She made a *humph* noise of obvious disagreement, but then again, her mind rarely reached into the realm of consequences and deadlines. *A free spirit*, she'd say, *doesn't limit themselves to time constraints. A true creative cannot work when they're feeling rushed.*

"Maisie, you're number one in your class. Valedictorian. It promises you a scholarship."

So I'd thought, once upon a time. Only I'd since realized that nothing in life was guaranteed, not when it came to Brentwood High and college funds. "Colleges like Stanford and Harvard cost more than some expensive, barely accredited coastal art school."

Now, *that* got her attention, because the blasphemy of my sentence could not be condoned. Mom would've been able to swallow me screaming the f-word better than that sentence. These were fighting words in the Matthews household. To the Matthews, that *barely accredited coastal art school* was basically the holy land.

"Do not compare your sister to you," Mom told me, and in an instant, her authoritative voice blew mine out of the water. I had nothing on the frightening way she controlled her tone, nor the completely flat expression she had when she wielded it. "And do not go off comparing colleges. I didn't raise you to be condescending."

"Are they even teaching her the basic courses at that place? Knowing art theory is *cool*, but so is learning basic courses for a degree."

"You sound like you're fifty-seven, Maisie, instead of seventeen. If your sister wants to learn art theory, you should be more supportive."

A stab of childish pettiness swept through me. "You and Dad are supportive enough without me."

"You shouldn't subscribe to what society says," Mom went on. "The arts *are* a valid career choice. It's disappointing to me that you're among the few who think it isn't credible."

I held my breath until my lungs burned. It wasn't that I thought arts weren't credible—I just didn't *get it*. I didn't get why Jozie got all the attention, all the money, all the support. Her art projects were always pinned up on the fridge. Couldn't they have pinned up one of my aced math tests? Jozie was forty-third in her class, and she was congratulated for being in the top fifty—couldn't they have congratulated me for being number one?

It was like they'd put all their enthusiasm into Jozie so they had no energy left to go through it with me.

Her once concentrated swipes across her tablet were now fueled by a rigid sort of passion, containing a bottled mix of anger and frustration. Without another word, I stalked off toward my bedroom, too tired to fight with her. Besides, it wouldn't do any good to talk now. Whereas I liked to tackle problems head-on and try to solve them, Mom simmered in her anger until she didn't want to anymore, and without resolving the issue, she'd act as if we'd never fought in the first place.

I turned toward the hallway, wishing that in that regard, I was more like her.

Jozie's bed greeted me first as I walked into my bedroom, reminding me how different the house felt without her. The dynamic was off. Jozie was the one who could always moderate between Mom and me, could soothe Mom's moods and get her back on my side. *Your and Mom's perspectives are too different*, she'd say. *Tell me what you want, and I'll get her to say yes.*

With a weight on my chest, I sat down on her bed. My side of the room seemed so much lonelier, with a few origami roses on my nightstand and my primly made bed. With a sigh, I pulled out my phone.

MAISIE

just so you know, I miss you

Her response came in a few minutes later, right before my screen auto-locked from lack of use.

JOZIE

I miss you BUNCHES! I'll try to call tonight so we can chat. Everything ok?

I'd been building a collection of things I could've confessed to her. The Most Likely Tos. The tumultuous situation with being valedictorian. Tutoring Connor Bray. My whole life, she'd been my confidant who'd always been there to share things with. I'd never kept anything from her before, and vice versa. Now, though, with her so many miles away, I couldn't imagine delving into any of it.

MAISIE

I waited for her next text, but this time, my phone auto-locked, and I sat on her bed for another ten minutes before I realized she wasn't going to respond.

$$+ - \times \div$$

I left my car in Brentwood High's parking lot and walked to the corner of Main Street and College Avenue. Car after car zoomed past, staring at the random high school girl standing like a statue. Thankfully, school let out an hour and a half ago, which meant that there'd be few, if any, peers driving past to spot me.

Just middle-aged folk wondering if I was selling Girl Scout cookies or something.

I readjusted my satchel strap where it dug into my shoulder, fighting for patience.

If Connor was late *again*, I was going to lose my marbles.

We didn't have any classes together, so confirming that we were still on for today was impossible, not that he would've appreciated my intrusion anyway. If I'd walked up to him, he probably would've pretended not to know me.

Ah, what a lovely dynamic we had.

There was a bench a few feet to my left, beckoning me closer, but I refused. Sitting down would be accepting my fate of waiting on him *again*. And I would not. I'd rather lose my valedictorian cord and watch him fail than to let him walk all over me again. I wasn't going to let it fly.

Except my feet were starting to ache...

The second I'd resigned to eat my words and sit down, a bright blue SUV drove up along the curb in front of me, window rolled down. I hadn't realized they'd stopped for me until a voice started speaking, one newly familiar. "Hop in. Now."

Connor leaned across the passenger seat and shoved the door open, staring me down until I stumbled into action. "Don't order me around," I snapped back at him. "I'm not a dog."

As soon as I shut the door, Connor peeled away from the curb, swerving back into traffic. I scrambled for my seatbelt.

"I don't know. Macy can be a dog's name."

"It's *Maisie*." My tone was biting, but then again, I'd met a dog or two with that name. I wasn't really helping my case. "Where are we even going?"

Connor readjusted his rearview mirror by a fraction, gaze flicking to it and then away. "Someplace where no one will find us."

"Because *that* doesn't sound sketchy as hell."

Now that I was looking at him, I noticed that his hair was wet, a few strands stuck to the back of his neck.

He wore normal clothes, a blue shirt, and droplets of water fell onto the collar. "Are you seriously that sweaty?"

"This is what we call a product of a *shower*," he responded in a condescending tone. "Heard of it?"

"I wondered what took you so long."

"I was barely five minutes late. But wow, now that I know you're a fan of what sweaty football players smell like, I'll keep that in mind for tomorrow."

I folded my arms across my chest, counting out the seconds. Now that he'd pointed it out, I could smell the clean sandalwood body wash he'd used. Begrudgingly, I could admit it smelled nice. "Where are we going?"

Connor stepped on the brake as the light before us flicked yellow, causing me to strain against the seatbelt. "There's a park in Jefferson that has picnic benches. Figured we could go there."

"Jefferson?" I felt my eyebrows rise. "You're the star football player and you're entering rival territory. What if someone sees you?"

"Please, it'll probably be just us in the park. Us and geese. Besides, if anyone recognizes me, they'll have no clue who you are. No offense, but you're not exactly memorable."

My jaw dropped. "Yeah, because that's *so* not offensive!"

"Well, I mean, you don't stand out much. At least until you open your mouth."

"You're making it worse." But then again, he wasn't exactly trying to come to his defense. He was being a jerk and didn't think twice about it. "Seriously, shut up and drive before I change my mind."

Connor obliged. He turned up the stereo using a button on the steering wheel, filling the interior of the SUV with The Cars. It was a band Dad liked listening to, the only one he asked me to load his phone up with a few months back. I wouldn't have guessed anyone our age knew them, and judging by Connor tapping his fingers in time with the beat, he knew them well. It was another weird stab of normalcy from him, and even worse, it was something we could connect on.

Gross.

We coasted into the city of Jefferson with Connor matching the speed limit. "Just What I Needed" morphed into "Moving in Stereo," and I knew where he was going the second he turned onto Huntington Road. Keystone Park was one of the biggest parks in the county and known for its hiking trails and the large lake at the center. I used to come up here three times a week and walk, admiring the scenery, but I hadn't been to the park in years. I didn't have a hiking buddy anymore.

As we turned in to the park, my mood simmered into something more sullen.

"We can go in the center," Connor said as the car bumped along. "Near the water. Prettier view than the parking lot."

"More secluded, you mean," I muttered, gripping my bag against my chest tighter. The nylon fabric scratched against my skin. "Whatever. Hurry up and park so we can get started."

"You're so demanding, you know that?"

"Says the guy who yelled at me to get into his car," I threw back with a sharp scoff. "And the guy who dragged me underneath the bleachers so no one would see me."

Connor rolled his eyes. "And you bit me for it."

"It's my charm."

He turned the wheel around sharply, causing my shoulder to slam against the edge of the door as he swung into a parking space. He unfastened his seatbelt and withdrew the car keys, giving them a shake.

The warm air hit me as the comfort of the AC dissipated, and I rolled up my striped shirtsleeves to my elbows. Hopefully this hour would pass quickly.

There was one picnic table by the large man-made lake at the center of the clearing, slight ripples vibrating the water. Geese littered the bank, ambling about like they didn't have a care in the world.

"Chapter one," Connor said as he dropped his book onto the table. "Gotta say, learning math here beats learning it in a stuffy classroom."

He wasn't wrong. Even though the sun was blistering hot, it was a pretty day, especially by the lake. Besides the geese, the only other distraction was an elderly woman decked out in a velour tracksuit, walking her small poodle. From here, I could see that he had on a velvet little shirt of his own. "Let's get started. I brought some notebook paper we can work through the problems on."

Connor seemed different now that we were out of the car, and as he peered at the book, the look in his eye seemed to sober up even more. "How many chapters will we do today? You said there are a lot."

"We'll go for an hour and see how you do. We don't need to hyper focus on every equation, just enough to brush up on the section. Flip open to page twenty-two. We're going to work our way from there and see if anything jogs your memory."

Once Connor had the book open, he turned back toward me, waiting for the next direction.

"I have a rule," I told him, switching into full-on tutoring mode. "When my students get frustrated or need a break, I have them put their palm on the book."

He glanced down at the textbook with an eyebrow raised. "My palm?"

"You're not allowed to get up and storm away. No yelling. If you get frustrated, put your hand on the page, and we'll take a timeout."

Over my two years of tutoring, frustration was an almost guarantee. Math brought out the Hulk in stressed students, which to a certain extent, I could understand. I'd once had a sophomore throw their textbook at me because they were too overwhelmed. Thus, the new rule —no temper tantrums. We'd take a break instead.

"Fine," Connor said after a moment, trepidation in his expression. "If I want a timeout, hand to the Bible. Got it."

The hour moved by slowly, but it hadn't started off as badly as I'd been expecting. Connor needed a refresher on what a number line looked like, so a process that should've only taken a few seconds turned into five minutes of explanation.

"These lines mean absolute value," I explained, tracing the straight line on the textbook's page. "So you want to find the absolute value of two minus seven."

He blinked at the sheet. "Which means..."

"You're starting at notch two on the number line." I tapped the second notch. "You want to move backward seven spaces." I moved my finger backward like a chess piece. "And what number are we on now?"

After counting the notches, he said in a voice that lacked confidence, "Negative five."

"But we don't focus on the negatives, only the number itself. So five is the absolute value of two minus seven."

Despite not liking who I had to tutor, after a while, I fell into my usual pace of it all, and found myself having fun.

It was not fun for Connor, but unlike many of the students I tutored, he didn't lose his cool when my explanations made no sense. I wasn't sure what I'd been expecting going into our sessions, but I hadn't expected him to be so patient. So determined. It left me wondering what had ever led him to failing in the first place.

Connor placed his palm gently against the textbook page, his fingers aligning with the top of the binding. "I don't understand," he said simply, refusing to meet my eye.

"Which part?"

"How you got this number."

I looked at where his finger pointed, figuring out where he lost me, and went from there. It was odd to watch his confidence waver. Throughout the entire hour, he only focused on the textbook and notebook in front of him. Or when he wasn't going through the papers, his attention darted at every little thing around us. The other picnic tables, the water, the geese, the rustling trees.

While he worked on the last few practice equations in chapter two, I pulled out a sheet of paper from my bag and smoothed it out on the picnic tabletop. It was a graded worksheet I'd gotten back today, with a red A+ in the top corner, and I creased it enough times that I could tear the rectangular piece into a square.

Origami was something Jozie had picked up in middle school, and as her younger, nosy sister, I'd had to learn it too. I could do simple things—boats, cranes—but my favorite thing to fold was paper roses. They didn't take too long, didn't take any complex folding, and it was a perfect way to bide my time. While Connor worked on his assigned equations, I folded.

He only glanced up once. His hair had dried in the sun during our session, the loose waves falling over his forehead. "What are you doing?"

"Origami."

"Ah, so a math lover *and* an origami lover."

"There's geometry in origami," I mused, delicately folding back the piece of paper. "Once I finish this flower, and I unfold it, the paper will have all kinds of lines on it, right? Those creases indicate intersecting planes and symmetry. If I were to mess up a fold, even by just a millimeter, the shape would be all messed up. It's fascinating."

When I looked up from the paper, I found Connor blinking slowly at me, as if he waited for a punchline.

The expression made me realize how lame I must've sounded. If Alex were here, he would've tried to cut me off before I got that far. Clearing my throat, I pocketed my half-finished rose. "It's about time to head back. You finished?"

"Yeah." There was a tinge of something sharp in his voice as he leaned backward, working a hand over his eyes. "We only worked through two chapters, though. That's not fast enough, is it? And won't the chapters get harder from here?"

"They'll build upon each other. They won't necessarily get harder, but there'll be more information to remember and work through."

Connor's lips tightened at my words, and now it was plain as day to see the nervousness wash over him. "How am I supposed to remember all this?" he demanded, gesturing at the book. "I'm not some math genius who can store equations and crap in their head."

"All you have to do is think them through." I began packing up the materials, sliding the notebook into my bag. "I have a few problems you can work through tonight—"

"I have homework from you, too? How am I supposed to juggle all this with my other classes?"

"Connor—"

"Do you and Mrs. Diego *want* me to fail, is that it?

Pile on all the homework possible and laugh when he cracks? I already have statistics homework to do—do you know how hard it is to learn two math classes at once?"

I barely stopped myself from pointing out that he'd gotten himself into this mess. I knew it wasn't helpful to say any of that, or to continue this line of conversation. Because even though Connor hadn't had much trouble in the first session, this was him stressing out. This was him overwhelmed. It was in the tension around his eyes, the line of his lips. A chaotic sort of energy that pulsed under the surface, like a shaken pop bottle. It was the same way I'd always felt whenever my parents would try to explain their art pieces or when Rachel and Ava gushed over the latest piece of gossip. It was easy to recognize in him after years of feeling it myself.

Before I even opened my mouth, my cheeks heated, my insides already withering at the prospect of what I'd say next. For every student I'd tutored in the past, though, this was an important step at keeping them from giving up entirely. When things got too stressful, too tense, it was important to switch topics to give them a break. And that was what I did.

All I had to do was kiss my dignity bye-bye. *Ugh.* "It's your turn."

Connor tilted toward me then, raising an eyebrow that didn't look interested in the slightest. "My turn?"

"You said you made a curriculum. For...love advice."

Now there was interest in his eyes, sparking behind the hazel color. It waved away the cloud of worry that'd been lingering there a moment ago. "Ah, so you *were* interested in that, huh?"

"You were the one who offered."

"And *you* were the one who said no thanks." He tilted his head, brown curls catching in the sunlight. "You really want to take me up on the offer?"

Okay, now I was seriously regretting changing the subject. "You can wipe the smirk off your face."

"You gave me a hard time about needing a math tutor. Isn't it fair I give you a hard time?"

I grabbed my satchel and stood, glaring at him. "Never mind. Take me back to my car. I have plans." Alex would be picking me up for bowling in thirty minutes.

Connor reached out before I could take a step away from the picnic table and grabbed me fast. His fingers wrapped around my pulse point, and I was sure that my heart spiked with anger. I distinctly remembered telling him not to touch me. "We'll start off with a big one," he said.

I waited, but he didn't go on. "A big one?"

"Physical touch." His fingers loosened around my wrist, but he didn't immediately let go. He held my gaze, almost daring me to retreat first. "A lot of guys like to be touched. Like when someone runs their fingers through our hair? *Mmm.* It's the key to our hearts."

I tried to think back to pinpoint a time I'd ever combed my fingers through Alex's hair. He had soft curls, so it *was* possible, but was that something I should've been doing?

Connor drew the tip of his finger along the backs of my knuckles, the tingling pressure shooting across my skin in a way that made me swallow. I tugged my hand back without thinking, my overreaction to the simple touch causing him to grin. "Touch his hair," he said. "Or his biceps. Back rubs are good. What I'm saying is that physical touch is key. I'm sure there's a science behind it or something, but all I know is that it works."

I turned away from him, knocking the knuckles he'd touched against my textbook. Physical touch. Easy enough. "I'll have to try it tonight."

"Tonight?"

"We're going bowling tonight at Allen's Alley." Speaking of, I glanced down at my phone. *Twenty-five minutes.* "We're meeting at six, so I should get going. Can you take me back to my car?"

Connor got to his feet and planted his palms on the picnic tabletop. "You'll have to tell me how it goes. And don't worry, for our next session, I'll come up with some more advice." He winked at me and picked up his book. "You know, tutor to tutor."

"Who's the bowling queen?" Ava demanded as she thrust her arms into the air, gazing triumphantly at the toppled bowling pins. The screen above the lane flashed with an anthropomorphic beaver holding up a sign that read *STRIKE*, flaunting a seriously creepy grin. "Ava Freaking Jenson!"

I bit down on the straw to my soda, unable to fight off a chuckle. "It's easy to get a strike with bumpers, Ava."

"Don't be a hater because *you* can't get strikes," she returned, practically skipping back to the seat beside me. "Rachel, you're up. But I'm sorry in advance, because you can't top *that*."

Rachel flipped one of her Dutch braids over her shoulder. "Has anyone ever told you that you take bowling too seriously?"

Alex, who sat at my other side, nodded. "You really do, Ava."

We'd only been at the bowling alley for twenty minutes—we had to wait the first ten for a lane to open up—but we'd already gone through three rotations. After

Rachel, I was up next, and notably doing the worst in the entire group. Even with bumpers.

"I got a new tip earlier today," Ava said, scooting closer to me and angling her cell so I could see. "Apparently Landon Settler has a new girlfriend. Which makes him the first of the MLT's to remedy their casting."

I frowned. "Remedy their...*casting*? What does that mean?"

"He was voted Most Likely To: Never Get a Girlfriend, and here he is, with a girlfriend. So he's the first to prove the list wrong. Before I post, though, I have to confirm it."

"I can't really remedy my casting."

She scanned through her *Brentwood Babble* for another moment before locking her cell. "Well, you can remedy it by just...not marrying a math book?"

I swatted at her, and she leaned back with a laugh. "When are *you* remedying *yours*, huh?" I asked her, thinking of her *Never Have Their First Kiss* title.

Ava's cheeks immediately flushed, causing her pale skin to become swamped with red. "Someday."

Rachel walked back to our table after she finished, the dancing beaver on the TV declaring she'd gotten a split. "We'll find her someone," she confirmed, squeezing Ava's shoulder affectionately. "We've got time."

Ava ducked her head into her drink, taking a deep pull from the straw.

Before I walked toward the lane for my turn, I stopped, turning to Alex. "Wish me luck?"

He glanced up from his own soda, startled. "Uh, good luck."

Physical touch, Connor had said. Okay, the way he'd said it sounded so simple, but it wasn't. *Touch his hair, or his biceps. Back rubs are good. What I'm saying is that physical touch is key.*

Running my fingers through Alex's hair now would've been weird. Doing *anything* now would've been weird, especially with Ava and Rachel and the drunk bowlers on lane eight as an audience.

Then again, I had all night to make that move. I had time.

When I got to the ball return, I picked up a light purple ball with green flecks, testing its weight. Again, I wasn't the best bowler, but my absolute garbage aim didn't lessen the fun. This was one of the rare things that I didn't mind being bad at. The company made up for my lack of skills.

Lining up with the pins, I narrowed my eyes, judging the throw.

And even with bumpers, I only knocked down three pins. *Sigh.*

I turned to head back to the table and found my friends staring, enraptured, toward the entryway. At least they'd missed my absolute fail, but when I turned toward whatever they were staring at, all the air knocked from my lungs.

Several people stood in the entrance, but my eyes latched onto one boy first. Connor Bray leaned one elbow against the shoe rental stand, an easy grin on his face as he chatted with the bald guy behind the counter. He wore the exact same clothes as he did at the park an hour ago, had on the exact same languid attitude, but seeing him here was jarring.

His gaze trailed my way, locking on for only a split second before lazily flicking away. As if the idiot didn't recognize me.

It was then that I noticed the entourage behind him, the gaggle of groupies that I only half-recognized. Jade and Madison, of course, because where Connor went, Jade followed, and where Jade went, Madison wasn't far behind. Reed Manning, Rachel's twin brother, chatted with a boy with reddish hair peeking out underneath a ballcap. I couldn't place him. At Reed's side stood a tall girl with dark skin and beautiful curly hair, lingering too close to be anyone other than his date.

Connor didn't, I thought to myself, glad I wasn't holding the bowling ball anymore. I would've dropped it as soon as I recognized him. *He didn't come here because I mentioned it. Why would he?*

That was a good question. Why would he come here, tonight, *this time* of all times? He made it perfectly clear he didn't want to cross paths with me outside of tutoring, and even that had to be top secret. But he knew I was coming to Allen's Alley tonight. He knew to dodge this place.

"It's your turn," I grumbled to Alex as I walked back to the table, but he was too focused on the group.

"What are they doing here?" he murmured, eyes wide. "I can't imagine Jade bowling, can you?"

"Absolutely not," Rachel returned, leaning her head onto her upturned palm. Her eyes fluttered as she blinked, caught in a dreamland. "But Connor? Yeah, I can imagine him bowling. God, he's probably so good at it."

"Probably not the only thing you're imagining," Ava returned, poising her cell phone at the group at the counter. The girl had zero shame. "What's a good headline?"

Alex's name blinked on the screen as it patiently waited for him to take his turn, but I didn't feel as patient. Everything in me prickled, especially once the group had grabbed their shoes, and they all walked straight for us.

Of course the one lane open was the one beside us.

"Hey, Bobcats," Connor greeted as he came up to the lane, knocking his knuckles on the top of their table. He glanced at his friends. "What a coincidence."

The jerk didn't even look at me. Coincidence. Yeah, right.

"Did Reed tell you we'd be here?" Rachel asked as she leaned forward, bouncing from person to person. "We come here every Thursday and hardly ever see anyone from Brentwood."

"It's because we're in enemy territory," Reed said, lips curving into a smirk. Even though he was Rachel's twin, our paths didn't cross often. I'd probably spoken to him five times in the entire time I'd known Rachel. They weren't really too much alike. Siblings, for sure, but not twins. Rachel had dark brown hair, whereas Reed's was more golden. He was taller at least by five inches. The only thing they shared was their brown eyes. "I guess we can make an exception this once."

The redheaded boy beside him chuckled a bit, glancing around the space as if he'd never been here before.

Connor wasn't the only one ignoring me. Madison pointedly looked away as she sat down to lace up her bowling shoes. Jade sat down too, but she was the only one who hadn't grabbed shoes. Instead, she was engrossed in her phone, like she wanted to be anywhere other than here.

I brought my straw between my lips and bit down until my teeth ached. It made a clogging sound as I ran out of soda, and I got back to my feet. "It's your turn," I reminded Alex, trying to keep my voice from leaking irritation. "I'll be right back."

He didn't even ask me where I was going. Instead, Alex nodded, striking up a conversation with Reed about who knew what.

Allen's Alley had an attached bar and grill, and I stepped up to the sticky countertop, waiting for the tatted-up bartender to glance over. "I'll be right with ya, hon."

"No rush." *Seriously*. In fact, I wished I could've stayed parked here until it was my turn again. My friends' attention spans had been cut in half by the Top Tier distraction, and it'd take a while for my name to blink on the screen again.

I focused on the TV above the bar, some football game I couldn't care less about.

Suddenly, someone pressed their body up against my side, sliding up along the bar and leaning both of their elbows on top of it. Before I turned, I recognized the clean, sandalwood scent.

"Hey, can I have two Cokes, please? Under lane nine." Connor knocked his knuckles on the bar, and I watched as the bartender bobbed her head. From the barest corner of his eye, he glanced over. "You know, your face is really familiar. Maybe it's the glasses?"

"What are you doing here?" I demanded. "You seriously brought all your friends when you knew I'd be here?"

"The alley's big enough for both of us."

Hard disagree. "Who's the guy?"

Connor glanced over his shoulder, lifting his chin. "Landon Settler. Quarterback. You know Reed, right? The girl with him is Cindy."

Cindy. I tried to remember if Rachel had mentioned her brother getting a girlfriend, but I came up blank.

"Anyway, I wanted to see if you'd put my advice into action," he went on, rubbing the sticky surface of the bar. "Judging by your boyfriend's face, I'd guess that's a *no.*"

"Maybe you should worry about your own relationship. Your girlfriend doesn't look like she's having a good time."

Connor raised a shoulder in a lazy shrug. "Jade rarely has a good time. Besides, we're talking about *you* and Aiden."

My head swiveled, and I glared at him, with the strongest *what is wrong with you* glare I could muster.

"You're so arrogant, you know that? You purposefully got his name wrong."

"Did I?" The only way to describe him then was *childlike*, like the way a kid beams when they know they did something purposefully bad. He traced invisible shapes along the bar, fingers creeping closer and closer to the edge of my arm. "Can you prove it?"

"I guess it wouldn't surprise me if you couldn't remember. You populars act like everyone is beneath you."

If he took offense, he didn't show it. "Psychology would say you resent us because you want to be us."

"If I ever need a psych tutor, I'll remember to come to you."

Connor leaned against the counter a bit more, peering down into my eyes with an intensity that almost felt intimate. Like it was a look he should've been giving Jade instead of me. "Do you need a demonstration for physical touch? I can give you one."

There was no explaining the rush of *something* sparking in my stomach at his words, nor the way my mouth suddenly felt dryer than the dirt parking lot outside. It reminded me of the sensitive way he'd coasted his fingertip across my knuckles an hour ago. I had no idea where the feeling came from, only that I didn't like it.

"Here you go, hon." The bartender placed two glasses down in front of Connor, the condensation already building from the humidity inside the alley. I tried not to let it get to me that she served *him* first when

I'd been waiting. He even got preferential treatment from strangers. Go figure. She turned to me, to my empty glass. "You need a refill?"

Connor swiped up his glasses, and before he turned away, he lowered his voice, leaning in to murmur, "Make sure you're taking notes."

I shook off the sensation of his words against my neck.

Rachel was finishing up her turn when I got back to the table. Landon had sat down beside Ava, and she'd taken the opportunity to ask him questions about his love life. To her, this would've been fate. If I hadn't felt so unsettled by all things Connor Bray, I probably would've laughed at how this night worked out for her.

Madison was at the ball return when I stepped up, and she stiffened as I got closer. "Hey," she greeted, because it would've been impolite to *not* say anything.

"How are you?" I asked, but swiped up a ball and walked toward the starting line without waiting for her response. I was convinced she wouldn't reply, anyway. Not with her friends watching.

I swung my ball toward the pins and knocked down four my first time—which was pretty good for me. When I turned around to wait for my ball to come back, I spotted Connor standing behind Jade's chair, his hands gently on her shoulders. He let them rest there, coasting his fingers over her sweater before he ducked his hands underneath her hair.

"Aim for the middle!" he called to Madison, who was lining up her ball with the pins. He smoothed Jade's hair behind her, combing through the strands. Though her attention was on her phone, she leaned into his touch.

My ball clattered back into the ball return, but my thoughts were stuck on his hands on her. His actions were so easy, simple. Natural. It should've been easy for me, too. I mean, it wasn't like I was jumping Alex in public—simply touching his shoulder shouldn't be a big deal. Why was it so hard for me to initiate it?

"You did great," Rachel said, giving me a thumbs-up. "Right, Ava?"

Connor leaned down and brought his cheek level with Jade's, whispering something to her. The level of awareness I had for them was alarming—and a little stalkery—but I couldn't bring myself to turn away. He told me to pay attention, and I couldn't help but note everything he was doing.

At least I wasn't *literally* taking notes. That'd be harder to explain.

Alex grabbed his green ball and wasted no time in bowling his turn, arcing his foot behind him like an expert. His form paid off—the ball sailed down the lane and clattered into the pins, sending them all scrambling. "He's giving you a run for your money, Ava."

"Yeah, yeah." Ava stared down at her phone. "One strike doesn't match my level of awesomeness."

"It comes close," Alex replied, and sat back down beside me. He leaned over and swiped up my soda, taking a drink from it.

With him leaning so close, it was my chance. Take Connor's advice, take initiative. Where would've been a normal place to touch? His hand? Wrist? Bicep? With how close Alex sat, contorting to touch his bicep would've been awkward. I couldn't touch his hand while he held my cup.

Whereas Connor made every move seem effortless, here I was, thinking through every scenario like I was rehearsing for a crappy school play.

Stop overthinking it, I told myself sternly, and laid my hand down on Alex's lower thigh.

He jumped at the contact, and that's when everything fell apart.

The bottom of his cup caught on the edge of the table, sharply upturning the glass and causing it to tumble from his apparently weak grip.

Straight into my lap.

I shrieked, but there was no dodging the pop as it immediately soaked into my white shorts. Alex jerked his chair back, trying to avoid the waterfall, and my hand fell from him.

For a moment, I just sat there with the crushed ice in my lap, listening to the sound of pop dripping off my legs and onto the floor.

The shocked silence of the two Brentwood Bobcats tables only lasted for a brief, heavenly second before Jade's voice crept through, tinged with amusement. "There she goes again. *Clumsy!*"

Alex swore, and Rachel jumped to find napkins, but my humiliation refused to let my awareness extend beyond that. Refused to see whether or not Madison was watching or averting her gaze, refused to see what

Connor's expression was. No doubt, he was fighting a laugh.

I hated him infinitely more in that moment because this was all his fault.

My bowling shoes slipped as I shoved away from the table, leaving Alex to sop up the mess, Jade's laughter ringing in my ears.

CHAPTER 9

$\mathcal{I}$ wasn't sure I'd ever leave the grimy bowling alley bathroom.

Why would I, when the Top Tier was no doubt still laughing at the waterworks fiasco?

I scrubbed a wad of paper towels along my denim shorts, hopelessly trying to work the pop stain out of the white material. In a distant part of my brain, I knew they were ruined, but right now, worrying over them was the only way to keep from totally falling apart.

Though I'd had a handful of embarrassing moments —like answering an equation wrong for a mathletes competition or getting into a minor fender bender with Nina Bradshaw's brand-new Ford Focus—there was only one memory that took the cake and frosted it, too.

Cheerleading tryouts. It all went back to cheerleading tryouts.

I let out a sharp exhale, focusing on the mirror. My eyes were red, but I hadn't let any tears fall this time. Back then, though, I'd felt much of the same. Embarrassed—no, *mortified.* I could still remember how my face had looked that day. The pawprints Madison had drawn on my cheeks had dissolved into black smudges on my skin.

The group audition was held at the football field, where we'd all perform to the same song at the same time. She'd grilled me on the exact footsteps, the pacing. Madison had told me the song, taught me the dance, and we'd memorized it to a T. To her, getting on the squad was the most important thing in the world.

Important enough to stab her best friend in the back for it.

Because instead of teaching me the song we were supposed to learn, Madison taught me a whole other set of choreography, ensuring that if anyone was going to be seen as ridiculous on the football field, it wasn't going to be her.

The bathroom door inched open, followed by a face and a soft voice. "Are you okay?"

Madison poked her head in the bathroom door and found me in front of the sink, dabbing hopelessly at my soaked white shorts with a paper towel. With the blotchy stain, it looked like I peed cola.

I turned away from her, but despite shielding my puffy eyes, there was no disguising my voice. "Y-Yeah."

"Are you crying?" I heard the door snap shut. "Maisie, it's no big deal."

"Why are you here?" I demanded, dabbing my jeans furiously. "I don't need you to check on me."

Madison's bowling shoes clicked against the sticky linoleum floor as she came closer. "I've never seen you cry, you know. Not even when you broke your arm in the fifth grade. And you're crying over your shorts?"

The callback to our friendship burned like a knife sliding between two ribs, a stinging pressure that left me breathless.

"Of course you wouldn't understand it," I bit out. "You don't know what it's like to be humiliated."

"Oh, I don't?" She propped her hands on her hips. "Sorry, Maisie, but you don't have the market cornered on humiliation."

"And *you* have no right to tell me whether or not something's embarrassing," I said, and finally glared at her when I said it. Her brows were drawn together like how she used to do when trying to mask her feelings. "If it were just my friends, it'd be one thing, but it's the fact that it's you and Jade and freaking even Connor out there that makes it worse. And you know it."

Madison's shoulders squared. "Who cares what they think?"

"Hypocrite."

The livid line between her blonde brows cleared as shock stole her expression. "Excuse me?"

"*You* care what they think. You always have. Don't be hypocritical and pretend that isn't the case." I gave up on the fruitless attempt of drying my pants and lowered the paper towel, staring my ex-best friend in the eye. "You voted me as Most Likely to Marry a Math Book, didn't you?"

I watched her expression transform from insulted shock to something more impassive. "Nobody knows who picks the names. It definitely isn't me."

I raised an eyebrow.

Now her defensiveness came in full-force. "Come on, Maisie. It's not exactly a secret that you like math. You were on the mathletes team for the past two years. You're always doing extra credit for Mrs. Diego. *And* you tutor. Whoever picked the labels had to have known that about you, which narrows it down to practically the whole school."

"You were voted Most Likely to Peak in High School, right?" I swallowed hard. "I guess they knew what they were talking about, too."

Her eyes flashed once, and this time, she didn't try to disguise the hurt. It tightened the corners of her mouth. My stomach twisted, but there was no taking the words back. Both of our labels suited us, and we knew it.

Madison didn't spare me another glance before she turned on her heel and stomped over to the bathroom door. As soon as she hauled it open, though, she revealed a figure on the other side, their fist lifted as if they'd been ready to knock.

Connor might as well not have been there as she brushed past him, and in the split second before the door began falling shut, I met his hazel stare.

He slapped his palm against the metal door, halting its movement. "Hey, uh, I found these in my backseat if you need something to change into," Connor said, voice stiff with discomfort as he offered a dark bundle over the bathroom threshold. "They're clean, I promise."

I stared at the fabric in his grip with a new feeling stirring, something suffocating. Not angry, not happy, not sad. Just...complicated, like a piece of string twisted into a knot. I held the wadded-up paper towels in front of me, trying in vain to hide the cola stain. "What is it?"

"A pair of sweatpants. For you to change into."

"Your friends are going to wonder why you're being so nice to me," I snapped, residual fire lingering in my veins. Madison walking out of the bathroom didn't cool it, exactly like wiping away my tears didn't erase all evidence of me crying. "I'd hate for you to risk your *discretion* over a pair of sweatpants."

Connor regarded the gray pants in his grip, as if thinking the same thing. In the end, he reached out and set them on the edge of the sink closest to him. "Put them on or don't," he said. "Up to you."

And then he let the door fall shut between us.

I turned back to the mirror across from me, swallowing hard against the lump in my throat.

Madison was right—crying over pop spilling on me was ridiculous, but it wasn't *just* the pop. It was Alex jerking away from my touch. It was the fact that I had witnesses. Not even just Top Tier, but everyone else at the bowling alley. Everyone's eyes had been on me, some laughing, some pitying.

Ugh.

And now I had Connor's stupid sweatpants. I didn't want to put them on. Something about them didn't sit right with me. If I put them on, it'd be like I was indebted to him somehow. It had me questioning his motives. Connor was not the kind of guy to help me out when his friends were watching—Exhibit A came from yesterday when he'd merely stood by while Jade laughed above me. He'd passed me my water bottle, but he may as well have pretended I didn't exist.

Then again, did I *really* want to walk out of here with now stained, pretty much see-through white shorts?

With a groan, I disappeared into one of the two empty stalls.

A soft knock came at the bathroom door, and it eased open a crack. "Maisie?"

"No one's in here, Alex," I called to him, kicking off my sticky shorts and stepping into Connor's sweatpants. Irritation laced through my words, because though I didn't say it, I was thinking *two people I barely know had to check on me first before you, huh?* "You can come in."

Despite the green light, Alex took a long time to open the door, almost as if he was afraid of what he'd find. His shadow poked underneath the stall, wavering like he shifted from foot to foot. "What happened back there?"

"What happened?" I echoed with emphasis, throwing the door open. Alex stood on the other side, cheeks a brilliant shade of pink. Whether because of him dumping soda all over me or because he was in the girls' restroom, I had no idea. "I made an idiot of myself, that's what. I'd be surprised if it wasn't on *Babble* by the time we got home."

"Ava doesn't post about us," Alex said in a voice that

was only a few shades of condescending. "And she wouldn't post about *you*."

"Just because she doesn't post it doesn't mean people aren't already talking about it." Jade had no doubt already snapped a pic and sent it to all her little minions. "Let's drop it, okay? It's whatever."

The urge to push the issue was strong. I wanted to demand why he'd flinched away from me, acted as if I was trying to stab his thigh instead of trying to rest my hand there, but my tongue tied up into a knot at the idea of saying anything. It was embarrassing enough that it happened—to know why he'd rejected such a casual touch from his girlfriend would probably leave me a few pegs past mortified.

Alex let the conversation go without objection. "Normally I wouldn't like the idea of you wearing another guy's clothes," he said, reaching out and tying the ties of the sweatpants into a tight bow. "But these are *Connor Bray's* sweatpants."

Of course that was his takeaway. I balled my pair of shorts up and headed for the door. "Aren't I so lucky?"

"Maisie," my English teacher, Mrs. Greer, called from the front of the class. I'd been skimming through a passage in *Pride and Prejudice* for our reading homework, attention fully absorbed in the text. Mrs. Greer withdrew her desk telephone from her ear, placing it back on the receiver. "You're wanted in the office. Go ahead and take your things."

I packed up my satchel quickly, shoving the paperback and homework sheet inside as I got to my feet.

Last night, a little after Alex had dropped me off, Ava had sent over her latest article for me to proofread. It was about the jocks showing up at Allen's Alley, but thank God she left out the soda pop fiasco. In hindsight, I knew Alex had been right—of course she wouldn't post anything about that. Mostly the article was about Landon and his new girlfriend, touching briefly on Reed and the girl he was with, and talking about how Connor and Jade seemed stronger than ever.

Hot news.

And of course, her readers ate it all up.

As I walked along the vacant hallways, I tried to think why they would want me in the office. Since they said to bring my stuff, it hinted that they might need me for more than the ten minutes left in class. Did I do something wrong? Maybe I left my headlights on, and they were calling me down for that?

In that moment, I imagined Madison going up to her mother, telling her about the argument that we had in the sketchy bowling alley bathroom. She wouldn't have. Even Madison had to realize I was right to be angry.

The office was hopping when I pulled open the door. One teacher stood by a desk chatting with the secretary, and another stood by the printer as copies pumped out of the machine. A boy lounged in one of the chairs by the principal's closed door, and *lounging* was the right word. He had his arms folded across his chest, black long-sleeved shirt covering his skin despite the summer heat.

"Maisie?" The secretary who'd been chatting lifted her attention to me. "Are you Maisie?"

"Yeah." I glanced around. "I was told someone wanted to see me?"

The secretary jutted her chin toward the boy. "Take a seat. Principal Oliphant will be out in a few moments for you."

Ah, so it *was* something about Principal Oliphant. If Madison told her mom about what I said yesterday...

I left one chair between the nameless boy and me, but that didn't stop him from glancing over. His eyes were the bluest I'd ever seen, as if he wore contacts. "Don't worry," he said, voice gravelly, like he'd recently woken up. "You're not in trouble. It's about the Most Likely to list."

I raised an eyebrow at him. "Is that why you're here?"

"Me? Course not. I'm not on the dumb list."

His voice was so flat that he almost sounded angry. He stretched his legs out in front of him further, daring everyone to either walk over his tattered Converses or trip. "Then how do you know that's why I'm here?"

"I recognize your name, for one. Maisie Matthews— Most Likely to: Marry a Math Book. New label. I bet you're honored."

I peered at him. "You don't seem like the type to have the list memorized."

That got a ghost of a smile from him. "Only the new ones. I know a couple people on it. My friend was called down yesterday. I guess Principal Oliphant is working her way through the names."

"What was your friend's label?" I asked him, but

before he had a chance to answer, Principal Oliphant's door opened. A girl I didn't recognize emerged. Her cheeks were pink, but before I could analyze her further, she ducked out of the office.

Principal Oliphant's demeanor brightened when she spotted me. "Maisie, darling, hello. Come in, come in. How are you feeling today?"

Darling? "I'm doing okay," I said as I stood up, following her into her office.

"Hey," the boy called after me right before I crossed the threshold, causing me to turn back. "Don't let the list bother you."

I nodded at him. "Tell that to your friend, okay?"

One corner of his lips tipped up. "Will do."

"Who was that?" I asked as I shut the door, gesturing at the central office. "That boy next to me."

"His name is Hudson," she told me, settling into her desk chair. "He's nothing but trouble. Best if you leave him be."

I sat down in the chair across from her, wincing at the firm seat. Principal Oliphant made a show of scattering some papers on her desk, letting them draw her attention for a brief moment.

"Was there something you wanted to talk about?"

"I've been told that the Most Likely To list has been circulating again this year. I know it does every year, but I can't help but hope that it would die out."

A part of me wanted to roll my eyes. "There'd need to be consequences for it to actually stop."

"I'd need to know who's doing it to dole out conse-quences," she returned, not unkindly.

Come on, she couldn't be truly oblivious, right? Maybe she was pretending she didn't know who was behind it. She was a Top Tier parent after all—she had obligations to give her friends' kids immunity.

"But I wanted to meet with you and talk to you about it," she said slowly, folding her hands on the desk. Some-thing about her tone struck me as totally disingenuous. "See how you're feeling."

"Because I'm on it?"

Principal Oliphant tipped her head forward a bit. "Well, yes."

"How does Madison feel about it?" I returned evenly. "Since she's on it, too."

If I thought Principal Oliphant would dodge the question, I was wrong. "I think it bothered her. More than she lets on. I think she's more hurt that someone would assume she's so shallow than that she actually believes it."

This time, I did roll my eyes.

Principal Oliphant inhaled softly, deciding to tackle it from another angle. "You know that it's for drama and gossip, right? The whole list business. It doesn't mean anything."

"I would hope not, otherwise I've got to pick a math book to spend the rest of my life with."

I'd meant it as a joke, but she didn't laugh. She merely peered at me as if I were an onion and she wanted to peel back the layers.

"How's tutoring coming? How is Connor absorbing the material?"

"It's a lot to learn in less than a month." I glanced around her office again. Everything that had happened—her lording the valedictorian spot over my head, forcing me to tutor Connor, and even simply being Madison's mom—set me on edge. "I think the stress of it is getting to him a little."

"It is a very stressful thing, having to catch up so quickly. Do you think he can do it?"

Another snarky barb sat on my lips, but with a sigh, I decided to be honest. "I'm not sure."

"Do you think he needs an additional week to study?"

At first, the question itself seemed harmless, a principal discussing a student. And then it hit me—"Are you asking because you'd give him more time?"

She simply tipped her shoulders, a blatant *I'm not saying yes or no* gesture. "I'm curious to hear your thoughts."

Biting my lip, I fought the urge to laugh. It was hilarious how dedicated she was to granting Connor anything he wanted. More time? Sure. Another extension? Yeah, no big deal. Another handout? What was next, she'd take the test for him?

It was weird, because on one hand I wanted to lobby for my student. I wanted to ask her for more time, ask her for a shorter test, for *anything* that would aid him in passing this exam. On the other hand, asking for special privileges for a guy who was used to freebies made my stomach turn. Maybe he needed to get knocked off his feet to learn that not everything would bend to his will.

I thought about the sweatpants he lent me last night. Alex agreed to take me home without finishing our game, and I'd practically bolted back to the table for my sneakers, head tucked down. Connor had been in the process of bowling, focused on the lane, so I didn't have to go through the awkward process of thanking him. I'd dodged everyone's gazes, especially Jade's. Strangely enough, she'd let me walk away without a scathing remark.

"Another week wouldn't do much," I told Principal Oliphant honestly. "It's a lot to learn in general. But we're getting through it."

She turned impassive, as if we were playing poker now. "You always do your best, Maisie. I believe that."

"There's only so much I *can* do."

"I believe that, too." But her voice sounded different now. More formal. "Connor is one of the school's prime athletes, you know. I've gotten many letters from schools saying they're sending scouts to our games, some even specifically asking about him. His abilities on the field are benefiting a lot of players in the long run. They're putting Brentwood on the map."

As soon as they asked me to tutor Connor, I knew this conversation was coming. The goo-goo, ga-ga fawning over a simple player like he was God's gift to Brentwood instead of just a boy with an above-average ability to run with a ball in his hand. Treatment that made my blood boil.

"If you have any ideas on how we can help Connor

pass this test, please let me know," Principal Oliphant told me in the same voice. "We want to see every student at Brentwood High succeed."

I'd known Mrs. Oliphant practically my entire life. I'd known her when she first started her principal position, had known her when Madison's dad had passed away, had known her when she'd won an award from the city for Teaching the Youth of Tomorrow or some crap like that. But as she spoke now, with a hypnotized expression and practiced words falling from her lips, I felt like I didn't know her at all.

Overhead, the bell rang, signaling the end of fourth period.

"Well, if you need anything else, I'm more than happy to help." She rose to her feet with her hands pressed against her desk. "I can set something up. But that's all from me for now. You can head to lunch."

Even though she'd given me the dismissal, something kept me glued to the chair, unwilling to move for a long moment. This whole conversation felt distinctly one-sided, and it left me with more to say. More about the list, more about valedictorian, more about Connor. But she didn't ask any of those questions, and I had no idea how to phrase the swirling storm of thoughts in my mind.

"About the Most Likely Tos," I began softly. "It might not be anything more than drama and gossip, but it does hurt to be singled out in a negative way. I'd think really hard about potential candidates for creating it."

"Any suggestions on where to start looking?" Her

gaze trained on me, and for a moment, it almost felt as if it were Madison eyeing me so curiously, so intently.

"I'm sure something will come up," I said instead of giving a straight answer. In all honesty, I couldn't gauge how she'd react if I told her that I suspected Madison and her friends. Would she act like a principal, or would she deny the possibility like a parent? There was no way of knowing for sure. "Thanks for the talk."

CHAPTER 10

"*A*va, pawprints have four fingers, not three." Rachel frowned sideways at her reflection in the mirror, cherry-red lips twisting back at her. She'd taken a play from Ava's book and scraped her hair up into two little buns on the top of her head, one gold ribbon wrapped around one bun and a blue ribbon wrapped around the other. "You have to add one more."

Ava stared at Rachel's cheek with intense focus, hand gripping the face paint marker so tightly that it shook. "I *am*. Be patient, sheesh."

"Did you just call the toe prints *fingers*?" I asked, hugging one of Ava's decorative lumbar pillows to my chest. The lacy edge tickled my throat.

Rachel shot me a grin. "Basically the same thing."

"Except animals don't have fingers."

"They have toe beans," Ava said, and then laughed.

The two were getting dolled up for the Brentwood football game tonight. Ava wasn't nearly as decked out as Rachel was, only wearing an oversized Bobcats sweater from a few years back. She didn't have a pawprint—yet.

They had a half-hour before they needed to leave for the game, so there was time to put on the finishing touches.

I sat on the bed and watched the whole thing, because even though I wasn't going, they wanted me here to spend time with them. It was times like this, hanging out with them outside of school, in their houses, that shocked me a little. Like a part of my brain couldn't believe we were close enough for me to be seeing them outside of school.

But coming off a friendship that'd lasted over a decade, Rachel and Ava taught me that you didn't always need years to form a tight bond with someone. Sometimes, moments like this—sitting on Ava's bed while she and Rachel bickered over pawprints, K-Pop filtering through Ava's laptop speakers—still felt a little surreal.

"I hope they win tonight," Rachel said. "They're up against the Chesterfield Vikings, and they haven't lost once this season."

"The season did just start." Ava shook the paint marker a little before touching up a stripe along Rachel's cheek.

Rachel lifted up her cell to peer at the screen. "Ooh, Jade posted a photo of the cheer squad doing warmups. They're there already."

Ava leaned in. "Aw, look how Madison styled her hair. I swear, she always comes up with the prettiest styles. We should try recreating them sometime."

"Or ask her to help us," Rachel whispered back, and then laughed, as if what she'd said was as controversial as removing sweets from the school vending machines. "Maisie, you should let us practice on you."

Despite being friends with them for two years, I'd never told them about my past with the cheerleader. Back then, we were just two nobody freshmen, which meant the fallout didn't reach nuclear proportions. Which meant that it was most likely just her, Jade, and me that remembered.

Or maybe it was even just me.

"Pass," I replied with a grimace. "The most I ever do with my hair is a ponytail. Braiding your hair like you're going to a wedding is silly."

Ava finished up the pawprint and passed the marker to Rachel, who took over, focusing on Ava's right cheek. "You're not coming tonight, right?" Rachel asked.

"Definitely not." I avoided football games like the plague. I didn't see the point in standing around a bunch of people to watch guys run around on a football field. The sport itself was stupid and dangerous and boring. "Alex and I are going out after, though. He'll fill me in on who scores a touchdown or whatever." And he definitely would.

Ava's bedroom fell silent as Rachel concentrated on drawing the pawprint, and I leaned back against her headboard, my mind filling up the space. Today was Friday, which meant no tutoring today, but I couldn't help but wonder if Connor had done the practice problems. The idea of him working through them incorrectly made me uneasy. We didn't have time for setbacks like that.

Thinking about Connor led me down Humiliation Highway as last night resurfaced for the millionth time. Stupid Connor with his physical touch tips and gray sweatpants. It made sense that his advice would backfire.

Love advice. More like "how to make your relationship awkward" advice. Ugh.

"Can you promise you'll come to a game this season?" Ava asked, and though she held perfectly still, she glanced at me from the corner of her eye. "It's our senior year. You have to come to at least one."

"As long as it's not—"

"Homecoming!" Rachel interjected, batting her lashes. "You *have* to come to homecoming."

Out of all the games, the homecoming game was the one I wanted to attend the *least*. The school spirit that was a step down from unbearable on normal game nights turned psycho on homecoming night. Like the spirit of Brentwood High possessed everybody. I'd need holy water to attend.

"It'll be so cool to see all the homecoming court candidates on the field," Rachel said, lifting a hand and beginning to count her fingers. "Landon was nominated to win, and so was Graham Ruiz. Madison was also nominated, but I can't remember the other girl. Obviously, Connor and Jade will win, though."

I twisted the tufts on the pillow in my grip, doing my best to stifle the scoff that rose in my throat. "Of course they will," I muttered, voice taking on a bitter edge. "They're treated practically like royalty."

"I agree, they shouldn't be shoo-ins because of being

the leaders of their sport teams," Ava said, backing me up. "Sometimes Brentwood traditions are so rigid, you know? Like there should be *some kind* of progression."

"You'd want to be queen?" Rachel asked, raising an eyebrow.

"Not in the slightest," Ava was quick to respond, shivering at the thought. "I'm perfectly fine watching all the drama, thank you very much."

The feeling stirring in my stomach hadn't necessarily been born from the fact that it was, once again, the jock and head cheerleader projected to win the homecoming title. It had less to do with sports, more to do with the people themselves.

And I couldn't figure out why I cared so much.

"Mom might need my help at the gallery that day," I told them, a cop-out that might've been obvious, but it was the only excuse I could come up with on the fly. "They're doing a Brentwood exhibit that week for school spirit. She usually asks me to help pass out pamphlets or something."

Rachel capped the marker and then pointed it at me, puffing out her bottom lip. "Think about it, okay? Please? We'd love it if you were with us."

Ava nodded with Rachel's plea.

And again, that surreal feeling was back. That, in a few years' time, I found friends who were truer than I could've asked for. That even though I sometimes spoke in fluent math equations, we still worked.

"I'll think about it," I allowed, my resolve weakening with a pleasant ache in my chest.

Ava burst into a bright grin, making a heart with her hands and peering at me through it. "That's all we can ask for."

In a close six-point lead, the Brentwood Bobcats defeated the Chesterville Vikings, Connor Bray scoring the final touchdown with seconds left on the clock. The tension in the student section had run high, everyone practically holding their breath as our team inched closer and closer to the end zone. And when Landon had thrown the ball, sailing perfectly into Connor's waiting arms, the entire bleachers had gone wild.

Or, at least, that was how Alex described it.

"You had to be there for the full effect," he said for what seemed like the millionth time, but this time, his words were garbled around a piece of french fry he chewed. He had ketchup on the corner of his mouth, and every time it caught my attention, my stomach turned. I hated ketchup. Fries with ranch were where it was at. "I swear, Maisie, it was awesome. And the cheerleaders— their new cheers were so good. Someone's probably already uploaded it onto social media, though. Maybe Ava even posted it on *Babble*. I'll see if I can find it."

Alex whipped out his cell phone, but I reached over, resting my fingers on the screen. "It's okay. I believe you."

"But you should *see* it."

"I don't want to."

He just watched me for a beat, gauging how annoyed

I was by my tone, before he put his phone away. "You're in a bit of a mood tonight."

The atmosphere of the Wallflower diner was quiet, though it wouldn't be for long. The quaint interior would soon fill up once the football players showered and changed. The diner was located right on the edge of city lines, but technically, its postal code was in Jefferson territory. Since it was so close, though, it was a race of which school team would show up first to claim the spot.

We really were in a time of greasers verses socs, except it was socs verses other socs.

Maybe that was why Alex had chosen to come here tonight, and maybe that was why I was practically inhaling my cheeseburger and steak fries, ready to leave.

"I'm just tired," I told him, and it wasn't exactly a lie. There were several things on my mind, though. My parents, Rachel, Ava, Jozie, Alex. Connor. I'd folded his sweatpants and stashed them in the top drawer of my dresser after I'd washed them, because heaven forbid Mom take them from the dryer and demand to know who they were from. "It's been a long week."

"Has anyone said anything about the Most Likely Tos? Or has it pretty much dropped off?"

"I haven't heard anything since the other day." Rachel's prediction of people losing interest after a week had been accurate after all. "Then again, my label isn't that interesting, is it? People are more fascinated by the relationship-oriented ones."

Alex grimaced. "Yeah, I know."

I knew he was thinking about being on the list last

year. His label had been a relationship-oriented one. "Your label did kind of stink, but it *did* bring us together. So that's good, right?"

He swiped a french fry through his ketchup, halting a little to give me a brief nod. "One of the good things to come from it."

As I wiped my fingers on my napkin, I couldn't help but wonder if there was anything good about my name being on the list. If there was, it definitely wasn't as obvious.

"I actually remember the first time I saw you," he went on, pausing to chew. "We were in the cafeteria. I think it was a day or two after the Most Likely To list came out? Either way, I was scanning the whole room for someone who'd make a good girlfriend. And then I saw you."

The story of our relationship had never been an overly romantic one—most of those mushy-gushy scenarios only happened in movies—but until that moment, I'd never known the full extent of how coincidental we were. How dependent upon the Most Likely Tos our relationship had been. It wasn't like he'd had a crush on me for weeks and finally mustered up the courage to ask me out. He'd gone *searching* for someone so he could *rectify his casting* or whatever Ava had called it.

And maybe deep down I knew that, but it was another thing to have him blatantly admit it.

"How's your tutoring coming along?" he asked as I sat back in my seat, struggling to wade through the wave of negativity that suddenly swarmed the Wallflower's small dining room. "Who are you tutoring again? I don't remember if you've said. Do I know them?"

"Probably not. It's a freshman." The lie slipped from my mouth smoothly, so long as I didn't look him in the eye. "And it's going okay."

"What did you do at home tonight? Homework?"

I had, in fact, read through the assigned *Pride and Prejudice* chapters, but also skimmed through the Algebra II textbook and wrote down practice problems for Connor to work on Monday. I needed the comfort of equations to keep me company. "I had to finish it because Ava's sending me an article to read through tonight."

Alex sighed. "You should've come to the game tonight, you know. Done something other than homework."

"I don't like football games." Jeez, was I caught in a time loop? That sentence might as well have been my catch phrase.

"Then come for the company."

"It's not like I can sit with you," I pointed out, folding my arms. "You're in the band."

"Well, I'm sure Rachel and Ava would love it if you went," he said, squeezing six fries between his fingers and swiping them through ketchup.

The door to the Wallflower swung open with a chime, and along with it came a flurry of new voices chatting. "Would *you* like it if I came?"

Alex's focus had snagged on something behind me.

Intrigue dripped from his voice as he leaned over the table, murmuring, "Jade, Madison, and Kyle came in."

My shoulders instinctively drooped. I shouldn't have looked. It was a compulsory movement, glancing over my shoulder. As soon as I turned, I regretted it, because I found the horror duo wading past tables with a boy, presumably named Kyle, trailing behind.

"Fancy seeing you two here," Jade said as she approached, because no way could she miss an opportunity to give her little digs. She eyed my plate as if it were a dead rat. "You know, that burger is *so* greasy."

My eyes were on Alex as he flipped a switch, going from curious to shocked to bedazzled as he gawked up at Jade. His eyes turned warm and melty, an expression he'd once given me whenever our eyes would lock. Months ago. Now it was directed at my archenemy, leaving me out in the cold.

"Careful," I told her, refusing to waver in the glare I sent her way. "With how clumsy I am, I'd hate for all that grease to get on your costume."

Jade and Madison wore their cheer outfits, the blue, pleated skirt falling way too high on Jade's mid-thigh. Her white sweater was pristine underneath the blue vest, not a grass stain or dirt smudge in sight. Like Rachel and Ava, she had pawprints drawn onto her cheeks, everything about her oozing Brentwood High cheer.

"Jade." Madison, who'd been lingering a step behind, tugged at her friend's arm. "Come on. Let's get a table."

Jade shrugged her off. "Go find us a good one, Mads.

I'm catching up with Alex and Math Book. Alex, how's the trombone?"

Madison ignored Jade's order, hesitating.

"He plays the tuba," I muttered.

Alex grinned. "It's great. You know, I'm one of the two tuba players in the entire band."

Without any further push, Alex went down the rabbit hole of geeking out over instruments, ketchup still on the corner of his mouth. I watched Jade fake her interest, her amusement, like he was a toy to entertain herself with. Behind her, Madison pressed her lips tightly together, as if she were debating on saying something else.

"Alex." Jade cut him off suddenly, leaning even farther over the table. "You're such a cool dude, you know that? The tuba...powerful instrument for a powerful guy."

Kyle's mouth scrunched up with disgust at the idea of her flirting with him. Same, Kyle. Same. "I'm going to sit down. Come join me when you're done gossiping." He flipped his hand underneath Madison's ponytail as he walked past, giving it a playful tug.

The door chimed once more as another person joined the fray. Connor's hair was damp, and he had his varsity jacket loose over his shoulders. It was too hot out for it, but he wore the ugly blue and gold thing anyway. When he spotted us, and how Jade towered over our table, he stopped midstride. "What's going on?"

"We're chatting." Jade pressed her fingertips to our

table, nearly upsetting my plate. "Waiting for you to park the car. What took you so long?"

"I had to parallel park." Connor didn't even look at me, but I squirmed in my seat. "If you're done talking, I'm starving."

Alex clamored to his feet, chair screeching as he shoved it backward. "Connor, man, you did great tonight. That final touchdown? Man, it *sailed* right into your arms, didn't it?"

Connor's expression brightened with the compliment, voice radiating charm. "Gotta have a solid pass for a solid touchdown. Landon did all the hard work. I was just in the right place at the right time."

Jade gave up her attempts at ambushing our table and walked over to Connor, pressing her palm on his chest and playing with the zipper of his jacket. It was a lingering touch, one that seemed highly inappropriate in the middle of the rinky-dink diner. "Don't downplay it, baby. You were great."

Without hesitation, Connor swiped up her hand, entwining their fingers. "Let's go sit down."

She let him lead her away, but only went a few steps before she pulled up short. The entire time, Madison stayed right behind her, and aside from her one comment, she'd been silent like her lips had been zipped shut. "Oh, and Maisie?" Jade gave her signature grin. "Bring Connor back his sweatpants on Monday. Don't be creepy and keep them in your closet."

There was a clear window for Connor to say anything. Something like *it's fine, no rush.* Something like *don't be a jerk, Jade.* He didn't laugh like she did, thank God, but he also didn't tell her to stop either. He didn't say anything.

Even though they'd walked off, the atmosphere they'd left at our table weighed me to my chair. Jade and Madison, I knew. Their attitudes weren't anything new. The glimpse of a halfway-decent person I'd seen yesterday wasn't Connor Bray's true self. This guy, holding hands with the head cheerleader and thriving off compliments from others, was the real one.

I was snapped from my thoughts when Alex grabbed his plate with one hand, swiped up his soda with the other, and acted like he was about to stand up. "What are you doing?" I asked.

"Let's go pull up a chair and sit with them," he said quickly. "There's enough room."

My hand shot out, latching on to one of his wrists. His Coke swished, almost like we were going to get a round two of Niagara Falls. "Are you joking?"

"Of course not." His eyes were round as he turned to me. "This is the perfect chance! I mean, they talked to us first. Let's go join them."

Did he honestly not pick up on the animosity emanating from Jade like a bad perfume? He didn't get it at all? I gaped at him, lost for words.

"I'm not sitting with them," I told him in a low voice, heart fluttering with something like panic. "If you're going over there, you're going without me."

Alex glanced over at the Top Tier table, the longing in his dark eyes crystal clear. He was going to sit down.

The hands holding his plate and Coke wavered, and he was going to put them back on the table. We were going to finish our food, and maybe round our date night off with getting a piece of Wallflower's signature chocolate cake. He was going to sit back down.

After a second, Alex did not sit back down. "Maisie."

That feeling definitely had been panic. "You drove me!"

Alex's excitement turned into desperation. He wore an expression of a kid begging his mom to buy him a toy from the store. "You brought your phone, right? I'm sure Rachel wouldn't mind coming to pick you up." He dropped his voice to a whisper. "Please, Maisie. This is my chance."

Chance. Chance to...what? Weasel his way into the Top Tier? *His chance.* At the expense of me. Except he didn't see that.

My grip loosened to the point where he easily pulled his wrist away. He hesitated only one more moment before saying, "I'll text you, okay?"

Please don't go, I said. Or maybe I thought it. Alex didn't stop. I didn't lift my head to watch him walk away, staring at my burger with a blurry gaze. Jade was right. Grease pooled on my plate, soaking into my french fries. My appetite was completely shattered.

Despite not moving a muscle, my lungs ached for air as if I'd finished running a marathon. A swell of darkness sweeping over me, ebbing my vision, threatening to completely take me whole.

It was freshman year all over again.

I glanced behind me once to see Alex positioning a chair alongside their booth, placing his plate on the table-top. Jade welcomed him with a grand smile, of course, because no doubt she was laughing on the inside. From the image, it was as if Alex fit in perfectly with the Top Tier.

Connor stared at Alex blankly, and there was no guessing what ran through his mind. It was perfectly, utterly emotionless. *He* was perfectly, utterly emotionless.

I'd never felt lonelier in my life.

My chair nearly overturned as I got to my feet, the screech loud enough to silence the entire diner. I tore away from the table, toward the door, barely seeing where I was going. A guy in a red and black varsity jacket was coming in as I ran out, and I slammed into his shoulder, knocking him back a step. He tried to steady me, quickly apologizing, but my shaking legs carried me forward without pause.

The air wasn't as cold as I wanted it to be, and it didn't cool the fire raging under my skin. I started sprinting down the street, sneakers slapping the pavement. My lungs burned for air, but I didn't slow. I wasn't much of a runner—hated it with a passion, actually—but I welcomed the ache. The denim of my jeans chafed against my thighs, and soon my sneakers picked at my skin uncomfortably, enough to build blisters, and my calves began to scream.

The toe of my sneaker caught on the edge of a pothole that I hadn't seen in the dark road, and it was a miracle that I didn't faceplant onto the gritty asphalt. I did stumble, though, tripping to a stop with a gasp. My heart pounded too fast, trampling in my chest, and the breaths I pulled in were too close together. *It's okay. It's okay.*

But it didn't feel okay. All alone on a dark street, feet aching with the newly formed blisters, it didn't feel remotely close to okay.

My cell phone in my back pocket almost felt like a brick, heavy and thick and weighing me down. Who could I call? Not Mom and Dad, who were too busy at an exhibit at the gallery. Jozie was too far away to do anything but be moral support, and with her track record lately, she might not have even been that. I couldn't call Rachel or Ava, because facing them right now made all of this so much worse.

There was no one *to* call. I had an hour's walk from home with only flickering streetlamps to guide me.

I'd been walking for five minutes when a wave of headlights swept down the road. I wasn't sure if the car saw me, but I ducked along the shoulder out of the roadway in case.

The SUV drove only a few feet past me before hitting the brakes, red lights lighting up the street. My pulse jolted, but before any ounce of fear could set in— because I *was* walking alone on a dark and sketchy road late at night—the driver's side door opened, and someone slender climbed out.

"Jeez, you got far fast," Connor said as he straightened his jacket. He rounded the end of the car. "Did you used to be a sprinter or something?"

I blinked, but the image didn't change. It really was Connor standing there with his stupid, shiny SUV beside him. But then again, of course the universe sent him. Even on our days off, I couldn't be rid of him.

"What the heck are you doing here?" My voice was shaky, but even with the tremor, it was still venomous. "Did you seriously follow me?"

"Evidence would point to yes."

"You shouldn't be here," I bit out, curling my hands into fists as I stomped forward. "I'd hate for anyone to find out you came to check on me."

Connor wouldn't let me pass by him. As soon as I got close enough, he blocked my path, forcing my steps to a halt. His varsity jacket was loose over his shoulders, the big blue B a glaring scream. "This is a rough part of town."

"I'll be fine."

I tried to sidestep him again, but this time, Connor's palms closed over my upper arms, stopping me. "It'll take you an hour to walk home. And it's dark."

I gritted my teeth, debating on yanking free of the touch, of shoving him away. "Why do you care?"

"I can't pass Algebra if you've been hit by a car."

The blackness in my heart had to have shown on my face, but his expression didn't even waver. "Mrs. Diego would find you a new tutor. Heck, maybe Principal Oliphant won't make you take the test. She would do anything for the football star."

"Not that, though. Believe me, I've tried to be convincing."

This time, I did shrug free of his hands, unable to stifle my scoff. "Go back to your loser friends," I said, ramming into his shoulder as I walked past.

And got about two steps away before he caught my wrist. "Wait—"

My wire-thin patience, and the pressure building inside me, snapped. "Let go!" I slapped my free hand against his shoulder, putting all of my force into the swing. The momentum knocked him back a step, his hand dropping mine in surprise. "You know, you could've said something back there. Could've stood up and offered me a ride home then. Why didn't you?"

Connor straightened his jacket, but the perfectly curated mask had already cracked.

"Because it's okay to talk to me when no one else is around?" Mortifying, hot tears filled my eyes, ones that burned with anger more than sadness. I shoved at him again, but this time, he'd planted his feet firmly. He didn't even fall back a step. "That's why you don't stand up for me when your girlfriend's being a jerk. Why you pretend like I don't exist. Why you wanted *discretion*. Because heaven forbid anyone connects you to Maisie Matthews. Well, guess what? I don't want to talk to you, even when no one's around to witness it."

Connor's hazel eyes grew hotter and hotter as I spoke, as if the fire burning my skin had transferred to him. "If I had said something at the diner, it would've been worse. Jade never would've let it go."

"Oh, *please*," I scoffed. "That's just an excuse. Your way of letting yourself off the hook for being a jerk."

Connor stared at the blinking taillights of his SUV, as if this time, *he* was the one fighting for patience. "If you want to be angry, be angry at your idiotic boyfriend. What kind of guy would ditch his date to hang out with people he barely knows? Real winner, right there."

His words were like a bucket of ice water. I tried to latch on to the anger that'd engulfed me mere seconds before, because anything was better than the sting of rejection, but it slipped through my fingers. "He wants his fifteen minutes of high school fame."

"And he's going to sacrifice you to get it?"

Earlier in the week when Alex had first broached the topic—*do you ever just feel like we're different?*—I thought it'd be a subject brought up for us to move on from, to grow closer about. Tonight, though, the conversation seemed more and more like a nail in the coffin of our relationship.

The summer breeze coasted across my face, drying my eyes, its way of saying *there, there.*

"Come on." Connor took a step backward, gesturing toward his car. He seemed to sense my wavering resolve, acting on it. "Let me drive you home. Or at least to Brentwood limits."

I wanted to yell at him again and tell him that he needed to take no for an answer, but it required too much energy. My anger had been a sparkler, and now it was all burned out. "You're going to risk being seen with me?"

"You can duck down when we see a car."

I didn't check to find out whether or not he was teasing. He probably wasn't. Walking home alone with nothing but my thoughts in the dark became an unbearable idea. Standing before me, in a way I never saw coming, Connor Bray was my last resort.

So, I started toward the red headlights and beacon of escape.

Connor drove slowly through Jefferson's residential district, tapping his fingers to the stream of music coming from the stereo. It wasn't The Cars this time, but a band I didn't recognize. Loud enough to make out the words, but soft enough to speak over if either of us wanted.

In our realm of quiet, I couldn't help but imagine what a certain Wallflower's booth looked like. Alex had sat next to Jade, but were they still there? Probably. What were they talking about?

I had to clear my throat a little before I spoke. "What'd you tell them?"

"Tell who?"

"Your girlfriend. What'd you tell her when you left?"

Connor caressed the steering wheel. "She didn't ask."

His expression matched his voice—even, neutral. "So you got up and left, and no one said anything?"

"I'm sure I'll get a text of her cussing me out later for bailing, but no, she didn't ask where I went." An oncoming car's headlights swept over him, causing him to squint as it passed. "She'll get a ride home with Kyle. She was too entertained by your boyfriend to focus on hers."

Alex's childlike excitement flashed across my mind again, weighing me down into the seat. Connor had to know that Jade wasn't entertained by him—she was entertained by the idea of it hurting me. "Alex will feel bad about it later," I told him as if he'd asked. "He wants to be in the in-crowd."

"It's overrated."

"Of course it is to you. You're in it."

Connor propped his elbow on the car door, considering my response. "Did you ever want to be part of the in-crowd?"

"Never."

He didn't answer. I didn't think he believed me.

The streetlights illuminated the roadway as we crossed from Jefferson into Brentwood, and I stared at the houses as we passed. There were families moving within some, TVs playing within view, and some houses had all of their lights turned off. I pictured myself in their shoes. Instead of sitting in the passenger seat of Connor's car, I was on the couch watching TV. Having a late-night snack. Anywhere other than feeling sorry for myself.

Connor turned onto my road without prompting, tires popping over the loose gravel. He dodged the potholes as best he could, flicking on his brights. "You said you were neighbors with Madison. Which house is it?"

"Mine is the blue one," I said, leaning forward to point. "With the gray garage door."

Connor twisted the steering wheel as he turned in to my empty driveway. The house was a ghostly figure, all windows blacked out, not a trace of light inside. He tipped his head to me once he'd parked the car. "Now thank me, because it would've taken you five times longer to get home."

I didn't thank him. I stared at the way his headlights hit the garage door, two spotlights on the gray paint. "Your tip didn't work."

Connor didn't even have to ask what I meant. "Yeah, well, it won't work on idiots."

"It seemed to work on Jade last night."

His hands loosely gripped the steering wheel, but hadn't paused their tapping, a flutter that held my attention. Focusing on his fingers was easier than looking at him. "The thing with Jade," he began slowly, voice a low murmur, "is that she's only interested when she wants to be."

His answer wasn't as satisfying as I'd been hoping. It wasn't a magic cure-all that I could implement in my own relationship. Was that how it was with Alex? He was only interested when he wanted to be? I thought about his attention to his videogames even when his legs were in my lap. How easily his attention was snagged by a couple of kids walking through the diner door.

I decided that if I was going to humiliate myself, I might as well go the full nine yards. "Do you two love each other?"

"*That's* overrated," Connor said, words accompanied by a scoff. "No one falls in love in high school."

I'd take that as a *no*. "You can fall in love in high school. I did."

"You call that love?" he demanded, casting that hazel glare over at me. An incredulous smile crossed his lips.

"Leaving someone to walk home alone for a chance to chat with people who are practically strangers? What you and Alex have, you'd call that love?"

I gripped the door handle tighter. Why hadn't I opened it yet? "He loves me."

"If that's love, I don't want it."

The bluntness of his response was sharp, simple. Detached. Words designed to make me feel stupid and naïve for believing in love in the first place. Stupid and naïve for wanting it. "No, you want a high-profile relationship," I shot back, turning on him. "A relationship that requires zero effort and one that people fawn over you over. You want to be the It-Couple—to hell with actual feelings, right? *That's* sad."

My throat ached from the severity of my words, and my ears rang with the silence that followed. Connor regarded me as a stranger might've—a stranger who bumped into them, jarring their shoulder. "If you're done insulting me, you can get out now."

I wanted to throw back at him that he'd started it, he'd insulted my relationship first, but his words settled like stones on my chest.

See? Even he doesn't want to be around you.

I popped the door open and stepped out into the night, not hesitating for a second before slamming it shut. Connor's headlights passed over me as he backed out of the driveway, tires crunching on the gravel, kicking it up in his haste to drive off.

And then all I saw were his taillights as they pummeled down the road.

Struggling to unlock the door, I was struck once more with how *lonely* I felt. Like I was the only person on the planet. When my key finally flipped the lock over, and the dark house greeted me, I couldn't help but feel like I had to be the only one who was having a bad night.

CHAPTER II

I woke up Saturday morning to my cell phone buzzing on my nightstand, and I had half a mind to ignore it. It had to be at least six in the morning, judging by the faint shade of the sky visible through my window, which was too early for a non-school day. Especially given how late I'd been up the night before, my face in my pillow to stifle my crying.

But my phone kept buzzing at an annoying level, and with a groan, I pressed it to my ear. "*Lo?*"

"Hey, May-May," the honeyed tone quickly quipped on the other end.

In an instant, I was wide awake. "Wow, I *do* have a sister. And here I thought I'd hallucinated her my entire life. Can you remind me, what's your name again?"

Jozie laughed. "I know, I know, I've been meaning to call. I had a big assignment due right off the bat, so I haven't had the chance."

I pressed my phone firmer to my ear if only to try and bring her voice closer, closing my eyes. "You could've waited a little longer to call, though. You're an hour ahead of us. It's only six here. On a *Saturday*."

"Waking up with the sun is good for the body and soul. Mom was saying you've been popping your knuckles again. Have you tried meditating? Try waking up before sunrise and—"

"If I'd known you were going to call to nag at me, I would've missed you a lot less."

"See, I told you that you'd miss me." Happiness radiated from her voice. "Fill me in on everything that's happened this week. How's school? How are your friends? How's Alex?"

The bubble of happiness that'd ballooned around me at the sound of Jozie's voice popped. Last night came back in scissoring memories, one after another snipping across my vision. Reality set in, and I peeled my eyes open to stare at the ceiling. "Everything's fine."

"*Beep, beep,*" Jozie said. "My lie detector's going off."

"I forgot how weird you are."

"Tell me what's going on. Seriously. Is it with school? Mom and Dad?"

It was a myriad of things, but I found myself wanting to tell Jozie about none of it. The Most Likely To list, losing valedictorian, everything with Alex, tutoring Connor Bray—I didn't want to ruin the one phone call I'd gotten from her in weeks.

I rolled onto my side and faced my window. From this angle, I only had the perfect view of the ever-lightening sky. "I don't really want to get into it."

"Just tell me who's grinding your gears," she said,

voice releasing a hint of impatience. "And we can let it go."

"Alex and I had a fight last night."

It was true, and it wasn't true. We didn't necessarily fight—no harsh words were exchanged, no one raised their voice. Still, it *felt* like we did. Like something happened last night that would be tough to overcome.

Jozie was quiet on the other end for a long moment, debating how serious she was about "letting it go." Apparently, not very. "Can I say one thing and we can drop it?"

My gaze slid to her discarded bed, sad without her endless supply of pillows and stuffed animals. All of those had gone with her in the move. "I don't know. I'm not in the mood to talk about everything." Especially not at six in the morning.

"Life's too short to spend it with people who don't make you happy," she told me, pulling on her big sister pants and giving the advice she would've given if she was home. "You deserve more than a guy who doesn't make you happy."

"You've never liked Alex."

"I never liked how he treated you," she corrected. "Your relationship has never really made much sense to me. You guys act more like dysfunctional friends than anything."

First Connor said that Alex treated me like an annoying sister, and now Jozie was saying that we acted like dysfunctional friends. Awesome. "Okay, you've said your one thing."

We talked for a little while longer, long enough for

the sun to rise higher in the window. I told her a bit about tutoring while leaving out the *who*, because even though Jozie had graduated last year, she absolutely would've recognized the name. She told me a little bit about her classes, which admittedly mostly went over my head. But I'd been content to simply listen to her voice, letting it calm a bit of my nerves that had carried over from the night before.

When we hung up, I realized Ava had never texted me last night with the article she needed proofed. It was a record for me, opening up *Brentwood Babble* so early in the morning, but I loaded up her blog page. She had ended up just posting the game's score, but just before I closed out the page, my eyes snagged on the second most recent post.

ALERT THE MEDIA—It Must Be Date Night!

It was a picture post from Thursday night, the image she'd snapped of Connor and his posse at the shoe rental counter. Connor smiled in the photo, and Reed's eyes were locked on Ava's camera, but that wasn't what had me faltering.

The top comment to the bowling post was another picture post, and this time, it was of me. It was five seconds post-Niagara Falls incident, with my mouth in an O-shaped letter of mortification, Alex's eyes round. The picture transported me back into the moment, bringing back the iciness of soda spilling onto my lap, the burning of my cheeks. And here it was, broadcasted for the entirety of Brentwood High to see. And reply to.

SmileyFace20: Why doesn't Babble post this stuff??? This is hilarious!

Anonymoose: Yikes, are those white shorts?! Guess someone got a show

BrentwoodBobs: Break out an umbrella. Probably got so nervous because the dream team showed up. Landon, Reed, AND Connor? I'd be a klutz too!

It didn't stop there. I counted ten comments before forcing my gaze away. My heart thrummed at the speed of light, thoughts running even faster. I couldn't do anything to the photo besides give it a frowny-face emoji, which it hadn't gotten yet. It'd only gotten laughing emojis and rain drop emojis.

I doubled back to the person who posted the picture, to the initial comment. It wasn't hard to guess who might've snapped the shot. From the angle of the photo, it could've only been taken from the table the Top Tier had claimed. When I read through the text, at who posted it, things became so much clearer.

JDBobcatBabe01: Did the weather call for rain?

+ − × ÷

Monday morning, I walked into Brentwood High with my insides in a tangle of discomfort. The weekend had gone by in slow-mo, dragging on as if someone had added four hours to the day. Mom and Dad had been at the gallery all weekend, leaving me to do nothing but home-work and feel sorry for myself. After impulsively checking *Brentwood Babble* for the tenth time, refreshing to see if any new comments had popped up, I'd ended up shoving my cell in the top drawer of my dresser, starting my self-proclaimed social media detox for the rest of the weekend.

Which meant that I didn't get Alex's apology text that'd come in Saturday night until I turned my phone back on this morning.

ALEX

hey, I know I should've texted sooner, but I didn't know what to say. I'm really, really srry for Friday, Maisie. Plz don't be mad at me. Can you call me when you see this? I feel like this is something I should apologize about in person. Plz?

I spun my combination, and as soon as I opened my locker door, a folded-up piece of paper fluttered to the floor. Immediately, my guard flew up, but I grabbed it anyway.

This time last week, I wouldn't have known whose handwriting this was. But now, after two days of getting to acquaint myself with it, the chicken scratch was easily identifiable even if they didn't leave their full name.

MEET ME BY THE FOOTBALL BLEACHERS AT LUNCH.

-C

Before I had a chance to react to the demand, to the absurdity of him slipping a note into my locker—because when would he have had time to do it, anyway?—a voice sounded right behind me. "Hi, bestie."

I turned to find Rachel and Ava standing behind me, the former offering me a sleepy grin, the latter gazing at me with a seriousness that wasn't like her. Seeing her, though, reminded me of the article from Thursday night, of the picture of me that she hadn't deleted from the text thread. It caused a dark emotion to stir in my stomach, and I crushed the slip of paper into my bag. "Morning."

Without wasting a second, Ava thrusted her cell phone at me, lit-up screen facing me. Her features were grim. "I got this submission last night."

My stomach dipped as I read the bold text.

Maybe they should change Most Likely to Marry a Math book into Most Likely to Get Dumped, because Maisie's boyfriend ditched her Friday night at the Wallflower to sit with the popular crowd. How embarrassing!

"People love to stick their nose into business that isn't their own," I muttered, trying to invoke the anger I knew was simmering *somewhere* in my body, but I felt more and more weighed down, as if I was about to sink into the floor.

Rachel took a step closer, lowering her chin. When she spoke, her voice was loaded with concern. "Did that actually happen on Friday?"

My silence spoke volumes; I knew it did. But I knew that if I were to say anything, there was no coming back from it. I could forgive Alex, but I wasn't sure that they would.

As I reached into my bag, the soft fabric of Connor's sweatpants grazed my fingers. I stared into the pit of my locker, but I couldn't see it anymore. All I could see was Connor in the driver's seat of his car, anger in his eyes.

Meet me by the football bleachers at lunch. Was he serious? After Friday, he thought he could boss me around?

I tried to imagine myself walking down the hallway, finding him before classes started, passing back the freshly washed pair of sweatpants. What would his reaction have been? Would he have thanked me for washing them? Snatched them back, embarrassed to be seen talking to me? Would he have pretended they weren't his?

The unknown answer had me passing the stupid things off to Rachel. "Here. Can you give these back to Mr. Popular for me?"

Without another word, I shut my locker door and flicked the combination before walking away. I wasn't sure if Rachel and Ava stuck around to talk to each other or whether Rachel went off to find Connor and return the sweatpants, but I didn't look back to find out.

CHAPTER 12

Even though the bell rang for us to go to lunch, Mrs. Greer hurried and got one last assignment in, leaving me scrambling to make a note in my planner. No one else bothered to stay around and write it down—some left even though she was talking—so I ended up being the last to duck out of the classroom.

I was one step away from starting down the staircase before a hand wrapped around my wrist, tugging me backward. My sneaker caught on the linoleum floor, creating a squeak that sounded like a scream.

When I turned around, I came face to face with Connor Bray.

"Would you stop getting all grabby-handy with me?" I demanded, wrenching my hand from his wrist, though he was quick to let me go. He wore a black hoodie and tan shorts, an odd combination for a late September day, but I only judged a little. "Seriously, there's this thing called personal space—"

"Is there anyone else left in the classroom?"

I frowned at him talking over me, squeezing my

fingers into a fist. "No, I was the last one." And then something weird hit me. "Wait, were you out here waiting for me?"

Connor's eyes bobbed around everywhere but at me—down the staircase, down the hallway, even peeking into Mrs. Greer's classroom to make sure no one was about to emerge. He was waiting for someone to catch him being too friendly to me. I wondered if he already had an excuse ready. "Did you not get my note?"

My mood darkened as a cloud covered my sunshine. "Lunch *just* started. There's no way I would've made it to the bleachers by now. Why did you want to meet me there, anyway?"

"I figured we could meet and talk about where we should go today for tutoring. Go over my math homework you assigned. Get in some bonus tutoring time. Maybe we could do *your* tutoring session. Except I assumed you giving the sweatpants to your friends was your way of saying 'not a chance.'"

He was right about that. I hadn't been planning on going. "How did you even know this was my class?" And then it hit me. "Rachel."

"Ava, actually. I asked her when Rachel gave me back the sweatpants. Which—" He turned back to me with a curious, raised eyebrow. "Going back to my above point, I didn't expect *her* to be the one to give them back."

"You shouldn't have given the pants to me in the first place. You're the one who preached about keeping this a secret."

"Only about the tutoring."

If it was any other student wanting to keep their tutoring sessions a secret, would I have thought twice about it? Would it have felt so much like an insult? Embarrassment washed over me all over again seeing Connor now. Seeing him launched me back into the creaky diner chair at the Wallflower, where my Friday night quickly turned into the Friday night from hell. Last *week* was the week from hell. And of course, Connor had a front row seat to most of it.

The sharpness of his tone when he dropped me off rang in my ears, and even now, the phantom ache in my throat as I snapped back a response rose up. Fighting with someone you barely knew, I realized, was almost as uncomfortable as fighting with someone you loved.

"Maybe I was right about what I said Friday," I said, rubbing my arm. "Mrs. Diego can find you a new tutor."

Connor's brow creased. "Why?"

"Because things are too complicated with us." *Us.* The monosyllable tasted awkward in my mouth. "We don't like each other, which is a pretty terrible student-teacher relationship."

"You don't like me?"

This time, his shocked tone made me laugh. "I know, someone not liking Connor Bray? Alert the media. But you don't like me either. Which is—well—whatever. We can hate each other and be enemies, and that's fine, but it means that I can't tutor you."

As my sentence drew on, Connor's eyes narrowed on me, and his head tilted to the side. I couldn't tell if he was amused or offended. "We're enemies?"

Okay, fine, I wouldn't have called him a strict enemy. Probably not, anyway. I'd reserve that term for two members of the cheer squad. "Maybe...frenemies." We *were* able to be friendly enough during our tutoring sessions, when the jerk side of his personality went into hibernation. "But either way—"

"I need you." Connor took a step closer until he'd entered my bubble of space, scenting the air with the smell of sandalwood and mint. There was no room to back up, not unless I wanted to take the plunge down the staircase, so I froze. "I need you to tutor me. I'm out of options at this point, and I don't have time to find another tutor. You need something too, right?"

A neon sign flashed in my head. *Valedictorian.* A gateway title that led to scholarships, potential full rides, no more worrying about what my parents had left for me in the college fund.

"Love advice," he filled in when my silence had stretched too long.

I snorted. "Not that your advice worked well the first time." I cast a glance down the stairs, the smudges on the linoleum from a morning's worth of shoe treads. Halfway down the stairs there was a landing, and then they turned, so I couldn't see the first floor. *Love advice.* The two words made me think of Alex, with a winter storm of nerves and feelings hot on its heels. None of it comfortable.

"Have you and Alex talked about Friday?" Connor asked, the words sounding suspiciously like small talk.

Filler. Like he didn't really care, but he knew he should ask.

"Did *you* talk to him when you went back to the diner? Become BFFs?"

"I never went back after I dropped you off. Jade and Madison got a ride from Kyle." Connor wavered on his feet. "He grovel at your feet for making you find your own ride home?"

If there was one thing that I didn't want to talk to Connor Bray about right then, it was Alex. The whole situation of Friday night. In fact, I wanted to strike that night from my memory, draw a fierce, red line through the whole evening. I started descending the staircase. "I don't want to talk about it."

"Macy—"

Not even five stairs down, I turned, craning my neck back up at him. "Are you pronouncing it wrong on purpose?"

If I didn't know any better, I would've said his cheeks appeared pink. "How are you supposed to pronounce it?"

"The S makes a *zee* sound. Not a *see* sound."

"Wait, there's an s? Where?"

I gave him a blank stare. "It's *M-A-I-S-I-E*."

He reached up and rubbed his fingers across his lips, the gesture almost self-conscious. "I'll have to write it down. I won't remember it unless I write it down."

Something about what he said had me hesitating. "Writing things down helps you remember?"

Connor shrugged and stepped down to the same stair as me. "Yeah, I guess. That's how I passed Spanish last year, anyway. It was way easier to remember conjugations after I wrote them down."

A little lightbulb went off in my head. "Where do you want to meet for tutoring today?"

Connor went down one more stair, glancing back. "What happened to our negative student-teacher, frenemy relationship?"

The way Connor looked up at me caused me to pull up short. His expression was more open now, almost relieved. That relief tickled something in my brain, reminding that small side that argued that there *was* more to Connor than his snarky attitude and popularity status. There was desperation in him, just like every other student.

I hated that reminder.

I stepped past him, gripping my bag strap tightly. "I think I've got an idea for tutoring."

"Do tell."

I didn't get a chance to, not before a voice called up the stairs. "Maisie? Is that you?"

Recognition blazed through me. *Alex.*

The suddenness of his voice—the instant fear of being caught—had me stumbling. My sneaker caught on the lip of the stair, and right before gravity sucked me down the staircase, Connor latched on to my arm.

The reaction was instantaneous, no room for hesitation before his fingers wrapped around the skin above my elbow. He yanked me back, his other hand wrapping around my waist to steady me further.

Connor's chest pressed flush against my back, the

world still caught in an uneven tilt-a-whirl. My brain quickly became aware of each point his ten fingers touched me. Even though he'd quite literally saved my life, the way his body was pressed against mine almost felt intimate, the way someone would hold the person they cared about.

Someone's heart was beating fast—I couldn't tell if it was his or mine.

As quickly as they'd risen to catch me, Connor's hands fell away. With the connection severed, clarity bolted through me. *Alex.*

Without turning back, I left Connor and hurried down the stairs. My heart still tripped even when I rounded the landing, finding Alex on the third stair from the bottom.

"I thought that was your voice," he said. He stopped when he saw me, one hand on the rail. It was the first time I'd seen him all morning, and he'd gelled his dark hair this morning so the curls were frozen off his forehead. From here, I could see the blue bandage on his upper lip. I guess he *was* shaving every four days. "Who were you talking to?"

"Some kid had a question about the English homework," I said hastily, hurrying down the steps. I needed to corral him away so Connor could come down. "We're late for lunch."

But Alex didn't come off the staircase, though he did pivot around. "I was waiting for you to come down. I want to say sorry, Maisie."

Lord, I didn't want to do this here. Not with Connor

above us on the stairs, no doubt able to hear every word. Whatever conversation Alex and I would have about our relationship didn't need prying eyes or listening ears. "Let's walk and talk—"

"You ignored my calls all weekend."

So we *were* getting into it. Fine. "You only called once."

"I wanted to give you space. I knew you must be angry."

"You humiliated me. Of course I was angry."

"I know." He at least had the good grace to pretend to be mournful, ducking his chin closer to his chest. "I feel awful about it."

I couldn't gauge the sincerity of the words, or maybe I didn't want to. Apologetic or not, it wasn't the sort of situation to beg forgiveness for. It definitely should've fallen under the *ask for permission* category. "Tell me, was sitting with the Top Tier the chance you always dreamed of?"

Alex didn't answer right away, weighing his words while biting his top lip. The fact that he wasn't gushing about Friday night hinted that no, it *hadn't* been everything he'd hyped it up to be. He just didn't want to admit it. That made me feel slightly better. "They talked about you."

Of course they did, because what else would Jade talk to Alex about? His super cool, super powerful tuba?

Alex came off the bottom stair and looked me in the eye, the curious sort of seriousness making me wary. "Did you really try out for the cheer squad back in freshman year?"

His words triggered an avalanche-like reaction within me, like little dominos tumbling over inside my brain. "W-Who told you that?"

"Jade said something. Said that you tried out but didn't make the cut."

A severe buzzing built within my ears, the hallway fading into pure background noise. Being friends wasn't a deep and dark, dirty little secret that I'd been fighting to keep, sure, but my stomach dropped anyway.

"Me, a cheerleader?" I asked, and though my heart was beating fast, my voice was calm. Level. I glanced toward the staircase, but Connor still hadn't appeared. "Can you imagine me trying out for the cheer squad?"

"Well, if I'm being honest, I didn't buy it at first," he said, one corner of his mouth quirking up. "With how much you dislike sports events, you would've been a depressing cheerleader."

The buzzing in my ears moved into my throat, the vibration closing off my airway.

"It's weird, though. Why would Jade say you tried out, then?"

It was the big question. Jade telling Alex about our history didn't make sense, and when things she did didn't make sense, it was never good. "She probably mistook me for someone else." Or maybe she tried to stir up conflict, her specialty. "But, uh, we should get to lunch. Before we run out of time to eat."

"Yeah, you're right." I let Alex pick up my hand,

curling his warm fingers around my clammy palm. PDA was rare for him—for both of us. We never hugged, kissed, or held hands in public, but here he was, grabbing my fingers without hesitation. My thoughts flashed back to Connor's hand wrapping around my arm, his other fingers gripping my hip, all to stop me from falling. The only reason my pulse stirred then was because I almost fell to my death, and the reason my pulse didn't stir now was because Alex's question left me shell-shocked. "I'm sure Ava and Rachel are waiting."

I let him lead me down the hall, hoping against hope that Connor hadn't heard any of that conversation.

CHAPTER 13

The more I thought about Jade bringing up freshman year, the more confused by it I became.

What purpose would Jade have, bringing it up to Alex?

"You're a million miles away right now," Connor said as we drove down Main Street. He had his elbow propped against the window, cheek pressed into his upturned palm. "Probably not the best time to zone out, huh?"

I glanced down at the worn leather steering wheel, gripping it tighter. "I wasn't zoning out."

"Uh-huh." Connor slouched in my passenger seat, a giant in the tiny car. His knees were folded awkwardly, legs too long to fit underneath the glovebox. He looked like an adult trying to squeeze into a Little Tikes Cozy Coupe. "Is there an airbag in this ancient beast?" he asked, rapping his knuckles on the top of the dash.

"Nope."

Connor tugged his seatbelt taut across his chest. "You want to tell me where we're going?"

"We're almost there." Traffic in Brentwood's heart of the city was heavy since most people were getting off work, one of the cons of meeting Connor for tutoring at four instead of right after school. Four-thirty, really—his glistening brown locks and sandalwood scent hinted he'd used the extra few minutes for a quick shower.

Ever since Mom started working at Center Inspire, I'd only been by a handful of times. The first time was when she'd given the whole family a tour of the facility and all the art exhibits. Halfway through, I snuck off to a deserted corner and read through a book on my phone, bored nearly to tears by the canvases and sculptures. On any given day after school, Jozie practically lived between those walls, soaking up whatever inspirational juices—her words—she could from the art.

Not me. I always felt too overwhelmed by the colors, the mediums.

But for a Monday afternoon, it would be the perfect place for a tutoring session.

"It's called Center Inspire. It's an art gallery."

"Brentwood has an art gallery?"

His thoroughly shocked tone caused a wave of amusement to hit me so suddenly that I couldn't stifle my snort. "It's mostly visited by the elderly or trendy, aspiring artists."

"I, admittedly, am neither."

"One thing we have in common."

Connor glanced over at me, as if contemplating

whether or not I was being serious. Surely, he couldn't be surprised. Nothing about me screamed *artist!* "Your sister was an artist, right?"

"You knew Jozie?"

"Brentwood's big, but not *that* big. She was prom queen last year, right?"

She had been prom queen, but it was one of those facts that I'd completely forgotten about until he said it. It wasn't something *she'd* been all too excited about, despite saving the plastic tiara on a shelf in our bedroom. It sat there now, collecting dust.

Connor readjusted his legs, banging his knee on the glovebox and causing it to pop open. As he tried to get it to latch, he said, "I'll be honest, you and your sister are nothing alike."

"Because she's pretty and I'm not? Because she has perfect vision and I don't?" Instinctively, I edged my glasses up higher on my nose with a knuckle. "She was popular enough to win prom queen, and it's not even something I'd bother dreaming about?"

Connor's face pinched as he raised one freaked-out eyebrow. "I was going to say because she's artsy and you like math, but it seems we've approached a sore topic."

I pinched my lips together and, without another word, I twisted the dial up on the stereo.

We rode the rest of the way to Center Inspire in silence, which, admittedly, wasn't that far. I slowed down when the boxy gallery came into view, all angles and modern lines, but my stomach dropped at the parking. Or lack thereof. I'd been hoping for a street spot that I could pull into, but there was only one spot along the curb—one that would've required coaxing the old coupe to parallel park in.

I circled the block slowly, hoping in the three minutes it took to go through the lights, someone would've moved.

Connor turned to watch the art gallery pass for the second time, pressing a finger to the window. "Is that not the place that we're going?"

Bitterly, I flipped on my blinker, beginning yet another rotation of the block. "I'm waiting for parking to free up."

"There was a spot right in front of the building. It wasn't handicapped."

Why did he have to be so attentive? "I don't want to park there."

He tilted his head. "Do you not know how to parallel park?"

"Of course I know how to parallel park." I made a right back onto Gunther Avenue, muttering a curse when I spotted the same empty space. "The perfect parallel parking job can be found using the Pythagorean Theorem. A squared plus B squared equals C squared. Mathematically, it's easy." The execution, though...that sucked.

When his silence stretched long enough, I glanced over at Connor, finding him rubbing his palm across his mouth. He might've hidden a grin, but it lit up his eyes, the amusement like a ray of sunshine. "You have a math-related answer for everything, don't you?"

"Not for *everything*. Probably about seventy-five percent of the time, though, yeah."

"That was technically a math-related answer." As we approached the art gallery once more, Connor popped his seatbelt undone in a swift movement. "Stop the car."

"What?" I looked over to find his fingers curling around the door handle, tugging against the lock. "Hey, wait!"

I stomped on the brakes as he unlatched the door, grateful there weren't any cars behind me. Before he shut the door, he waved a hand at me. "Get out, and I'll park."

The sheer ludicrousness of his demand and the fact that we were parked in the middle of the road had me fumbling to unbuckle my belt. "You'd win the award for world's most annoying person," I muttered, begrudgingly opening the door. "Seriously."

Connor was unfazed. I was sure he'd been called worse. "I'll A square plus B square equals C square this parking space."

"Don't hit another car," I warned him as he rounded the coupe, appraising the front end as he did so. I stepped onto the sidewalk. "I'll make you pay for my hiked insurance."

"Yes, ma'am."

Connor looked squished behind the steering wheel, and though his legs must've been cramped underneath the dash, he didn't edge the seat backward. Instead, he put the car into drive and aligned perfectly with the car in front of the parking space. He twisted the wheel sharply, expertly easing the coupe into the empty space before straightening out.

The whole process probably took five seconds.

Show off.

Once he climbed out, Connor leaned the front seat over to reach into the back, grabbing his backpack and my satchel, the neon orange fabric a shock of color in his grip. Instead of offering it out to me, he fit the strap over his shoulder. "Well, Ms. Matthews, shall we?"

Center Inspire had the industrial vibe going on without feeling empty, with exposed ductwork and studs. To me, it always smelled like wet paint and Caribbean Waters air freshener. The displays and exhibits were constantly rearranged, which meant new coats of paint would be layered over the drywall for a new feel. The last exhibit Mom prepared for was jungle-themed, and they'd painted the walls a tan color. Before that, the postmodernism exhibit had called for the walls to be a sky blue.

I understood none of it, but apparently picking out the correct color scheme was almost as important as the art itself.

We checked in at the front with the bright-faced girl who gave us pamphlets with artist information on them.

"What made you think of this place?" Connor asked, glancing up at the ductwork.

"My mom works here. She's a curator." Among other things. Her job description was like a laundry list of art-related tasks.

Connor's lips twitched. I knew what he must've been thinking—*she has to be adopted.*

I led Connor through the maze of artwork without glancing at one piece, but his head kept going back and forth periodically, eyes tracing every canvas he had time to admire. I studied the line of his jaw when he wasn't looking, examined the interested way his attention was drawn to nearly every hanging piece of art. Connor liking art wasn't out of the realm of possibility, but it struck me then that I didn't really know much about him. Was there more to his life than football?

You know there is, the angel on my shoulder whispered, trying to remind me to cut my cynical ways. Maybe later.

There were two tables available to guests in the back area of the gallery, set up between a huge sculpture of a mermaid going fishing and a sculpture of a mother and her ducklings, except the ducklings had human feet. I never understood the two—especially the feet—but they were two of Mom's favorite sculptures. "We can sit in here."

I watched as Connor took care to unpack the Algebra II notebook filled with notes and math equations we'd worked on last week. In this setting, with how focused on the task he became, it was easy to be swayed by how different he seemed.

"So what's your grand fix-all, oh dearest tutor? You said you had an idea for helping me."

I angled the Algebra II book toward Connor. "I want you to copy this entire page."

"Copy?" he echoed, disbelieving stare going from me to the page in front of him several times. "Like, write everything on this page down?"

"That's what I said." I stretched my legs out, hamstrings screaming in response. They were *still* sore from the flat-out sprint on Friday. Another reason why I hated running. "Copy all the practice equations on these two pages and the next two pages. Everywhere it's explaining something, copy it down."

His lips twisted in distaste. "What, I'm plagiarizing my own math book?"

"Plagiarism insinuates that you're trying to pass this off as your own. Seeing as how you failed Algebra II the first time, I don't think anyone would believe—"

"Isn't this wasting time? Copying everything down?"

"You talking is wasting time." Like he gestured at me in the car, I waved my palm at him now. "Come on, get writing."

With a grumbling sigh, Connor tipped his head toward the book, slowly picking up his pencil. I waited for him to bring up what Alex said earlier, to ask, "you used to be friends with Madison and Jade?" but he never did. He dutifully copied the algebra page in silence.

While he worked, I scrounged around for a scrap piece of paper from my bag. It wasn't until I unfolded it that I realized it was the note he'd left me this morning.

MEET ME BY THE FOOTBALL BLEACHERS AT LUNCH.

-C

Smoothing out the wrinkles as best as I could, I went to work on folding the paper flower, creasing and un-creasing his writing in the quiet of the gallery.

Well, it *was* quiet until his complaining started. "I'm getting a hand cramp."

I didn't even look up. "Get over it."

"Do I really have to copy this whole page?"

"Isn't that what I said?"

The *click-clack* of heels rapidly approaching caused both of us to lift our heads. When a figure stepped into the doorway of the exhibit room, I froze.

Mom's work uniform was the picture of cleanliness. Straight blazer with a matching skirt, navy pumps, minimal jewelry. Her hair was wound back into a small braid. It was very sophisticated, like one look at her and you couldn't tell she was an artist herself. The monotone colors, though, were for a reason—she could blend in while the art stood out.

"How did you know we were back here?" I asked, having enough presence of mind to finally rise out of my chair. It was too late to fully intercept her—she was already halfway to our table—but I cut her off before she got too close.

"The secretary thought it was you who walked in," Mom said, spotting the boy at the table. "Hello, I'm Maisie's mom. You look a little familiar, but I don't think we've met before, have we?"

Of course she thought Connor was familiar—she was a Brentwood stan who never missed a game. With his posters hanging around the fenced-off field, it'd be weird if he didn't look familiar.

Connor's chair scraped back. "I'm Connor," he returned, coming close enough to offer his hand. It was the first time that he'd willingly acknowledged me in this universe, and of course, it was with my mother. He gave her his most dazzling expression. "Your daughter is tutoring me."

"She's really good at that," Mom said, even though she wouldn't have known. "Why'd you pick here?"

"It's quiet." But I was starting to wish I'd picked someplace else. With Mom's full schedule and the upcoming week-long exhibit next week, I thought she'd be busier. Then again, I should've bet on the fact that she'd come to investigate if someone told her I showed up.

"I've never been," Connor supplied. He had tucked his pencil behind his ear and stuck one hand in his jeans pocket. "I've never really been to any art galleries, but this is a great addition to Brentwood."

His flattering words hit their mark, because Mom's lips went from a polite tilt to a full-on beam. "It's taken a lot of work to get it here. We have a big exhibit next week celebrating Brentwood spirit in honor of homecoming, incorporating pieces from local artists, and it's been all hands on deck for that."

"I'll have to see if I can swing by."

"And bring your friends," Mom said happily, clasping her hands together. "Or your parents, if you want to."

Connor's easy smile faltered at that, only a blip in the perfection simulation, but I caught it.

"Okay, Mom." I started waving her back a step. "We've got to get to work."

"Fine, fine. There'll be someone coming through in a

little bit with a few sculptures, though, so be prepared for an interruption, okay?"

I nodded quickly, trying to end the conversation as quickly as possible. Mom's appearance unnerved me. Just a little. Our tutoring session had crossed into personal territory for me, and I didn't like the thought of Connor knowing more than he needed to.

"She seems nice," Connor said as we sat back down, gaze drawn in the direction she'd walked. "You two sound alike."

"The extent of our similarities," I replied, picking up my near-finished paper rose and turning it over in my grip. One of the creases was off by a millimeter, but it would require re-folding. "Once you're finished, flip to the homework section, and we're going to problems one, five, and ten." That way, there'd be a varied difficulty level he'd be working with.

"But we didn't go over—"

"Trust me," I said firmly. He had one elbow planted on the tabletop and his head propped on his hand, fingers woven through his hair. Those hazel eyes were already on me. "I want to see if you can work through them."

I waited for his skepticism, but it didn't come. His stare felt probing and curious, like there was a math equation written on my forehead he was tasked to solve. "You know, you let Alex off the hook a lot easier than I thought you would today. All because you secretly tried out for the cheer squad once upon a time?"

My stomach did a somersault, a stumbling one that

almost didn't stick the landing. "You must not have heard the part where I said I *didn't*."

"Jade's not a liar."

Ha, was it bad that I doubted that? "So you're saying *I'm* one?"

"I'm saying you let Alex off the hook awfully easy." Connor lifted his chin so he could size me up. "He hurt your feelings."

"And he apologized."

"But it hurts. It hurts when the people we trust the most betray us. It's allowed to upset you."

I hated how he could tell. Even though we were practically strangers, he could see straight into me, past all the defenses I built as if they were made of glass. Feeling exposed with anyone wasn't fun, but I hated that out of everyone at Brentwood High, I felt exposed with *him*.

Connor flipped his pencil around between his fingers, much like a drummer might twirl a drumstick.

"Problems one, five, and ten," I said, slamming the door shut on the conversation and turning back to my origami. My fingers trembled as I unfolded the paper, starting from the beginning. "I want to see if you can do them."

He listened to me this time, flipping his notebook back open and using the eraser of his pencil to trace the problem. The first thing he did was copy down the problem onto the paper, and then from there, he began to simplify the equation, pencil scrawling in slow spurts. We both worked in silence, but I kept a careful eye on his progress, trying my best to translate the upside-down numbers and variables.

It took him a few minutes, but soon he finished the three problems and turned the notebook for me to see.

"You didn't factor the exponent correctly in number five," I told him, pointing at the error. "You dropped it in the second round of simplifying. But otherwise, the rest of them are right."

Connor nodded a little, scrubbing his eraser across the page to try again. "It wasn't that much different from the last section."

I turned the notebook back toward him. "I think it has something to do with writing things down," I said, tapping on his notebook. "You're able to visualize things clearer after you write them down, right? I think that's going to really help you here. Writing down the intro instructions can help you remember the steps when it comes time to solve the problems. Have you ever done that before with math?"

Connor eyed the book like it'd transformed in the blink of an eye, turning from a simple book to something akin to a wild animal. "No, I've never copied the instructions down."

"It's not going to be the magic fix-all for understanding stuff, but I think it's something that will help." I sorted through the slick pages of the textbook to the next section, doing a quick scan of the topic. "Let's do the same with this part since you have that previous section covered. *Polynomial functions*. Copy down the instructions on this page now."

We worked a bit longer than our normal hour today since we had so much to go over. Connor copied down expression for expression in terms of instructions, and when he didn't have questions, I passed the time by folding paper roses. The silence, though, gave me time for my mind to wander, straying off the path of *here and now*. When I caught myself thinking about things—like Madison and the Most Likely To list—I jerked back to the present like my thoughts were on a leash.

He ended up having a bit more trouble with this section, the polynomials confusing him more than the previous simplifying. Even so, we finished up two sections by the end of our tutoring session, which left me feeling more confident about his progress than before.

Once the hour was up, Connor began packing up his supplies, and I gathered the four paper roses I'd made. Two of them I'd attempted to fold with a piece of paper that wasn't square, so the outcome was a bit lumpy, making it destined for the trashcan. "How are you feeling with everything?" I asked him. "What's your confidence level like?"

"Better after today, I guess. Writing things down beforehand helped. Some things are still confusing, though."

"Which is okay. Practice makes perfect. You can work on some of those equations as homework if you'd like, but no pressure. We have two weeks to go through everything."

He nodded a little, and then his demeanor changed. His relaxed posture straightened as he sat forward, stacking his hands underneath his chin and giving me his undivided attention. His hazel eyes were bright underneath the gallery's lights, and from this distance, they came off more green than brown. "Have you ever tried playing hard to get with Alex?"

Jeez, that subject change nearly gave me whiplash. Was this our segue into his tutoring session now? I simultaneously wanted him to drop the whole "love advice" play and wanted to hear what tip he'd have for me this time. "Playing games is stupid."

"Depends on the game. Some guys like the chase. After almost a year of being together, maybe he *needs* more of a chase. You shouldn't have let go of Friday so easily."

We were back to that? "So, what? I should've been a jerk about it?"

"It's allowed to upset you," he replied. "And you're allowed to want an apology—one that's more detailed than a simple 'sorry.'"

The entire weekend, I had wanted to make Alex work for my forgiveness. It wasn't often that we came to a disagreement like this—nothing this important had ever come up before. We'd stumbled upon that road, and maybe Connor was right. Maybe I let it go too quickly. But if the choice was letting Friday go or having to explain the nitty gritty past of Jade and Madison and cheer squads, I'd choose the former.

And explaining that to Connor...it meant delving deeper into the situation than I wanted to.

So I shrugged. "Well, I already forgave him. What now?"

"You can still play hard to get," he said. "Nothing major. Nothing bad. Like, maybe the next time he offers to hang out, say you'll think about it before instantly saying yes. Sometimes just that 'I'll think about it' line is more exciting than an instant yes, you know?"

No, I didn't get it. "Why would that be exciting?"

"There's a sort of anticipation to it. Will you say yes? Will you say no?" Connor's eyes crinkled at the corners. "Exciting."

There was anticipation in that? Excitement? It all sounded stressful, complicated, and super annoying. I wondered if this was how students felt trying to learn math.

Before I had a chance to respond, a voice coming from the hallway had me freezing—more specifically, a *name*. "Madison, I'm so glad it was you who stopped by. It's been so long since I've seen you, sweetie."

Connor and I both jerked toward each other, our thoughts following the same trail at the same rate. *Madison.*

I shot up so fast that it was a wonder my chair didn't tip over, but I wasted no time before grabbing Connor's wrist, dragging him toward the only door in the room— the storage closet. Praise God it was unlocked. It was pitch black, the perfect space to hide in.

The only problem was that the area, packed with boxes and mid-sized sculptures, was the size of a measly coat closet, and there was hardly room for two teenagers to squeeze into. As soon as Connor tugged the door shut behind him, he shuffled directly into me, nearly knocking me over. I bumped into a shelf, causing the contents to clatter. There probably was a light switch, but I was afraid the glow would be visible from underneath the door, so we stood in the dark.

"You didn't have to hide," Connor whispered, his voice startlingly close. His warm breath tickled my neck, his sandalwood scent was everywhere. The combination of the two caused a shiver to bolt across my skin. "It wouldn't have been weird for her to see you here."

"It was instinct, okay?" I hissed back, shoving blindly. My hand connected with something firm—his chest? "Do you have to stand so close?"

"I currently have a sculpture poking where pottery shouldn't poke, so yes, I do."

"Oh, I wonder where she went." Mom's voice seeped through the thin walls, causing Connor and me to tense. "She was tutoring someone in here."

"That's great that she's still doing that," Madison told Mom kindly, but the discomfort in her voice was clear. "I didn't mean to interrupt. Where do you want me to put this box?"

"Oh, any of these tables," Mom replied, and her voice sounded a bit louder, as if she drew nearer. "Thank you for dropping off these drawings. I was going to ask Maisie if she could pick them up for me."

I couldn't help but huff, and Connor jumped at the soft sound.

"I've been meaning to stop by the gallery for a while.

This totally suits you, Mrs. Matthews. I know doing something with art has always been a dream of yours."

She was doing with my mom exactly what her mom had done with me once upon a time—bringing up history that had long since been buried.

When Connor drew in a breath, his chest brushed against my arm, and there wasn't any more room to inch backward. However, in the buzzing white noise of the quiet, my heart kicked up in its beating. Surely it was because Madison was on the other side of the door, seconds from stumbling upon us, and not because I was literally chest to chest with Connor. It made me think of earlier today on the staircase, how he'd hauled me back against him. Now it was the same sensation. I couldn't tell if it was his heart beating fast or if it was mine.

He shifted again, only this time when his chest grazed my arm, I jumped. "Sorry," he whispered.

"*Shh!*" I slapped both of my hands against his chest, as if the action would chase the sound out of the air. But it only brought us closer, and I could feel all the firm, taut muscles of his torso underneath my splayed fingers. Rachel had mentioned how nice Connor's butt looked in his football uniform when she really should've been talking about how toned his shoulders were.

Holy...

And then—horror. Icy horror, washing all over me like a bucket of ice water. Because my fingers still pressed against his body and my thoughts still hiccupped on the verge of insanity, and I actually audibly *swallowed*. I snatched my hands back and crammed as far from him as possible, debating on whether walking out of the closet and facing Madison would be as bad as staying in it.

"Well, I should get going," Madison said. "But I'll be sure to swing by again soon so you can give me a proper tour."

I closed my eyes. Thank God this was almost over. And thank God that the closet was dark enough to hide my no-doubt flaming cheeks.

"Let me put this box in the storage closet, and I'll walk you to the front," Mom said, and it took me several seconds to realize that she meant this closet. The same one we were standing in.

And before I even had a chance to react, the closet door was already shuddering, trying to open inward but getting stuck. I didn't move, waiting for her to unjam it and stumble in, finding us in this awkward, compromising position.

Except she didn't. "I didn't even know this door locked," she muttered to herself, trying again to force it open.

I reached out to check to see if there was a lock, and that was when I felt Connor's hand wrapped around the doorknob. His knuckles were taut beneath my fingers, holding the knob firmly so it didn't turn. As long as it didn't turn, the latch wouldn't pop undone.

His reflexes were insane. Maybe that was why he made for a good football player. *That and those muscles...*

Maisie, get a grip.

Connor and I stood impossibly close, holding our breath and waiting for the moment to pass. My eyes were starting to adjust to the near-blackness, and I could see the faint slope of Connor's jaw inches from my eyes.

Mom gave up trying to force the door open, and after a moment, her and Madison's voices faded. It took us both several moments to thaw from our frozen positions. "We should get going," I whispered to him, too afraid to talk too loudly. "I have to drop you off at your car."

"Okay." The one word was practically a reverberation in the air, spoken in a low enough tone that the goosebumps were back. The knob made a soft creaking sound as Connor twisted it open, letting a sliver of light into our dim space. Enough to illuminate a section of his face, and his eyes seemed to glow. Closer than ever before, I could see the individual flecks of green in his eyes, tiny pools coiling in the brown, almost like a painting themselves. "Lead the way."

CHAPTER 14

It rained Wednesday morning, heavy enough to begin flooding the football field, according to the PA system. During last period, one of the secretaries made a school-wide announcement that cut into Mrs. Diego's explanation about limits and continuity.

"*Attention all J.V. and Varsity football players: practice for today is canceled due to the rain.*"

Because that was definitely necessary for everyone in the school to know. I knew what the turn of events meant, though. If Connor didn't have football practice, that meant we could tutor right after school. I wouldn't have to linger in my car for an hour, roasting because the coupe could barely cough out enough AC.

Then again, where would we go to tutor today? If we met up while everyone was filtering from the school, someone would see us together. The problem-solver in me went into overdrive trying to figure out a possible alternative.

We couldn't go to any restaurants or cafés around here in case anyone from school had the same idea. Not the school's library or public library, since Connor seemed allergic. Definitely not my house. If Madison saw his car, we were done for. If I thought the attention I got from Jade now was bad, I couldn't imagine the living hell she'd turn my life into if she knew I was hanging around her boyfriend.

What kind of living hell would she give me, too, if she'd known how close Connor and I had gotten Monday? Remembering what his chest had felt like, the brief touch of muscles, sent my brain into a tailspin.

I needed to get a grip.

When the dismissal bell sounded, I was quick to pack up my things. "Maisie," Mrs. Diego called, slowing down my retreat. She waited until every student had left the room before speaking again. "I wanted to check in with you. How is the tutoring coming?"

"Good." The breakthrough Monday had gotten us further than I would've thought. Learning that Connor could recall things better after writing them down made for an easier way to tutor—the night before the session, he'd copy down the instructions for the next chapter, and we'd work through any questions that he had the next day. "I think he's starting to remember the material now. It's a lot to review in a few weeks, but I think we've found a good pace."

Mrs. Diego glanced at the door before stepping closer, lowering her voice. "Mrs. Oliphant sent me an email yesterday. She's told me to only test him on half of the units—so two units instead of four."

I blinked. Half of the initial exam—even *less* than what his peers had tested on last May. "Why?"

"Like you said, it's quite a lot to go over in only a handful of weeks."

Little baby fire ants marched underneath my skin, leaving a trail of heat. We were already almost finished with unit two. If she was slashing the amount he needed to learn in half, there was no question at all whether or not he'd pass. With so little to cover, his A was practically guaranteed.

I clenched my bag strap tighter, pulling it hard against my neck. "It's not really fair that he isn't tested on all the material like everyone else was."

"Believe me, I'm on the same page as you with that." Mrs. Diego rubbed her fingers against her temple, leaning against the edge of her desk. "I'm glad he's absorbing the material, but we're jumping through a lot of hoops for him."

It was all I could do to not dig in my heels, to not snap at the unfairness of it all. "Why is this happening, again? Because of some sort of clerical error? He's getting so many free passes because someone screwed up?"

Mrs. Diego sighed a little, but before we had a chance to carry on the conversation, a student walked in with a Calculus question.

The resentment built back as I walked out of Mrs. Diego's classroom, much more annoyed than I'd felt when I walked in. They were cutting the exam down to practically nothing. What would be next—the only question on the test was going to be his name?

Alex found me on my way to my locker. "Got much homework?" he asked in greeting. "I have a mountain of math. Maybe I should have you tutor me, huh?"

"Sorry, my roster's full this semester." Full of star football players getting preferential treatment.

Alex trailed behind me as I got to my locker, and a few doors down from mine, a homecoming poster hung taped to the metal. The homecoming dance was a little over a week and a half out, the first Saturday of October, but people were already hunting around for dates. Rachel had turned down two proposals last week. I glanced at my boyfriend from the corner of my eye.

Quite honestly, I'd forgotten all about homecoming. I hadn't even gotten a dress yet.

He watched me fiddle with my combination. "It feels like I need you to tutor me if only to get a little time with you."

"Yeah, let's go down *that* road," I said, surprised by how light my voice was. "Last time we hung out, you ditched me."

"That was—"

"And then the time before that, you were focused on videogames." Once I finally got the lock to click, I gave him a meaningful stare. "Don't go pointing fingers."

Plus, I wanted to add, *you were the one talking about compatibility.*

A piece of paper fell out of my locker, sucked out by the breeze of the door opening. I couldn't move quickly enough. Alex swiped it off the floor before I even had a chance to bend. "Is someone leaving you love notes?" he asked as he unfolded the paper.

I tried to snatch it away from him, but he leaned out of reach. "Of course it's not a love note," I said, heart in my throat. "Give it."

"'Meet me by the west side staircase?'" Alex read, frowning. "Who's C?"

Thank *God* that Connor hadn't written his whole name. He must've anticipated this exact moment happening. "The, uh, kid I'm tutoring."

"The freshman?"

"Yeah, the freshman."

He let me pluck the paper from his fingertips then, and I quickly scanned Connor's handwriting. The west side stairs—why on earth would he want to meet on school property? Sure, we'd had our conversation Monday on the stairs, but that was during lunch when no one was around. Now it was the end of the day, and students would be milling about collecting all their stuff for at least ten more minutes.

"Maybe Friday night, you can come with me to the game," Alex said. "We could go to the movies afterward. The drive-in over in Hatchfield is open late on weekends."

For a long moment, I almost was sure I'd heard him wrong. "You know I hate football games."

"Yeah, but you love me, don't you?"

"I wouldn't even get to sit with you," I reminded him. "We've talked about this, Alex. You have to sit with the band."

Alex picked up my hand, and this time with an infinite amount of gentleness. He gave it a squeeze before lacing our fingers together. "I'll come sit with you when I have my breaks. And I promise, at the movies, my full attention will be on you the entire night. I'll let you get two snacks. There'll be no ditching you, no ignoring you —just Alex and Maisie time."

I stared up into his eyes, bouncing between them, searching for any ounce of insincerity. But there was none. The brown hue was warm and familiar, and the promise on his lips should've made me happy, but I hesitated instead. *Alex and Maisie time.* Where was this coming from?

What was it Connor had said? Play hard to get? I didn't get the psychology behind it, but something in me dragged its feet. "I'll think about it," I decided on at last, feeling awful for not immediately accepting, but I needed to give Connor's advice a chance. I pulled out my Algebra II textbook. "I'll text you when I've made up my mind."

"I'll do my best to convince you before Friday." He smiled broadly, proud that even though it wasn't a win, he hadn't gotten an outright no. "Come on, I'll walk you to the staircase."

"That's okay," I hurried to say, glancing around. The west staircase was around the corner, and I was too afraid Connor would be waiting there. There'd be no possible excuses then. "I'm a big girl. I can wait by myself."

To my complete and utter surprise, Alex leaned down and pressed his mouth to mine. It was a chaste kiss, one that had me jerking back in surprise. A pair of passing freshmen let out a peel of giggles. "Alex and Maisie time," he repeated, completely unfazed by the audience, words sounding like a promise. "Think about it, okay?"

I was too stunned to call after him, curling my fingers into a fist to keep from pressing them to my lips.

Even though the freshmen had walked past, they weren't quite out of earshot. "Wasn't that the math book girl?"

"Yeah, marry a math book. She's a lot prettier than I thought she'd be."

"Who was her boyfriend? She trying to make her math book jealous?"

That caused an eruption of giggles, one that almost made me straighten from the wall. I'd show them how much *my math book* weighed.

Swallowing my violent thoughts, I trudged toward the west side staircase.

It'd been about ten minutes since the bell rang, which meant the hallway had cleared out for the most part. Connor, though, wasn't by the stairs when I approached. No one was. Maybe he was waiting until the coast was fully clear? How long was he going to make me wait for him this time?

Not even two seconds passed before a hand wrapped around my wrist and tugged me backward. I only had time to register that I'd been pulled into a small room I'd never noticed before until the door shut, sealing me inside.

My heart lurched with the sudden movement, but any anxiety was quickly quelled. It was funny how instinctively I knew who it was—there was no light in the room to see, but the scent was easy to place. The sandalwood wasn't as sharp as normal, since he wasn't fresh from a shower, but still warm and heady, completely invading my senses.

"There," Connor said, sounding satisfied. "I don't think anyone saw, do you?"

Fighting off a shiver, I punched him hard in the general direction of his arm, but I wasn't sure if I ended up hitting his bicep or his chest. Either way, he didn't flinch. "Dude, seriously. Stop *tugging* me places. A simple, 'Hey, Maisie, come into this closet' is much better than trying to rip my arm off."

"I was trying to be sneaky."

"You don't have to give me a heart attack in the process." I readjusted my satchel on my shoulder, scowling deeper. "Hate to mess with your plan, but we can't tutor in the dark."

Connor drew away like a wave receding back into the ocean, only he took his body heat with him. He clattered around, cursing as he tripped, until the room suddenly filled with light. An exposed lightbulb was the only thing illuminating the space, and its dangling chain swayed back and forth. "Ta-da."

The space was only marginally larger than the closet at Center Inspire, but equally filled to the brim with stuff. Boxes of jerseys, those little square scooters we used to ride in elementary school, other various sports equipment. Someone had stacked a few cardboard boxes in front of the shelf, presumably what Connor tripped over.

The space seriously lacked something called *organization*. There were a few tiers of boxes so tall that I could've hidden behind them.

"What's this room for?"

"It's the storage closet," Connor said, glancing around with a weird expression of happiness, as if he was proud of the rinky-dink space. "Mostly for gym equipment. No one'll interrupt us here, don't worry. Everyone knows that if the door's shut, no one goes in."

I couldn't imagine why someone would want to be in here in the first place. It smelled like three generations of sweat. "It means something if the door is shut?"

Connor cleared his throat. "It means someone's in here."

"But why can't they come in if someone else is in here?"

"Ah, well. Some of the seniors come here for...privacy."

He wouldn't look me directly in the eye, and in an instant, I realized why. I clutched my satchel to my chest in horror, glancing around the space with a newfound sense of disgust. "You brought me to a place where people—where people—are you *kidding*?"

"No one will bother us!" he insisted and turned to where he'd propped his backpack against the wall. "It's fine. Come on, sit down. Sorry there aren't any chairs."

Sit down? On the germ-infested floor? Once images

filled my mind, there was no way I'd be sitting down. "The library has chairs."

"And it has other people."

And in that instant, I *really* would've liked to be around other people. "It's creepy to be in here with you."

Connor peered up at me from the ground, some of his brown hair falling into his eyes. The hazel was definitely darker in here, nearly entirely brown. "It's not like we're in here for *that* reason. Get your mind out of the gutter."

"*My* mind? Yeah, because coming here in the first place hinted at a totally innocent train of thought!"

Connor patted the floor beside him.

"I can't believe you. Seriously. I'm reconsidering making you pay me."

Dragging my feet, I drew a scooter off the shelf. Absolutely no chance was my butt touching that tile. Science wasn't my subject of choice, but I knew enough to figure there had to be at least a billion germs crawling around on the dingy, hadn't-been-mopped-in-ten-years floors.

Once I got situated on the small pink thing—one that my butt barely fit on—I dug my heels into the floor to keep the wheels from wiggling.

"You look like a third grader on that thing."

"Yeah, well, at least I'm a third grader who's not going to catch a disease." I refused to look at Connor, sure my cheeks were burning. "You know, you shouldn't leave notes in my locker anymore. Alex found your note today."

"Did he figure out it was me?"

He probably would've, if I hadn't lied my butt off. "No, but—"

"If I can't grab your arm, at least let me write the notes." He sat back against the wall with a little sigh. "I like being all secretive. It feels like we're in an action movie."

"More like a horror movie." I could barely suppress my groan. "Give me your notebook."

He flipped the cover over and passed the wire-bound notebook to me, clicking his mechanical pencil a few times. I scribbled down my phone number and then wrote my name above it in case he forgot who the seven numbers alluded to. *M-A-I-S-I-E.* "This part—" I traced the tip of the pencil along the *A-I-S* part. "It makes a *zee* sound. Not a *see* sound."

Connor took the pencil from my grip and wrote underneath my letters. His handwriting was smaller, letters a compact doodle. *M-A-I-S-I-E.* "Maisie," he echoed. "*Zee.* Got it. Now that I've written it down, I won't get it wrong again. I promise."

We both glanced up at each other at the same time, and with our heads bent over the same notebook, we were...close. Too close. I shoved my scooter backward, knocking into a cardboard box. "Uh, where's your homework? I'll check your answers."

Connor took a second to fish the sheet out from between the textbook pages, the corners rumpled. He settled back against the wall and stretched his legs out, but since the space was so cluttered, he couldn't stretch them fully. "You know, we've been meeting for a week, and I know nothing about you. Jozie, apparently, is your sister."

"Uh-huh. Open the textbook to the next page."

He obliged, thankfully, because if he'd ignored me, I might've hit him. "What's your favorite color?" he asked.

"I don't have one."

"Who doesn't have a favorite color?"

I let out a long sigh through my nose.

"My favorite color, for example, is red. Not bright red, but the shade that's almost purple? Is that maroon or burgundy? I always get them mixed up."

I couldn't keep my composure anymore and jerked my head up. "Why are you so chatty today?"

Connor gave a lazy shrug. "Just trying to get to know you more. You can't say you aren't curious about me too, right?"

"Not really." But for some reason that I couldn't explain, I *was* kind of curious about the Connor Bray beyond the football star.

Surprise flickered across his features. "Rude. You could've lied."

A burst of guilt speared through me at the thought of hurting his feelings, but it was so unsettling that I focused back down at the graphs he'd etched onto the piece of notebook paper.

"So, with Alex," he began, segueing into a new topic. "How are things?"

Even though the kiss had happened only moments ago, the lingering sensation was gone now, replaced by my teeth digging into my bottom lip. Connor would've been pleased to hear that I took his play-hard-to-get advice, but I couldn't bring myself to admit it aloud. "Things are fine. Let's focus on math."

"*Yawn.* How many chapters do we have left?" Connor thumbed through the book at his side, peering at the pages. "Probably about two units worth, right?"

Mrs. Diego must not have told him about the change in schedule, that he only had to learn the first two units. My mind processed the information in a whirl. Should I tell him or keep going as initially planned? What would it hurt to go over every unit? Pretend as if Principal Oliphant *hadn't* forced Mrs. Diego to alter the test, and review all the units. He deserved to have to learn all of it, like every other student who might've taken the make-up test.

But then that would mean more time tutoring together and more of a risk he'd fail if he was filling his brain with information he wouldn't be tested on.

It's not fair, I thought. *One person shouldn't get so many free passes.*

"You got this one wrong," I told him, using my heels to scoot myself closer to him. I stopped by his knees, coming as close as I could without running him over. "This can be factored through further." I went through the process of showing him how everything could be divided out in the rational expression, using the tip of my finger. "It can fully factor to $5x(2x+3)(2x+5)$."

After a moment of silence, I looked up. He wasn't focusing on the paper with confusion, though—he watched me the same way he'd regarded the math problem. A complexity that I often regarded Mom's scribbles with. "Did you memorize the answers to these problems or something?"

"No. Why?"

"You got that within, like, fifteen seconds." He didn't seem impressed; his face was more freaked out. Like I'd confessed to him I was an alien with a sixth toe on one foot. "Jeez, you really are a math genius."

Instead of feeling proud of getting the answer so easily, so quickly, I had the overwhelming urge to clamp my mouth shut and flee from the cramped room. His words might've been innocent enough, but they triggered an avalanche of other thoughts, other voices ringing in my ears. *Marry a Math Book.*

"Was that the only one?"

I blinked, tearing my eyes away from the paper as he took it back. "What?"

"Is that the only one I got wrong?" Connor tipped his head to peer at me. From how close I sat and how slouched against the wall he was, our eyes were nearly at the same level. "I'm doing pretty good, huh? Guess I needed this one-on-one time with the biggest brain at Brentwood High."

"It's okay that I like math," I said, the defensiveness in my voice enough to plow down a linebacker. "It's not that big of a deal. It's not weird."

I decided that I hated Connor's attention on me. I felt too much like an insect under a microscope, too much like he was trying to dissect me. Maybe it was because he pushed my buttons more than anyone else I'd tutored. He was more attentive than I'd previously given him credit for, too *aware*, and I hated it.

"It's not weird," he agreed, voice surprisingly somber. It lacked any and all traces of the humor I'd come to expect from him. Instead, he looked at me seriously. "Does that bother you? Being known for being good at math?"

I started popping my knuckles before jerking away, dropping my hands back to my lap. "It's..." The words trailed off. I knew how I wanted to finish the sentence, but the words were too honest, too vulnerable, and there was no way I could share them with him. *It's just that when people look at me, that's all they see.* Even more so since the stupid Most Likely To list. "Why is me liking equations dorkier than you liking running around on grass, waiting for people to knock you over?"

"Touché." One corner of his mouth twitched upward.

I didn't want to talk about this anymore, and I sure didn't want him looking at me like that anymore. "Let's get to work."

"How about we start with my tutoring today, yeah? Love advice is in session. I've thought long and hard about this lesson, but I think it's good."

I let out a little sigh, the tutor side of me wishing we'd start learning the more important part of things, but the student in me perked up. I was also glad we'd veered away from that topic. "Okay."

"For this lesson, I will need to be able to demon-strate." Connor held his palms up toward me, all wide and innocent. "Can I touch you?"

"*Touch me?*" I recoiled so sharply that I nearly upturned the scooter, catching myself at the last second. "Did you seriously bring me in here to make a move? *Seriously?*"

An abrupt laugh burst from him, accompanied by an expression that was amused in every sense of the word. "Jeez, of course not. It's easier to show you rather than to explain, that's all. I'd touch your cheek." He poked at his own cheekbone. "Your hair. That's it, I promise."

I could...I could deal with that. I mean, it wasn't like he was going to kiss me. It wasn't *that* kind of demonstration. He would've found his protractor shoved down his throat if that were the case. If recapturing Alex's attention meant I had to let Connor touch my hair, my cheek, I could do it.

Ugh, but I didn't want to.

I gave my head an annoyed shake. "Fine. If it's necessary."

He grabbed the edges of my scooter and angled me in front of him, moving his legs so they weren't a barrier between us. And then he leaned closer. "Today's topic: building tension."

"That really needs to be a lesson?"

"Patience, grasshopper." Without warning, Connor reached out and brushed a few strands of hair out of my eyes, the gentle, close touch making me jump. "Building anticipation is important."

The confidence this boy possessed was like no other. I tried to imagine myself in a reversed role, tasked with tutoring him on the lessons of love, and no way would I be able to offer a demonstration. It was just *awkward*. But he dove in without hesitation, as if this was the most normal thing in the world.

Awkward atmosphere or not, I swallowed hard as he continued to explain.

"Sets the stage, ups the heartrate. Think about it. Going in for the kiss without the proper buildup sucks the fun out of it."

I didn't know where to look, because looking at him while he explained building anticipation—while he *demonstrated*—was way too weird. Way too...charged. "Fun?"

"Sure. You can't tell me your heart has never fluttered, waiting for someone to kiss you."

I could still remember my first kiss with Alex. My first kiss ever. We'd gone out to see a movie, and when he pulled into my driveway to drop me off, my heart had fluttered something fierce. My stomach had been in knots the entire night, wondering—hoping—to end the night on that note.

Of course the flutter had disappeared after a year together. That was normal, right?

"Building the tension helps get that spark back," Connor mused, as if reading my mind. The soft quality of the sentence felt like a soothing blanket to the stir of feelings a moment ago. His words earlier had unsettled me, but now...I couldn't pinpoint what I was feeling. "So touching his hair before a kiss, touching his cheek—it helps."

Once he tucked the piece of hair behind my ear, his

thumb coasted along the edge of my cheekbone, and I froze. It was such a soft touch, almost barely there, a whisper of contact, that couldn't help but tickle. His skin was cool against my flushed cheeks—wait, when had my cheeks gotten flushed?

Alex never touched me like this. Any bouts of affection came in bursts—quick, sharp, sudden. Like the kiss earlier in the hallway. There was no buildup, no time for my heart to flutter. It was then that I realized that Connor was absolutely right—building tension *was* important. Something I craved.

The scooter rolled a fraction of an inch closer.

Connor's hand skidded along my jawline, and he had to feel how hard my pulse beat against my throat. Had to. And even though that was a mortifying thought, I was still frozen, letting him touch me.

Something shifted in his gaze. The arrogant confidence that simmered there seemed to harden into something else as he looked at me, and for a split second—just a split second—I could've sworn his eyes dropped to my lips.

"And then," he whispered in the same murmuring tone, "before anything happens..." He drew his thumb along the apple of my cheek, the slight vibration that made my heartbeat stutter. "Pull away."

Connor sat back against the wall in a swift movement, shattering the moment into thousands of pieces as he placed his hands on his knees. I reeled from the touches—and then the sharp lack thereof—as my brain struggled to process what happened.

"When you do that, he'll chase after you," Connor told me, blinking innocently at me. "The key is to make *him* want it, you know?"

I swallowed a gasp of air, both of my lungs aching from the ten seconds I'd been holding my breath. My skin tingled and hummed from the touch across my cheek, emotions hitting me in a whiplash of movement. Shock came first, surprised that such a small touch could trigger a physical response like that. Guilt, hot on its heels, because it *had* triggered a physical response.

Before I had a chance to even wrap my head around that, the door to the closet rattled as something heavy—a fist or a body—slammed into it. "Anyone in here?"

I jerked away from Connor—when had we gotten so close?—the scooter skipping across the floor, sending the wheel careening over my fingers that had been splayed against the ground. Red-hot pain lanced across my knuckles, sharp enough to spot my vision with sparks, painful enough that I let out a yelp before pressing my other hand against my mouth.

I hadn't stifled it in time, though. "Whoa, uh—sorry," the voice came again. "Didn't mean to interrupt the festivities. Number?"

My pain-riddled brain took longer than necessary to realize that the mystery boy asked a question, one that I had no idea what the answer was supposed to be. I cradled my fingers to my chest and looked up at Connor, who rubbed a hand across his eyes.

"Number?" the voice came again, and the doorknob clattered as someone tried to open it. "Don't make me get the keys from coach. No one will be having a good time then."

Connor let out a heavy sigh. "Twenty-two."

The doorknob stopped rattling. "*Bray?*" The disbelief was a thick sound, and I could almost imagine the dropped jaw and widened eyes that must've accompanied the tone. "Oh, uh...okay. Aye-aye, man. Hey, Jade."

I locked eyes with Connor, absolutely frozen. Of course the guy would think I was Jade—who else would Connor, Jade's *boyfriend*, be in a make-out closet with?

"Sorry to interrupt," the voice called, and the person rapped his knuckles against the door once more. "Walking away now."

I winced, curling my fingers ever so slightly. My middle knuckles had a nice track mark through them, the dirt from the wheels of the scooter dusting across the inflamed skin.

A dull thud sounded in the small space, and I found Connor with his head leaning against the wall, his forearms on his propped knees. He had his eyes shut. "How are your fingers?"

"Not broken." I gave them an aching wiggle. "What was it that you told that guy? Twenty-two?"

"It's my jersey number." He raised his eyebrows once, even with his eyes closed. "It's kind of like a password. Or, in my case, like the nail to my coffin, because Jade's going to kill me once she finds out I was in here with someone else."

My pulse skipped a beat. "Why would she know?"

"Jade's cheer practice moved to the gym since it's

raining, which means she can't be in here with me right now. Once Kyle—the guy who knocked—figures that out, she'll be the first he'll go to." Something about his words triggered him into motion, and he began collecting his things. "We should pack it up now, just in case."

My brain filled in the unspoken meaning. Before *Jade* comes to investigate. Panicking, I gathered my things and carried the scooter back to the shelf. Yeah, her showing up when we were literally trapped in a closet sounded like the opposite of a fun time. I tried to imagine what would happen if the cheerleader came knocking. In every scenario, I'd be dead meat.

"Maybe if she asks, you can say you were in here by yourself."

Connor didn't answer. Gone was the gentleness to the hazel gaze, replaced with a hardness that I'd come to recognize as a trigger of negativity. I wanted to say something to alleviate the tension, something to take away a bit of his stress, but not a single line came to me. For the first time, my mind was blank.

Connor tucked his book underneath his arm and went to the door. "Wait!" I caught at his arm. "Where are we meeting next? We need to go over—"

"I'll work through it at home and text you if I have any questions." He withdrew his hand, expression as hard as stone. "Wait five minutes and then go."

"But what if someone sees me?" I asked, but I'd finished my question too late. Connor already unsealed the door and disappeared through the small opening, leaving me in the skeevy closet all alone.

CHAPTER 15

"We need to paint the walls in Room C and organize the brochure table right when guests walk in," Mom was telling Dad that night at dinner. They were breaking one of their biggest rules: no work at the dinner table. Mom had her tablet open in front of her, tapping her stylus against her chin with one hand while trying to stab pasta with her fork in the other hand. "The entryway needs to be as organized as possible. Did Regina check to see if we have enough business cards?"

"She had to order more for the gallery, but Talia dropped off some for the school's fundraiser department earlier today."

Talia. Principal Oliphant.

Mom checked something off her list and studied it for another moment. "You're going to be busy these next few days. You have all the supplies you need?"

When Jozie was still present for family dinners, instances like this were rare. With her, someone who spoke a mile-a-minute and hated silence of any sort, there was never enough time to be distracted by something else. And even if work overwhelmed our parents on rare occasions, I was never left sitting in silence on my own, like a fly on the wall.

"I'll be painting tomorrow and then building the sets for Exhibit A hopefully the day after. I have the blueprints in the maintenance office to show you tomorrow, and we'll get that finalized."

My fork clattered against my plate, too sharply for it to sound accidental. "Uh, *hello*. Is this dinner really turning into a business meeting?"

They weren't shamed. In fact, they both looked up, startled, as if they'd forgotten I was there. Mom blinked. "The Brentwood High exhibit is going to be big for Center Inspire. We need to make sure all our ducks are in a row." She went back to her tablet. "Check with Casey tomorrow to see if he's got everything on the checklist. And to make sure to label where each student's piece is in what room."

I wondered what Jozie was doing right now. An hour ahead of us, she most likely would've already eaten dinner. Would she be with friends right now? Drawing something? Getting ready for bed? I wished that I knew.

My phone vibrated in my pocket, making an obnoxious noise against the wooden dining chair. I stiffened, the urge to check it strong. Even though my parents were breaking a rule, I was hesitant to.

It could've been anyone texting me, really. Alex, Ava, Rachel—Connor. He'd said he would text me if he had any questions, and since then, my phone had been silent. Until now.

That was important. And school-related. I could totally make that argument. Sneaking my cell out of my back pocket, I peered at the screen.

AVA

Can you proof this when you get a chance?

My stomach dropped once I scanned the first line.

Jannor On the Rocks?! Connor Bray already moving on to someone new?

"I—I'm finished," I gasped out, throwing my napkin on top of my plate and shoving my chair back.

"It's your night for dishes!" Mom called after me, because my socked feet were already sliding down the hallway. "Maisie!"

"Bathroom!" There, let them fight me on *that*.

As soon as I got to my room, I shut the door behind me and fell against it, practically bringing my cell phone to my nose.

My sources tell me that Connor was allegedly caught in the equipment closet after school today, and he wasn't alone. Though no one caught a glimpse of his closetmate, his

*girlfriend, Jade, was at practice
when this occurred. Is Jannor officially over? Is Connor Bray a
cheater? Say it isn't so!
Let me know in the comments below:
who do you think could've captured
Connor Bray's attention, and his
heart?!*

"Oh, God," I gasped, rereading over and over but not fully comprehending the words. Someone told *Brentwood Babble* about Connor being in the closet with someone who *wasn't* Jade. It'd gotten out, exactly as Connor had said it would.

The line only rang twice before Ava picked up. "Was the article riddled with mistakes? Or are you calling because you don't have time to proof it?"

"Y-you know, it's kind of an invasion of privacy, isn't it?" I asked, pausing to crack my knuckles against my leg. There was no sugarcoating the wire-thin quality to my voice, a piece of string on the verge of snapping. "The whole article, I mean. That's why I'm calling. Like...who really cares who Connor was spotted with?" I winced after I spoke, hoping it didn't sound too offensive.

"You're so funny," Ava said with a chuckle, one that only made my panic tick higher. "I totally get that the gossipy stuff isn't your thing."

"It's just—"

"This is big news, Maisie. Like, imagine if the world

discovered that 2+2=5 instead of 4. Connor cheating on Jade is insanity. Literally does not compute." She made a humming sound on the other end of the call. "Maybe *he* should've been voted Most Likely To: Cheat on Their Partner."

I dropped my head onto my drawn knees with a thunk. It wasn't even *me* that I was most concerned about. But it was Connor who'd been in that closet—who'd given his jersey number. Connor, who was caught with someone who wasn't his girlfriend.

Think, Maisie, think. "Maybe it's a big misunderstanding. Is there proof that it was even him in the closet?"

"Someone said—"

"Ava, writing an article like this without proof would be horrible." My voice was clearly high-strung as I cut her off, but I tried to keep my tone firm. "What if it's not true? You know how the gossip mill at school works. An article like this could really hurt him."

Ava fell quiet for a long moment, and when she spoke again, her words came out sounding small. "You think so?"

I knew Ava never posted things out of malice. If there was ever a person who embodied sunshine, it was her. Sometimes she didn't think about the repercussions of things. She was focusing on the present, on what would get the most engagement, what would deliver the shock factor.

A few weeks ago, I might've rolled my eyes at the article, but I wouldn't have protested like this. I wouldn't have cared enough to. I tried not to think about that. "Is it possible to wait until someone confirms it? Until you get more information?"

"That's a good idea," she said softly. "This was such a good story, but you're right. I'd hate to make things bad for Connor if it's not true. I don't want *Babble* to be known for spreading misinformation."

Some of the tension lifted off my chest. Air leaked back into my lungs. "I'm sure something else will come up."

Even after we hung up, I left my phone pressed against my ear for several moments, staring into the dark area of my bedroom. The sun had dipped low enough in the sky that its rays didn't reach my window anymore, leaving my room shadowy. I had a clear view of Jozie's bed from here, stripped of her normal blankets, replaced with the multi-colored quilt.

If my sister were here, she would've said something stupidly positive. Something you'd read out of a self-help book. She was good at that, spouting off flowery stuff that sounded good.

With a groan, I pressed my fingers against my eyes. Connor and I were only tutoring! Then again, who in their right mind would go *there* for tutoring? Connor had taken one too many tackles, apparently. How early do brain injuries occur in football players?

I sat perfectly still while my mind sprinted on the uneven terrain.

A wave of headlights swept into the bedroom, reflecting on my wall. Stepping back temporarily from the edge of panic, I stood up and walked over to my window. The car hadn't pulled into our driveway like I'd thought—no, it'd turned into the Oliphant's and shut off its headlights.

The passenger door popped open, and Madison unfurled from the car. She had on her Brentwood Babe varsity jacket, blonde hair tied back by a blue ribbon, as if she'd come from cheer practice. That wasn't the case, though—practice would've ended hours ago.

I knelt down so she wouldn't see me, and though I squinted, I couldn't see the driver from here. It was too dark, and the windows were too tinted. All that I knew was that the car wasn't Jade's—she drove a souped-up SUV with a pink stripe painted down the door, and this black car was free of any stripes.

Madison had almost made it to her porch before the driver's side door swung open, revealing a boy I'd never seen before. He turned toward her, which was coincidentally away from *me*, so I couldn't get a good look.

I did, however, get a good look at his red and black varsity jacket, with the clear cursive *Jefferson High* scripted on the back.

I blinked once, and then twice, but the words didn't change. *No way*, I thought, watching as she turned around. *There's no way she's hanging out with a guy from Jefferson.*

If I thought Jade would kill me for hanging out with Connor, she would crucify Madison for fraternizing with the enemy. Madison was crossing enemy lines, and that was treason. Like, head-on-a-pike treason.

But as the boy reached up and traced his hand across her jaw, I realized Madison had not only crossed the line, but had blown a hole in it.

Inspiration struck like a match, blazing through me, jerking my body into motion. A puppeteer tugged my strings now, brought my hand up, cell phone in my grip. The frame was blurry, slightly out of focus, but it was enough. It showed the blue and gold colors mixing well with the red and black.

Brentwood mixing with Jefferson.

A seed of discomfort lodged behind my ribs as I snapped the photo of my ex-best friend. This was self-preservation. Madison had made a decision similar to this one years ago. Now it was my turn.

I opened up Ava's text thread.

MAISIE

This might be more interesting than the whole Connor ordeal.

When I got Ava's text back, I knew I had won her over. For now, Connor and I had dodged a bullet.

AVA

!!!

+ − ✕ ÷

"I'm telling you, it was Madison Oliphant," I told my friend group for the millionth time at lunch the next day, sighing. "I live next door. It's her."

Ava bit down on her lower lip as she unpacked her food from her lunch bag. "She says it wasn't her."

"Who else would be standing on her front lawn?"

"Is it even her lawn?" Alex asked, glancing at me. The skepticism might as well have been tattooed on his face. "It's hard to tell in the picture."

"I literally took the photo from my window," I said, impatience seeping into my voice. "None of you believe me?"

Ava raised her palms level with her shoulders, her potato chip pinched between two fingers. "Hey, we believe you. *Madison* is the one saying it wasn't her."

Which made sense. If I were her, I'd deny being spotted with a Jefferson High athlete too. It also made me uncomfortable, knowing that I threw her under the bus to save my skin, and I was the reason she had to deny anything.

"I still think you should've posted the Connor article," Rachel said, but thankfully, she kept her voice down. If there were any listening ears, they wouldn't have been able to pick up his name. "That was insane."

"If I get proof, I'll post it." Ava gave me a small, grateful smile. "You were right, Maisie. Any good journalist needs proof. Otherwise they're a scummy tabloid writer."

Even though I was sure I appeared calm, I hoped to God no proof would ever come to light.

I channeled as much nonchalance as possible as I searched through the cafeteria. Connor hadn't texted last night, meaning he didn't have any questions about the material. I didn't see him after a few minutes of probing. Or Jade. Or Madison.

That felt like a bad sign.

As discreetly as I could, I reached into my satchel and found the square slip of paper in one of the inside pockets, smoothing it out enough to read. I'd specifically told him yesterday how he shouldn't leave notes anymore, but when I opened my locker this morning, I found this gem waiting for me.

I'VE GOT A BETTER PLACE FOR US TO TUTOR TODAY, DON'T WORRY. ONLY IT NEEDS TO STAY BETWEEN US.

WAIT FOR ME AT THE CORNER OF COLLEGE AVE AGAIN @4:30, OKAY?

—C

Alex nudged me in the side. "Do you have any plans tonight? We could do something."

Connor's voice filled my mind, almost like he was whispering in my ear. *Play hard to get. Build the anticipation.* I picked up the fork on his tray and took a bite of his broccoli salad. He never ate it, but he always got it for me. "Would you rather hang out tonight or tomorrow night?"

Alex raised his eyebrows. "Wait, does that mean you'd come to the game?"

"What?" Rachel leaned forward over the table, eyes wide. "You're coming?"

"He made quite the hard bargain," I said with a theatrical sigh, stabbing a piece of overcooked broccoli in the heart. It crumbled off my fork. "We're going out afterward."

Rachel's expression was as perplexed as I'd ever seen it. "But...you never come to games."

Ava smacked Rachel's shoulder with a grin. "Don't question it! She's coming! Wait, what will you wear? Do you have any spirit gear?"

Spirit gear. "Uh...no?"

"You'll come over and get ready with us," Ava said with a nod, no room for negotiation. "I have a sweatshirt you can borrow. We'll do your hair too."

I knew it was not worth arguing over, but I had one rule I'd stick to. "No pawprints."

Ava crossed her heart, but I wouldn't put it past her.

With five minutes left in the lunch period, I packed up my things and headed to the bathroom. As soon as I stepped out into the hallway, I saw them.

Jade and Connor stood down the hall, and even from their stances, I knew this conversation wasn't one I wanted to pop in on. Her little fists were clenched at her sides, and she'd backed Connor against the wall. Not that he seemed too bothered—he had one eyebrow raised, wearing the stupid mask of confidence that always irked me.

He obviously had a death wish, giving that expression to Jade.

"*Brentwood Babble* might not have posted it, but do you know how many people texted me?" she demanded, her voice low but filled with heat. "Kyle told Riley, who told practically everyone on the cheer squad. Who were you in there with?"

"It's not what you're making it out to be, you know."

I took a step backward because I knew there was absolutely no way I was going to walk past them mid-argument. Quite honestly, it was a miracle they hadn't seen me yet. Jade had her back to me, but all Connor had to do was turn his head to the side.

Jade let out a little scoff. "Are you kidding me right now? We've talked about this. We're *good* together."

"Are we?"

"What about king and queen, huh?" She shook her head a little. "We need this."

Connor's voice came out with a little sigh, sounding something like defeat. "I know."

She stepped up closer to Connor until there wasn't enough space between them to fit another person. In that split second before she spoke, Connor's gaze finally found me, but a hand wrapped around my upper arm tightly and jerked me to the side before he had a chance to react.

I barely registered Madison hauling me through a doorway before we ended up in the girls' restroom, and I stumbled to get my feet underneath me.

"What the heck is with you jocks?" I demanded, trying to find my balance with the bulky backpack weighing me down. "Ever heard of personal space?"

Madison stood by the sinks with her arms folded, her reflection in the mirror portraying her fury. She wasn't wearing any makeup today, which was out of the norm for her. Without the concealer under her eyes, she looked tired. However, when she spoke, her voice was filled with energy, almost as angry-sounding as Jade's. "Ever heard of *privacy*?"

My stomach dropped as if I was on a rollercoaster. "I don't know what you're talking about."

"Denying it makes you look stupid, you know. The only spot that photo could've been taken was from your bedroom window." Her normally full lips thinned. "And now you're over here eavesdropping on Jade and Connor? What, you run *Brentwood Babble* now?"

I couldn't see it, but I could feel my cheeks flame, irritation spiking in me. "I couldn't care less about stupid gossip."

"Oh, yeah? Then why did you take a picture of Logan and me last night?"

Logan. I didn't recognize the name, but then again, as a girl who pretty much surgically removed herself from that part of school life, not knowing wasn't a surprise. "Maybe I wanted to get back at you," I told her, forcing my lips into a thin line. "Maybe this is payback."

She knew exactly what I was talking about. "Oh my gosh, Maisie, come on. You didn't know the choreography."

"Yeah, because *you* taught me the wrong routine."

Her chest rose and fell fast, as if she'd finished sprinting around the track field. "If you were serious about cheer, you would've made sure you had the right choreo yourself."

"I didn't expect my best friend to sabotage me."

Madison let out a sharp groan and turned toward the mirrors, bracing her hands on the porcelain sink. "You don't get how big of a deal it is, being caught with him. I could get kicked off the squad."

The seriousness of her words connected with me in a way I wished they hadn't. We were in the same boat, and she didn't even know it. Or maybe *we* weren't, not really—I didn't have any skin in this tutoring game aside from getting valedictorian. My friends would be mad that I kept it a secret, yes, and scholarships, but otherwise, Madison and *Connor* were in the same boat.

When did it begin to feel like Connor's fate intertwined with mine?

"Maybe this wasn't payback," I said, but there was no heat to my voice anymore. Apparently, bathroom confrontations with Madison were a new regular for us, but I had too much weighing me down for a proper argument. "Maybe it was karma."

Madison took a sharp step toward me, enough that I almost flinched back. "I did you a favor, and we both know it."

In the sea of laughing people all those years ago, she'd been the only one I'd focused on. Ironically, she'd been the only one *not* looking. She'd ducked her head, too embarrassed for eye contact.

Squaring my shoulders, I took a shuffling step backward. "Maybe one day you'll think the same of me," I said, wrapping my hand around the bathroom door handle. "That I did you a favor."

Before I had the chance to tug, the door swung open,

nearly clipping me in the forehead. Jade pulled up short of storming into the narrow bathroom, and before she schooled her features, I caught a glimpse of the true emotion. Frustration simmered in her eyes and worry tugged at her mouth—two emotions that seemed out of place on her.

And then, when she registered who stood before her, it was all wiped away by a twist of annoyance. "Excuse you," she said by way of a greeting, in true Jade fashion, and brushed past me. "If you don't mind, Math Book, I need to talk to my best friend."

Without meeting anyone's eyes, I slipped back out into the hallway, slouching forward as if someone punched me in the stomach. My knees were shaky, an aftershock of bringing up the past.

I did you a favor, and we both know it. So even now, all these years later, she couldn't see that what she did was wrong.

She didn't do me a favor—she did herself one.

With a sigh, I straightened. The spot where Connor and Jade had been standing was empty now, but the hall clung to the tense atmosphere. Jade didn't sound as mad as I would've expected her to be, hearing her boyfriend could potentially be cheating. Then again, Connor didn't seem that desperate to convince her otherwise, either.

Curiosity ate at me as I tried to imagine where the conversation had gone, my mind replaying the snippets that I'd heard.

Jade's bare irritation. *We've talked about this. We're good together.*

Connor's detached reply. *Are we?*

Connor had said that he didn't believe in love in high school, but I couldn't help but wonder what was keeping them together if it *wasn't* love. How had they lasted two years without a deep connection? I didn't have an answer, but as I headed back into the lunchroom, I remembered Connor's words from once upon a time. *If that's love, I don't want it.*

CHAPTER 16

Once I buckled myself into Connor's passenger seat, I leaned back with my book bag in my lap, knotting the strap around my hands. The sandalwood of his bodywash was a warm and familiar scent that greeted me, putting me at ease. "What, you didn't think the germ-infested closet was good enough for round two?"

"It might not have been my best idea." Connor grimaced as he got the words out, wrinkling his nose. "No, scratch that. It was probably the worst idea I've ever had."

"Did you get things sorted with Jade?" It felt weird asking, like I was crossing a line, but then again, we talked about my relationship with Alex. Was it weird to ask him about Jade?

He let out a disparaging sigh. "Don't ask."

His tone wasn't rude, but it definitely was clear. The door on *that* conversation was padlocked. Blocked by barbed wire. I glanced out the passenger window, recognizing one of the residential areas of Brentwood. "Where are we going, anyway?"

"We're going to my house."

"I'm sorry, your *what*?" My words came out more high-pitched than I'd wanted them to, and I stiffened. "Is —is that not weird?"

"It's not weird if you don't make it weird."

I hated how casual he could be about everything. Everything was super surface level for him—heaven forbid he think deeper about things. Like spending time at his house alone felt...well, *weird*. Not as weird as hanging out in a closet couples normally flocked to, but still strange. Personal, like we were something more than tutor and student.

Most of the houses we were passing were small and cluttered, with disheveled lawns and broken-down cars parked in the driveway. "You don't live around here."

"I don't?"

"You live on Bleeker Avenue."

He glanced at me from the corner of his eye. "Okay, when I called you my stalker before, I *had been* joking."

The only reason I knew where he lived was because I had ridden with Mom once when she dropped Jozie off at his house for a party. Besides, it wasn't like his two-story, modern-day mansion was easily forgettable. The white siding and stone building had columns, for crying out loud.

As we drove farther and farther down the road, there was not a column in sight.

Connor spun the wheel down a side street. "We're actually going to my grandma's house."

"Your—" *Grandma?* That was even weirder than

going to his own house! "Are you seriously taking me to meet your grandma?"

"No, I'm taking you to my grandma's house so you can tutor me. Add this to our frenemy secret pile," he added with a serious expression, though it wasn't focused on me. Those hazel eyes were latched onto the road, fingers fluttering against the steering wheel. "I mean it, okay? If this shows up on *Babble*... It just can't, okay?"

I almost asked why his living accommodations would be worthy of gossip, but knowing Ava, she would post anything to bring in the views. "Yes, because so far in our tutor relationship, I've spilled *all* the beans."

"Your sarcasm is noted." He looked at me once more, his eyes considerably softer. "And so is the fact that you haven't said anything. This is something that's extra important, okay?"

It wasn't long after that Connor turned in to a short driveway, parking in front of a closed and dented garage door. The garage was attached to a house almost the size of mine, but a smidge smaller.

I opened my mouth, but he was already out of the car, swinging to the backseat and ducking in to grab his backpack.

It's not weird, I told myself, staring up at the structure, a bit of anxiety leaking through. *It's not weird if you don't make it weird. You're great with grandparents. You can do this.*

It did feel homey, though, like a little old lady could totally live here. A little old lady I was about to meet. *Gah.*

I went to shut the door behind me, but instead of clicking into place, it shuddered and bounced back open. "You have to twist the doorknob a little to get it to latch," Connor instructed. "Something's wrong with the lock."

The front door let us directly into the living room, and the warm scent of cinnamon greeted us, perfect for fall. There were two mismatched sofas with throw pillows that didn't quite fit either—they were a little too new and modern for the space. The coffee table was an antique-looking glass one, filled with magazines and paperbacks with worn spines. "It's cozy in here," I told him as I glanced around, spotting the family portrait on the wall. He resembled his mother the most, but his eyes were the same as his dad's. "Our living room is like an art gallery." And a cold one at that.

"Connor?" a raspy voice called from deeper in the house, followed by a clattering of what sounded like dishes. "That you?"

"Yeah, I'm home," he called back, turning to me once more. He slid his hands into his pockets, and for the first time since I'd met him, he looked *nervous*. More than nervous, uncomfortable. Like *I* was the one putting *him* under a microscope this time. "Kick off your shoes and pick them up—if it's okay with you, I thought we could sit out back and work."

I did as I was told, slipping off my sandals, toes sinking into the plush gray carpet. As I straightened, a tall woman stepped into an archway on the other side of the living room. She had a pink paisley print bandana wrapped over her hair, which was only visible by her gray bangs peeking over her forehead. A kitchen apron hung from her frame, one that was a bright blue, and wore a pair of green sweatpants. The fashion combo made me smile. "Oh. I didn't realize you had a friend."

"This is Maisie, Grandma," Connor said, pronouncing my name perfectly. Ever since I'd spelled it out for him, he'd never gotten it wrong. "She's tutoring me in math for my retake test."

"It's nice to meet you," I said, ducking my head in an awkward half-bow. Nice, Maisie, nice.

"A tutor?" Connor's grandma asked, squinting at me. "Thank God. You needed one, kid. Thank you for helping him, Maisie. You can call me Joy, dear. You look like you'd be good at math."

Connor jumped to say, "Grandma—"

"Thank you," I told her, nudging my glasses with a knuckle.

Joy offered to make us refreshments, which Connor declined with a shake of his head. His excuse was that we wouldn't be tutoring long, and if we were thirsty, we could come in ourselves. With a final farewell, Connor led me through the house to the back door, propping it open so I could pass through first.

For being a house in town, the yard was huge, practically double the size of my backyard. It was fenced in, too, the chain link a little warped in some areas, but sturdy. "We'll sit here," Connor said, gesturing toward a white wooden picnic table set up underneath a tree. "A lot different than a closet, huh?"

"A lot less scandalous, too," I retorted, looking up at

him. In that moment, with the sun catching in his brown hair, it struck me how odd it was to see a genuine smile from him. "So, we only have one week left of tutoring, but we're pretty far in our chapters. I think we might finish early enough for you to take a practice exam."

"I did have a bit of trouble last night," he confessed, dodging my eye as he withdrew a piece of paper. "I wrote everything down like we talked about, but I couldn't figure out the logarithmic functions."

Once he passed over the homework sheet for me to scan, we began our tutoring session. His error was small. "So you applied the theorem incorrectly here," I told him, and began the process of explaining the distortion. Even in layman's terms, logarithmic functions were tricky to explain, and Connor pressed his palm to the textbook a few times for clarification. Our back and forth, though, was as smooth as I could've hoped for.

"Can we take a break?" Connor asked about a half hour into the session, rubbing his fingers into his eyes. "My brain's going to explode."

I folded my hands on top of my textbook, covering the words. "Sure."

Connor traced one of the knots in the wooden picnic table, picking at a chip in the paint. "How often are your date nights with your boyfriend?"

The sudden question caught me totally off-guard. "What?"

"Jade and I used to do date nights two times a week last year. Mondays and Saturdays, and then games on Fridays. How often do you and Alex go on dates?"

"We hang out a few times a week," I said, unable to stop the touchiness from leaking into my voice. "We'll work on homework together or chill on the couch at his place. We haven't been hanging out much since I have to tutor you all the time."

Connor tipped his head to the side. "But how often do you go *out?*"

Date nights with Alex where we actually went out of the house were few and far between, especially when it was just us. We went bowling every week with Rachel and Ava, but a night of just Alex and Maisie time? Rare. And I so didn't want to admit that to Connor, not when he'd bragged about his booming dating life. "Not everyone has an endless amount of money to go on dates," I said, crossing my arms. An obviously defensive gesture, but I couldn't help it.

He bobbed his head slowly, and then wisely backed off. "I saw Madison take you into the bathroom today at lunch. I'm assuming it had to do with a certain picture that was posted to *Babble* last night?"

Now it was my turn to focus on the picnic table, not making eye contact. "What makes you think that?"

"Her face might've been blurry, but I recognized her porch from when I dropped you off the other night."

Of course he would've picked up on that. He was more observant than I'd ever given him credit for.

"I'll admit, I didn't expect you to be so...vicious."

"*Vicious?*" I demanded, jaw dropping. I half-expected him to be joking, but he just blinked at me. "That wasn't vicious!"

"No?"

"It—it wasn't vicious. Besides, it was *your* fault I posted it!"

Connor pressed a finger into his chest. "*My* fault?"

"Someone submitted a tip to Ava about you being in the closet with someone. She was going to post our stupid closet tryst on *Babble*—she'd drafted a whole article about you cheating and everything—and because I couldn't tell her the truth, I had to come up with something." The tirade was cut short by me gasping for a breath; I hadn't realized I'd been speaking so fast. "So, no, *not* vicious. It was necessary."

Connor's lips had slowly been turning upward as I spoke, and by the time I'd finished, the grin had taken over. It made the lines around his eyes crinkle. "You did it for me, huh?"

Did it for— "I did it for *me*," I said quickly, jumping to deny. "If your girlfriend found out I was the one with you in the closet, she'd—"

"Does this mean we're becoming more friends than enemies?" Connor leaned as far back on the picnic table as he dared, letting a few locks of hair fall into his eyes. "Am I growing on you, Maisie?"

"My annoyance is growing, yes. Is our break over yet?"

He shook his head with a laugh. "Five more minutes."

Connor tipped his head up toward the sunshine, soaking up the Vitamin D. With his throat exposed, I could see faint lines in some places, no doubt old scars from sports. Noticing his throat, though, had my eyes trailing elsewhere, over more details of him. Like how he had a freckle underneath his jaw, and how along his jaw there was the faintest trace of stubble. I couldn't help but think about Alex and his frequent razor cuts, shaving when there was no hair to get rid of. Connor, though, he must shave.

I shook off the comparison, shifting in my seat.

I forced my eyes down at the homework sheet we were working through, at Connor's scrawling handwriting. The familiar equations blinked back at me, on a little bit of a slant from how he wrote it. I brushed my thumb along the graphite, smudging it a little.

"What do you do for fun?"

The array of supplies around us caught my attention, and I fixated on where his calculator was by his elbow. "I do calculus worksheets sometimes. Mrs. Diego finds me hard problems on the internet to solve. And I watch TV." I only tacked on the last point so he didn't make fun of me, but embarrassment crawled over me for being honest. Like I should've said I liked painting like Mom and Jozie or building stuff like Dad. Something...cooler. "How about you? What do you do for fun?"

"I haven't really had time for fun lately. Go to school, go to football practice, tutor with you, finish up the rest of my homework, and then bed." He opened his eyes to little slivers. "And then do it again the next day."

"Should I get out my tiny violin?"

A spark of triumph burst through me when Connor grinned. "You're ruthless, you know. You weren't even going to pretend to pity me."

It wasn't pity that I felt for him, he was right. There wasn't the *oh, I feel so bad for you* sort of feeling stirring in my chest. It was more like *how can I help take some of the pressure off?* If he was too overwhelmed, he'd fail the Algebra II exam again.

Belatedly, I remembered that if he failed, no more valedictorian. I couldn't let that happen. That was the only reason behind the feeling. The only reason.

"Well, let's do something fun, then." I shut my math book and swung my legs out from underneath the picnic table. "A five-minute game."

Connor tilted his head curiously. "What kind of game?"

"You pick. Does your grandma have cards or anything?"

A sudden boyish glint lit in his eyes as he got to his feet, curbing the table and heading to a small shed near the house. When Connor came back, he had a grin on his face and a football in his hand. The ball was sunbleached and cracked with age. It clicked then what he meant, and I immediately began shaking my head. "This is not a game. This is a *sport*."

"What's the difference?"

"Sports require physical activity. And sweat. And I'm wearing sandals." I cast a glance around at his grandma's yard, still muddy from yesterday's downpour.

Connor raised his eyebrows at me, tossing the football up into the air and catching it with ease. "It doesn't matter what kind of shoes you have on when you play catch."

Oh, great. Catch. I had vivid memories of basketballs and volleyballs slamming into my face during gym class, breaking my glasses on at least two occasions. Why not add a football to that list?

Connor stopped about fifteen feet from me in the grass, tossing the ball up once more. "Five minutes, like you said. It's been a long time since I've played a casual game of catch."

"You literally have football practice every day!" And besides, how was *catch* even a game? For a couple of kids, maybe, but not for me.

He didn't give me a response this time and didn't wait for me to object further. Without warning, he drew his arm back and lobbed the football at me.

My hands went to my eyes, shielding my glasses as I ducked out of the ball's path, and it bounced against the grass a few feet behind me.

"I know it's a weird concept," Connor called, a laugh clear in his tone, "but you're supposed to *catch* the ball when playing catch."

I fought the urge to flip him off. "I literally have never thrown a football in my life," I told him with a twisted grimace, picking up the ball and weighing the thing in my hands. It was smoother than I thought—my fingers could hardly get a good grip on it. "I'd probably break one of your grandma's windows."

"You're not even facing the house. If you manage to break a window, I'll be impressed."

This time, I did flip him off.

"Put one foot back a bit," he said, demonstrating from

his safe distance away. He set a leg behind him, leaning into that hip. "And then twist your body forward as you throw."

I was breaking all sorts of personal rules I'd set for myself. One of the main ones was to stay as far away from football as possible, but here I was, doing exactly as Connor instructed.

Stupid. This was stupid. I was stupid. Why was I letting him talk me into this?

Drawing my arm back as he had, I put all my weight into the throw, the ball spinning unevenly through the air.

Connor had to hop back a few steps to snatch it, a happy laugh permeating the air from simply catching a ball. "That was good!"

Triumph swelled within me even as my shoulder ached.

My friends would absolutely lose their minds if they saw me right now, playing catch with the most popular guy in school. Two things I practically cursed two weeks ago, and now I begrudgingly could admit that I was having fun. More fun than I'd had in a long time.

Because with each throw, Connor would take several steps backward, forcing me to throw harder and farther. If the ball came up too short, he'd sprint to catch it, going as far as to nearly div into the grass at times. The throws he sent me were softer, of course, starting out underhand while I built my confidence before throwing it overhand.

I wasn't sure how long we'd been throwing the ball—more than the previously agreed upon five minutes—

when my sandal snagged on a patch of uneven ground as I hurried backward to catch the football. I lost my balance, body wincing from the slight twist to my ankle, and I ended falling butt-first in a pile of mud.

The football landed about a foot away from me, splattering in the dirt.

Connor's abrupt laugh from across the yard carried, and he pressed a hand to his mouth as he hurried over. "Are you okay?"

"I'll let you know when I can feel my butt again." Despite the predicament, a short laugh burst from me as I frowned down at my sandals. The strap of the one that had gotten caught had snapped, rendering the shoe useless. My toes were filthy from running back and forth in the mud. "I feel like a kid, getting all dirty from playing outside. Joy's not going to let me back in the house."

"I shouldn't have thrown the ball so hard." Connor stretched a hand down to me, bottling down his own amusement. "This is the part where you say something about trajectory and how you should've seen that coming."

"It's not a trajectory error—I totally would've caught the ball."

Connor gave up trying to bite back his smile, and even though he kept the curve to his lips small, it reached his eyes in an instant.

I wrapped my fingers around Connor's and let him tug me to my feet, his other hand coming up to cup my arm. The broken shoe remained stuck in the mud, and to keep from fully planting my bare foot into the mud, I leaned against him, gripping his shoulder for support.

His arm immediately wrapped around my back to steady me, and I could feel all of his fingers even through the thin material of my T-shirt. My chest was pressed against his side, getting up close and personal once more with the firmness of his muscles. He was close enough that I could see where a few locks of his hair were sticking to his temples from the sun, could see that the tops of his cheeks were beginning to grow pink.

Without warning, Connor brushed the pad of his thumb along my cheekbone, causing time to freeze. "How did you manage to get mud on your face?" he asked with a quiet sort of humor, teasing with me the way a friend might. I swallowed hard, my head inexplicably tilting toward the touch. "Maybe playing catch in sandals wasn't a good idea."

"I'm always right," I told him, trying to pack as much strength into my voice as possible, even though my lungs felt like they were lacking enough air. My head swayed as my thoughts ran in dizzying circles, and my heart...why was it beating unevenly? "That's what I get for doing something physical. With math, the only risk is a paper cut when I flip a worksheet over."

"You play it safe, huh?"

I wanted to pull away from him but was unable to bring myself to. "Apparently."

Connor bent down and picked up my broken sandal, patting me lightly on the shoulder. "Come on, let's get you a pair of sweatpants to change into."

CHAPTER 17

This was the second time I had to wear Connor's pants. Why did this keep happening?

But that wasn't the weirdest part of it all. When Connor led me to a bedroom down the hall, I'd been expecting a basic guest room. One with floral sheets and maybe an antique dresser with knickknacks littering the surface. I hadn't expected to find a room that clearly belonged to Connor.

He left me alone to change, and I dressed into the sweatpants quickly, tying them as tightly as they'd go around my waist, and went to investigate.

There was a small desk near a set of closet doors, and I picked up a graded US History homework sheet from last week. There was a hamper in the other corner of the room filled with dirty clothes, and even though the twin-sized bed against the far wall was technically made, the blankets were a bit rumpled, like someone had straightened them in a hurry.

There were also several cardboard boxes stacked

around the entire perimeter of the room. *Connor's Clothes, Connor's Games, Connor's Trophies.* All the boxes with the labels facing out had his name on them.

There was a soft knock at his door. "They work okay?"

"You can come in," I said, taking a healthy step away from the desk.

The door cracked open a second later, and Connor poked his head inside. His gaze immediately went to the sweats hanging from my frame, and then it jerked back up. "I can get a bag for your shorts."

"Are you living with your grandma?" I asked, the question coming off about as blunt and nosy as it could, but my curiosity had totally taken control of my tongue.

He stiffened with a short inhale. "Uh, yeah. That's why I said this needs to stay in the vault."

"Why don't you live with your parents?" I peered at him closer. "What happened to the house on Bleeker Avenue?"

He dodged my eye as he stepped farther into the space, his stare jumpy. Discomfort clung to him like a second skin, evident by the stiff line of his body. He sat down by the footboard of his bed, rubbing his palms over his knees. "My parents...lost it. Last May."

"Lost it?" I echoed, jaw slackening. I opened my mouth to fire off another question, but froze. The area around his lips was tight, jaw a sharp line, screaming of uneasiness.

Shuffling closer, I sat at the headboard of the bed, giving a good distance between us. The bed creaked slightly under my weight, and I pulled one of my legs up. "You don't have to tell me," I said softly, nearly coming close to touching him before I forced my hand on the bed between us. "But you can if you want to. It'll stay in the vault."

Some of the tension ebbed from his posture. "Promise?"

Without verbally answering, I stuck my hand out to him, pinky raised. He gave a soft exhale, one that sounded like a chuckle, as he accepted the pinky-swear. For a moment, we both held still. His pinky wrapping around my own was enough to make my heart race.

And then he finally told me the story of why he bombed his Algebra II exam last year.

"Last May, my parents' years of debt caught up with them," he began quietly, settling back against the foot-board and studying his hands. It was a vulnerable posture for him, one that almost had me feeling like I was sitting in the bedroom with a stranger. "They stopped making payments on the house, and the bank stepped in. Instead of letting them foreclose the house—and then fall from the graces of their friends—my parents sold it for dirt cheap. They told everyone they sold it to move someplace nicer, but really, they moved to a one-bedroom apartment in Jefferson."

I glanced around his makeshift bedroom, at all the moving boxes. "That's why you live here? With your grandma?"

"It was either here or a couch four steps from the kitchen."

"They couldn't afford a smaller house? Or a bigger apartment?" I could understand downsizing from the behemoth of a place they lived in before, but it seemed extreme to go from a home with five bedrooms to an apartment.

Connor's fingers fluttered against his denim jeans. "They were...deep in it. Debt collectors calling every day, people showing up at our house. Dad made bad investments, Mom had a shopping habit, and things caught up to them."

He spoke so clearly, so easily, as if moving out of his childhood home, being separated from his parents, wasn't a big deal. His body language, though, hinted at his true feelings. His cheeks were still pink, warm, and his limbs had stiffened as if replaced with lead.

"I've been pretending everything is normal. With everyone. Keeping up appearances is the only thing they care about. The guys from the team know I moved, but I always make excuses why they can't come over. The only person who knows is Jade."

"You don't have to tell me this," I told him, curling my fingers into themselves. It was clearly making him uncomfortable diving into this. And this was something so secret, so personal. If only one other person knew, I couldn't imagine why he'd want to add me to that list. "I promise I won't say anything. I don't need to know the details."

"My parents sold the house the week before exams, and I was so busy with packing up my stuff that I didn't have time to study." He turned his face toward me, but his eyes didn't follow. "That's why I'm telling you now. I'm not a guy who blows off class. I think I had a B- in the class to begin with, but bombing the exam tanked my grade."

Connor having a B- made a bit more sense when it came to why he never had a tutor earlier in the year. His grades were average, but average grades meant that failing a test worth a hefty percentage would do damage. Big damage. This entire time, I'd been judging him for not paying attention when, in reality, I wasn't sure I'd have been able to pay attention either.

He cleared his throat, and as he shifted, the whole mattress creaked with the movement. "That got heavy fast. I—I just wanted to explain myself." And then he finally turned to me. It was a tentative stare, ready to flick away any second. "So you could understand me a bit better, maybe."

His words did something to me, like they reached into my heart and thawed something frozen. Thawed the rigid pre-established perspective I'd carved of Connor Bray. He didn't fail Algebra II because he slacked off last year. It was because he'd been in the middle of one of the hardest things he'd ever had to go through. And he told no one about it. *Keeping up appearances*, he said. His parents hadn't wanted anyone to know about their situation, either. Had him lie, had him go through this alone.

It felt like all of my convictions about him crumbled down, because the golden boy that everyone at Brentwood High worshipped wasn't as perfect as he seemed—he was going through hell and smiling through it.

I looked at Connor closely, at his stiff frame, at how he was rubbing his palm over his knuckles. A strange unfurling sensation swept through me, starting in the center of my chest. His discomfort—strangely enough, I wanted to ease it.

"I lied before," I confessed, thinking back to Monday. "I...I did try out for the cheer squad. Back in the ninth grade. I tried out with Madison. She taught me a few cheers and taught me the routine. We were going to do it together."

I remember my heart had been pounding in my chest because dancing in front of so many people was a bit outside my comfort zone, but having Madison at my side had bolstered my confidence. I could do it if she was there. The head cheerleader stood among all the new recruits, about to play the song everyone was supposed to have learned for tryouts. Madison stood on one side of me, Jade on the other.

Before we started, I'd turned to her and gave her a thumbs up. *"You're going to do great, Mads."*

"They played a different song than the one Madison and I had been rehearsing all week," I told Connor. "I didn't realize until, like, ten seconds in that everyone danced to a completely different routine. Even Madison."

Connor leaned forward, narrowing his eyes on me. "Wait, she taught you the wrong routine?"

I nodded, remembering.

Madison hadn't looked at me while she danced, not even when I tried to keep up, tried to keep smiling even though I didn't understand what she was doing. She hadn't looked at me when I stopped smiling, not even when I stopped dancing, the wave of ugly realization crashing into me. I didn't check to see whether or not she looked when I ran out of the gym, but I knew deep down that she hadn't.

It was the first time Jade's expression was filled with so much disdain, though, and the first time I felt like an outcast. That I felt like a *geek*.

I suddenly felt very awkward. Very exposed, especially with the way Connor watched me. I wanted to snatch the words back, go back to pretending I wasn't that pathetic. "Anyway, now we both know a secret about each other." My secret wasn't as important as his, of course, nor as life-changing, but I hoped it gave him a bit more peace of mind about letting me into his house. Letting me see a side of him that very few got to see.

Except my words hadn't seemed to soothe him. "That makes me... Jeez, that makes me furious, Maisie."

Furious. It was such a charged word, and the way he said it caused a strange feeling to stir within me. Almost like he'd dragged his thumb across my cheekbone again.

It was weird that he was angry on my behalf. I tried to think of what Alex's reaction would be if I told him that story—I didn't think he'd be angry. I'd expected a solemn nod, a nonchalant "that sucks," but not *furious*.

"It's high school." I forced myself to shrug. "Crappy things happen to people every day."

"Yeah, but it happened to *you*." Connor's frown deepened.

I wanted to ask him why I was different from anyone

else at Brentwood, why the emphasis was important. I wanted to ask, but...I didn't. I was too afraid of what his answer would be.

Connor let out a soft breath, as if realizing how serious he'd gotten in an instant. When he spoke again, his voice was significantly lighter. "So, you wanted to be a cheerleader, then?"

"I think I wanted it because Madison wanted it." The confession increased the awkward tension between my shoulders. "But, you know, I'm glad that didn't work out. Could you picture me as a Brentwood Babe? *Ha.*"

Connor stretched his legs out beside my hip. "I think you might've made a good cheerleader," he murmured, tilting his head. "But do I see you fitting in next to Madison and Jade? Obsessed with the latest *Brentwood Babble* post? Threatening to go to war over being spotted with the rival school's quarterback?"

The thought made me cringe. "Yeah, the probability of that happening is low."

He scrunched his nose. "Was that another math line?"

I stretched my legs out like he'd stretched his. "It wasn't intentional." We both chuckled together, and I knew we should've gone back out to the picnic table at that point—we'd both unloaded our baggage and could now move forward—but there was one question that had been on my mind as soon as I saw him today in the hallway. "Are you going to tell Jade it was me in the closet?"

"I didn't plan on it. I don't know how she'd react, but

I don't think she'd believe me if I said we were just tutoring."

"I don't know if Alex would believe me either if he found out." It was the truth, too. How would he react if he found out I was hanging with *Connor Bray* every day after school? Except we weren't hanging out. It was strictly business, totally professional, and yet...would Alex see it that way? Or would he see the part where I lied? Repeatedly.

"I never should've asked you to keep it from him," Connor said, and then gently, he knocked his foot against my hip. "You should tell him. If he can't keep the secret, it's fine, but I never should've asked you to lie to people who are important to you."

Telling Alex would open a huge can of worms now, worms that would wiggle their way back to Rachel and Ava. I didn't think that Ava would post it without my permission, but the paranoid side of me wasn't sure. And if something about it came up on *Brentwood Babble*, then what? "We're coming down the home stretch," I said, mimicking him and knocking my foot against him. Except, since my legs were shorter, my toes hit his thigh. "We have four days next week and then your test on Friday. He won't have to know."

Connor laid his hand on the top of my ankle, right over where the hem of his dark sweatpants kissed my skin. My mind flashed back to all the times Alex would prop his feet onto my lap, his dirty socks emitting a smell practically ingrained into my memory. I'd hated it then and hated when I'd have to touch his feet to readjust them. Here Connor was now, touching my foot—which had a smear of mud on the top of my skin—like it was no big deal.

Physical touch, his words whispered in my ear, my brain bringing up that once-upon-a-time conversation. *Physical touch is key. I'm sure there's a science behind it or something, but all I know is that it works.*

The air I'd been drawing in lodged in my throat, trapped by the pressure building there. I knew I needed to pull away, but I couldn't do anything but stare, stomach twisting. *What is going on?*

CHAPTER 18

*A*va looped her arm through mine while Rachel forged through the crowd Friday night, elbows uncaringly clearing a path. She brushed past people who shot her dirty looks, her head held high. "I'm happy you came tonight," Ava told me, squeezing me closer. "You don't know how long I've wanted you to come to a game."

"I think I've got a bit of an idea," I responded, thinking back to the countless times they'd asked, the countless times over the years I'd said no, using every possible excuse in the book. Hearing how happy her voice was, though, caused guilt to spread through me. "I'm sorry I didn't come sooner. I didn't realize it was important to you."

"You're here now." She gave me an infectious sort of grin, one so bright that it rivaled the sun. "Hopefully we can find some good seats."

The game hadn't started, which meant the bleachers weren't filled completely yet, but there weren't a lot of empty spaces left once we got to the student section. Several students had made signs and held them in their laps, waiting for the football players to come out onto the field.

"Oh, look," Ava whispered to me, nudging her chin. "It's Connor's parents."

It was funny how quickly I was able to find who she meant. I spotted Joy first, wearing a vibrant blue shirt with the numbers 22 written in glittering gold. Beside her sat a woman with a dark pixie cut. She, too, was wearing Brentwood Bobcat spirit gear, with an oversized sweatshirt over her frame. Connor's father sat on the other side of her. He, too, showed school spirit by wearing a baseball cap, and he was turned, chatting it up with a few men behind him.

They were all smiles, exuding happiness at getting to support Connor. An outsider looking in would have no idea that things were so tumultuous underneath the surface. That was where Connor got his mask from. *Keeping up appearances.*

"Can we sit here?" Rachel asked a blonde girl in the front row who seemed as out of place as I felt. Instead of blending into the sea of Brentwood blue and gold, she wore maroon pants with a black motorcycle jacket two sizes too big for her. Her blonde hair was fading out near the roots, growing in a deep brown, but it looked pretty.

"Only if you talk to me," the girl responded with her eyebrows raised, and I noticed the sparkle of her nose ring. "Nothing's worse than sitting by yourself. You'd think people would've sat down because it's the front row, but it's like I've got the plague."

"The front row is worth the plague," Ava said

happily, squeezing us in tight. "And we're always down to make new friends."

I sat down on the chilly metal bench and tightened my jacket around me. It was a colder night tonight, fall starting to make an appearance. Ava had given me her Brentwood zip-up hoodie, which was a bright blue, and though I had escaped the horrors of a bobcat pawprint on my face, Ava did insist on drawing little sparkles on my cheeks with her paint marker. No doubt I'd already smudged them.

And don't get me *started* on the braid crown on my head. It pulled so tightly that I was sure my hairline had begun to recede.

"Do you go to Brentwood?" Rachel asked the girl, leaning across Ava.

She nodded. "I'm Lacey." The girl stuck her hand out to me first since I sat right beside her, and her nails were a shiny black. "Senior. You're Maisie, right?"

I blinked. "Uh, yeah. How'd you know?"

"My cousin pointed you out the other day. Most Likely To: Marry a Math Book, right?" Before I had a chance to feel offended that *that's* how she knew me, she jerked her thumb at herself. "I'm Never Get a Boyfriend."

Ava gasped a little from my other side. "Really? That's you?"

"Yep." Lacey shrugged, totally unbothered. "At least I wasn't Most Likely To: End Up Alone. That's, like, the ultimate single. But it's all right."

"Wait, so you're Never Get a Boyfriend," Rachel

repeated. Her dark eyebrows were drawn together. "That means you're Landon's Lacey?"

"*Landon's Lacey.*" She smiled a little, one corner of her red-painted lips lifting higher than the other. "I've never been anyone's Lacey before. Is that weird that I like how that sounds?"

"Is he super sweet?" Ava demanded, leaning over me this time. She was a gossip bloodhound—could sniff out anything that would make front-page social media news. "I talked to him the other day. He seems like he'd be super sweet. Shy, maybe, but sweet."

"Once you get to know him more, he's definitely got golden retriever energy." Lacey tucked some hair behind her ear, shrugging again. "We're different. But what is it that they say about opposites attract?"

I felt like I was watching a tennis match, glancing side to side at each speaker, and the atmosphere felt frostier than it had been when we sat down. "Well, good for you," I said in a bright voice, flattening my hands along my knees. "Good for you for sticking it to the stupid list by getting a boyfriend."

"We love love," Rachel chimed in, giving Lacey a thumbs-up.

More people clambered up the bleachers, and someone caught Rachel's attention, drawing her out of the conversation. Ava's eyes had shifted to her phone, thumbs typing quickly.

The student section filled in, everyone seeming to come in at once, and almost at the same time, the football players took to the field to begin their warmups. Ava was right for getting here when we did. One out of five students gripped a homemade poster board, supporting any given player. However, from a quick glance around, Connor Bray was the favorite. One person even had a poster with his face printed on it.

It occurred to me then that I was completely out of my element.

I wore the Brentwood Bobcat attire like a true fan, but while everyone cheered and waved their signs, I shrank back, attempting to morph into the metal bleacher. Blending in was impossible.

It wasn't so bad, though. Lacey didn't rush to her feet and cheer for the team, either. Instead, she placed her palms against her ears. "Are they always so loud?"

"I wouldn't know," I called back to her, but I was sure the words were lost over everyone else.

A few of the football players sat on the grass and stretched to reach their toes, much like they'd been doing during their warmups the day I'd gone to confront Connor at the field. A few were off to the side tossing a football back and forth. Some were standing near the sidelines already, chatting with the coach.

Despite myself, I trailed over the players—more specifically, the torso of the players.

What was it that you told him? I'd asked him in the closet. *Twenty-two?*

It's my jersey number.

I squinted but couldn't spot the number.

The cheerleaders bounded their way to the grass in front of the bleachers, rustling their pom-poms with every step. For a second, just a split second, I imagined a life where things had been different. Where Maisie Matthews wasn't stiff in the student section, wasn't forcing herself to cheer on the football team. A life where Maisie Matthews hadn't been rejected by the cheer squad.

What would I have looked like among them? Would I have felt comfortable wearing the mini skirt and turtle-neck? Would I have enjoyed the cheers and songs? Would I have been a base or a flyer in any of the routines?

I found Jade easily, because instead of wearing a blue top like the rest of the squad, Madison and Jade wore gold tops. Signifying their co-captain status, probably. But she wasn't with the rest of the squad, fluffing their pom-poms, ready to start the night of cheer. Instead, I found her by the water cooler for the players, and she had her arms wrapped around Connor's neck.

"Oh! Photo op!" Ava quickly brought out her cell and pointed the camera at the couple, zooming in as far as she could. "Well, Rachel, you owe me five bucks. Looks like they've made up from the whole closet thing already."

I squeezed my fingertips as I watched them. They were much too far away for me to be able to read their lips, but I couldn't help but wonder what they were talking about. If they *had* made up. They certainly looked like it.

We'd gone back to tutoring not long after sharing our heart-to-heart, but I hadn't been able to fully shake off the lingering strangeness of it all. Not even focusing on my paper roses had helped. As soon as Connor closed his Algebra II book, I'd told him I was okay enough to walk back to the school to get my car. I'd needed time to clear my thoughts. It was his confession that had thrown me off, peeling back the curtain, showing his true self underneath the smoke and mirrors he used on everyone else.

And now I had a pair of his sweatpants, *again*.

Jade grabbed the collar of his shoulder pads and pulled him down, sharing a kiss for all to see. Ava's phone caught it in high definition. Guess they'd made up.

I forced my eyes away, trying to ignore the strange, uncomfortable twisting in my stomach.

"How's our lovely student section doing tonight?" Madison shouted to the crowd, eliciting a response from nearly the whole bleacher set that made my ears ring. She had a plastic sort of smile painted on her red lips, and much like Ava and Rachel, little pawprints were trotting along her cheeks. "Everybody in the stand, let's give our Bobcats a big hand!"

Everyone else clapped along, a sort of electric energy running through them. It skipped right over me. I might've tried out for cheer before, but now I cringed a little at the mere idea of wiggling pom-poms.

As the Bobcats took to one side of the field, and the other team, the Haven High Ravens, took to the other, one blue and gold jersey stood out against the rest. The glittering numbers caught my eye immediately. He was walking away from the bleachers, the number on his back in full view. 22.

Even from here, I could finally see what everyone

was talking about. Football pants *were* good. And then I wanted to kick myself for looking.

Once the game started, some of my dread ebbed away. There was something to do other than stand there —watch the players. And though it wasn't nearly as exciting as everyone made it sound, it was interesting to see how each player would converge on the runner with the ball. Even though I had no idea what half of it meant —like how the referee kept throwing a flag into the air or what a "first down" meant—it wasn't as boring as I'd always preached it to be.

Only one thing truly got on my nerves: the cheers.

"Y-E-L-L, everybody, yell, yell!" the squad all chorused, smashing their pom-poms together in unison. Madison's voice stood out above the rest in this chant, her shimmery blue eyeshadow bright as she blinked. Her hair was braided in a crown too, a bit too much like mine. She was in her element, though, following a choreographed dance without missing a beat. "BHS, BHS, let's go BHS!"

The chant went on again, this time the student section joining in with the spelling. I didn't cheer along, but, begrudgingly, I did find myself clapping.

Ava held up her cell phone sideways seconds before halftime, snapping a pic of the whole field. "We're so going to win tonight. I'm going to start drafting the blog post now. *Bobcats Win Big.*"

"They're only six points ahead," I told her, squinting at the scoreboard. I wasn't sure how the scoring system actually worked in football, but I knew it was easy to catch up fast. "You think they'll win?"

"We haven't lost a game yet this season," Lacey said from my other side. "Landon said that their only true competition will be Jefferson for the homecoming game."

"Ugh." Rachel's lips twisted at the mere mention of the rival. "He shouldn't worry. We'll knock them out of the water."

"Or off the field," Ava quipped, thumbs speedily typing. "Maisie, you can dodge football games all you want, but it's against Brentwood Bobcat law to skip out on homecoming. They'll expel you if you don't show."

I couldn't help but snort. "Is that a promise?"

My words caused Lacey to chuckle on the other side of me, but she tried to mask it by taking a drink of her slushy.

"Let's give it up for our Brentwood High marching band!" the football announcer cried into the microphone, eliciting scratchy feedback that was almost as loud as his words. The crowd's response to the band wasn't nearly as animated as it'd been for the football players, but then again, the majority had retreated to the concession stand to stock up on popcorn and hotdogs before it closed.

The halftime performance kicked off with a bang, quite literally a slam of cymbals clamping together. The band moved onto the field in tandem with the cheerleaders, who were doing cartwheels between them.

I could spot Alex instantly, because even though the tasseled and bedazzled uniforms were all the same, the tuba was like a neon buoy bobbing in the water. Anyone else might've thought it was dorky, but it was so *him*.

Though it was a bit shaky, the song they played was

obviously the Bobcat fight song, because everyone around me clapped along to the beat.

I let myself melt into the moment, rooted to the metal bleacher. My two friends at my side, Alex on the field, the fight song ringing in my ears. Normally, I would've spent a night like tonight in my bedroom with only the company of homework or books. It wasn't a bad sort of existence—because, let's be honest, I was a total couch potato—but there was no denying the slightly infectious quality of being among other happy people. Listening to the cheers, the music, watching the players—there was something energizing about it. Like learning a new math subject.

Of course, I'd never tell a soul about it.

Once the football players came out of their halftime huddle, some of them took to the field while some waited on the sidelines near the student section. Connor was one of the ones who lingered, his helmet dangling from his fingertips, his dark hair wet-looking under the lights. He stood about twenty feet away down on the grass.

A little boy ran up to him carrying a case of plastic water bottles, passing one to number twenty-two. Connor reached his fist down as he took a drink, and the boy pounded his knuckles. The sweet interaction lasted two seconds, but it made me smile nonetheless. Connor looked at where the cheerleaders assembled briefly before roaming over all the posters and people in the student section. Half a beat later, he got to the front row, finding me.

One corner of Connor's mouth quirked up a little,

akin to his normal condescending smile but...not. More amused, more friendly. Both of his eyebrows were raised in a *well, well, well* expression.

"You've got this, babe!" Jade shouted to him, causing a few of the other cheerleaders to shake their pom-poms. She broke the connection entirely, because without another glance, Connor donned his helmet and turned toward the field.

Once the game was back in motion, the cheerleaders resumed hyping up the crowd, and after a big internal debate, I found myself cheering along with the crowd by the fourth quarter. Soft muttering, for sure, but it was still cheering. Maybe I needed an exorcism after this, but for now, I enjoyed it.

Tomorrow I would shake my head at how easily my mood had shifted, but in that moment, I couldn't help but smile a tiny bit at my predicament. Two days in a row, I found myself pleasantly surprised. I didn't know why my thoughts on all things Brentwood football were changing, but I couldn't say I was fully upset by the prospect.

Against all odds, I was happy that I'd come tonight.

CHAPTER 19

$$\frac{x}{a} + \frac{y}{b} \quad X = \frac{\underline{\quad\quad}}{2}$$

$$\sin(\theta) = \frac{opp}{hyp} \qquad a + 0 =$$

$$d = \sqrt{(x_2 - x_1)^2 + (y_2 - y_1)^2}$$

After the game ended, I waited for Alex by the closed concession stand, stirring my straw around to suck up the last drops of the slushy Lacey had convinced me to get. I hadn't expected such a sour taste, but it had to be laced with something, given how addicting it was. As Ava had predicted, the Brentwood Bobcats demolished the Ravens in a thirty-two to twenty-six score. It left every Bobcat passerby beaming as they headed to their cars, waving their homemade signs happily.

Alex had only been gone five minutes—he'd been adamant that he'd take his tuba to the school himself and come back for me—and the walk back to the school with the heavy thing had to be at least ten, but the crowd had thinned considerably. I was one of the few remaining people left by the field, and though the stadium lights were on now, they wouldn't be for long.

"I'm surprised to see you here." Madison walked up to me with her letterman jacket slung over her shoulders, cell phone in her hands. Her makeup had smudged through the night, the pawprints smearing along her skin, now resembling polka dots. Though she seemed polite enough at the moment, my guard went up. Our previous conversation hadn't exactly been friendly. "No offense, but you're the last person I'd expected to see in the stands."

"My friends have been wanting me to come to one for the longest time."

"Ava and Rachel, right?"

Was she keeping tabs on me or something? "Uh, yeah."

"It's Ava who runs *Babble*?"

Yeah, my guard was up, and maybe my sword, too. "Yes."

But Madison just nodded, like the question had been a random one to fill space. Her discomfort was obvious as she took a step forward, planning her escape. "Well, it was nice seeing you."

"Can I ask you something?" I glanced around, but everyone had cleared out by then. Everyone but Madison, it seemed. The question that bubbled up was one I couldn't let go any longer. I'd tried to shove it down, pretend that it didn't really bother me, but it was like a little splinter wedged into the heel of my foot. Small but excruciating. "Why did you name me for the Most Likely Tos?"

"I didn't put you on the list," Madison said, staring me in the eye. Weirdly enough, that used to be the way I could tell she was being truthful. Whenever she was lying, she looked away from me. Like for her next line, she focused on my shoulder as she said, "I don't even know who does the list."

"Liar."

Her features pinched, pissed I wouldn't buy the b.s. she was selling. "Believe what you want."

"Who put *you* on the list?"

In that instant, she was no longer Madison Oliphant of the Bobcat Babes, one of the top performing cheer squads in the county. She wasn't even Madison Oliphant of the Top Tier. For a split second, she was a girl with insecurity plain on her face, as easy to read as a basic math equation.

She straightened her spine, nearly causing her jacket to slip off her shoulders. "My ride's here," she said suddenly, voice thick. "Have a nice night." She gave me a tight-lipped expression before walking on, ponytail swishing with her step.

I dragged the toe of my shoe through the dirt. I couldn't help that if, like Connor, Madison had more going on than anyone else realized. Maybe she *wasn't* living the happy-go-lucky life in the Top Tier like she'd always wanted. She'd been hanging out with Brentwood's rival, and the quarterback, at that. She'd been put on the same list her gaggle of friends created, basically stabbed in the back.

I did you a favor, and we both know it.

"You know, I almost didn't recognize you with a Bobcat sweatshirt on," a voice said, startling me enough that I nearly dropped my phone. "Oozing school spirit isn't exactly your thing, but you look the part."

Connor walked toward me in the same direction Madison had come from, grinning. He held his shoulder pads in one hand and helmet in the other, with his duffle bag strap banging against his hip with each step.

"I was told it was against the law for me to attend a game without showing some *school spirit*."

"It's actually a felony, I hear." The stadium lights behind him cast his face in shadow, and he stopped a few feet from me. Enough space that someone could've assumed we weren't together. "I don't want to get too close," he told me, lifting his helmet to gesture at the tight black athletic shirt he wore. "I'm waiting until I get home to shower."

"Thanks for the warning," I said, slipping my hands into the hoodie pocket.

His eyes lingered on me for a moment. "Your sparkles."

I touched my fingertips to my cheek, immediately picturing the little sparkles the girls had drawn on earlier. No doubt, like Madison's pawprints, mine were smudged. "They're silly."

"I like them."

My cheeks warmed, and there wasn't the summer heat to blame it on. For some reason, talking to him like this had my heart pounding, the fear of anyone spotting us at any second keeping me on edge. "You guys did great tonight."

Connor turned, casting a glance at the scoreboard. "Did we?"

"I don't know. I thought that's what people say."

A short laugh burst from him, and he shook his head. "So, what are you doing out here by yourself? I know you might be new to school sports, but everyone usually goes home once the game is over."

Connor was *teasing* me. I wasn't sure whether it irked me or made me want to laugh. "I'm waiting for Alex."

"Ah, right. Date night." Connor readjusted his grip on his set of shoulder pads in one hand, helmet around his other fingers. The fidget was accompanied by him casting a glance once more over his shoulder, inspecting to make sure we were still alone. "You should come to the homecoming game next week. It should be a good one."

"How can you be so sure?"

"I'll make sure it's a good one if you show."

His words settled oddly in my mind. Maybe it was the way he said it, with his usual half-smirk and light eyes. Instead, it was genuine.

"You'll have passed your math exam by then," I told him. "All this tutoring nonsense will be behind you."

After next week, after next Thursday, there wouldn't be a reason to meet after school anymore, wouldn't be a reason to see him anymore. There'd be no more lessons in love, no more talking about equations, no more worrying about anyone finding out. In all honesty, after Thursday, my life wouldn't be as complicated. I should be looking forward to it.

Then why did the thought deflate my good mood?

Connor had been shifting on his feet, like he was debating stepping closer. "You know, we could—"

"Babe!" The voice was a sudden shout, causing

Connor to turn around and me to stiffen. Jade rounded the corner where the field lockers were, with three football players behind her. I didn't recognize any of them. "There you are."

Connor took a large step back from me, but even he had to realize there was no playing it off. "Hey."

Unlike her co-captain, Jade's makeup hadn't smudged at all through the night—either that, or she'd touched it up. Her pawprints were intact and her eyeshadow glittered both blue and gold. Even from here, it flashed like a disco ball. "Oh, wow, did you get lost on your way to the library?"

I inwardly sighed. "The library closes at eight."

Two of the three football players kept walking, tossing a "see you in a bit, Bray" before heading toward the parking lot. The only three that remained were Connor, Jade, and the one other football player. After a moment of staring, I recognized him as the guy from the Wallflower last week, when Alex ditched me to sit with them.

Speaking of, was Alex reading his tuba a bedtime story before tucking it in? I glanced off in the direction of the school, squinting, but I couldn't see anyone coming this way.

Jade wrapped her arm around Connor's waist and leaned in. "What were you two talking about?"

"She congratulated me on the game," Connor replied, voice as stiff as his spine, and he edged away from his girlfriend. "We should get going. I need to shower before we head to Ashton's."

"I'm surprised you're here," Jade said as if Connor hadn't spoken, raising an eyebrow. "Have you been to any football games, like, ever?"

I made a soft noise under my breath, trying to appear unaffected even though my blood burned hot. "I'm touched that you noticed."

"Jeez, sorry," Alex gasped as he practically slammed into my side, catching at my arm to steady himself. "Mrs. Peters asked me...to help her put away...the music stands." Each phrase was punctuated with a wheezing inhale as his chest heaved. "Took forever. But I'm here."

Alex seemed to notice the Top Tier members surrounding us for the first time, because his body locked up with surprise. He went from nearly hyperventilating from running all the way here to not even breathing. "H-Hey."

"Hey, Alex." Jade's voice was significantly lighter when she spoke to him, as if she was speaking to a child. "I was saying how surprised I was to see Maisie here tonight."

"Oh, I know." Alex picked up my hand and gave it a hard squeeze. His eyes were bright, the way they got whenever he got the attention of someone popular. "I finally got her to say yes. Bribed her, really, with a date night."

Connor watched Alex quietly—really, he surveyed the whole scene quietly. He straightened his duffle bag strap, shifting on his feet like he was moments from walking away. The mask was in place with an effortless sort of ease, and I had no idea what kind of emotion lingered underneath.

Jade gestured at my school spirit apparel. "You probably would've preferred to stay at home with your math book, huh?"

"We do have a wedding to plan, after all," I deadpanned.

She blinked once and then laughed—like, *really* laughed. As if what I'd said had been the funniest thing in the world. Alex joined in, obviously only laughing because Jade was. She placed her hand on Connor's chest, leaning in as close as she could. "Did you hear that? Because she was voted Most Likely To: Marry a Math Book."

For the first time since the interruption, Connor's attention slid to me. Even though we'd spent nearly every weekday together for the past two weeks, it felt like we were launched back to square one in our tutoring relationship. Like he was back to the Connor Bray I couldn't stand. For having been to his grandmother's house and learning about his home life—and divulging a secret of my own—it almost felt as if we were strangers.

The hardness in his expression, the flatness, belied no connection at all. "Yeah, I heard." He gave Alex one of those chin nods. "Have a good date night."

I curled my fingers into fists, waiting for him to look over once more, but he didn't.

Jade huffed a little at Connor's abrupt departure, but it did the trick—she began following him, the other football player on her heels. She didn't even have time for a proper comeback, hustling to catch up with her boyfriend.

I stared at the back of his shirt, at the stiffness in his shoulders, until the shadows grew too thick. The only way to describe Alex when they walked away was *bedazzled*, the one-minute-long conversation more than enough to make his night. It took him a moment to turn to me, giving my hand another squeeze. "You ready to go to the movies?"

As I stared up at the pure, blank innocence on his face, I fought to recapture the happiness of earlier. Where I was standing next to Ava, Rachel, and Lacey in the crowd, when Connor's fleeting look of surprise and amusement made me chuckle. Now, I had a bad taste in my mouth.

"Can I get a raincheck?" I asked him. Alex's hand latched on to mine, but I felt very, very far away. "I'm not feeling very well."

Alex was quick to agree. "Sure, sure, I'll drive you home. A few guys from the band were doing a live tournament on our videogame, so that actually works out."

We made our way to the car silently, and the drive back to my house was even quieter. Why did I feel so... unsettled? Discomfort clung to me like a second skin, holding my happy thoughts hostage. Alex and Maisie time had been the whole reason I went to the stupid football game. But the thought of going to a movie with him, plastering on a false smile, left me too drained.

And *why* did I need a fake smile?

Alex waited until I got the front door unbolted before

backing down my driveway, flashing his lights once in farewell. I lifted a hand to wave, but he was already down the street.

The house was dark and empty as I let myself into it, basking in the quiet for a long moment. Our shadowy foyer was adorned with a few art pieces Mom had either acquired or painted herself, and I stared at a black and gray one. The different shades of colors were splattered across the canvas in a way that looked half-finished. I pressed my thumbnail against my mouth, wishing, not for the first time, that I could understand what they all went crazy over.

Instead, all I saw was a confusing, jumbled canvas of nothing.

That's what my insides felt like, really. Confusing, jumbled. Maybe I could relate with the art piece after all.

My steps were heavy as I ventured down the hall, not flicking on any lights, basking in the darkness. I sat down on my bed, wondering if Connor had gotten to the party yet.

Never in my life had I ever loaded up *Brentwood Babble* for gossip myself, but tonight, I opened the webpage. Ava had a little search bar on the main blog, and with slow fingers, I typed in one name. **Connor**.

And just like that, I fell down the rabbit hole of articles.

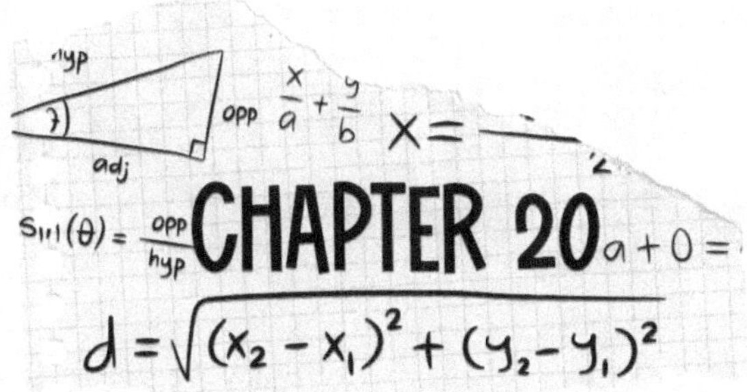

CHAPTER 20

Connor had joked about me being his stalker, and now it potentially could've been the case. I knew more about him than I should've.

My eyes burned as I scrolled through article after article, consuming so much content that my brain felt a little like goo. Words stopped making sense, but I read the blog posts anyway.

Connor Bray and Jade Dyer—New Power Couple???

Brentwood Star Athlete Scores the Winning Touchdown!

POLL: Jannor Is Off Again—When Do You Think They Will Reunite?

Ranking the Football Players—

Spoiler Alert: Connor Is At
the Top!

POLL: How Should Connor Ask Jade to
Junior Prom?

All of Connor's articles were entwined with football or Jade, like one couldn't exist without the other. Of course, I read all of them. I found myself neck-deep in it all. Jannor first got together September of sophomore year and had broken up a total of five times since. He was nominated MVP last year, something completely unheard of for a junior. For junior prom, Connor asked Jade by spelling out 2, 4, 6, 8 – *WILL U BE MY PROM DATE* in flowers on her front lawn.

That would've been around the time his parents lost their house, but in the photo attached to the *Brentwood Babble* post, with Jade at his side, he was beaming from ear to ear.

As I clicked on another article, my phone buzzed with a text message. It was one of Jozie's good morning texts, and I quickly sent back a heart emoji before going back to scrolling.

A second later, my phone began ringing with an incoming call.

"What are you doing up so early?" Jozie demanded, shock a heavy weight in her voice. "It's, like, five in the morning there."

My no-doubt bloodshot eyes widened. Sure enough,

the sky was a faint blue, hinting at a sleepy morning stretching across Brentwood. I'd been on *Babble* for hours. *Hours.*

For how zombie-like I felt, my answer came quickly. "I did what you suggested. Waking up before the sun, meditating, all that anxiety-reducing jazz."

Jozie made a smacking noise with her lips. "Fine, let's say I believe you. So, you know how I follow your friends on social media?"

"Okay?"

"Rachel posted an interesting photo last night. It was of the football game. Guess who I caught sipping a slushy in the background?"

I couldn't help but wince. "I was forced. At gunpoint. Ava can be very persuasive."

"Hey, I get it, I get it. It makes sense you're more interested in the school stuff your senior year." There was amusement in Jozie's voice, though, that lilt that sounded like *I-told-you-so.* "Sports can be fun, right?"

Inspiration struck at a possible segue. "Yeah, it wasn't that bad...and the football players aren't as bad as I thought."

"Ooh, like who? Did you talk to them? Anyone I know?"

I probably could've told Jozie about tutoring Connor. She was miles away at her art school. She didn't even check *Babble* anymore. I couldn't imagine her saying anything to anybody, but after weeks of keeping the information, I couldn't break my promise to Connor now. "Well, Landon Settler was really nice. So was..." Crap, what was another football player's name? Without thinking, I added, "Reed Manning."

"Isn't Reed Rachel's brother?"

"Uh, yeah." Her brother who had also quit the team this season. Thankfully, Jozie wasn't aware of that. "And Connor Bray was really cool, surprisingly. I talked to him a bit after the game. Do you remember Connor?"

It was a stupid question, because *of course* she remembered Connor. She'd graduated last spring. She was slow to respond, though, and I knew by the hesitation that I'd screwed up. I should've been more careful. "Why are you asking?"

Well, I guess my stealth went out the window when I was running on zero sleep. "Oh, uh—trying to make conversation."

"If you're thinking of getting involved with him... don't, Maisie. Okay?"

The thought stirred my stomach, like a bird was fluttering around in it. "Ew, Jozie, I'm not *getting involved with him*. I was only asking a question. Besides, he's dating Jade." My brain easily conjured up the image of her kissing him on the football field, like she was marking her territory.

"I'm just saying, everything he does is *super* scrutinized. Connor's the poster child for Brentwood, and I know you know that. I mean, look at your friend's blog, for crying out loud."

I had looked at Ava's blog. For five hours straight. My lips twitched into a frown, though, uncertain where she was going.

"I'd hate for someone to snap a picture of you talking to him and have it spiral out of control. Those people do things for the attention. It's toxic, and not something you want to get caught up in."

Like nearly being spotted in the equipment closet with him? *Ha.* "Yeah, I know, I know."

The other end of the line grew quiet for a moment, leaving a white static sort of sound in my ear. I picked at the edge of my comforter, feeling where the material had thinned from years of plucking at it. "I was on the Most Likely To list this year."

I wasn't sure why I'd told her, or why I blurted the words as if they were some grand thing. Bringing it up now didn't make sense. I'd put all that behind me. I'd already dealt with it. It wasn't a big enough deal, and definitely not something I wanted to talk about with my sister, who had never been on the list.

"It's whatever," I said immediately, grimacing. "It's not that big of a deal. Ava was on it too. It's like a rite of passage, right?"

Jozie didn't respond right away, almost like she was thinking about her words first. "What was your label?"

"It was a new one—Marry a Math Book."

Jozie fell quiet once more on the other end, and I had to check to make sure the call hadn't dropped. Talking to her like this, in the early morning, reminded me of times that we'd both stay up chatting.

I closed my eyes and brought my blankets up to my chin.

"Don't get caught up in it," Jozie said at last, her voice

considerably quieter now. "I know you. You say it's not a big deal, but you've probably thought about it a million times since. But seriously. Don't get caught up in all that drama."

It's too late, I wanted to tell her. "You know me," I said, searching for levity to interject into my voice. My well was running empty. "I'm dramaphobic. I repel drama. No drama for me."

Jozie's ghostly laugh filtered over the phone. "Go to sleep, Maisie," she said softly, and I could almost pretend she was in the same room now, like her words were tucking me in. "It's too early to be awake, even for me. We can talk more later."

A weird seed of disappointment blossomed in me, but drowsiness finally tickled my eyelids. The dark was starting to lull me closer, and my sister's smooth voice wasn't helping. "You didn't ask why I asked about Connor," I mumbled, the words practically gibberish.

"I'm going to pretend you didn't. I'm going to forget you asked anything about him. And Maisie?" She hesitated, making sure she had my full attention. Sleep tugged me again, and this time, I gave in. "You should forget about him, too."

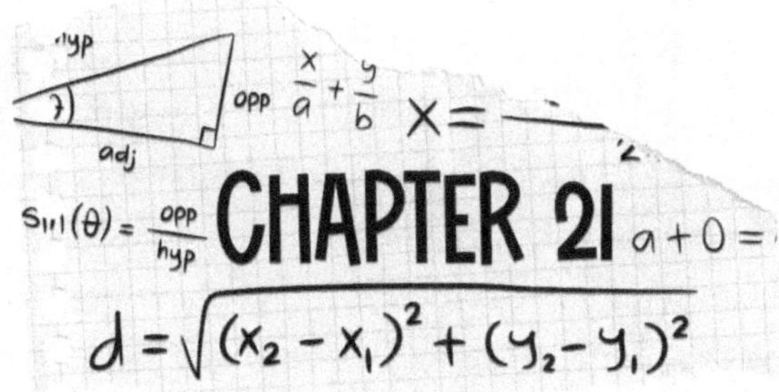

CHAPTER 21

Spirit week. The week where everyone went all-out dressing for whatever the day's theme was. Everyone's goal was to be the top-voted outfit for the day, and the poll could be found on *Brentwood Babble*, of course. It meant that the outfits were crazy, over the top, or full-on glam.

AKA, the week from hell.

"Today is pajama day," Ava said as I walked up to her in the hallway Monday morning, eyeing my jeans with distaste. She wore a matching silk pajama set, the pink and white stripes making her look like a glammed-up jailer. "Where are your pjs, girl?"

"I didn't get the memo," I responded apologetically as I clutched my backpack strap. As soon as I stepped into the building, I'd sought her out, and of course she'd been at her locker. "Hey, I have a question—"

"Ava posted it on *Babble*," Rachel interrupted as she came up to us, carrying her books in one arm. She wore a simple black top paired with a pair of pajama pants, ones with little rubber ducks on them. She even had an eye mask perched on her forehead. "You really didn't see?"

I wondered if she posted it *after* my Friday night deep dive. If not, I didn't know how I'd missed it.

Ava patted me on the shoulder, passing over her cell. "Here, I can send you a screenshot if you want me to."

I took the phone reluctantly, peering at the screen.

Monday — Pajama Day
Tuesday — Twin Day
Wednesday — Country vs City
Thursday — Athletes vs Mathletes
Friday — Blue & Gold!

"Athletes vs mathletes?" I read, forehead puckering. "How does someone dress up as a mathlete?"

"Glasses with tape in the middle, suspenders—the whole nine yards," Alex said as he came up to us, placing his heavy hand on my shoulder and giving it a squeeze. He wore a pair of gray sweatpants, not going too far out for today. "Not all mathletes are like you, Brain."

I shrugged it off, his words sparking annoyance in me. It felt like I was running into joke after joke about math, and I was starting to become a ticking time bomb—who knew when I'd blow. "So the stupid 'stereotypical' smart person? That's such bull."

"It *is* dumb," Ava insisted, shutting her locker and turning to me. Her expression was sympathetic, and she gave my arm a squeeze. "Don't sweat it, Maisie."

The question that had been bouncing around in my mind all morning resurfaced, but I couldn't figure out how to bring it up without being obvious. Especially not in front of Alex, who eyed me strangely. "What?" I asked him.

"You seem like you're feeling better," he responded quickly. "You hadn't texted all weekend, so I thought maybe you were still sick."

"Still—" I cut myself off sharply, remembering all at once my excuse to get out of date night. "Oh. Yeah. I'm— I'm starting to feel better."

Rachel and Ava didn't say anything, but they looked at each other, clueing me in that they could see through the lie. I wondered if Alex could too, or if he couldn't read me as well as they could.

"Well, maybe we can hang out tonight? After you're finished with tutoring?"

Warily, I gave him a nod. "That could work."

The five-minute bell rang above us, and Alex was the first to back away. "I'll see you all at lunch?" he confirmed with a thumbs-up, turning to head to his homeroom.

Rachel went off next with a little wave, and I looped my arm through Ava's. "Can I ask you a question?"

"Fire away," she said as we started down the hallway, dodging student after pajama-wearing student. "Although I'm half asleep, so my answer might suck."

"Did anything happen over the weekend?" I asked, hoping I sounded casual. Nonchalant. "Like, anything...dramatic?"

Ava stopped, interest piqued. "Did you hear something?"

"No, no." I swallowed hard. *Think!* "I mean, I thought I heard that there was a party Friday night, and you never sent over an article for me to proof."

Ava gave a soft laugh. "I knew about the party. It was a 'Jocks Only' party. Everyone who attends is super tight-lipped about what happens. I never get any tips from those." She puckered her lips. "In fact, things have been slow all weekend. I am glad, though, that Jannor is okay after the whole equipment closet incident. I guess it *was* a misunderstanding."

We'd gotten to the classroom door then, but I didn't pass through. The unsettled feeling from Friday night had been biding its time, finding me once more as I passed through the halls of Brentwood High.

Ava halted on the other side of the threshold, turning back to me. "You okay?"

"Yeah," I said, but took a step backward. "I forgot to stop by my locker this morning. I'll be right back."

"You've got three minutes!" she called after me, but I'd already turned down the hallway.

My locker. I hadn't stopped at it this morning. My history book was in my backpack from last night's homework, so I didn't need to grab it this morning, but I couldn't stop thinking about my locker. Something other than textbooks might've been inside.

I stopped in front of the metal door, staring at the smooth blue paint. My heart fluttered strangely in my chest, wondering—hoping—that something would be waiting for me.

With a slow hand, I spiraled through my combination, easing the door open. A piece of paper fluttered to the ground. It was a ripped-out piece of notebook paper, edges frayed, with handwriting that I knew as well as my own by this point.

> MY GRANDMA NEEDS HELP WITH SOMETHING AFTER PRACTICE, SO CAN WE MEET LATER TONIGHT INSTEAD? AROUND SEVEN? THERE'S A COFFEE SHOP IN JEFFERSON CALLED EXPRESSO WHERE WE COULD MEET?
>
> —C

I read the message once, and then twice, before crumpling the paper into my fist. By the time I started back down the hallway, practically sprinting before the bell, my mind already raced along with me with possible excuses to give Alex.

$$+ - \times \div$$

I'd been expecting a quaint little café when I walked into Expresso's, but was instead greeted with an almost warehouse-like space, more industrial than cozy. The exposed ductwork along the ceiling paired with brick walls was aesthetically interesting, and did a great job at holding my interest as I waited for Connor. The smooth jazz leaking from the speakers was top quality, a quiet soundtrack as I flipped absently through the Algebra II textbook.

This time, Connor's lateness didn't bother me. I could've sat there all night, inhaling the scent of crushed coffee beans, the sweetness of the sugar.

The doors chimed a few times as new customers walked in and waded out, and some stuck around to work on homework themselves. I recognized a guy in the corner—or, really, I recognized his varsity jacket, which was the red and black colors of Jefferson High. He was sipping from his disposable coffee cup, scrolling through something on his phone.

Each time the door chimed, he looked up as if he were expecting someone too.

My awareness of him disappeared as the coffee-house's doors swung inward once more. "Sorry I'm late," Connor said in a rushed voice, hair blown a bit to the side by the wind, clutching his backpack in front of him. "I'll buy your coffee to make up for it."

"I don't drink coffee," I said, watching as he deposited everything into one of the chairs across from me. "But I do drink hot chocolate."

Connor knocked his knuckles against the table's surface, eyes softening on me. "One hot chocolate coming up. Don't go anywhere."

I snorted a little at the prospect, reaching across the table for his duffle bag. Might as well unload his book while he got our things. We were starting the second to last chapter tonight, all about descriptive statistics, which is one of the harder elements of Algebra II. I brought out Connor's notebook, flipping it open to a random page.

My name greeted me on the paper, mixed in with equations and number lines. My first thought was that it must've been from the day that I wrote my name down for him, but my cell number was nowhere in sight. And my name wasn't in my handwriting. It was in Connor's.

I'll have to write it down, he'd said. *I won't remember it unless I write it down.*

I turned the page to the next blank one and dropped it onto the table, tenderness tugging at my heart.

"Large hot chocolate for the math queen," Connor announced as he set the to-go cup down in front of me, a red lightning bolt printed on the side of the cup. "And one for me. It's late for coffee, anyway."

"Thanks," I said softly as he eased into the metal chair across from me. The last time I'd seen him had been at the football game on Friday, and the once easy atmosphere seemed stiff now. "We should dive right in. This is one of the last sections, and it's a confusing one."

Connor took a drink from his hot chocolate before setting it aside, digging a pencil out of his duffle bag. "Aye, aye, tutor."

He worked diligently, with the smooth jazz keeping pace. As he copied down the instructions, following the new routine we'd established, I tried to picture him scrawling my name in his notebook, but it felt too bizarre. Bizarre, but the image made me smile. Just a little.

I brought out the note he'd slid into my locker earlier today, flattening it out and tearing off an edge until it was a square. "How was your weekend?" I found myself asking. Even though such a casual question was weird to ask, there was no way to *not* ask it. Not when my pestering curiosity was going to eat me alive.

"Uneventful," he responded without elaboration. "How was yours?"

I thought about my phone call with Jozie and our topic of conversation, and brought one corner of the paper across itself. "Uneventful."

"How was your date with Alex?"

The question settled over my skin thickly, one that had a straightforward answer and an answer that felt more truthful. "I think you were right."

Connor's pencil halted in its transcribing, and he looked up with only his eyes. The warm glow of the café made the hazel in his gaze appear golden. "About which part?"

I traced a finger along my origami in progress, but I didn't feel happy on the inside. Instead, I was a ball of confliction. "You said that you didn't think people could fall in love in high school. I...I think you're right about that."

"What happened?"

"Nothing happened. Nothing at all. I've been thinking. About me, about us—I mean, Alex and me." I paused in my folding to grab my hot chocolate cup, bringing it to my lips. "I mean, I'm only seventeen. What do I know about love?"

The hot chocolate scorched my mouth as I took a

drink, burning a trail of fire down my throat. Connor did nothing but study me.

"I'm slacking," he said finally.

"Slacking?"

"I'm a terrible tutor. My love advice isn't working."

I nearly snorted at the seriousness in his tone. "Maybe I should've chosen someone who isn't fighting with his girlfriend all the time. Although it looks like she forgave you for the closet thing."

"You're talking about the kiss at the game on Friday?" he guessed, picking his pencil back up and tapping it against his notebook. "Trust me, if people weren't around to witness it, she wouldn't have been kissing me."

"She only kissed you because there was an audience?"

"She does a lot of things only because there's an audience." Connor went back to work copying from the textbook for only a moment before he paused again. "I change my answer."

"You have an eraser," I said, pointing at his pencil. "Except you're copying down the practice equation, so the steps should be right."

"I think you can fall in love in high school. As long as it's with the right person."

His words caused both relief and a debilitating sense of unease to wrench through me, two halves of a confusing whole. "You think?"

He slowly nodded. "I do."

I focused back on my rose. I'd stopped mid-fold and had no idea where to pick back up. My brain stalled out on what fold came next, unable to work through the geometry in front of me.

If I didn't love Alex, would I have been so upset when he left me at the Wallflower? But then again, if I *did* love Alex, wouldn't I want to spend time with him, even if it meant watching him play videogames?

If I did love him, would I be wondering *what if?*

Connor placed his hand over mine, half-obscuring my paper rose. His palm was a little rough against the top of my hand, but the warmth radiating from his skin was undeniably pleasant. Once more, the topsy-turvy roller-coaster sensation flipped my stomach. I tried to swallow down the strange feeling, but it roared up like a fanned flame, surrounding me.

"You have to show me how to do this sometime," Connor said, trailing his fingers over the edge of the flower. The touch was delicate, careful not to dent the paper. "They always look so cool. You said origami counts as math, right?"

"That's geometry, not Algebra II. I'm only tutoring you for Algebra."

"Dang," he breathed dejectedly, but he ran a hand over his lips to cover his smile.

These feelings. It was in that moment that their meaning hit me. It was as if I told a doctor about my symptoms and they came back with a clear answer, one that hit the nail on the head. The weird fluttering in my stomach, the way my heart would skip a beat. *Do you like Connor Bray?*

The door chimed as someone walked in, and I jerked

my hand back, dropping the rose. *Deny, deny, deny,* my body screamed, but I couldn't.

And then I didn't have time to. My gaze caught on the person passing through the doors, recognition blasting through me. It was the sort of full-body jolt, like an electric current ran through my body, adrenaline chasing on its heels. Because the person who'd walked through the door lasered in on me, jaw dropped.

Madison.

CHAPTER 22

$$d = \sqrt{(x_2 - x_1)^2 + (y_2 - y_1)^2}$$

adison looked dressed for a date, with a blue floral sundress and a light jean jacket thrown over her shoulders. As soon as she spotted us, her wide gaze went from me to Connor and then back again, almost as if she were watching a tennis match. Each back and forth, she appeared more and more alarmed, until her gaze finally settled on Connor's hand stretched across the table.

Once Connor turned to find what I was gaping at, he cursed.

Steeling herself, Madison began her storming, shoes creating little clicks as she came across the room. "What is going on?" Madison demanded in disbelief, voice a low tremble. "Seriously. What the hell is going on?"

My heart launched into a dead sprint, barreling in my chest without hopes of calming down anytime soon. "Madison—"

"No, don't *Madison* me. Okay? Because you're going to explain what *that*"—she gestured frantically at the table where our hands had been—"was while explaining why you're—" Madison pressed a hand to her forehead, cheeks pink with frustration. "Dear God, *please* tell me you're not here on a date."

"No! Of course not." I grabbed the edge of his Algebra II textbook and wiggled it. "I'm tutoring him. See? *Math.*"

She glanced down as if seeing the materials for the first time, noting the hot chocolate cups. It was one of Connor's rules—discretion—and I'd crossed the line. Then again, we were backed into a corner. I didn't have a choice. "Tutoring," she echoed, skeptical.

Connor rubbed a hand through his brown hair, tugging on the ends. "I have to retake my Algebra II exam on Friday. Maisie's been helping me study."

Her voice was accusing. "Jade never said."

"Jade doesn't know," he returned, voice flat. "No one does."

Madison's mind was whirling a mile a minute; I could see it in her eyes. Her lips twisted in their pixie-like grimace. I expected her to ask why we were keeping it a secret—it was a legitimate question. The boy who'd been sitting at the window had stood up and was now focused on our table. No, not focused on our table, focused on *Madison.* Like she'd been the person he'd been waiting on.

"You two are seriously..." She trailed off with a harsh laugh, glancing around the café in disbelief. "You have a death wish, you know that? Lie to your girlfriend, check. Meet up *in public*, check. What if I was someone else, huh? Someone with a cell phone to text *Babble?*"

I inwardly flinched at the idea of someone submitting a tip to *Babble*. To have Ava find out that way was almost as scary as Jade finding out.

"That's what happened in the hookup closet, right? Don't be so surprised. I knew you were in there with someone, Connor. It was Maisie, right?" She turned to me. "You were tutoring in there? What the hell is wrong with the library?"

My thoughts had practically mirrored that sentiment exactly.

The boy who had been watching the conversation stepped up behind Madison then, his head appearing over her shoulder. His blonde hair was long and tucked behind his ears, his bright blue gaze focused only on her as he gently trailed a finger down her arm. "People are beginning to stare."

The familiarity in the stranger's voice caused me to squint at him, that and the delicate way he touched her. Madison relaxed ever so slightly at the contact, knowing exactly who it was without even looking. "You asked *Maisie* to be your tutor?" she demanded of Connor, who focused on the table like Madison wasn't there. "Seriously?"

"It's not like Brentwood has a lot of tutors."

"Did you ask her before or after the Most Likely Tos?"

If possible, Connor froze further. I couldn't figure out why the answer mattered. Who cared if he needed a tutor before or after I was nominated Most Likely To: Marry a Math Book? Connor didn't break her stare, the mask of zero emotion perfectly in place. "Don't tell Jade."

He had to see that it was a ridiculous request. Madison had declared her loyalties to Jade years ago—no way Madison would double back on her simply because Connor asked.

"Oh?" She folded her arms across her chest. "And why not?"

"If you tell her about the tutoring, I can tell her about this." Connor tipped his chin at the boy over her shoulder. "Because I'm pretty sure I remember you telling Jade you'd stop seeing him."

The two were caught in a stare down, one that made me shift uncomfortably. I couldn't bring myself to check and see if anyone at the coffee shop *was* starting to stare, like the blonde boy had claimed, but I couldn't deny that it felt like we were causing a scene.

"You wouldn't," Madison said finally. "I know you, Connor. You're too much of a peacemaker to snitch."

It was funny—as soon as she said it, I had to agree with her. I couldn't imagine Connor truly using this as blackmail. "I would." I sat up straighter, totally over letting her plow her way through the conversation. "I've done it before. My best friend runs *Babble*, after all. I could have her posting about it in minutes."

Once more, we were in a standoff, waiting for the other to back down first. Madison narrowed her eyes at me, like we were caught in a no-blinking contest. I wouldn't be blinking first.

"Fine," she ultimately said, voice deceptively light.

She spoke to Connor's profile, voice icy. "I won't say anything. But when everything blows up in your face, I'll be the first to say I told you so."

With one last, well-placed glare at both Connor and me, Madison turned on her heel, grabbed ahold of the blonde boy's hand, and strode straight out of the coffeehouse.

The residual tension lingered even after they both walked out, too thick to talk around. I stared at the textbooks in front of us, and for the first time, math read like gibberish to me. My limbs shook as unused adrenaline worked its way through my bloodstream. What had we been expecting, meeting in public like this? Madison was right—it was a wonder we hadn't been caught yet.

Connor's mask had slipped at some point after Madison stormed off. Tightness lingered behind his eyes now, along with something similar to worry.

"I don't think she'll say anything," I told him, desperate to ease the stiff atmosphere. "And I don't think anything will blow up in your face."

In an instant, the mask was back in place, shielding his inner thoughts from me for the first time in a long while. Connor picked up his pencil and tapped it against his notebook twice. "Yeah, you're right. Let's get back to our tutoring session."

Connor began copying the rest of the page down, but even when it was time to walk him through the steps, everything had shifted. His mood, my mood, the friendly banter between us. Madison's appearance had dashed all of that. It felt more like my previous tutoring sessions now, less personal, more surface level. By the time I brought my hot chocolate to my lips, the temperature had cooled considerably, leaving a lukewarm taste in my mouth.

My happy place was anywhere a mathematics worksheet was, even if that place was the Center Inspire art gallery. Mom had enlisted my help after school Tuesday to fold up brochures, and once I'd finished—about a thousand paper cuts later—I was free to finally work on a sheet Mrs. Diego had given me. After spending so much time on Algebra II with Connor, it was a breath of fresh air to get back to the wonderful world of calculus.

∫cot²x dx equals to...?

Without missing a beat, I filled in the circle of the multiple-choice question. *-cot x − x + C.*

It was easy to get lost in functions and integrals, and with the way that life was playing out lately, math made for an easy distraction.

Until Mom stepped into the doorway of the small curator's office, putting her hands on her hips. "Maisie, this isn't what I asked you to do." She peered around for the box she'd left with me. "Did you finish folding up all the brochures?"

I reached down and tugged it out from under the desk, the folded flyers visible on top. "Yep."

"Are you sure you folded them the right way?"

I wasn't sure if there was another way to trifold a

flyer, but I nodded. "I did it exactly how you showed me to."

It'd actually been a project perfect for me. Jozie would've been the one to help hang posters and pick out where each art piece should go, but folding brochures was a lot like my origami, each little line a new geometric point.

Despite this, Mom had to double-check my work, and she sifted through the pamphlets with a sharp eye. "The exhibit starts tomorrow, so things need to be perfect."

"Odd that these weren't folded earlier."

"The printer was delayed in dropping them off. Trust me, it shaved off a few years of my life when they were delivered unfolded."

She probably wasn't lying about that, since even in the snapshot of this moment, Mom looked *tired*. Pinched lips and a slouched posture. Mom loved her job, but it was clear the Brentwood exhibit was more taxing than her previous ones. It made sense, given that this was one of the biggest displays with the most art pieces they'd put on yet. And especially since it was homecoming week, everyone was all Brentwood High crazy.

Her gaze dropped to what lay on her desk. "Do you have to be doing that right now?"

"My homework?"

"Why don't you come help me set up some artwork?" she said, putting her hand on the back of the desk chair, angling me around. "Or come help your father finish some touchup painting for the sculpture room."

"I'm not a worker," I objected, rooting myself in the

chair. I was totally okay with pitching in a little with the brochures, but the idea of doing either of those things made me frown. "Why can't I just stay here?"

"You should do something other than coop up with your math sheets." Without giving me a chance to respond, Mom swiped up the integrals worksheet, folding it in half and stepping away from the desk. "Come on, let's find you something to do."

"Mom," I began, but she was already sauntering out of her office, leaving me and the brochures behind.

I slumped back in the desk chair, staring at the abstract canvas on the wall near the door. I still had my pencil, but the distraction I'd desperately needed had been abducted. Of course it had. Heaven forbid I cooped myself up with *math*. If I'd been Jozie, working on a sketch, would Mom's response have been different?

No doubt. She'd probably have offered to sharpen my pencils for me.

I wished we could've seen eye to eye. That even though I didn't fit the Matthews mold, Mom accepted my passions. Maybe even a little bit, I wished I *did* fit the mold.

With a sigh, I rose out of the desk chair to follow her out into the gallery, thinking, not for the first time, that it would've been nice if she'd understood.

CHAPTER 23

It was Wednesday night that I got a phone call. I'd been in the middle of deciphering a Calculus II worksheet Mrs. Diego printed for me when the vibration shook my desk, the loudness in the previously silent room startling me. Mom was still at the gallery, and Dad had gone to take her leftovers from dinner. With ten minutes until ten o'clock, I'd been finishing up this worksheet before going to bed early.

Until Connor called.

"Are you home?" His words came immediately, a rush to beat me before I could even say *hello*.

"Why?" I asked, but put the pencil down, knowing my concentration had been shot. "What's wrong?"

"Nothing's *wrong*, I, uh—I'm in your driveway."

The words speared through me as sharp as an arrow. I was already moving when I demanded, "You're *what*?"

And sure enough, when I parted my curtains, his SUV was parked in the driveway, lights off. I could just make out a figure sitting in the driver's seat. "Can we talk? Are your parents home?"

The two questions should've been easy enough to comprehend, but I found myself reeling, as if he were speaking a different language. Connor Bray was *here*. And he wanted to...what? *Come inside?* I blinked hard, but the car didn't disappear. "N-No, they're not home, but—I mean—I guess you can come in."

Connor Bray was here, and he wanted to talk, and I'd said *yes*.

Frantically, I pushed my glasses up onto my forehead to scrub off the acne cream that I had on, yanking down my hair from its loose pony. I'd already changed in to my pajamas, which of course had to be a nightgown with a snoozing owl on the front—it would've been perfect for PJ day—and I couldn't find my robe anywhere. There was absolutely no way I was opening the door in my nightgown, but his knock echoed through the house, indicating that I had no time to change.

Gritting my teeth, I grabbed a throw blanket from my bed and wrapped it around my shoulders, rushing to the door.

When I eased it open, I found Connor on the other side dressed in his pajamas too. His dark green pants had little footballs on them, and his shirt had a logo with a pair of headphones in the middle and words curved around them. He didn't grab a jacket, but then again, it wasn't that cold out. "Hey."

I tightened the blanket around me. "Hi."

Connor glanced down at the welcome mat. "Can I come inside?"

"Oh. Right." Jerkily, I stepped back, allowing him

enough room to step into the foyer. He seemed so much bigger in the small space, taking up too much oxygen in the room. "You don't have to take your shoes off."

Connor toed the sneakers off anyway, not bothering to untie the laces. He had on a pair of black socks, but they were mismatched, one a solid black and the other black with a white stripe across the toes. "You were right," he said as he tilted his head up at the art on the walls, purely impassive. "It does feel like an art gallery in here."

Connor looked at the art piece that had always puzzled me, all the gray tones and splattering. "You came over to check out the décor?" I meant to sound teasing, but the shrill note to my voice ran along the words. It'd been weird for me to go to his house, but it was absolutely bizarre that he was at mine.

He pulled out a piece of paper from his pocket, unfolding it and smoothing out the creases. "Can you check my answers?"

"You came over so I'd review your math problems?" I glanced from the paper extended in his grip to his face, and gave a slight chuckle. "At ten at night?"

"Apparently so."

"You could've texted me a picture of them, you know. Or waited until tomorrow."

"I'm getting nervous," Connor admitted. "About the test. About passing."

His presence made a bit more sense now. It wasn't about checking these answers; he was seeking reassurance. "Let's go sit in the living room."

His footsteps were silent, but the floorboards creaked ever so slightly. Our living room wasn't that big, which meant there weren't many places to sit. There was the three-person couch or the recliner in the corner of the room, but the recliner was too far from the couch to make conversation natural. So when Connor sat down on the couch, I sat down on the opposite side, leaving a cushion between us.

"I'm sorry I came over without checking with you first," he said as I started scanning the problems. He'd done the review set that I was going to have him attempt tomorrow. "It's kind of terrifying, the weight this test has. I mean, if I fail, I won't graduate on time. That's...insane."

I used my finger to follow through the math expression, wincing as I caught an error. "Did you check your work?"

He tensed. "Ah, no. I didn't think to."

"Here, check your work before I grade it," I said, passing it back. I picked up one of the colored pencils on the coffee table; Mom left them littered everywhere. "You can use this to change anything if you spot it."

Connor's expression was grim. "I'll have to remember to double check my work Friday."

"Triple check." I leaned against the couch arm, pulling one leg underneath me. The blanket's warmth made me a wee bit less uncomfortable, thankfully, as did the even breaths I drew in and let out. "And don't worry. You've absorbed the past two weeks' information really well. It'll be okay."

And I believed that. I'd thought the past two weeks

would've been so much harder than they were. He continually surprised me.

"I keep thinking about how terrified I am of anyone finding out."

It made me think of Madison showing up Monday night, threatening to spill the beans we'd kept sealed this entire time. Even after everything, he was so worried about what others thought. It made me shake my head. "I'm sure you're not the only athlete who's failed a class before."

"You can fail a class, but you can't fail a grade. It's like an unspoken thing."

"Well, it's a stupid thing. You shouldn't worry about what other people think of you."

I stared at his hands as they gripped the paper. Some people bit their nails when they were nervous, but he portrayed his nerves in a different way, from fidgeting his fingers to drumming them along the tabletop. They were always moving when he was anxious.

Connor let out a soft sigh. "After tomorrow, we won't see each other anymore."

"We'll see each other at school."

Connor didn't respond, and I wondered if he was thinking the same thing I was: even if we saw each other at school, it wouldn't be the same. We wouldn't say hi. We'd lock eyes for a few seconds, maybe even get close enough to speak, but neither of us would. Connor wouldn't because he couldn't step outside of his world, and I wouldn't because I'd be too afraid that he wouldn't say anything back.

"Thank you for helping me," he said at last, glancing around my living room. "I wouldn't have a chance if it weren't for you. And...thank you for keeping it a secret."

"I'm sorry I wasn't more understanding in the beginning."

Connor gave a little laugh. "You truly weren't. You bit me. I think I still have the mark."

I reached over and hit his shoulder, but it did nothing more than cause him to laugh. It was a nice break from the tension in his voice, a reprieve from his unease. I wanted to make him laugh again.

"Where are your parents?" he asked then, glancing around the empty living room. "It's a little late for a weeknight, isn't it?"

"They're at the gallery. Mom has that big Brentwood school spirit exhibit this week, so she's been staying late. The big night is Friday, and she's being neurotic about every little thing."

Connor's eyes were focused on me. "You're not like them, huh? You prefer numbers over paints."

"You don't know how many times I wished I was more like them." I let out a little exhale. "If only to understand them when they gush about that stuff. If only so they'd understand me when I want to gush about stuff."

"I can't picture you liking art instead of math, you know. You're very...analytical. Straightforward."

"My mom says straightforward art is the worst, because there's no deeper meaning. There's no emotion behind it."

Connor frowned, a severe twist to his features. "You're not a piece of art."

I shrugged a little.

"I like you like this, though." Connor dipped his chin a little. "You know what you want. What you like. You don't play games, don't beat around the bush. Any less straightforward and you wouldn't be you."

I pinched my lips together to keep from grinning, because his words speared through me, leaving heat to trail in their wake. "I bet you're used to that, huh? Girls who play games?"

My thoughts went to Jade, who played with Connor's feelings as if they meant nothing to him. As if they never meant anything to him.

"I should apologize to you," he said slowly, staring down at his paper. "I shouldn't have given you love advice. I...I wasn't in a position to offer it."

"Because you don't believe in love in high school?"

"I haven't told anyone this, but—"

I reached across the couch cushion and placed my hand on his shoulder, digging my fingers in instinctively. "This is another secret? I can't keep any more secrets, Connor," I said helplessly. "There's already so much I'm keeping from my friends. From Alex."

"But I—I want you to know." Connor angled toward me, shifting closer into the middle cushion, approaching the line. "You should know it."

"What's the point? Like you said, after tomorrow, it's not like we'll talk again. I don't need to know."

His chest rose and fell steadily as he breathed

through his nose, looking on the verge of saying some-thing for several seconds, but he marinated on whatever thought was in his head. *It's not like we'll talk again.* It was a valid point, but then again, why not learn just one more secret, then? If we weren't ever going to speak again, what would one more secret hurt?

"We could still talk," Connor murmured, setting the piece of paper he'd been gripping down. "We could still be friends."

I let my hand slide off his shoulder to rest on the couch between us, the words echoing in my mind. "Are we friends?"

"There's that straightforward quality," he said with an easy chuckle, sobering quickly. "I'd like to think we're friends, Maisie."

"I can't be secret friends with you," I whispered. My voice came out small even though I hadn't meant for it to. "I can't keep you from Alex." *Or Ava or Rachel,* I should've tacked on, but I didn't. I didn't know why I didn't.

Even though there were so many things I wanted to say, to ask, I bit my tongue, waiting for his response.

"I don't want you to be a secret friend," he said, tracing my hand with his eyes. "You deserve more than to be a secret."

I tried to exhale, but it got stuck in my windpipe. When had he become this way? So quiet, vulnerable? When had he gone from a stuck-up jock to someone I enjoyed being around? Little things about him coming to light in pieces, slowly forming the entire puzzle.

And I liked the puzzle.

He still watched my hand. "I wish things were different."

"Different how?"

Connor didn't reply. Instead, he reached out and drew his finger along the couch cushion just beside mine, coming as close as he could without touching me. Something about it caused my heart to kickstart. If I moved my hand just a fraction of an inch, we'd be touching.

There was a soft knock at the front door, and it startled me away from Connor. As our voices lowered, we'd both ended up tilting across the middle cushion. I pushed to my feet to give myself distance, refusing to look him in the eye, not even thinking about who could've been on the other side of the door.

If I'd stopped to think, I would've realized how odd it was that someone was knocking at almost ten o'clock at night. If I'd stopped to think, I would've told Connor to duck down behind the couch in case it was Madison, having spotted his SUV out front. Because when I opened the door, Connor was in plain view on the couch.

It wasn't Madison, though.

I found Alex on the threshold, hands in his shorts pockets. "Hey. That car out front. You know, it looks a lot like"—he'd been doing a quick scan of the room behind me, locking on to the figure sitting on the couch—"Connor's car."

You could've heard a pin drop, my living room was *that* silent.

"Connor Bray?" Alex said a bit more firmly, stepping

past me and into the house. Neither Connor nor I moved. Not an inch.

He's not really here, my brain chanted in denial, but I slowly got to my feet. *You're imagining Alex in your living room at ten at night.*

Except the rigidness of Connor's spine told a different story. "H-Hey, man."

"W-What are you doing here?" I asked. Shock fully consumed Alex's reaction, but I was certain at any moment a different emotion would take over.

"I wanted to stop by and see if I could borrow a pair of your old glasses for tomorrow," Alex said slowly, and to his credit, he sounded more confused than angry. *Very* confused, as if he was questioning the reality of this moment. "What...what are *you* doing here, Connor?"

"Maisie's been tutoring me," Connor said quickly, and he rose from the couch as he did so, putting distance between him and me. "In Algebra II. I have to retake my exam."

For how long he'd been pressuring me to keep the secret, the truth of the situation rolled pretty easily off his tongue. The confusion hadn't left Alex's eyes, though. "In your pajamas?"

I looked down at my nightgown, then at the blanket I'd dropped on the couch in surprise. *Crap.* "I was about to go to bed."

"With him here?"

"No!" I tried to keep my voice level, but it came out sharp. "Of course not."

Alex crept deeper into the living room, glancing

around. "If you're tutoring," he said slowly, "where are your books?"

Even though I knew I'd only find empty space, my gaze darted to the coffee table, to the couch cushions. The excuse I'd used with Madison on Monday, gesturing at the Algebra II textbook, wasn't available in this situation. Connor had only brought the piece of notebook paper, not any of his other things. My math book was all the way upstairs. Yes, I *had it*, but Alex would no doubt ask why I didn't have it out if we were studying.

But there wasn't a drop of anger in Alex's eyes, only bewilderment. He genuinely couldn't decipher the situation in front of him. For zero reason at all, that caused heat to spike through me, expanding from the center of my chest. "I've been tutoring him for two weeks now. You can ask Mrs. Diego."

"*Two weeks?*" Alex's eyes widened. "You've been tutoring him for two weeks, and you never said anything?"

"I told you." My voice was wickedly calm for how fast my heart was beating. "It's confidential."

"You—you—I would've thought that if you were tutoring the most popular guy at Brentwood High that you would've told me."

Something in me snapped. I sidestepped the couch while folding my arms over my chest. "Why? Would you have shown up at our tutoring sessions? Thought that would've been your 'in' into the popular crowd?"

"What's wrong with showing up? We could've talked, could've gotten ice cream—"

"Only because Connor would've been there," I cut him off, the burning in my chest increasing to a sweltering degree. "Because you wouldn't have done that with just me."

The severe words had come from a small corner of me that wanted to see a reaction from him, that wanted to knock the bewilderment off his face.

"You'd never come to my tutoring sessions if I was teaching someone else," I went on, squeezing my fists. "Alex, *we* don't even go out and get ice cream! Sounds like you should be dating him instead of me."

Alex listened to my words with only a small crease in his forehead, as if at some point I'd switched into speaking a different language and he stopped being able to understand me. Gosh, did he ever? I'd been so desperate for his attention all this time, but he wasn't *seeing* it.

It was then that I remembered Connor stood behind us, a silent spectator to an argument that was about him but...not. He was tucked out of my peripheral, so there was no telling what his expression might've been.

"Connor." My voice was hard. "You should go before it gets any later. I'll check your work tomorrow."

Alex looked at Connor, lips parted in puzzlement.

I could hear Connor fold his worksheet back up, but he was hesitant to walk to the archway of the living room. "See you two tomorrow," he said finally, and I could feel his eyes on me.

I didn't look at him as he headed for the front door,

and even once we heard it click shut, Alex and I faced off in the silence of my house, waiting for the other to start.

"I'm not mad," Alex tried to reassure me, but it only made me feel worse.

"Why not? For two weeks, I've lied to you about where I've been, who I've been with—"

"You didn't, though. You told me you were tutoring, and you were. You were just tutoring *Connor Bray*." Alex scrubbed a hand down his cheek, still in awe. "I can't believe you could keep it a secret this whole time. I don't know how you did it. Was it hard tutoring him? Was it intimidating?"

His words came like a quick rapid-fire, each one making me feel worse than the last. "Intimidating?"

"Because it's Connor Bray," he said, like *duh*. "Do Ava or Rachel know? Probably not, right? Ava would've put it on her blog. Jeez, they'd freak."

They'd freak. Strangely enough, I thought of how Madison reacted. It would've made sense if Alex's reaction had been even a fraction of Madison's, but it wasn't. His expression only held confusion, perplexity, like he couldn't even begin to figure out how Math-Book Maisie was hanging with Hot-Shot Connor Bray. Like I must've been intimidated, because Connor was better than me.

It was that mentality that made me hate the athletes at Brentwood High. It was that mentality that had me hating Connor at first until I learned that he didn't think that way. But Alex...Alex did.

"I think you were right," I finally got out, releasing a slow breath. I didn't know how long I'd been holding it, but finally exhaling came as a relief to my lungs, like I'd been holding my breath for years. "I don't think we are compatible."

Alex blinked in surprise, recognizing the word. "Are you breaking up with me?"

Much like how I'd felt when Connor said the words Monday at the coffeehouse, my body froze. My first instinct was to deny it, to snatch the words back out of the air. How could I break up with Alex, the first guy who'd truly *seen* me? How could I throw away the history stretched out between us?

But my mind was quick to remind me of the longing I'd felt for the brief physical interactions with Connor. And I couldn't go on with Alex when I was having feelings like that with someone else.

"You think I'd be intimidated by a guy like Connor Bray because I'm Most Likely To: Marry a Math Book, right?"

"You know—" He stopped, processed the urgency out of his voice. "You know I don't care about that."

"You don't?" I squeezed my arms tighter around me, wishing I'd kept the blanket. "You cared about the list when you were on it. That's why we're together, right?"

Alex tilted his head, the way a dog might after getting a confusing command. "We're together because I like you, Maisie. I think you're cool, nice to talk to—"

"You think Rachel's cool and nice to talk to, right? And Ava?" As soon as I said it, I knew. That was how it was between us—how it had been for a while. There'd been no spark because there'd been no *romance*. We were essentially two friends who'd given each other a serious label. We hung out, talked about surface-level things, but the romance was gone.

"I've been doing better, haven't I?" Alex asked. "We've been doing better. I've been trying to make us work."

Alex and Maisie time. That was the first thing that came into my head, but it was quickly overshadowed by the memory of him ditching me at the Wallflower. He'd left me alone without hesitation. He walked away from me like he might've walked away from Rachel or Ava, not thinking twice. "Why?" My voice came out quiet. "Why are you just now trying to make things work?"

He glanced around my living room, growing more and more exasperated. "Because we're good together."

That was exactly what Jade had said to Connor. "You said we were too different. You said that—"

"I don't want to be single again!" he burst out, but there was no heat behind his words. He had the good grace to appear embarrassed, though, rubbing his fingers into his eyes. "All right? I didn't want to go back to being Most Likely To: Never Get a Girlfriend. I thought you were going to dump me after the Wallflower thing, so I just...tried harder."

The one thing I told myself throughout our relationship, as a sort of affirming mantra, was that if Alex only dated me because of the Most Likely To list, he would've broken up with me long ago. Except...that wasn't the case at all.

A numbness spread through me as I realized the

affirming mantra was the equivalent of me claiming that 2+2=5. Now the truth stood before me, and I could barely recognize it.

What should loving someone feel like? Electric? Safe? Like sunshine? It shouldn't make me feel less than, right? Shouldn't leave me sitting alone at a diner. Shouldn't ask me to change who I was to fit the mold it desired.

Maybe I didn't know what love felt like, but I'd been telling those three words to him for a while now. They weren't a lie then, but they'd be a lie now.

"Okay," he said with a sigh, staring down at his shoes. For a moment, I thought my words were actually hurting him. It was the hunched curve to his shoulders, the way he breathed slowly. "Fine. I guess we can call it quits, then. But I'm the one breaking up with you. If anyone asks, it was my choice."

Well, that was the *last* thing I expected him to say. And to have said it so calmly. "Wh—" I shook my head a little, trying to clear the confusion. "Why does that matter?"

"Because I don't want people thinking I'm a loser who got dumped," he answered quickly, easily, like it'd been something he'd thought about before.

So I would be the loser who got dumped? Lovely.

"I could've gone on like this, I think," he went on, sounding perfectly rational. Almost like he was talking about the weather, explaining why the sky was blue. Here we were, ending our relationship, and he sounded nothing but calm, cool, and collected. "How we were, I mean."

That day all those weeks ago resurfaced in my mind, him voicing his thoughts for the first time with his feet in my lap and the videogame roaring between us. *I just think we're too different.*

Alex smiled a little, as if remembering too. "I'm sorry it ended this way, though."

He could've at least pretended to be sad. With a few weeks until our one-year anniversary, he was walking away with ease. And, despite how my feelings had shifted, it stung.

"Maisie?" Mom's voice filtered into the house like a snap, breaking through the tension. I could hear her shuffle inside, and my dad's soft murmuring joined her. "Maisie, what have I said about leaving all the lights on?"

Alex turned around to the archway as Mom stepped underneath it, her purse in the crook of her elbow. Dad stepped into view behind her, surveying the scene. "Ah, I thought that was your car out there, Alex."

"Alex!" Mom greeted happily, lasering her sights on him as she lumbered closer. She'd already kicked off one of her shoes, limping along with the other kitten heel still on. "Oh, it's been too long. Your hair is getting so curly!"

He tore a hand through his curls with a little embarrassed expression, obviously uncomfortable with all the attention on him. Or maybe he was uncomfortable, given the fact that my parents walked in on our breakup.

"What are you doing here?" Dad asked him, holding Mom's arm as she kicked off her shoe. "It's getting a little late."

I could've said something, could've told them what happened, but I suddenly was overwhelmingly tired.

"I stopped by to see if Maisie had something for spirit day tomorrow," he explained, casting a cautious glance at me. "It's athletes vs mathletes day, and I wanted to borrow something. My friends and I are all going as mathletes."

Mom gave a little gasp. "Oh, so you need things like suspenders, collared shirts, and things like that? Oh, we have a few things, don't we, Ty? We can make you totally geeky, Alex."

I looked between them all, feeling as though I was screaming at the top of my lungs. "I was on the mathletes team for two years, and never once did I wear suspenders."

She ignored me. "Come on, Alex, I'll show you where Ty keeps his ties."

"I'm going to bed," I grumbled, brushing past them. There was no way I was taking part in their stupid scavenger hunt for "geeky clothes," and quite honestly, I didn't have enough energy to fake my way through more conversation. It felt weird to be walking away from such a monumental thing—to leave my now ex-boyfriend in the presence of my parents—but I didn't stick around.

CHAPTER 24

Mrs. Diego was sipping a mug of coffee when I walked into her empty classroom Thursday morning, her hair tied back into a loose bun. When she spotted me, she removed the glasses from her nose. "Maisie, good morning. What brings you by so early?"

"I wanted to check in before Connor's final tutoring session today." That, and I wanted to avoid the hallways as much as possible. I'd been trying to brace myself for the slew of "geeks" and "dorks" I'd be seeing today. There'd be way more mathletes than athletes—what fun was it to dress up as a brainless dumbleweed? "Do you have his exam already written up?"

"I do. You know me, always on the ball." She chuckled a little as she said that, removing a piece of paper from a folder on her desk. "Like I said earlier, it's two questions per chapter for the first two units. Per Principal Oliphant's request."

I scanned the sheet of paper, eyes trailing along the equations, brain absorbing it in an instant. From simplifying equations to finding equivalents, it seemed like a pretty easy test. Connor had to get fourteen questions right to pass. Fourteen. He could do that.

"If he fails," I said slowly, turning the paper over, "he'll get sent back a grade?"

Mrs. Diego leaned back in her chair. "It's a complicated situation. He'll be a senior, but he won't graduate with his class due to not enough credits. He can't take two math courses at once, so he'll have to retake Algebra II this year and take Calculus over the summer." She massaged the front of her forehead. "He'd also be removed from the football team for the season, since technically an athlete's grades have to be in good standing for them to play. If he failed Algebra II, his grades wouldn't technically be in good standing. And with Principal Oliphant hoping they'll go to championships, it'd be...it'd be a mess if he failed."

A mess for Connor, presented to him on a silver platter. Because if he failed and had to go back a grade, there'd be no keeping that a secret. "How did this happen, anyway? You said it was a clerical error?"

Mrs. Diego gave a little sigh, shoulders seeming to weigh her down further. "It was my fault. I'd misplaced his exam at first and didn't find it until after school let out for the summer. I inputted the grade, but since it didn't go through the system, it wasn't flagged that he failed a core class until school resumed."

I shifted on my feet. It wouldn't have been a mess if he failed—it already *was* a mess, for more than Connor. What Mrs. Diego didn't say, I picked up on. Sure, she may have inputted the grade late, but it wasn't her fault that no one caught his final percentage. And here she was, carrying the brunt of the worry.

"You know, Connor told me—" I cut myself off, weighing the words in my mouth. "He told me that the reason he failed in the first place was because he had family problems going on. Is there, like, a break he could get for that?"

Mrs. Diego arched an eyebrow. "Wouldn't you say Principal Oliphant is being more than generous?"

"Of course, yes," I said, closing my eyes. She was being more than generous. I'd taken the Algebra II exam —it'd been six pages with questions on both sides. The test Connor was going to take was only one sheet of paper, front and back. More than generous. "I—I want to see him succeed, I guess. And I don't want you to be in trouble."

"And you really want that valedictorian spot," she added softly.

Sometime through this all, I'd forgotten that had been my initial goal, the carrot dangling over the messy and complicated situation. At some point, it'd turned into less about me and more about him.

"Don't doubt your tutoring skills," she encouraged, taking the test back when I offered it. "And if you think he's going to do well, I believe in him *and* you."

The first few days of our tutoring, I hadn't been so sure of Connor's ability to pass. It was a ton of information to fill up on in a few weeks, combined with other schoolwork and sports. But in those weeks, his dedication toward it—maybe more like desperation—made me more and more confident in him. He could do this. I had faith.

I stopped by the bathroom before heading toward first period, but as soon as I stepped inside, I heard the obvious sound of someone crying. The choking breaths, the sniffling nose. Instantly, the sound cut through me, and I looked at the only closed blue stall.

I stepped up to the stall door and hesitated before rapping my knuckles against the metal. Whatever was wrong, she probably didn't want to talk to a stranger about it, but I couldn't ignore her. "Is everything okay?"

The girl's sniffles cut off almost instantly, and her voice was a soft croak. "Y-Yeah, I'm okay."

"Need someone to talk to?" I was *so* not the optimal person for cheering someone up, though. In our friend group, Rachel was the funny one, I was the logical one, and Ava was definitely the encourager. But from years of being their friend, I could figure out a way to channel them. "I have a few minutes before I go to class."

With how big Brentwood was, I hadn't expected it to be anyone I knew. But when the stall door opened, my eyebrows shot up in surprise.

Madison froze as soon as she saw me, her puffy eyes widening. For athletes versus mathletes day, it was clear Madison wasn't participating with her simple pink sweater and denim jeans. Her golden hair was smoothed into a low ponytail, but what really caught my attention were the black smudges under her eyes from her mascara mixing with her tears.

Everything inside me lurched as I was thrown back in time.

I pivoted on my heel and went to the paper towel dispenser, extracting a sheet and dampening it under the sink. "You know," I said slowly, offering the wad to her. "I haven't seen you cry since the fifth grade."

I've never seen you cry, you know, she'd told me two weeks ago at the bowling alley. *Not even when you broke your arm in the fifth grade.* It was funny—the exact time she'd expected me to cry was one of the few times I'd seen her cry. She'd cried my tears for me that day.

Madison sniffed, going to the mirror and dragging the paper towel underneath her eyes. "At least I'm not crying over shorts."

Weirdly enough, I found my lips twitching like they were about to smile. "What's wrong?"

The question came before I gave too much thought to it, but I found myself genuinely curious about the answer. What upset her badly enough to cry in the girls' room at school, where anyone could've found her? I couldn't even begin to guess what could've been the reason.

Madison studied her reflection in the mirror. Most of the mascara was gone now, replaced with a faint gray sheen. Her voice was filled with barbed wire. "Do you really care?"

"Yes." I folded my arms across my chest and leaned against the sink beside hers. Her chest shook from crying, intermittent sniffs that quivered her frame like a hiccup. "I promise it won't show up on *Babble*."

She gave a short, humorless chuckle as she tossed the paper towel into the trash, flicking on the faucet. "I don't want to talk about it," she returned, but her voice wasn't unkind. After dipping her hand underneath the stream of water, she pressed her fingers to the side of her neck where redness had started to bloom. "We both know you wouldn't have knocked if you knew it was me."

Was that true? If I had known it was Madison in the stall, would I have knocked? Would I have walked out? I didn't know, but I did know that seeing her cry triggered something in me. The same sort of protective affection that I thought had died years ago. Like despite everything that happened, that one sisterly thread still could tug on my heart.

Instead of saying that, I flipped open the flap of my satchel and dug around. Once my fingers closed around the tube, I held it out to her. "What?" I asked as she eyed the mascara. "A math geek can't wear makeup?"

"That wasn't what I was thinking."

"You think my lashes are naturally this voluminous?"

Madison's lips tipped upward. She looked on the verge of crying again, a haziness filling her eyes like tears about to spill over.

The strange affection surged in me again, and like a puppet on strings, I stretched out a hand to touch her shoulder. It was then that I knew, even with our history between us, I'd never be able to walk away when she needed someone.

I pressed the mascara tube into her hand and didn't say anything more before turning away. The five-minute bell rang overhead as I pulled the bathroom door open. "Whatever's going on," I began gently, feeling awkward the moment I opened my mouth, but forging ahead anyway, "Don't let it ruin your makeup."

Her face crumpled again, but Madison didn't say anything as she let me walk out. Really, there wasn't anything left to say, anyway.

I didn't see Connor until the end of the day for our final tutoring session. He drove to a dirt road where the elevation was higher, parking at a spot the locals called Lookout Ledge. It was a hill with a road carved into the side of it, the elevation barely high enough for the view to clear the tops of the trees. Still, even though the view wasn't that spectacular—a lot of houses and subdivisions —it was peaceful with the lingering summer breeze.

Connor opened up the hatch of the SUV, and we sat in the back, legs dangling against the bumper. He was working on practice test number two, and we had one left after this for him to take. I didn't want to overload his brain, but I wanted him to be as prepared as possible.

The math equations from the official test danced in my mind, a few clear as day. Especially the multiple-choice ones. It felt weird having insider information, like at any point I could tell him what the answers would be.

Connor tapped his pencil against his paper, creating a hollow fluttering sound. "Perpendicular bisectors, that's—"

"I'm not helping you," I hurried to say, closing my eyes to bask in the breeze. No paper rose today—I couldn't settle my thoughts enough to focus on the lines. "So try to figure it out on your own."

"You know, I think that's a phrase in the 'What a Tutor Should *Not* Say' handbook."

"This is a practice test. As in, you're pretending that this is the official exam. Which, in case you forgot, I can't help you for."

I hadn't used the practice test that Mrs. Diego put together, since hers only focused on the first two units. Since I taught Connor the entire book, I included all four units, but felt guilty for it. Maybe I should've told him they were lowering the amount he tested on. Maybe that would lessen his stress.

But still, the small part of me still annoyed at how everything played out bit down on my tongue.

Connor sighed, quite dramatically, might I add, and leaned back against the side of his car. Without another word, he pressed his palm down on the closed Algebra II book at his hip. "I want a timeout."

"Finish your test, and then you can have a timeout."

"That's not how your timeouts work," he argued, and put the practice test down on the floor of the car. "I am allowed it if I ask, as long as I don't throw a tantrum. This is me, acting perfectly civil."

I waved my hand at him and granted his wish. "So, were you an athlete today or a mathlete?"

Connor was wearing sweatpants and a t-shirt now, but that was his usual post-football practice attire. His hair was almost dried in the wind, only the tips twisted with water. "I didn't dress up." He arched a brow. "What about you?"

I glanced down at my jeans and striped t-shirt with a hole near the collar. "Athlete, obviously."

Connor rolled his eyes as he propped his arm on one of his drawn knees. "Speaking of costumes, did Alex get what he came for last night?"

I knew the daunting subject was going to come up sooner or later, but I'd been hoping for the latter. I'd told Ava and Rachel at lunch today about our breakup, and though they'd been upset I hadn't told them earlier— "Maisie, you should've called us!" Ava had said, and Rachel added, "We would've been over to your house in a heartbeat"—their support reinforced even more that I'd made the right decision.

Alex had already integrated perfectly back into his friend group, fitting at their now-full lunch table.

Despite my mood, there was no pushing down my soft chuckle. "Was that your way of trying to do a smooth segue, Connor?"

And there was no stopping the pull of his. "Maybe."

"Alex wasn't mad. He was just..." *Confused.* "He asked me if I was intimidated by you."

"Have you ever been intimidated by me? I mean, you *bit* me. Was that you intimidated?"

We were close in the small trunk, so it was easy to reach over and swat at him, the movement familiar and easy. "That was me asserting my dominance."

"Of course."

I held Connor's gaze and let myself feel every emotion that surfaced. Confusion, relief, unease, anticipation. Every little thing that I'd been bottling down these past few weeks, brushing off, appeared now, and I let myself feel it. *Tell him you're single*, my brain ordered.

But I couldn't, because even though I was single, he wasn't.

"I'll figure it out," I finally said, leaving out any and all mention of the breakup, and nodding my chin toward his worksheet. "Is your timeout finished yet?"

"If it must be," he said with another sigh. He leaned out of the path of the sun's rays, squinting down at the page. "I should get finished. There's a party tonight I have to swing by."

I tried not to feel curious. I really tried. "Another party?"

Connor looked up at me. "Yeah, a guy on the team is having a bonfire at his house to celebrate game day tomorrow."

"Is it a Players Only party?"

Connor leaned forward, only inches away in the cramped space. The summer breeze suddenly felt way, way too hot. "My, my. Is the social butterfly, Maisie Matthews, fishing around for an invite?"

"As if I'd want to hang out with a bunch of jocks." I scoffed, gazing out at Lookout Ledge. The tops of the trees danced with the wind, their green leaves swaying this way and that. "Underaged drinking is so lame. Like, why do people *voluntarily* kill their brain cells?"

"There's that judgey side I love so much coming out to play."

"You hate it."

"No, I hate when I'm on the receiving end." Connor knocked his knuckles against the rubber side of my shoe, drawing me back to him. "You should come tonight."

I looked into his hazel eyes. In this light, they were definitely green, the different colored flecks easy to get lost in. They almost seemed to glow, beckoning me closer. "I'm helping out at the art gallery tonight. I wouldn't be able to go anyway."

"Bummer." His shoulders drooped briefly before he shifted, leaning against the side of the car and facing me straight-on. "Should we dive into our last love advice lesson?"

It was ironic that my love life had actually *deteriorated* since the start of all this tutoring, but I didn't have the heart to tell him. "We should focus on you. Your lessons are more important."

But Connor wasn't convinced. He shook his hair out of his eyes and leaned closer, putting a hand on his knee. "Be honest about how you feel. With anything. A relationship with no honesty, no transparency... It's never going to last."

Over the course of my relationship with Alex, there were definitely things I kept to myself. I never told him about Madison and the cheer squad. We never talked about how I felt after Jozie left. And when it came to things about him, we never talked about anything deeper than surface level.

"Sometimes you need to just be brave," Connor went on. "Sometimes it's scary to talk about certain things. But you might regret *not* saying something, you know?"

Maybe we should've talked about things when we first started drifting apart. Maybe I should've started the conversation, been honest with what I'd been feeling. There was no way of knowing whether or not it would've made a difference in the end, but it was something I regretted, not being open about things earlier.

We sat so close in the trunk that I could hear Connor's soft inhale and exhale as he waited for my response, and the overwhelming desire for something *different* stung at me. *Be honest with how you feel. Sometimes you need to just be brave.* But what happened when you had no idea how you were feeling? What did you say then?

"Thank you," he said after a beat, voice low enough to nearly get caught in the wind. "For helping me with this. With tutoring. I know I kind of tricked you into it."

"It wasn't all bad."

"So that means it was a little bad?"

I laughed at that, tilting my face up toward the sunlight. It was warm on my skin, a delicate touch made bearable by the accompanying breeze. It was easier to not look at him, to sever the connection his eyes always seemed to swipe me up in. "I shouldn't have judged you so much in the beginning," I confessed. "I'm sorry for that."

A faint tickle grazed the side of my bare arm, and I opened my eyes to find Connor's knuckles grazing me there. Though it was obviously a casual touch, my skin tingled, mind pretending it was more affectionate than it was. He nodded solemnly. "Likewise."

It felt like we were stumbling upon the last page in a book that I could've sworn would have at least one more chapter. A math equation that I'd been working on for hours only to discover there was no true solution. This was it. The last tutoring session. The last time we'd share a space like this, the last time we'd laugh together. Mrs. Diego would give me a new student to tutor, Connor would play at football games and go to parties, and this would all be a blip in time.

Two people who knew each other's secrets, fading away to be nothing but strangers.

Sometimes you need to just be brave.

I urged all of those thoughts down deep until they stopped resurfacing. They weren't helpful anyway. "Okay," I told him, and then reached out to tap his practice exam. The paper wavered under my touch. "Time to get back to work."

He looked on the verge of saying something, probably adding more to the one last love tip, but something held him back. *Say it,* I thought. *Take your own advice. Tell me what you're thinking.*

But he ultimately nodded, turning back to his practice exam. "Let's see where we end up."

CHAPTER 25

The art gallery's patrons began dying off the closer it got to the top of the hour, which left me sighing in relief. The gallery had extended its hours this week due to the Brentwood High Spirit exhibit, catering to those who were caught in after school practice and PTO meetings, but ordinary attendees of the exhibits were used to the seven o'clock closing time. However, this week only, Center Inspire would be open until eight, which meant that I would be stuck there until then.

If not longer. Who knew how long Mom would linger? If she had it her way, she'd stick around until the cleaning crew was finished.

Earlier, I'd been helping Mom pass out pamphlets with student artist information and singing the praises of Center Inspire. "Oh, it's a woman-owned art gallery, the only one of its kind in all of the county," I'd say, or "Center Inspire has a mix of European artists as well as local—we live to celebrate every success from every walk of life."

Apparently, when Mom gave me the script to read off of, she didn't hear how plasticky it sounded.

After my feet got too tired from standing the majority of the night, I'd found a bench near a few student displays and listened to them explain their artwork. It'd been the night designated for them to show their work to their families, so for practically the entire night, Center Inspire was filled with grandparents going gaga over sculptures and paintings.

Most of the Brentwood High students had left now, though, and I would've bet money that the majority were heading straight for the pre-game party.

Connor would've been there by now. I wasn't sure if Rachel and Ava decided to go—they'd invited me to tag along, but if football games weren't my scene, parties were a definite no-go.

It didn't mean that I *wasn't* checking *Brentwood Babble* for updates, though, in case Ava decided to post an article without proofing it first. I refreshed the page every ten minutes.

I sat in the room at Center Inspire that I'd tutored Connor in last week, listening to the faint classical music pumping through the speakers, gaze constantly drawn back to the closet we'd crammed in. The way his body felt against mine still lingered in my memory, and I shivered, practically able to still feel his breath on my skin.

Get a grip, Maisie.

Now that I'd broken things off with Alex, these thoughts—the intrusive, unavoidable thoughts—were overwhelming.

"How's your first big exhibit, May-May?" Dad found me sitting in the room, sauntering up to my table. He wore his nicest pair of blue jeans and a black button-down, because even though this was an art exhibit—one of the biggest it had had since opening—Dad wasn't a suitcoat kind of guy. "Think you might want to be a curator like your mother one day?"

I didn't think it was a joke, but the question made me laugh anyway. "If anything, I know what I *don't* want to do."

"Too bad Jozie couldn't be here for this. This is totally in her wheelhouse, huh?"

He probably hadn't meant it as a backhanded comment, but it stung like one.

His hand came down gently on my shoulder, giving it a squeeze. "We appreciate your help, May-May."

"The front desk girl better not be sick tomorrow, that's all I'm saying," I tried to tease, attempting to portray a humor I didn't feel. "It's not like I had anything else to do anyway."

Except possibly attend a party.

"You about ready to go home?"

"There's..." I checked the time on my phone. "Fifteen minutes until closing."

"Your mother and I drove separate." He took a set of car keys from his pocket, letting them dangle between us. The fob looked futuristic compared to my rusty coupe's key set, but it was the same opportunity: freedom. "You can head out if you want. I'll ride home with her."

I wasted no time in curling my hand around the fob,

snatching the keys before he tried to jokingly take them back. "And this is why you're the best dad in the world." I pushed to my feet and squeezed him around his middle. "Should I say goodbye to Mom?"

"She's been talking with Mrs. Oliphant for the past twenty minutes, so I'd say you can head out."

"Mrs. Oliphant is here?" Now I was glad I'd tucked myself away in the back room. No doubt she'd grill me on how Connor would do on his test tomorrow.

"Madison isn't with her," Dad said quickly, assuming that's why I'd reacted the way I did. "Talia stopped by to see the exhibit. 'Bout time, if you ask me, since we've been showcasing the students' artwork all week."

I smirked at his annoyance, happy I had one person on my side in the Oliphant/Matthews civil war.

I stepped around a hip-looking couple on my way to the front door, twirling the fob around my finger. As soon as I got home, I was kicking off these stiff flats Mom made me wear and changing into sweatpants. The flats were hers, which meant I had to cram my toes into a shoe one size too small, and don't even get me started on the skirt she'd gotten me to put on.

In my purse, my phone vibrated with a text notification, and I scrounged for it. My fingers curled around the plastic phone case when I slammed into something hard—some*one*—and before I could ricochet off them and onto the floor, their hands came up and gripped my forearms, steadying me.

"Whoa, easy there," a smooth voice said, tone a teasing lilt and one immediately identifiable. My heart began slamming in my ribs even before I looked up, and when I did, it was mid-gallop as Connor grinned down at me. His hands were cool on my arms, touch grounding and gentle. The music played over the speakers of the gallery, but faintly, as if someone cupped their hands over my ears. "Where's the fire?"

"W-What are you doing here?" My words came out in a pathetic whisper, but then again, I was impressed I'd spoken at all. After spending the last hour refreshing *Babble*, waiting for an article about him asking Jade to homecoming or something, Connor showing up here was the last thing I expected. "Why aren't you at the party?"

Really, the first thing I almost said was *there are people from school here.* Earlier today, I'd resigned myself to the closing of our chapter, and honestly, he'd been lucky no one had found out about our tutoring. No one except Madison. His desire for discretion had been fulfilled, and he was going to risk it all now?

"Connor mentioned the art show," a new voice joined in, startling me enough that I jumped back out of habit. Joy stood behind him in the doorway, partially blocked by his frame. She had another bandana wrapped around her hair, though this one looked silkier, matching perfectly with her pearl-colored blouse. "It's been a long time since I've done anything this fun."

"I wasn't sure what you wear to art exhibits," Connor said a little awkwardly, looking down at his clothes with a boyish grin. "Are jeans okay?"

Connor had changed since I'd seen him earlier. Like my dad, Connor wore a nice pair of dark jeans, no tears or frays in sight. Mom would've called them Church Jeans. He had on a thin gray sweater, sleeves pushed up to his elbows in an effort to fight the lingering summer heat. With his hair sloped over his forehead, he looked ready for a magazine shoot.

"Jeans are perfectly okay," I returned, tugging on the hem of my blue skirt. "I'd be wearing jeans if I could."

His eyes swept over me, warming the blood in my veins. "You still look pretty."

Do not smile like an idiot, my brain ordered my lips, a drill sergeant yelling at a recruit. *Do not, do not, do not.*

Except all it took was one soft whisper from my heart to have the corners of my mouth tugging up. *He thinks you look pretty.*

Joy cleared her throat, and if my face wasn't flaming hot before, it was now. It was a happy sort of embarrassment, but later it'd probably morph into something more firmly mortified—because here I was, grinning at Connor like all the other smitten girls at Brentwood High. *But he thinks you're pretty.*

"You heading out?" Connor asked, eyeing the key fob in my grip.

"Oh, walk her out to her car, Connor," Joy ordered sternly, sidestepping his frame and gazing up at the exposed ductwork. "I'll meander around. Are there any refreshments, dear?"

And then suddenly, my dad was there, stepping up to Connor's grandma with the world's warmest expression. He offered his hand down the hallway where the cookies and drinks were, the perfect usher. "We absolutely have refreshments. Champagne and non-alcoholic beverages."

Joy, pausing in being corralled off in the opposite direction, pointed a finger at Connor. "You're driving."

"The last thing she needs is alcohol," Connor retorted with an exasperated smile, glancing down at me. "Well, I guess I'm walking you to your car."

"You don't have to," I said, taking a step back. "Someone might see."

Connor slipped a hand into his pocket, and the relaxed way he regarded me caused my insides to flutter. "I meant what I said before, you know. You deserve more than to be a secret friend."

The shadows on the side street were heavy as the sun disappeared behind the horizon, the lampposts slow to flick on. I pressed the key fob so that the lights would blink, and I found Dad's car a few spaces down from the door, perfectly parallel parked.

Connor noticed it immediately. "Did you figure out the Pythagorean Theorem, then?"

"One day, one day." I gripped the strap of my purse, glancing up at his profile as we walked down the sidewalk. "So, why aren't you at the party?"

"I figured a party probably wasn't the smartest idea for a guy who has a big test tomorrow."

"Good call."

We got to the trunk of my car far too soon, and I hesitated by the taillights. It felt like a gift, his sudden appearance at Center Inspire. One last hurrah. "Can I ask you a question?"

He gave a soft nod. "Hit me with it."

"Do you ever wish you didn't have to hide things from people? Like, with your house, with the tutoring. Do you wish you didn't have to keep all that a secret?"

"Before," he began, slow to pick out his words, "I never wanted that. After I started getting so much attention, it was all I wanted. I would do things just so people would talk about me."

"Like?"

Connor gave a soft, shallow sigh, thinking. "Throw parties, pick fights with players from Jefferson...date Jade."

"What do you mean, date Jade?" My jaw dropped open a bit. "You started dating her for a popularity boost?"

"Don't say it like that." Connor walked along the side of the car and leaned against it, crossing his ankles slightly in front of him. He tapped his fingers against his thighs, unable to keep them still. "Then it just sounds awful."

I sputtered for a solid five seconds. "Wait, so you're saying it wasn't *real*?"

"It started off genuine, of course. I mean, we really liked each other at first. But once people picked up on the whole 'it couple' thing, the attention got to the both of us. Once *Babble* started posting about us, it was fun to see what people would say next." Connor tilted his head to the side to peer at me, and even in the low light, I could see the pinkness in his cheeks. "Somewhere along the way, she and I lost our spark, too."

I tried to think back if there were any signs of their disintegrating relationship, any dead giveaways, but there hadn't been. Not any that I'd seen. The only one that was slightly telling could've been how quickly Jade had gotten over the equipment closet incident. *We talked about this*, she'd told him when I'd caught them in the hallway, her voice more annoyed than anything else. *We're good together.*

And Connor's dejected reply. *Are we?*

My mind went back even further, to the time he drove me home from the Wallflower. *No one falls in love in high school.* We'd been in the same boat all along, and I'd never noticed. For one brief moment, I wondered what Ava would say if she found out that *Jannor* had been more or less a Brentwood High publicity stunt.

Jeez, the personal question was going to be fully transparent, but I couldn't keep myself from asking. "Are you going to rekindle the spark or...end things?"

He gave a short laugh, kicking the toe of his shoe against the back tire. "Things have been over between us for weeks now. Since summer."

And here I thought my jaw couldn't drop further. "*What?*"

It was clear that my shock amused him, judging by the way he rubbed his fingers across his lips. "I mean, we never said 'hey, let's only act like a couple in public' or anything like that. But we never see each other outside of school or sports. She'll do things when we're in public.

Like the kiss on the football field. Her arm around my waist. I guess that's the thing with attention—it gets addictive."

I gaped at how casually he leaned against the car while I was fully absorbed in disbelief. This entire time, he and Jade had been...what? Letting people think they were together? Letting *me* think they were together? The past twenty-four hours of me struggling with my thoughts, my feelings, and they weren't together? *"Why?"*

"Homecoming king and queen relies on us being together. It's important to her." His voice softened, eyes getting a faraway look. "And it was important to me, too. My dad was the quarterback, did I ever tell you that? Homecoming king, too. When Coach picked Landon for quarterback over the summer, my parents were so disap-pointed. That'd been Dad's dream for me, to follow in his footsteps. And I couldn't change that, but as long as I was with Jade, there was still a chance to be homecoming king. Just like he was."

I let out a breath. His words made sense, but...*not.* He'd been so conditioned to live in the world of social hierarchy, to focus on what people thought of him—to *obsess* over it. That was why he kept tutoring a secret, hid the fact that he had to move in with his grandmother, dated Jade even though they'd lost their spark. A lifetime of being put on a pedestal had made him terrified to fall off.

But then again— "Wait a second, let me get this straight." I held up a hand between us. "Your whole relationship was a hoax, and yet you offered to give me *love advice?*"

Connor pressed his fingers to his bottom lip, but it did nothing to hide the boyish smile. "I guess I thought I could fake it 'til I made it."

"Except it totally backfired in nearly every way."

"I should've made you sign a waiver."

I scoffed out a laugh, leaning against the car beside him. Our shoulders brushed, but he didn't lean away from the contact. Neither did I.

It was suddenly too hard to swallow, too hard to breathe, too hard to do anything but look at him. The weight of his confession and the fact that he shared it with *me* had me drawing courage of my own. "Alex and I broke up."

Connor's eyebrows went up in a flash, the surprise on his face no doubt mirroring mine a second ago. "What? When?"

"Last night." I flattened my fingertips across my skirt, tracing the floral pattern. "I wasn't going to tell you."

His shoulder pressed into mine more firmly, sending sparks along my side.

"I didn't realize how suffocated I felt until after. Trying to stuff myself into a mold to fit what he wanted me to be." And who was that person for Alex? Someone who was more outgoing, had more normal hobbies. Who I was now hadn't been it for him. "He always looked down on me, and I knew it. Not on purpose, I don't think —Alex isn't cruel."

"You give him a lot of credit," Connor muttered. "I'm not that generous."

But he didn't know Alex like I did. "He wants to be like you, the cool guy everyone looks up to."

"It's overrated," he said, and my mind flashed back to the night that Connor had driven me home from the diner, to our conversation then. Even back then, I'd been giving Alex an excuse. *He just wants to be in the in-crowd.*

And Connor's monotone reply. *It's overrated.*

"If I could trade places with Alex, I would," Connor went on, shaking his head. A few cars passed by us with a soft zoom, but it didn't burst our quiet bubble. "He can be the guy everyone scrutinizes. Because I know what it feels like to be suffocated, too."

Of course he did, and my heart squeezed with sympathy. All of his secrets, all of his lies, all to keep up the image everyone expected from him. Mr. All-Star Player, who had everything he wanted. No one wanted to look underneath the mask; no one wanted to risk finding out that the guy they worshipped was as flawed as they were.

"I wish I figured it out sooner. That we wouldn't work. I wouldn't have had to worry about keeping all this from him." I tried to think back to pinpoint an exact moment when things had begun falling apart. But when had it happened? It'd been a gradual build, beginning two weeks ago with the resurfacing of the Most Likely Tos. Two weeks ago, when I'd begun tutoring Connor. "Figured out that I...wanted more."

Like someone who would make my heart tumble over itself.

I blinked a few times, the dawning understanding enough to render me speechless.

"You deserve more," he murmured, and before I knew what was happening, Connor picked up my hand from where it was still tracing my skirt. He wrapped his fingers around my palm, the warmth of his skin spreading like wildfire through me. "You deserve the world, Maisie Matthews."

All of Connor's love advice came flooding back in a rush, consuming all rational thought.

For the first time in my life, I allowed myself to be bold. To channel the energy every jock seemed to possess, to be as confident as Connor and Madison were. I twisted my hand so that my fingers could thread through Connor's, watching as they fit so perfectly into the spaces his created.

And without hesitation, Connor's fingers curled around mine. The wildfire was nearly everywhere now. I was a field of paper roses, swallowed by flames.

When our gazes locked, the heat inside me seemed trapped in his eyes, an emotion seeming to melt the brown tones in his eyes while brightening the greens. Something low in my stomach shifted.

It'd been the reaction stirring inside me for days now, the gnawing sort of longing that I couldn't place. Until now. Until I looked him in the eyes, and the places my thoughts went were no longer *wrong*, despicable, awful. Looking at him was allowed now, but I still felt the strongest urge to pretend I wasn't feeling what I knew I was.

Instead, the desperate craving to throw the consequences to the wind swept over me, charging the air between us. *Sometimes you need to just be brave.*

And so, ignoring everything, throwing caution to the wind, I leaned forward and pressed my lips against Connor's.

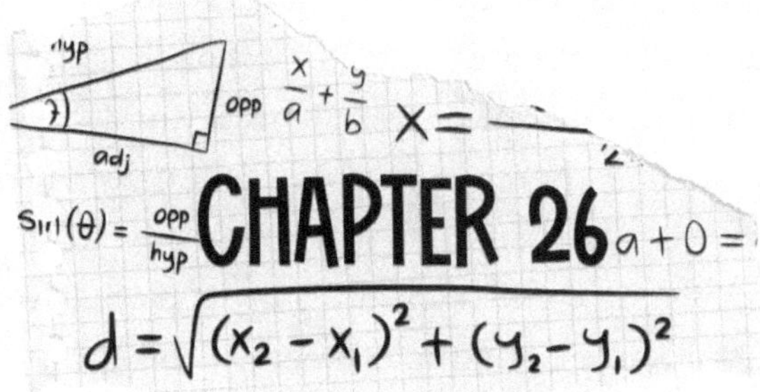

CHAPTER 26

When I'd first kissed Alex, we'd both gone in the same direction, our noses smashing together as we tried to line our lips up. We'd laughed about it and tried again, and though the mishap had taken some of the pressure off, the magical firework kiss I'd been wondering about my whole life hadn't been there. The wick had been lit, but it fizzled out.

A current of pleasure zipped through me the second I pressed my lips to Connor's, causing my heart to spasm in my chest. As soon as Connor broke out of his shocked stupor, he threaded his free hand through my hair, angled my head, and kissed me back. His mouth urged me on, assuring me this was okay, that he was just as in this as I was.

That he wanted it just as badly as I did.

I'd never let myself imagine this. Connor was gorgeous, yeah, but it would've been cheating on Alex to picture what his lips would've tasted like. Would've been cheating to imagine how he'd react if I kissed him. And quite frankly, that wanting that had been a constant swirl in me had made no sense until a few seconds ago.

But now it was okay, it was allowed, and I knew that my imagination never would've done this moment justice.

Connor shifted closer, catching my body between the warmth of his chest and the coolness of the car. I curled my fingers into the material of his dress shirt, feeling his hard side through the material. He kissed me like the desire had been bottled up inside him for so long, and it was finally his chance. The scent of him was everywhere, thrilling and intoxicating as the sandalwood mixed with the late September air.

I pulled him closer, smiling against his mouth, unable to get enough.

And the world's greatest kiss ended with one over-whelmingly familiar voice. "Wow. Just...wow."

Connor and I broke apart to find Jade standing on the sidewalk a few feet from us, Madison lingering over her shoulder. Madison looked more shocked than Jade, with her wide blue eyes and parted lips, where Jade looked more annoyed. She was all crunched eyebrows and twisted lips.

Connor edged slightly in front of me, as if he could hide me over his shoulder. For the moment, that was fine by me. My cheeks burned as if someone had taken my internal temperature and turned up the furnace. "What are you doing here?"

"My mom asked me to stop by to see the exhibit,"

Madison said, rapidly blinking. "We were going to Ashton's party after this."

"Which will be the perfect place to drop *this* new development." Jade folded her arms across her chest, clicking her tongue. "You know, when Kyle told me he heard you in the hookup closet, I never would've *dreamed* you'd be in there with Maisie Matthews. I wonder if everyone else will be shocked, too." She took a step closer, her shoes clicking against the sidewalk. Her attention slid to me. "I might not be able to get your friend to post about it, but I don't need *Babble* to call Connor a cheater."

They were the words that triggered my flight reaction, because though they were deceptively soft-spoken, it felt like she was inching toward a checkmate in a game I hadn't realized we were playing. And they weren't even really targeted at me.

I edged out from behind Connor. "You're not going to say anything," I said, but the probability in my head wasn't absolute. It was greater than fifty-fifty, but less than one hundred percent.

"No?" She blinked innocently. "And why wouldn't I?"

"Connor goes from dating you to kissing a girl like me—what would everyone think?" My voice wasn't firm, probably because my heart trampled in my chest like it was trying to break free. It wasn't even about me. Brentwood wouldn't care who Maisie Matthews was kissing, but they *would* care about the golden boy cheating. And after everything he'd been through, he couldn't be hurt again. "If he chose me over you, who's the real loser?"

"You're giving him too much credit, Maisie," she said, her words eerily echoing what Connor had said a moment ago about Alex. "I hold his reputation in the palm of my hand, and he knows it. Don't you, Connor?"

Connor didn't reply, but when I looked up at him, there was not an ounce of emotion in his expression that could've hinted at what had happened a few seconds ago. I found nothing but a clenched jaw and a hard stare.

"I know about your parents," Jade said, ticking off the numbers on her fingers. "I know about how you live with your grandma. I know you failed Algebra II."

At Jade's elbow, Madison dropped her gaze.

"You know we're a package deal," Jade said, taking another step closer. "I can't win homecoming queen without you."

"Why not?" Connor demanded, his voice flat.

"*I'm* not Brentwood High's star player. *I'm* not the one the student body shows up week after week to see on that field." She gave him a gooey smile, one that, if anyone were watching from the outside, would've seemed flirty. "I need the prized running back, Connor Bray, and I've got too much on you for you to ditch me. We're too deep in this for you to back out now."

I gave a little scoff, despite the load of her threat. "So you're piggybacking off him?"

"Just like you are?" Jade raised her eyebrows. "You're only tutoring him so you can get valedictorian, right? Sounds like I'm not the only one using someone to get what we want."

"The difference is that I'm not hurting other people in the process."

"I don't know." Jade drew in a breath through her teeth. "You trying to sabotage Madison at cheer tryouts sounds a bit like that to me."

I stared her down, the buzzing in my ears growing louder and louder. In my head, I could see it: me, standing out like a sore thumb, the only person flailing her arms to a beat that only lived in her head. "We both know that's not what happened."

"Trying to embarrass her by dancing to the wrong routine, but ultimately only embarrassing yourself."

"You think I'm embarrassed about something from three years ago?"

Jade looked me up and down. "Seeing as how you didn't tell your boyfriend about it, yeah, I do. And maybe that's not the embarrassing part. Maybe the embarrassing part comes when everyone sees how once upon a time, the math book-loving geek desperately wanted to be popular, but couldn't hack it."

I felt Connor's fingers skim the inside of my wrist, and it was almost enough to have me backing down. Almost. "Or maybe people will see how threatened you are by me," I returned, pulling my arm away. "You, Top Tier cheerleader Jade Dyer, threatened by a math book-loving geek. That's why you stole my best friend. Why you helped Madison skew my squad audition. That's why you put me on the Most Likely To list."

For the briefest second as I spoke, Jade had faltered. The confidence in her expression had cracked, revealing the insecure girl underneath. But by the time I got to my last line, the blip of emotion was gone. As if I were on a rollercoaster, my heart dropped to my feet as Jade raised her eyebrows. "The list. You want to know who *truly* put you on the list?"

"Jade." This time, it was Connor speaking from behind me, warning her to stop.

But I was already shaking my head. "I don't even care anymore." And it was the truth. The song and dance of the list exhausted me, and I was ready to lay it to rest. "You have whatever blackmail material that the video is supposed to be. Take it out on me, and leave Connor out of this."

"But Connor's in it," Jade said, biting down on her bottom lip to suffocate her smile. It didn't work, though, because the patronizing gleam was clear as day. "After all, *he* was the one who put your name on the Most Likely To list."

My first response was to laugh, a short, hard sound that ripped out of my throat. He wouldn't have put my name on the list. He didn't even know me then. The day he walked up to me in the hallway and asked me to tutor him, he didn't even get my name right. But then again, he *had* known I was Maisie, the math tutor.

"If you're in the Top Tier, you have to nominate someone for the list," Jade went on, voice conversational now. Lighthearted. "If you don't nominate someone, you're put on it. That's why Landon was on the list this year. Why our sweet Madison was on it."

Over Jade's shoulder, I could see tears swimming in

Madison's eyes, shimmering underneath the dull lamplight. I couldn't figure out why they were there.

"Connor, though, came up with that label all on his own. *Marry a Math Book.* It's kind of clever, right?"

Clever. The label that had dug its claws into my mind, *clever.* The label that had me questioning everything about myself. *Clever.*

When I risked a glance over my shoulder, I found Connor with his eyes closed, like he was annoyed she'd told the truth.

Like it *was* the truth.

"It was you?" I demanded, staring up at him, taking a page from his handbook and carefully curating an expression of utter blankness. My teeth felt like chattering, but I kept my jaw clenched. "*You* put me on the list?"

Connor's chest rose and fell sharply, and he shook his head a little as if to clear it. "I—yes, but—"

"That's another reason you wanted to keep the tutoring a secret, then, isn't it?" The ache behind my eyes trailed all the way to the back of my throat, but I swallowed past it. "You wouldn't want it to get out that you're a hypocrite, making fun of me and then asking for my help."

The lies, the secrets—all piling up, accumulating to a crushing weight.

"Were you ever going to tell me? Of course not," I went on with a scoff. "Not all the bribery in the world would've gotten me to tutor you then."

Connor drew in a shaking breath, closing his eyes as if he were in pain. "Maisie."

This entire time, I thought it had been Madison who'd given me the label. But it wasn't. He didn't know me at all, but he put me on the list.

Like little dominos falling into place, Madison's comment from the other night at Expresso's suddenly made so much sense. *You asked Maisie to be your tutor? Did you ask her before or after the Most Likely Tos?*

"Don't be too mad at him," Jade said, breaking through my rampant thoughts. "It's not something you'd understand, but to stay on top, you'd do anything. Even throw your best friend under the bus. Right, Mads?"

Connor caught my hand, and when I glanced up, I saw it. *Pain.* It cracked into the hazel of his eyes, interjecting the color of sadness there. Just like before, that desperate urge to do something—anything—to alleviate it swept over me, but there was nothing I could do. It was like the sun shining down on a road, creating a water-like mirage on the pavement.

"Maisie," he began, barely audible. "I know that it sounds—"

"Let her go, Connor," Jade said, and this time, she came close enough to put her hand on his shoulder. "I won't air your dirty laundry. I won't tell the whole school you're a cheater. We'll win king and queen, and we'll stay being the top of the Top Tier. That's what you want, right? What you've always wanted?"

It was clear what Jade wanted. She'd said it herself. *To stay on top, you'd do anything.* Even sink her claws into a guy who was trying to break away, all for the sake of *Brentwood Babble* articles and people fawning over their "it couple" status.

The funny thing was—it *stung* that Connor put me on the Most Likely Tos, sure. It hurt my feelings. But it was nothing compared to the way that he, after a brief moment of hesitation, did as Jade directed. His fingers slowly uncurled from my wrist, letting it fall.

I just keep thinking about how terrified I am of anyone finding out.

The rigid line to his shoulders made sense. He knew this was it—the moment everything could come crashing down. Instead of standing up, he backed into familiarity, afraid to lose it all. Even now, after he'd kissed me, he was too caught up in the popularity game. Before, I'd never pitied Connor, but now...it hurt to look at him.

I'd been wrong before. *Now* we'd stumbled upon the final chapter, flipping the book to a close.

Connor didn't try catching my hand again, and I didn't look at any of them as I rounded the car. I didn't look at any of them as I started it up and accelerated out of the parking space, nearly clipping the bumper of the car in front of me.

Once I was a block away, the trio absent from my rearview mirror, I swiped a hand across my mouth. There was no wiping away the lingering trace of Connor's lips against mine, though. I could, however, wipe away the tears that had begun to fall, flowing as if they'd never stop.

CHAPTER 27

The hallways were quiet when I got to school the next morning, and that was a rare scene. With over three hundred students in my grade alone, the halls were never empty, but I'd shown up a half hour early today. Mainly, it was because I couldn't sleep at all the night before. Connor was taking his test today. This was his make it or break it moment. Between where we left things and the weight of what today would bring for him, sleep had been totally out of the question.

I couldn't even lie to myself that I was worried about valedictorian. Something I was once so desperate about was now weighed down by things so much more important.

I made my way to my locker in utter silence, save for the light *thud* of each step. I glanced at the blue and gold lockers and at the posters hung up on the walls. Several were advertising the homecoming dance, with bright colors and cursive fonts.

Homecoming. A time when Brentwood High could

not be more spirited, and a time when everything had fallen apart.

"Maisie?"

I turned to find Principal Oliphant walking down the hallway, donning a polka-dotted raincoat and gripping an umbrella. She shamelessly dripped water onto the floor as she strode toward me. "You're here early," she murmured as she got closer. "I was hoping to get a chance to talk to you before classes started."

Ironically, I thought back to the lengths I'd had to go to once upon a time to get on her jam-packed schedule, all for her to turn me away after two minutes. "Why?"

Principal Oliphant leaned her umbrella against the blue and gold lockers and popped open her work bag. I watched the water pool on the linoleum. "I was waiting to tell you," she said, digging in her bag, "today is Connor's retake test day, meaning your tutoring is over, and that means—"

"Are you reinstating the valedictorian award?"

She found whatever it was that she was searching for, tearing a paper out and offering it to me. She radiated excitement in a way that my numb heart couldn't get in on.

The Brentwood High logo greeted me on a piece of printer paper, along with the words,

To Whom It May Concern,

After much consideration, the Brentwood High school board has

elected to reinstate the valedicto-
rian and salutatorian awards for
the current school year.

I stopped after the first line, even though the notification went on for over a page. There were signatures at the bottom, along with an illustration of our school mascot. "That's great," I told Principal Oliphant, and even I could hear how tired my voice sounded. "I'm glad it was brought back."

"Now, it's premature to say this," she said, taking the paper back from me, "but of course you'll be valedictorian, Maisie. There isn't another student who is close to your perfect GPA and weighted courses. As long as you keep your grades up, of course."

I looked up at the principal, taking in the brightness in her gaze and the wide spread of her lips. She'd gotten what she'd wanted—me to tutor Connor. This was her, holding up her end of the deal. If she sensed she did anything wrong with using the valedictorian award to bribe me, she didn't show it.

Four weeks ago, I would've been over the moon at the news, at the promise, but now it only tasted bittersweet.

"Thanks for everything, Principal Oliphant," I said flatly, shutting my locker door. "Go Bobcats."

And then I turned my back on her and her dripping raincoat, wondering why, even though I'd gotten what I wanted, it didn't feel like winning at all.

I walked to Mrs. Diego's classroom, clutching my bag

strap tightly. I could hide out in her room until it was time to go to homeroom, time to face the music. I had no idea if Jade had spread the word about me kissing Connor. Ava and Rachel hadn't texted demanding answers, so I had a feeling that Connor went along with her demands. And then I started wondering *why*, jumping down a new rabbit hole.

To my surprise, Mrs. Diego's door was already open, her lights already on. When I stepped into the doorway, I froze.

Mrs. Diego sat in her chair, but someone else took up one of the desks in the front row. My heart lurched at the sight of him, so unexpected that for the longest moment, I stood there, staring.

Connor had his head in one hand, hair rucked up by how his fingers were woven into the locks. Even from his slumped-over posture, I could see that he had on his football jersey, a vibrant blue and shocking gold that celebrated homecoming. He was slouched over the desk, a piece of paper in front of him. His Algebra II exam.

I backed out of view, but Mrs. Diego had already seen me, rising from her desk. "I'll be right back," she told Connor, and a second later, she appeared in the doorway. "Good morning. You're here early."

I took another step back from the doorway, afraid he'd hear my voice. "Is he taking his exam?"

"Yes, he started a few minutes ago. He wanted to get it out of the way before school rather than after. However, he *was* surprised when I gave him such a short test." Mrs. Diego raised her eyebrows. "You didn't tell him we altered it?"

I gave her a weary smile. "Guess it slipped my mind."

"He asked for the full-length exam, said he didn't want the advantage, but I didn't have one to give him."

A little flutter stirred behind my ribcage, like a hummingbird moving around. *It doesn't matter*, I tried to tell myself. *It doesn't matter if he tried to do the right thing.*

Quickly, I flipped open the flap of my satchel and dug out the Algebra II textbook. "I—I came by to return this."

Mrs. Diego examined the cover and then squinted at me again. "Did you get enough sleep last night?" She sounded like a mom with the worry in her voice, and with the crease in her brow, she looked like a grandmother. "If you promise not to send Connor signals, I can let you rest your head on one of the desks before classes start."

She'd been teasing about the first part, because she knew that goody-two-shoes Maisie would never help him cheat, but my insides instantly rebelled. Facing Connor now? Not happening. "I'd hate to distract him." I took another step back from her, drawing my bag closer. "I'll see you in last period."

"I know it's a half-day today, but stop by my room when school lets out. I should have his test graded by then."

So there was even more pressure on this day. More to anxiously await. It kept building, trying to flatten me underneath it all. Without another word, I turned on my heel. From here, I had no idea where I'd go, where I'd hide out. *Could hide out in the equipment closet*, I thought bitterly.

I'd gotten probably twenty feet down the long hallway before I heard it, the screech of sneakers squeaking against the floor, followed by a voice. "Maisie!"

When I turned around, I found Connor jogging down the hallway toward me, expression urgent and desperate.

"What are you doing?" I demanded, heart jumping into my throat. "You're literally in the middle of your exam."

"I saw your book," he said as he got closer, "and I wanted—" He cut himself off as he stopped right in front of me, drawing in an unsteady inhale. I stared at the 22 in glittering gold. "I *needed* to talk to you."

I'd begun shaking my head even before he finished his sentence. "Now that you've had how many hours to think of an excuse, now you want to talk?"

"Maisie—"

"You want to talk to me *now*," I cut him off sharply, hating my voice for already beginning to tremble. "When there's no one else around to see it."

He breathed hard, as if he'd finished sprinting a mile, as if his heart was thundering in his chest just as hard as mine. "She would've made everything worse," Connor rushed to say. "She would've told everyone that we kissed, she would've told everyone you were the one to sabotage Madison, she would've—"

"Who cares?" I squared my shoulders, trying to come

off braver than I was. Over his shoulder, I spotted Mrs. Diego standing outside her classroom door and watching us. "I'm not embarrassed to be seen with you."

"I'm *not*." His voice was fierce as he lowered his head to look straight into my eyes. His own were wide, as if he were trying to convey as much truth as possible. "I'm not embarrassed."

"Prove it. Otherwise, you're exactly like Alex." My eyes began to fill with stupid tears. It was ridiculous to be crying over this, but my insides truly felt like they were being squeezed into mush. "You care more about what people think than about me. And I can't—I can't do that again."

He winced as if someone had stabbed him, and I knew that I was the one holding the hilt of the knife. There'd been a time once when all I'd wanted to do was hurt him, back when I'd barely even known him. Now, with the opportunity, the pain in his gaze was enough for me to drown in, and I absolutely *hated* it.

Mrs. Diego had taken a step down the hall at that point, no doubt coming over here to draw Connor back into the classroom. The thought of her seeing me with tears in my eyes filled me with an intense sense of mortification.

"Maisie," he whispered, and his eyes started to seem blurry, too.

"I just can't, okay?" My voice caught, and I forced my features into a scowl, hoping my angry frown would chase away the water blurring my vision. "I can't be a secret friend. A secret anything."

He reached out to me, but I jerked away before his fingers could graze my skin, terrified that the touch would transport me back to last night, to when he kissed me back and elicited a wave of warmth. Terrified it'd break my resolve. "Don't forget to check your work."

And for the second time in twenty-four hours, I walked away from Connor, fighting for composure, and for the second time in twenty-four hours, he let me.

Every part of me trembled as I hurried down the hallway, half-blind by the swarm of tears turning my vision fuzzy.

I didn't stop. Not when I got to the double doors to the parking lot, finding the skies pouring their tears, too. I didn't stop until I was safely in my car, because I'd changed my mind. There was no way I could face today.

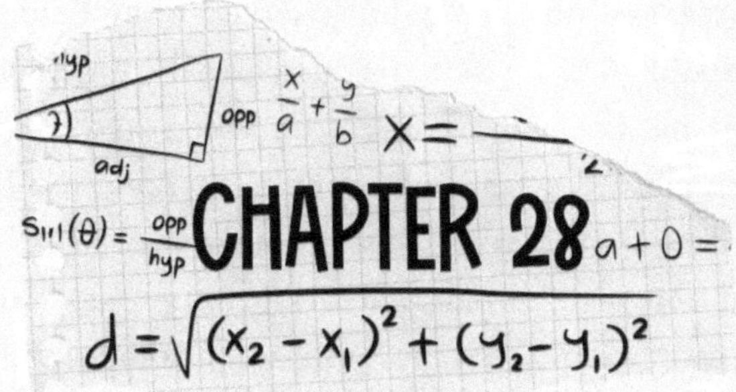

CHAPTER 28

"*Maisie?*"

I stirred at the sound of my name, blinking my eyes open to find my mother leaning over me. She wore her usual Center Inspire attire—a beige pantsuit with a pair of dark heels. Water droplets had bled onto the shoulders of the fabric, and her hair glistened with the rain.

"Mom?" My voice came in a bleary murmur. "What are you doing home?"

"I left my cell phone," she answered and raised her eyebrows at my reclined figure on the couch. "But I could ask you the same thing. Why aren't you in school, young lady?" Though she'd tacked on *young lady*, the words weren't strict or upset. If anything, there was more concern in her voice.

"I wasn't feeling good."

She placed the back of her hand against my forehead, a definite *Mom* move. "You aren't very warm, but I know you didn't sleep well." When I gave her a questioning look, she said, "You left your door open, and I could hear you tossing and turning all night."

I sat up from the couch and ducked my fingers underneath my glasses to scrub my sleepy eyes. "What time is it?"

"Almost ten o'clock."

Ten o'clock. School would've started by now.

"You do *look* sick," Mom amended, tilting her head affectionately. "Do you need some medicine?"

It wasn't medicine that would make me feel better. What I truly needed was to pull the plug in my mind, let all the worries and negativity run down the drain. "I'm sorry I'm not more creative," I said, pressing my fingers firmer against my eyes. "I'm sorry I'm so analytical and straightforward."

Mom didn't say anything at first, taken aback by the sudden subject change. No doubt she was trying to figure out how our conversation train had arrived at *that* station. "Why is that something to apologize about?"

"I know you and Dad wish I was more like you. More artistic. Like Jozie is."

She let out a soft sigh as she sat down on the couch beside me, the cushions shifting under her weight. "Your father isn't very artistic, you know."

"He paints all of your sets for the exhibits."

"Yeah, and you know something about painting sets and walls?" Mom nudged me, forcing me to pry my fingers apart to look at her. "You have to be precise. Patient. It's not as creative as painting a canvas."

I guess I knew that to some extent, but I wasn't sold. "He goes to galleries with you all the time."

"He likes to look at the sets and exhibits," Mom said, amending, "though he likes art too. He thinks it's fun to imagine how someone might've been feeling when they painted a piece. I'm more into searching for hidden meanings, but he likes looking at the psychology behind it, I suppose."

"There's psychology to art? I've never thought about that before."

Mom watched me, eyes betraying no emotion. "You should ask Jozie about the relationship between psychology and art sometime. You might find it interesting."

I hadn't spoken to Jozie since our late-night chat Friday night, but she had texted me a few times, just her normal encouragements. And of course today, the day that I needed that encouragement the most, she hadn't texted.

"But, Maisie." Mom lifted a hand to tuck a piece of hair behind my ear, careful not to let it hook around my glasses frames. "Just because you don't like art doesn't mean you aren't as valuable. Don't apologize for having different passions, Maisie."

"You and Dad were so supportive of Jozie going to art school, and I'm afraid you won't be as supportive of me going for a career involving mathematics."

"What do you want to do with mathematics?" Her smile seemed a little sheepish. "I don't think I've ever asked before."

I didn't think she ever had either, because it felt like I was speaking my answer for the first time. "I think I want to be a math teacher. Maybe a professor in a more advanced math course, even. I just know I like teaching the formulas and finding ways to help students understand it."

It was rare that I ever knew what Mom was thinking. Her mind was a maze to me, hard to navigate, to fully understand. But as she looked at me, expression filled with warmth, I could practically read her mind. "I think that would be a wonderful path for you." She wrapped her arm around my shoulders. "Your father and I will always support you in whatever path you choose. As long as it doesn't involve drugs."

"Wow. Supportive to an extent, huh?"

"Everyone has their limits." Mom gave me a squeeze before looking at me with a serious gaze. "I'm sorry that we took money from your college fund for Jozie's. I didn't realize it might've put stress on you until you asked about scholarships. It wasn't right of us to ask."

"It was okay to ask," I murmured, inhaling her perfume. "I guess it was kind of nice, knowing you believed in me."

"Always."

She kissed the top of my head, and for the first time in a long time, everything felt okay. Especially with her. We could fight tomorrow—and given our history, it was totally possible—and we both might say the wrong things, but at this moment, we understood each other. I smiled at our shadowy reflections in the turned-off TV. That was all I could ask for.

With one last squeeze, Mom let me go and got to her feet. "I have some time before I have to get back. I'm going to make some coffee. Want some—"

"I don't drink coffee."

"—pancakes," she finished, casting me a chastising glare. "Jozie's the one who likes coffee, and *you* are the one who likes blueberry pancakes."

For the first time all day and for a brief moment, I felt happy. It was something small, but it was exactly what I needed in that moment. "I'd love some pancakes."

"You *what?!*"

The pitch both Ava and Rachel's voices got to was enough to splinter my eardrums, but then again, if I'd been expecting anything less, I was kidding myself. When school had let out at noon, I texted Rachel and Ava and asked them to come over. They'd assumed my no-show had something to do with my breakup, and wore twin expressions of worry as soon as I'd opened the door.

However, with nothing left to lose, I dropped the bomb.

Both bombs, actually. One—I had been tutoring Connor Bray for the past three weeks.

Two—I'd kissed him last night.

"You *kissed Connor Bray?*" Rachel shrieked, pressing her palms over her mouth. Rachel and Ava were sitting on my bed while I sat on Jozie's. I figured distance might be a good idea. "No way, no way, no way."

"I'm still hung up on the fact that you've been *tutoring* him, and we never knew," Ava said, digging her elbows into her knees. Her expression was stunned. "You've been living a double life these past few weeks."

"I wanted to tell you," I said earnestly, clutching one of Jozie's pillows to my chest. "Really. But he was embarrassed and wanted to keep it a secret—"

"Who cares about tutoring?" Rachel demanded, excitedly slapping Ava on the arm. "Maisie, you lived my *dream*. Which, just so you know, if you weren't totally heartbroken, I'd be mad at you for ignoring my dibs."

"Heartbroken? I'm not heartbroken."

Ava raised an eyebrow, somehow managing to come off tender with the lofty expression. "You are."

"Totally are," Rachel agreed. "You have sad little bags under your eyes and everything."

I poked my under-eyes, trying to tell if they felt puffy. I explained the full situation to them, how Jade came across Connor and me kissing and ripped the entire moment to shreds. I told them about how she threatened to smear Connor's name through the dirt. "No one was saying anything at school? No one posted any videos or anything?"

"No, I haven't seen it anywhere," Ava told me. "I didn't get any submissions to *Babble*, either. As far as the student body knows, Connor and Jade are still together."

My suspicion *had* been right. Jade hadn't posted

anything. Nothing negative or horrible or humiliating. No one knew what happened.

"You think she'll use it as blackmail or something?" Rachel frowned. "Not that it's *that* big of a deal, but I'd hate for you or Connor to be put on blast. It's lame that she's trying to stop love."

"I can always post something on *Babble*." Ava was already lifting her cell phone. "I can expose her for faking her relationship."

"Connor would be caught in the crossfire." And that was the absolute last thing I wanted. I squeezed my pillow tighter. "I guess for now, we'll wait and see."

Both of the girls fell silent, stewing over other possible alternatives. There truly weren't many. Jade had a handful of wild cards.

"I can't believe you kissed Connor Bray," Rachel said, retreating back to that conversation. "I know we're mad at him, but you have to spill—was he a good kisser?"

"You kissed *who*?"

All three of us turned to the doorway, and the last person I expected to see took up residence on the threshold. "*Jozie?*"

I almost didn't believe what I was seeing at first. My sister stood in the doorway, looking much different from the last time I'd seen her. She had chopped half of her hair off, her dark brown locks now coming to her collarbones. She had on bright blue eyeshadow, a color that clashed with her green sweater and plaid pants. That was Jozie—a fashion nightmare. At least the duffle bag she had slung over her shoulder was a safe and neutral black.

"What are you doing here?" I asked, utterly dumbstruck by her appearance. "I didn't know you were coming."

"I'm here for homecoming, and yeah, we kept it from you so we could surprise you, but *none of that* matters." She spoke rapidly and then waved her hand in the air, batting the topic away. "Who did Rachel say you kissed?"

Ava stood up, gesturing for Rachel's arm. "I—I have so much homework I should get started on—"

"It's a Friday," Jozie told Ava, seeing through the lie.

"Never too early to get started," Rachel chimed in, grabbing Ava's arm and shooting me a wide-eyed nod. "We'll see you tonight?"

I almost asked her what tonight was when I remembered the homecoming game. I couldn't imagine going, but I *could* imagine how disappointed they would be if I backed out now. "I'll text you."

Admittedly, there was a bit of betrayal lingering under my skin when they shut the door behind them, leaving me alone to fend off my sister, who looked like a wild animal ready to lunge.

"You kissed Connor Bray?" she demanded, dropping her duffle bag down on her bed beside me. "When?"

There was no point in dodging the truth. She'd figure it out eventually. "Last night."

Jozie nudged me over so she could sit cross-legged beside me. If it weren't for the old quilt on her bed and not her usual comforter set, it would've been exactly like old times. "Didn't I tell you to stay away from him?"

I told her about how Connor had asked me to tutor

him, and how initially I'd said no, but with a little persuading—and a little lying to a teacher—he'd convinced me to help him. I told her about the relationship advice and about Alex. I had to start at the beginning, and once the words started, I couldn't stop. I expected her to cut me off, because the Jozie I knew had a terrible time listening without interjecting comment after comment, but she just sat, rapt, the entire time. Eyes wide, lips parted, growing more and more...alarmed?

"You kissed him," she repeated, blinking, "and he kissed you *back*?"

"Y-Yeah, I think so." I thought about the way he'd pressed my body against the car, fingers knotting around mine. "Yeah, he did."

"So he likes you?"

I bit down on my lower lip. "I think so."

Jozie tapped her nimble fingers against her chin, mind running a mile a minute judging by the fluttering of her gaze, which didn't land on one thing for more than a moment. "So, what are you going to do about it?"

"It doesn't change anything. He and Jade are going to continue their little charade to win homecoming."

My sister didn't like the answer, features twisting. "Maisie."

"You were the one that told me to stay out of the drama. This is me keeping my nose clean."

"Sometimes things are worth fighting for, you know."

It was a conversation I couldn't go into, not now. Not when everything was so fresh. So, instead, I squinted at her. "You know, you owe me an explanation."

"For what?"

"For blowing me off." I reached out and pinched her bony knee. "It was like you forgot I existed when you went off to college."

Jozie fell back onto the bed with a sigh, squishing a pillow underneath her head. "College, Maisie. It's harder than I thought it'd be. Which sounds dumb, right? But... can I tell you a secret?"

I laid down beside her, shoving my shoulder against hers. "Always."

"I was afraid I made the wrong choice."

Instead of whipping my head toward her in disbelief —because *wow*—I grabbed ahold of her hand and gave it a squeeze.

"I thought it would be amazing, focusing on art. But I've never forced myself to be creative for a class, you know? So it was...a lot."

"So you were dodging my calls because you were having an existential crisis?"

Jozie snorted, a loud, pig-like sound that I hadn't heard in months. It caused me to laugh, affection wrapping its arms around my chest and giving it a squeeze. "I have to break it to Mom and Dad, but I dropped a class. Computer animation—which, thinking about it, might've been too ambitious for me anyway. My advisor suggested it to ease myself into everything. I'll have more free time soon to call you."

I couldn't stop myself from smiling, only a little. It sucked that she had to drop a class, but the selfishness in me won out. "I miss you not being here. I miss having you to talk to when I can't sleep."

"How about this?" Jozie rolled on her side, elbow digging into the covers. She narrowed her blue-eyeshadowed eyelids. "When you can't sleep, text me. I'll make sure to leave my ringer on. And you promise to actually reply to my good morning texts, yeah?"

"Deal." I leaned my head against her shoulder, inhaling her strawberry-scented perfume. "Can you explain the psychology of art to me?"

"You mean art theory?" I felt her tilt her head, attempting to look at me, but I snuggled closer.

"Please? I want to hear."

It wasn't necessarily the psychology behind art, or art theory or whatever, that I wanted to hear, but more just her voice. Her slightly raspy, deep voice that always made me feel better, no matter the situation. It'd been far, far too long since I got to be with her like this, and I wanted to soak up as much of it as I could. Even if we were talking about art and even if it went over my head, I needed this.

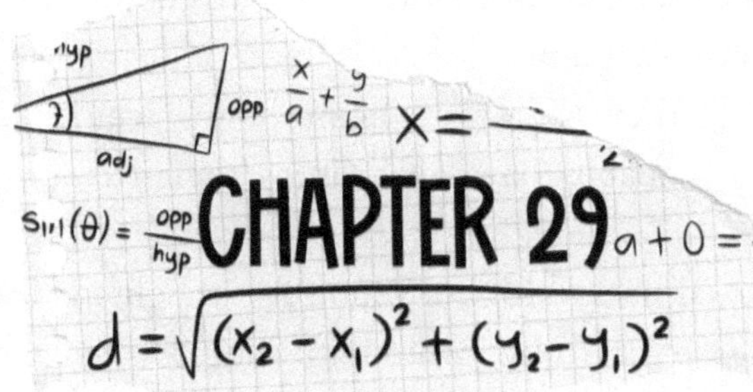

 f I thought the crowd was highly invested in the football game last Friday night, they were ten thousand times more energetic for homecoming.

Almost every student in the student section thrashed signs around in the air, and everyone was wearing their signature blue and gold Brentwood garb. The cheerleaders were nearly drowned out by the dull roar the section created, joining in on the chants.

"They're insane," I said bluntly, staring at the section in the corner of the bleachers. "They've snorted too much blue and gold glitter. Seriously."

Jozie tossed a handful of popcorn into her mouth, speaking around the kernels. "It's the homecoming game. You expect anything different?"

I shouldn't have. Thank God Jozie agreed to sit in a different area. Ava and Rachel were somewhere in the mass of insanity, and though they'd been a bit bummed I hadn't sat with them, I was happy to be excluded from the mosh pit of school spirit.

"I don't see Jade or Madison," I said, craning my neck to spot the co-captains.

"Well, they were on homecoming court, right? They're probably changing into their dresses for halftime."

I rocked backward, but promptly straightened when the knees of the guy behind me dug into my spine. "Right, right."

I watched Connor throughout the game, wincing as his shoulder pads would slam into the Jefferson players, who truly looked built like giants. Quickly, I learned that I hated when Landon passed Connor the ball, knowing that a tackle would inevitably follow unless he crossed the end zone. "Why do people like watching football?" I asked, knotting my hands in my lap. "It's so violent."

"It's an American pastime."

"That's baseball." I watched as the Brentwood Bobcats got into their little formation, the Jefferson Bulldogs facing off. "A contactless sport. Nice and peaceful."

Jozie reached over and patted her hand against my conjoined ones, keeping me from popping my knuckles. "Look at their butts. It'll make you feel better."

"I might've been able to if we hadn't sat in the nosebleeds."

Jozie went from patting my hand affectionately to giving my skin a sharp pinch.

All I had to focus on was either the field or the scoreboard, which counted down the minutes until halftime. I wondered why I hadn't felt this at the game last week.

A Jefferson player slammed into Connor mercilessly,

ramming him into the ground. Even from here, I could see his helmet ricochet off the grass. I sucked in a breath, though the sound was lost in the cheering of the crowd. "Why is our crowd cheering?"

"See how close he is to the end zone? They only need twenty yards." Jozie peered at the scoreboard. "Two minutes left on the clock until halftime."

Two minutes until the weight would lift from my chest. Except it came a whole lot sooner than expected, because before the next play began, a Bobcat hurried toward the lineup to replace number twenty-two. Connor jogged from the field, drawing his helmet off and shaking his head when he got to the sidelines. Like before, the little water boy came up to him with a bottle, gazing up at Connor all starry-eyed. Connor wasn't focused on him, though. His gaze scanned the student section, pressing a hand against his side.

Jozie squeezed my hands once more before letting go. "You know, you could've stayed home. It's not like you're sitting with your friends."

Connor walked over to a cheerleader, ducking his head to say something to her. Probably looking for his girlfriend. *I shouldn't care, I shouldn't care.*

"You shouldn't stare," Jozie went on, lowering her voice. "If you don't want to get caught up in drama, that is."

"Don't poke fun at me," I grumbled. "It's not nice."

Before she had a chance to respond, the crowd erupted in a scream, and everyone surrounding Jozie and me lunged to their feet. I flinched at the sharp noise, which was only followed by the obnoxious sound of the buzzer.

"And that's halftime, folks," the announcer called into the microphone, and the football players on both teams began to make their way off the field. The Bobcats retreated into most likely the field locker rooms while the Bulldogs went off to the far corner of the field, huddling away from the crowd. "Which means it's time for the halftime show by our very own Brentwood High marching band and cheer squad! Let's give them a hand!"

Jozie clapped good naturedly, even though her faced twisted. "Does the marching band still suck?"

"They sound good, but their choreography could be better," I said, thinking of last week where the players stumbled into each other. "Alex was excited about the one tonight."

"Alex," she grumbled. "Your love life is sucking for you lately."

Yeah. Tell me about it.

"Do you want to go get a hot chocolate or something, then? I can ask someone to make sure our seats don't get stolen."

I watched as the band filtered on to the field, wearing their decked-out uniforms. Alex was easy to spot with the tuba wound around his body. "I'm okay," I said honestly. "I might as well watch."

Most likely, this would be the last football game I ever attended. With their win record, the Bobcats were well on their way to the State Championships, but it wasn't like there were many games of the normal season left anyway. Although, it did seem fitting that I was here for the last homecoming of my high school career. It was a weird realization.

The marching band got into their formation on the field with the cheerleaders sorted among them, holding their pom-poms. With a few blows from the student conductor's whistle, the band began their performance, starting hard with a flurry of instruments.

Jozie flinched, putting her hands over her ears. "Yikes."

"Shh," I hissed, dropping my voice to a whisper. "What if one of their parents is sitting behind us?"

"Then they need to invest in some lessons."

I didn't notice Rachel climbing the steps to our bench until she was almost beside me, and she waved her hand in my direction. "Hey, come chat with us while it's half-time. A lot of people went to the concessions, so it won't be as crowded." Before I had a chance to argue, Rachel grabbed my hand, hauling me to my feet. "Jozie, I'll bring her back in a sec."

"Get me another popcorn while you're up!" my sister called after us.

I wanted to dig my heels in, didn't want to go hang out in the student section, but Rachel's unrelenting grip wasn't giving me a choice. Ava was sitting on the bench seat in the front row, thumbs working rapidly on her cell. When she saw me, she scooted over, patting the space beside her. "Hey, you."

"Jozie wanted a popcorn—"

"We'll get it in a second," Rachel assured, forcing me

to sit. She glanced backward at the field where the band members and cheerleaders weaved their way through the song. Alex, in the back, was swaying his tuba back and forth, totally in the moment. "How are you feeling?"

I glanced around at everyone around me. *Way* too many listening ears. "I'm okay."

"I'm glad you came tonight." Rachel placed her hand on my knee and gave it a squeeze. "Things work out the way they're supposed to, don't they?"

Did they? Was that why I sat here now, in the last place I ever thought I'd be, single, with the guy I liked too afraid to stand up for me? This was what was supposed to happen? "I guess so."

"Okay, Brentwood, before we get back to the game, let's take a second to recognize the high school home-coming court!" the announcer proclaimed over the mic, and the field became a flurry of movement as the band shuffled into a corner of the grass, playing the fight song. Three couples from each of the grades congregated on the field, wearing their best dresses and suits.

Madison was the first I spotted, and Jozie had been right—she *had* changed from her cheer uniform. Madison now wore a glittering blue floor-length gown that hugged her curves in a way that totally suited her, and her golden-brown hair hung in perfect coils around her face. She had her arm wound around Landon's, who still wore his football gear. She smiled at something he said, beaming underneath the lights.

But they weren't the couple I focused on.

There was no denying that Connor and Jade were a

cute couple. Underneath the stadium lights, Connor gleamed like he was under a spotlight. Like Landon, he wore his shoulder pads too, and the brilliant blue jersey was the perfect match to Jade's rich golden dress. Brentwood High colors. The perfect football player/cheerleader pair. Jade's dress was just as beautiful as Madison's, and with her hair pulled back into a loose bun, she definitely looked like royalty material.

Looking at them, you'd never be able to guess it was fake.

I'd never even entertained the idea of being on homecoming court, but I wondered, in a different universe, what it would've been like to be the one on his arm.

"And then, finally, our last couple in the running for homecoming king and queen! We have Brentwood football player, Connor Bray, and co-cheer captain, Jade Dyer!"

Jade tugged Connor forward a step to separate them from the lineup, giving the crowd her best princess wave. Connor didn't wave; he wasn't even smiling. Instead, his attention seemed to sort through the crowd, never settling.

Until he found me.

Even though my heart ached, it apparently hadn't gotten the memo, because it gave a slow, longing-filled *thump*.

I watched as Connor looked over—not at Jade, though, but at Madison, who'd already been waiting for him to return her gaze. She tilted her chin down, and it took me several seconds to realize it was a nod.

Connor dropped his arm, forcing Jade to drop hers.

She tilted her head at him, and it was obvious she was asking him a question. His lips moved in response.

"You think he's about to ask her to homecoming?" I muttered, insides wincing at the prospect.

Rachel, on one side of me, picked up my hand and gave it a squeeze. Ava, on the other side, picked up her cell phone.

Madison suddenly broke away from Landon's arm and grabbed her best friend's wrist, snatching Jade back from pursuing her boyfriend. My heart seemed to know what was happening before my brain did, racing as Connor strode from the field with determination written across his features.

He isn't coming over here. Don't get your hopes up. He wouldn't.

Except...he did.

Connor stopped in front of the student section, beside where a small gaggle of cheerleaders crouched. He stood back enough so that he could see past the railings, tilting his head to look at me, and drawing in a deep, shaky breath. "Maisie."

"What are you doing?" I whispered, as if the entire student section wasn't already rapt.

He hauled himself up onto the edge of the bleacher railings, clutching the bar with one hand, and now I was the one tilting my head to look up at him. He leaned down, picking up a bouquet of flowers one of the girls passed to him.

"Maisie Matthews," He spoke my name clearly, as if

he wanted to leave no room for confusion. "Will you go to homecoming with me?"

I blinked once. Twice. I would've thought I'd be more mortified in this situation, but all I felt was a thick and dumb amount of shock.

Utterly, truly speechless.

I turned to Ava, finding her with her cell phone propped up. My wild-eyed expression was reflected in the camera lens.

After my brain kickstarted back into gear, I realized the bouquet he held wasn't filled with white flowers— they were *paper*, folded together to create a bouquet. Something I'd always done during our tutoring sessions, something that, though I hadn't taught him, he'd learned how to do on his own.

"You can say no," Connor went on, those hazel eyes focused solely on me. His hair was damp, curling at his temples, and his fingers trembled where they gripped the metal bar, hinting at his nervousness. But he didn't back down. "I'd understand if you said no. I've made mistake after mistake with you, but you're the only one I want to go with."

"Connor." I let my gaze drift past him, but I couldn't see Jade on the field anymore. "She's going to—"

"I don't care," he cut me off, eyes wide and earnest. "She can post all she wants about my family, who I live with, how I failed Algebra II—I don't care about any of it. I never should've cared about it. And I realize now why I don't anymore."

God, there were so many eyes on me, and a distant

part of my brain knew it, but I was wholly and totally swept up in *his* eyes. "Why not?"

"Because, Maisie Matthews, none of it matters if I lose you in the process."

It was like the entire student section behind me gave a collective gasp, one that echoed like a rush of wind in my ears.

Connor's lips tugged into a boyish smile, but I knew it wasn't due to their reaction—it was because of mine. My jaw was practically on the ground. "I was the one supposed to be giving you love advice, but it was *you* who made me realize I wanted more. I wanted to be with someone who makes me laugh when I don't feel like laughing. Someone who lets me write them notes so they can make paper flowers out of them." He laughed a little. "Someone to teach how to parallel park. You're the only person in the world who's ever made me feel like it's okay to be *me*. And I don't want to keep it a secret anymore."

With her free hand, Rachel pushed at my shoulders, practically shoving me to my feet. My knees wobbled, uncertain if they wanted to support my weight as they carried me to the edge of the bleachers. Connor offered the flowers to me. The six origami roses glued in place were sloppy and crinkled but wholly perfect, causing my heart to expand in my chest.

Connor's gaze roamed my features, and his now free hand came up to smooth a hair back from my cheek, careful not to nudge my glasses. It was a tender touch I'd found myself longing for over the course of these past few weeks. "Whatever happens, I want to face those consequences with you. Only ever you."

"That was really romantic," I told him, and though my voice sounded deadpan, my insides felt like a giant exclamation point.

"Can—can I kiss you?" he murmured, a searing warmth in his expression that I wanted to lose myself in. Before I could respond, he added, "I kind of stink."

I gave a short, nearly strangled laugh. "I'm a fan of that sweaty football player smell."

His lips split into a grin at that, one that caused my lips to do the same. And then, for the whole bleachers to see, Connor wrapped a hand around the side of my head and pressed that smiling mouth against mine.

Immediately, my free hand came up to rest against the collar of his shoulder pads, fingers pressing against his hot skin. Just as they'd cheered when someone scored a touchdown, the student section erupted behind us. Not only the student section—the *entire* bleachers.

I broke away from him to duck my head, feeling my cheeks flame. Connor laughed quietly, the musical sound stealing some of my tension. "Meet me by the concession stand."

"Right now?"

He glanced back at the scoreboard, checking the time, and gave a nod. "Right now." And then, with one last quick kiss, he jumped back onto the ground.

When I turned around, Ava's cell wasn't the only one trained on me. I couldn't even count the amount of people who pointed their cameras at me, people who I didn't even recognize. It was kind of like that dream where I stood before a giant crowd in my underwear—I felt *that* exposed.

Ava lowered her cell phone first. "Wow," she said and nodded once, letting out a soft, contented sigh. "I've never felt more single in my life."

CHAPTER 30

"Congratulations, Maisie."

"Yeah, congratulations. I'm so happy for you."

"Were you the girl from the closet?"

"Oh, those flowers are *so* adorable."

I gave an awkward, nervous laugh to each person who walked up to me, clutching the flowers closer to my chest as if they were a shield. Then again, fat chance I'd be invisible now. I just kissed Connor Bray in front of the entire school. Ava was probably putting it on *Brentwood Babble* right this instant.

What ship name would she give us? *Maisor?*

I looked down at my flowers, and though they made me smile, I couldn't help but cringe a little.

Some of the band members walked past me on their way back to the bleachers, and I spotted the tuba among the sea of students. Alex's face, though, stayed in my blind spot, and though I felt a little guilty, there was no denying that I was happier this way.

Connor, still dressed in his full football gear, dodged

a band member as he jogged off the field. When he got close, Connor wove his fingers through mine and drew me underneath the bleachers, tucking us back into the shadowy corner we'd ducked under weeks ago.

"There, not so many eyes," he said softly, trailing his thumb over the backs of my knuckles. "I've got five minutes before I need to be back on the field. Coach wasn't happy I skipped out on our halftime huddle, but this is more important."

"I didn't think you'd do something like this," I admitted breathlessly, looking down at the roses. "I wasn't even expecting it."

"You deserved to be more than a secret." His lips twisted into something more serious. "I should've said something last night. I shouldn't have let Jade get to me, should've done *something*." Connor ducked his head to bring his forehead level with mine. "I let you down, but I swear to you, it's not going to happen again."

I'd never dreamed of Connor Bray saying things like that to me, making promises like that to me, but here he was. The promise settled over me like a warm blanket, tucking me closer, turning my insides into a gooey pool.

"I don't want to care about what other people think," he went on, bringing my hand up between our chests. "And I don't when we're together. When I'm with you, I don't think about anything else *but* you."

I looked down at the roses once more. I pictured him looking up a tutorial online, pictured him attempting to fold the edges right. "What about Jade? She'll be angry."

"I meant what I said. She can have my reputation,

and she can do her worst." He blinked, concern flitting across his features. "Wait, are you—are you worried about you? About her spreading lies about you?"

"I'm not." That was another thing that had changed over the course of the past few weeks, funnily enough. Maybe it was because I'd grown more confident in who I was. Maybe it was because Connor helped me see that. "I'm just...I don't know."

Connor dropped my hand then to loosely frame my face with his palms, eyes suddenly becoming desperate. "I never should've put you on the stupid list. It was horrible and childish and cruel, and I've regretted it ever since."

I shifted the bouquet of flowers in my grip, listening to them crinkle. "I think you do need to explain to me, though, why you put me on the Most Likely Tos. And how you came up with the label."

His cheeks reddened, but he gave a solemn nod. "The Top Tier votes the first Friday of the school year, and then someone—I honestly don't know who—compiles everything to go out in the list. I wasn't going to vote. Ironically enough, that was the same day that Mrs. Diego and Principal Oliphant called me to the office." He reached up and rubbed the side of his neck. "Told me about the retake test, told me about getting a tutor. They mentioned you—said you were in advanced math, best tutor in the school. That you did math worksheets for fun."

"Wow, Mrs. Diego didn't hold back, did she?" I grumbled.

He chuckled once, but pushed on. "It was fresh on my mind when I needed to pick a label. I said it without really thinking." And then everything about him sobered. His hand trembled as it came up to coax my hair back, and then he spoke again. "But I never, *ever* should've done it. I didn't realize how hurtful it'd be. That day when you said it bothered you, it—it nearly tore me apart, knowing it was my fault you felt that way."

I pressed a palm against his shoulder pad, shaking my head. "It's okay. Seriously." Looking back, being on the Most Likely To list wasn't all a bad thing. It showed me that it *was* okay to have my own passions and embrace them. It stung at first, but being on the list showed me that it was okay to be *me*.

And then it dawned on me. "Just *please* tell me that after all that, you passed your exam."

Connor raised his eyebrows, eyes sparkling. "Why? You wouldn't date a guy who failed math?"

"Unfortunately, it might be a deal-breaker."

Connor spread his palms a little, gesturing at himself. "Well, good thing you're looking at a senior who passed Algebra II."

Laughing, I wrapped my arms around him and leaned in, the flowers crinkling as I gripped him tightly. The hug was awkward due to the shoulder pads, but I didn't care. It was one last weight off my shoulders, one less worry. He'd done it, despite all his fears. He'd passed.

His hand smoothed up my back. "I tried to take the longer test."

I smiled over his shoulder. "I know."

"I wanted to do right by it. By you."

And he did. Oh, did he ever.

The embrace only lasted for a moment, though, before I leaned back. "You really do stink."

Connor laughed, but he did let go enough to swipe up my hand and press a kiss to my knuckles. The action was so tender, so sudden, that my pulse surged in surprise. It took the humor out of the moment and swept it away, replacing the amusement with something that felt a lot more charged. "Are we the real deal?"

"As real as it comes." I rose up onto my tiptoes and pressed my mouth against his. His lips were just as soft as they'd been for our first kiss, just as firm and toe-curling. I traced my hand down the material of his jersey, basking in the way he touched me, the way that I was now allowed to touch him.

The kiss deepened to the point where I nearly cast my flowers to the side when a voice cut in. "Hey!"

Connor and I sprang apart to find Madison standing at the opening of the bleachers we'd ducked under. She was back in her A-line skirt, her hands on her hips. "As sweet as you two are, the game's about to start, Connor, and unless you want Coach to bench you for the rest of homecoming, you should probably get out there."

A burst of alarm crossed Connor's features, like he'd forgotten about the game entirely.

Madison raised her eyebrows at him. "And you should brace yourself, because your buddies are going to tease you for such dramatic PDA."

"I don't care," Connor replied easily, smiling. "I only care about what one person thinks."

"And I'll tease you about it tomorrow," I promised, fighting the urge to reach back out for him. "Go, though. We'll talk more after."

"After you *win*," Madison added, smirking.

Connor lingered on me for another moment, staring until I waved him on with a chuckle. Without another word, he ducked out from underneath the bleachers, leaving the co-captain and me alone. I wanted to follow after him, half worrying that Madison would burst my happy bubble, but I had to know. "How's Jade?"

"Pissed," she said, but her voice came off amused. "But I think she realizes that she lost the game she was playing. Or maybe she realized that she was the only player."

It wasn't exactly the stance I was expecting from Madison, and I definitely hadn't been expecting the smile. "Did you help him?"

She reached up and tugged on the end of her ponytail. "He came to me and said that he wanted to go public with you. I helped him brainstorm ideas."

I raised my eyebrows. "And you thought asking during the homecoming game was fitting?"

"It was the most public way he could say he cared about you." She laughed, as if knowing it was totally opposite of me. "You have to admit, it was perfect."

Quite honestly, if I were to take the bit of embarrassment away, it *was* kind of perfect. It left no room to doubt Connor's feelings. The one way to be sure. "Why, though? Why help him? I thought you said you'd be the first to say 'I told you so.'"

Madison took a step closer, even though her hesitation was clear. With the way she was looking at me—nostalgia mixed with something else, something like remorse—it threw me back to the time when things had been drastically different. "I know it doesn't make up for freshman year, but I wanted to be a part of something that made you happy. I could make a million excuses, but...you didn't deserve what I did to you back then."

"We don't have to talk about it now." It was a conversation I wanted to have, for sure, but another part of me wanted to keep tonight as it was. On a happy note. I wasn't sure if we could ever go back to the way things were before—the rift between us seemed too big—but I was open to talking things out. "Not on homecoming. We can talk later."

Her expression was a bit uncertain, but she nodded. "Are you excited for the dance tomorrow?"

"I don't even have a dress," I said with a chuckle. These past few weeks had gone by in a whirlwind, and even though I'd planned to go with Alex, we never got around to coordinating. I didn't even think I had anything in my wardrobe that would work.

"You can come look at my closet, if you want," Madison offered softly. "We used to swap clothes all the time, do you remember that? I'm sure I have a dress that would look good."

Wistfulness stirred in her gaze. I could see myself reflected in her eyes, could see the history stretching out between us. Looking at her now, the anger I'd always felt was absent. Maybe it was because she helped Connor. Maybe it was because, for the first time, she chose me over Jade. Maybe it was because I was on cloud nine.

But right in that moment, when she waved the white flag, I found myself accepting it. "I'd love that."

Even though our paths diverged back in freshman year, there'd always be the years before that I couldn't erase. The years where we were each other's best friend. The years we planned out our weddings and watched movies and put up posters on our walls. And even if I could erase them, for the first time, I wasn't sure that I would've.

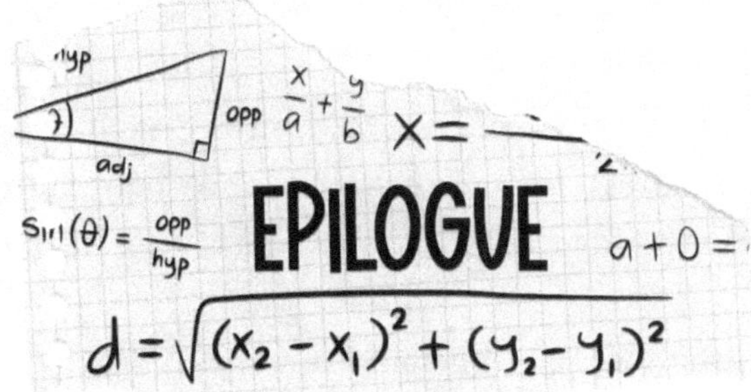

Can someone say SWOON?! Friday night, at the homecoming game of the century, Brentwood High's very own Connor Bray stepped out into the limelight with his new leading lady—and can I just say, as that leading lady's BFF, EEEEK!

Wait, you live under a rock, didn't go to the homecoming game, and don't believe me? Shame on you! But here are pics to prove it ;)
#TEAMCONSIE4EVAH

"Oh my gosh, who sent in the photo of us underneath the bleachers?" I demanded as I scrolled through the photos on *Brentwood Babble*, my jaw dropping. Someone had snapped a picture of the moment we hugged, getting a great shot of my back and Connor's content, closed-eyed expression. "How did they know we were even under there?"

"People are sneaky," Ava said, sitting on Jozie's bed. Her white dress accentuated her pink hair perfectly, which was braided over her shoulder. "Are you almost done?"

"Putting on the finishing touches," Rachel said, swiping her eyeshadow brush once more across Ava's lids. Rachel's dress was a long-sleeved red one, filled with sequins. "Besides, Maisie, you got to admit—some of those photos are adorable."

Of course, she wasn't wrong. Though many of the photos were blurry—Ava had posted pictures that others had submitted through the anonymous box—there were quite a few good ones, like Connor beaming down at me while I looked at the flowers. Or the photo taken a second before he pressed his lips to mine.

Trying not to grin like an idiot, I saved them all to my cell phone. "Team Consie," I echoed, looking at the hashtag. "I like it."

"*I* like your dress," Rachel said as she turned to me, giving my outfit a nod of approval. "Madison came through, huh?"

The dress was a soft baby pink, off the shoulder with a hemline falling a smidge above my knees. There was a bit of tulle too, and though it was a little scratchy against my skin, it gave the dress a perfect amount of puffiness.

When I picked out the dress, we still put off the conversation about our friendship. It seemed like there were things she needed to come to terms with first before we could talk things out, and I understood that. But for me, even though our years of friendship had been lost, buried under years of hurt, I could finally look at my old best friend and feel okay.

She was a bit like Connor—so wrapped up in the popularity of it all, but I had a feeling that things would change for her.

And even though things weren't like they were, I knew that if Jade waged war with Madison for picking Connor's side, I'd be right behind my old best friend, pitchfork ready.

I pushed to my feet and dusted my palms down the front of my dress. I wore my white sneakers, because Maisie Matthews in heels was a safety hazard, and with my hair curled, I felt perfectly myself. Just the dolled-up version. "Anyone have the time?"

"Connor will be here in ten," Jozie answered from the doorway, holding a coffee mug in her hand. Even from here, I could see the rolling steam. "And then Mom will assault the two of you with photos, so get ready."

"Please, *I'll* be assaulting you with the camera," Ava said, flashing me a wink. "Brentwood wants some inside pics of their new favorite couple."

I gave her a look that consisted of pressed lips and raised eyebrows.

Ava sighed. "One photo."

"And then..."

"And no more articles on the two of you without permission," she muttered, slouching her shoulders. "Not that I'd ever do that."

"Except for this morning."

When Ava and Rachel showed up to the house to get ready, the first thing Ava did was show me the article as well as all the photos everyone had taken of Connor and me. Thus, our new rules had been born.

Rachel chimed in. "In her defense, you kind of owed it to her. You kept it a secret from us literally until the day the whole school got to find out."

"That's why you had one pass. Now, we're practicing boundaries."

I didn't want Brentwood High glorifying our relationship the way they glorified his and Jade's. They worshipped it so much that they couldn't even tell that it wasn't real, and I didn't want that. Navigating whatever the future with Connor looked like, I wanted to do that privately. Just him and me.

And maybe I'd let Ava take photos here and there.

"I'm pretty sure Jade is still going to win homecoming queen," Ava said, peering at her phone screen. "Everyone casted their votes before school let out yesterday, so I'm assuming they all still voted for her."

Rachel reached out and squeezed my shoulder. "I can't believe Connor pulled out of the running."

Yeah, *that* news had shocked the entirety of Brentwood High. Ava had dropped the bomb last night on *Babble*—with Connor's permission—and from what she'd said, the responses hadn't stopped coming in, all summarizing in *WTF*.

I didn't blame them. Connor quitting homecoming court the day before crowning? Blasphemy. But he was taking his life into his own hands, living his life for himself and on his terms, and I was happy for him.

"Maybe Landon will win, then. He'd be a great homecoming king." Rachel helped me put in a pair of teardrop earrings Ava had picked out. "Thank you for being there for me," I told them, sentimental all over again. "And for not hating me for keeping secrets."

"If anything, I'm mad at Connor," Rachel said with a frown. "How can he ask you to lie to your best friends?"

"Not a lie," Ava corrected, patting my shoulder. "But we're always here for you, Maisie. No matter what."

I'd struck gold when Ava and Rachel had welcomed me into their friendship duo—it was something I always thought of, but now, more than ever, I *knew* it. They were two people in the whole world who would always have my back. And even though we didn't have a decade of friendship under our belt like I'd had with Madison, it didn't make it any less special.

"Oh my goodness." Mom appeared over Jozie's shoulder and put a hand to her mouth. "You three look so beautiful!"

"Waterworks alert," Jozie muttered, and ducked out of reach when Mom tried to slap her. "Hey, hey, careful. I've got coffee."

"Maisie, that dress looks so stunning on you," Mom gushed, stepping into the room. She picked up my hand and drew me to my feet. Jozie had accurately predicted it; tears filled Mom's eyes. "My little baby. I can't believe it's your senior year. Soon it'll be prom, and then graduation...Oh, and your valedictorian speech!"

Even though the attention made me a bit uncomfortable, especially with my friends bearing witness to Mom's antics, I found myself smiling under her watery gaze, feeling seen. This time, her tears were for me. "Get ready for me to practice it, like, *all* the time."

"And this time next year, you'll be off to college, too," Mom went on, and she seemed to realize how dramatic she was being. Frantically, she swiped at her eyes. "I'm fine, I'm fine. Look away."

I reached out and patted Mom's shoulder. "You've got me for a while."

Once more double-checking that my laces were tied, I looked at my reflection in the mirror. My dark hair was loose and wavy. My lips were pink with gloss. With happiness in my eyes, I just waited for my football player to get here.

And not even a second later, his face appeared over Jozie's shoulder in the hallway. "Is this where the party's at?"

We all jolted when Connor's voice interjected, and my heart immediately jumped into my throat, especially because he had a total view of my messy, pre-homecoming-cluttered bedroom. Rachel had left the can of hairspray uncapped on my dresser, and there was some form of eyeliner stick or foundation bottle *somewhere*.

But holy, he looked *amazing*.

And everyone was totally smitten.

I, though, had the good grace to be embarrassed by literally every girl in the room staring. "Jozie! You were supposed to be on boy duty!"

"I didn't think he'd sneak in like a spy," she said with a chuckle. "Connor, good to see you again."

Ava surged forward and grabbed Jozie's wrist, drawing her back out into the hallway. "Hey, will you come take some pictures in the living room? My mom will probably say she didn't get enough earlier."

"Of me too!" Rachel followed after them, shooting Connor a sweet smile. "Love the tie."

"Get ready," Mom said, glancing between us with her hands clasped in front of her. "I'm sure between Ava and me, you'll be posing for pictures all night."

"Sounds like a plan." Connor grinned down at her, and once the peanut gallery had dispersed, I could finally get a better look at him.

Since I didn't know what color my dress would be until this morning, I'd told Connor to go with a plain black tie, and he looked drop-dead gorgeous in it. He didn't style his hair, and it fell in its normal loose waves. His hair was a bit like my sneakers—though we were dressed up, we had something that was us.

Connor's eyes roamed over me in a way that made my toes curl, like I was the prize he'd been waiting for. "Passable?" I asked, flaring my skirt to the side.

"You're perfect." He came close enough to rest his hand on my waist, and I leaned into the touch. "Absolutely perfect."

I pressed a soft, sweet kiss against his lips. "You know, I still have your sweatpants," I said, trying *not* to beam like a doofus. "I'm going to keep them, though. I guess I'm just a total creeper, hiding them away in my dresser."

"Now I just need something to remember *you* by."

I wrapped my arms around his waist, peering up at him. "You have me."

Connor hooked a dark curl behind my ear and allowed his fingers to trail over my cheek, the exact same way he'd done once upon a time in the kissing closet. It still made my heart flutter. "I do have you, and you're all I need."

This time, he was the one to kiss me, with that one hand gripping my waist and the other delicately touching my cheek. My head swam with the sweetness warring with the intensity, but I matched him touch for touch, kiss for kiss, wishing I could do this all day.

Connor pulled back with a slight gasp, his cheeks pinking. "We should probably go before they come looking for us."

"Probably."

He wound his fingers around mine, bringing my knuckles to his lips. "You know, I should've asked you to homecoming in a math-related way. Something like, 'You're sweeter than pi.'"

I cringed as I led him down the hallway, laughing. "My answer would've been different."

"What about, 'You are the square to my root'? Would that work?"

"I see our next tutoring session needs to be on math-related puns."

He gave my hand a squeeze.

Mom corralled us outside when we got into the living room, claiming the better lighting and backgrounds were against the brick of the house. Connor was a great sport about all of it, watching as I posed with Ava, Rachel, and Jozie. He even snapped a photo of me with my parents, his smile visible even from behind the camera.

Rachel, standing next to Ava and Jozie, began clapping her hands. "Okay, pose, pose, pose. We need photos."

"One photo, Ava," I told her, holding up a finger, positioning myself at Connor's side. His arm wrapped easily around me, hand landing at a respectable spot on my waist, like he'd been doing it for a while. Like he'd been *wanting* to do it for a while. I leaned into Connor, laying my other hand against his chest. "One."

She winked at me. "No, I only get to *post* one. I can take as many as I want."

Connor ducked his face into the top of my head, and his slight chuckle shivered its way down my spine. Mom fumbled for her camera as Dad surveyed the scene with a serene expression. Jozie stood beside him, her arm looped through his.

All of my favorite people.

While Mom and Ava were trying to find the perfect light, I tipped my head back toward Connor, pushing my hair back from the breeze. "I've got a good one. 'I was supposed to solve for x—so glad I found u instead.'"

Connor tried to stifle the laugh, but it was impossible. I chuckled along with him, chest swelling with triumph, skin warming as he ducked his face into my hair.

Ava gasped. "Ooh, hold that pose! That's a good one."

I tried to be professional after that, to keep the dorky smiles at bay, but when Connor readjusted his grip on my waist and pulled me closer, whispering in a low voice that no one could hear, I couldn't fight the goosebumps. "I'm glad I found you, too."

I looked up at Connor, chest swelling with an emotion that threatened to burst inside me. That hazel gaze of his, equally green and brown in this light, was as tender as a touch, skimming my features.

Instead of listening to Ava, I stretched onto my tip-toes and kissed his cheek, feeling Connor smile beneath my lips. I'd been wrong before. Our story hadn't been over before. In fact, it was only the beginning.

Thank you so much for reading!
Order Book 2 in the Most Likely To series, Dreaming
About the Boy Next Door today and fall for the best
friend's brother!
Keep reading to see the first kiss from Connor's point of
view!

CONNOR'S POV

Over the course of my high school career, so many things had been engrained in me that I'd never stopped to question whether or not they were true.

One: Football is life.

Two: Popularity is key.

Three: Never let anyone see behind the mask.

And here Maisie Matthews was, making me second guess all of it.

I'd never thought the girl beside me would become as important to me as she was now. God, I'd never felt this way before, where my chest seemed to buzz at the prospect of our tutoring sessions.

And I knew better. I knew my heart wasn't beating faster at the idea of logarithmic functions.

But transparency had never been my strong suit. It'd been easier to throw up wall after wall than to be tackled to the ground, forced to lay everything bare.

Except apparently, Maisie used to be a linebacker in her past life. I swear, no one got me rambling about the things I kept under lock and key the way she did. It was more than that, though. She didn't force it out of me—I wanted her to know it all.

"Alex and I broke up."

The words jolted me from my thoughts, and I turned toward her. She leaned against the side of her car beside me, her shoulder touching mine in a way that I shouldn't have thought twice about. With her, there were a whole lot of *shouldn'ts*. "What? When?"

"Last night. I wasn't going to tell you."

Why? I wanted to demand, a desperate buzzing in my ear. *Why weren't you going to tell me?* After all the love advice, me practically operating without a license in that regard, she should've told me as soon as it happened. Should've ripped me a new one.

My thoughts slowed up, cleats skidding in the grass. If she wasn't going to tell me before, what made her change her mind?

Maisie lifted her chin. "I didn't realize how suffocated I felt until after. Trying to stuff myself into a mold to fit what he wanted me to be." Her voice was soft as she spoke, enough for each syllable to make me feel like the air was way too thin. She traced the pattern of her skirt, unable to look me in the eye. "He always looked down on me, and I knew it. Not on purpose, I don't think—Alex isn't cruel."

I could think of a million descriptors for the meathead, and cruel probably was one of them. Maybe not purposefully cruel. I'd never met anyone as air-headish as that kid. But still. "You give him a lot of credit. I'm not that generous."

"He wants to be like you, the cool guy everyone looks up to."

Hearing that made my lips want to twist into a grimace, the words leaving a bad taste in my mouth. It brought back blind conviction Number Two. "It's overrated. If I could trade places with Alex, I would." As soon as I said it, panic bolted through me, as sharp as the pain of a muscle being strained too far. Much too transparent. I scrambled to cover my tracks. "He can be the guy everyone scrutinizes. Because I know what it feels like to be suffocated, too."

I glanced at Maisie, analyzing her expression. It was oddly calm for our conversation, for the weight of it all. Her eyes behind her glasses were clear of any tears, and I couldn't see any sadness there, either. Her brown hair hung over one shoulder, a few strands twisting with the wind, and I had the sudden urge to comb my fingers through it.

Not the time, Connor.

"I wish I figured it out sooner. That we wouldn't work. I wouldn't have had to worry about keeping all this from him. Figured out that I...wanted more."

Her words speared through me, ringing true with a corner of my heart I'd beaten into submission over the years. The section of my heart that bowed down to the convictions. Football is life, popularity is key, and never let anyone see behind the mask.

I wanted more. Weeks ago, when I met Maisie for the first time, I never could've dreamed of how much her feelings seemed to mirror my own.

Like I said, Maisie Matthews had been the one to make me second guess everything. The one to make me want more.

My body moved before I even gave it permission, desires overriding my brain, though not for the first time when it came to her. I thought about the closet, tracing her cheek. I'd been able to stop myself in time then—before I got us both into serious trouble—but I couldn't stop myself now.

I picked her hand up off her skirt and held it, praying mine wasn't sweaty from how badly I wanted this. *Please don't pull away*, I thought. "You deserve more. You deserve the world, Maisie Matthews."

She held perfectly still for a moment, looking at our hands in a way that I couldn't even begin to guess what she was thinking. My words—jeez, they were probably overly sentimental, but I believed them with my whole heart. She deserved the world, and I'd do anything to get it for her.

Please don't pull away.

Maisie maneuvered her fingers underneath mine, and for a split second, I thought she was going to drop my hand. I didn't know what I would've done then. There'd be no playing it off like this was a love advice session. It had to be obvious. *I* had to be obvious. With how smart she was, she had to know.

She threaded her fingers through mine, bringing our palms closer, tightening the grip she had on my hand.

I'd held hands with a lot of girls. I couldn't count how

many times Jade had grabbed my hand, flaunting our relationship for all to see.

But when Maisie pressed her palm flush with mine and then looked up at me with her soft brown eyes, I nearly lost my mind. I sure as hell wasn't breathing.

She moved before I could. Trust me when I say that if she hadn't literally rendered me motionless, I would've moved first. The thought that had been lingering in my mind for days now had resurfaced with a need so strong that I would've leaned in first, but Maisie was too fast.

She kissed me first, and just like that, it was game over.

The hesitation behind her kiss was obvious from the barely there pressure of her mouth, almost like she thought I'd pull away at any second. As if. With a sharp breath in, I threaded my fingers through the hair at the back of her head, relishing the softness that slipped against my skin like silk. I angled her head back and kissed her for real.

Any hesitation? Gone.

The way her lips moved against mine was nothing like the forceful claim I'd been so used to over the past few months, and that alone caused the electricity to build underneath my skin. She kissed me because she wanted to, because after all of our sessions together, we hadn't been building to an algebra exam—we'd been building to this.

I'd never been challenged the way she challenged me, and for the first time in my entire life, I didn't care about any of it. Not about football, not about popularity, and not about hiding my feelings. Not right now. Not with her. With her, in this moment in time, none of it mattered.

If only I could've held on to that confidence, to that newfound conviction, bottled it up and kept it safe. I didn't realize how easy it would've been for the old convictions to seep back in. Didn't realize someone would be there to smash them to bits.

But for this one moment, as I pressed Maisie against the side of the car, I let myself believe that anything was possible. As long as it was with her.

Dreaming About the Boy Next Door

Kissing your best friend's brother is never a good idea, but I went ahead and did it anyway.

Order your copy today!

ACKNOWLEDGEMENTS

This book has been such a whirlwind to work on, and it feels like the time just flew by! I started writing this one in November of 2021, but I'd started outlining it way back in July of 2021. And now, here we are, at the acknowledgements!

This book really has touched my heart in so many ways, and I'm so excited to share it with you. So first and foremost, thank you, my sweet readers, for picking up this book and giving it a chance. I hope it made you smile, swoon, and cheer right along with the characters.

Thank you to my INCREDIBLE editors, Jessi and Zeze, who saw this book in a pretty rough state. Your encouragements as well as your critiques helped me along the path, and there's no way I would've gotten here without your keen eyes.

Megan, thank you for yet another gorgeous cover. Every time I look at it, I get serious heart eyes!

No acknowledgement section is complete without thanking my amazing parents. They've listened to every stress, every plot hole, and every confusing explanation of the chapters. Even though my brain is crazy and hard to follow, thank you for your constant support and suggestions.

Mom, thank you for talking through this new series through with me. Your excitement is what really spurred me on when I was feeling discouraged.

Dad, thank you for talking the business side of things through with me. I know you think the boy should've had a head on the cover, but I still love you.

And thank You for always guiding my steps and for keeping Your hand on mine. I'm never alone with You, and I know none of this would be possible without Your blessing. Thank You for giving me this passion.

What Are Friends For?

Who said falling for your best friend was a good thing?

Out of My League

Fake dating the captain of the baseball team is all fun and games until someone catches feelings.

If the Broom Fits

How do you move on from someone you never fell out of love with?

Can't Catch My Breath

Can she break free of the past and find true love?

Two Kinds of Us

Diamonds meet rock n' roll and secrets meet their end.

Christmas As We Know It

Meet me underneath the mistletoe.